HUNGER MAKES THE WOLF

"Gritty and engrossing, I [...]
side when the revolution [...]
Mur Lafferty, John W C[...]
of The Shambling Gui[...]

"The story is a fast-paced, edge-of-your-seat space opera, tied together with the characters' struggles, adventures and mishaps. If you've ever thought, 'You know what *Dune* needed more of? More magic and a biker gang!' then this book was written for you."
The Canary Review

"I was expecting a fun, quick space adventure read, but this story is so much more than that."
Helen Lindley

"Wells had me at space bikers, but what keeps me coming back to this world is its ass-kicking, subtly complex heroine. I'll ride in Hob's sidecar any time."
Matt Wallace, author of Envy of Angels *and*
Rencor: Life in Grudge City

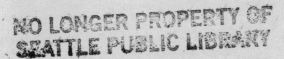

ALEX WELLS

HUNGER MAKES THE WOLF

ANGRY
ROBOT

ANGRY ROBOT
An imprint of Watkins Media Ltd

20 Fletcher Gate,
Nottingham,
NG1 2FZ
UK

angryrobotbooks.com
twitter.com/angryrobotbooks
Feed me

An Angry Robot paperback original 2017

Cover by Ignacio Lazcano
Set in Meridien and Bourgeois by Epub Services

Distributed in the United States by Penguin Random House, Inc.,
New York.

ISBN 978 0 85766 644 4
Ebook ISBN 978 0 85766 645 1
Printed in the United States of America

9 8 7 6 5 4 3 2 1

*For Mike, who believes in me
even when I don't believe in myself.*

PART I

CHAPTER ONE

They were on the return leg of a routine supply trip to bustling, dusty Primero when Hob Ravani saw the great eagles circling above the rolling sea of red dunes. The enormous birds were laboratory creations that had been brought along by the first settlers, a mix of eagle and vulture that could smell water from kilometers away – useful on a planet where there was no surface water for most of the year. They were also very, very good at smelling blood.

The two older mercenaries from the Ghost Wolves chattered back and forth on the short wave circuit, shooting the shit about their most recent job. It had been a simple escort across the salt flats between Shimera and Walsen that begged for a bit of spice if it was going to be of use to catch the attention of any town girls. Their tinny voices were loud over the sound of wind, the soft hum of the electric motors and the metallic whine of chainmesh and steel tires propelling the motorcycles over the sand barely audible through Hob's helmet.

"So, shall it be eight bandits, or only six?" Coyote's snobby accent and slightly nasal tones, there. He was the shortstack of the team, a good fifteen centimeters shorter than Hob at her lanky two meters, nearer thirty centimeters shorter than the dark mountain that was Dambala. He tended to make up for what he lacked in size with sheer, grinning craziness.

"Weren't any bandits 'tall." Dambala's deep, rumbling bass.

"You're rather missing the point, Bala." Coyote huffed out a long-suffering sigh. "You lack vision."

"You lack honesty."

Hob laughed – it was impossible not to, listening to the Coyote and Dambala comedy hour – but it was pure habit. Her eye was fixed on the eagles as a third soaring shape joined them.

"You seein' what I'm seein'?" she asked, her voice activating the microphone in her helmet.

"See what?" Dambala asked.

"Eagles circlin', 'bout two o'clock."

"So it would seem," Coyote said a moment later. He sighed. "I suppose we ought to check on it."

Him saying that as senior on the squad was more form than anything else; they'd already turned course, aiming for the dunes below those eagles. The command structure of Ravani's Ghost Wolves tended to be more of a suggestion backed up with the occasional fist fight. Older Wolves called the shots over the younger ones out of respect, and by grace of being more cunning and less likely to get het up and run off with their cocks hanging out Only when it came to the commander, Nick Ravani, did *yessir* and *nosir* magically pop up in anyone's vocabulary, and Hob thought that was half a matter of a tradition that stretched back to the first colonization of Tanegawa's World, and half a matter of Nick being crazier than a shithouse rat and seven times meaner. There was always a Ravani in charge, to the point that *Ravani* had come to mean *commander* and *boss*. It was a name you earned, a name you took when the old leader died and a new one clawed his way to the top through sheer cunning – most of the time.

Somewhere out in space there was a government, and laws, but they might as well have been ghosts for all this dusty, desert world was concerned. Here, there was only TransRift, Inc and their private security company Mariposa, and neither much cared if someone was dying in the desert. Most of the time, if someone ended up in the dunes it was because the company had put him there.

But Hob, Coyote, and Dambala weren't TransRift employees, and even those under the thumb of the company had rules. Number One: never leave someone stranded to die, because you didn't want the same to happen to you some day. It was bad luck, bad karma, bad everything. And the unspoken rule the Ghost Wolves added to it was this: if you were going to leave someone out in the dunes, well, you shot them in the head first. Because sometimes a quick death was the only kindness available.

They crested a dune, and Hob caught sight of a dark huddle in the sand, full in the punishing afternoon sun. "Think it's already too late for that one," she commented.

"Might have a note for his wife or somethin'," Dambala said. "Better check."

They pulled up at the base of the dune, parking their motorcycles with wide stands designed to not sink into the sand. Hob pulled her helmet off, the two tight plaits she kept her dark brown hair in plopping down onto her shoulders. Staying still for any length of time made the helmet into a personal, head-sized oven. Relative cool or not, she regretted her decision immediately as the strange, burnt death stink coming off the body hit her, thick enough to chew.

Corpse it would be: only the unconscious or dead would stretch out facedown in the sun like that, and there was enough rust-brown spatter around to show that some carrion eaters had already worried at the person's flesh. She could also tell it had likely been a man, from the cut of his clothes – it was rare for women to wear men's clothing like Hob did, except for the few who fought for a place deep in the mines, where the money was best.

His suit had probably been a good one before he was picked apart by animals, and strangest of all, he still wore his jacket. As a rule, people who got blacklisted and thrown out into the desert weren't wearing their Sunday best – and they sure didn't keep on anything more than they had to once the punishing heat hit. He had no hat, likely either gone on the wind or forgotten entirely. The patches of hair visible against the burnt skin stretched taut across his skull were gray, neatly trimmed.

Hob glanced at Dambala and Coyote. Both still straddled their bikes, waiting for her to make the check. Of course they were; they'd both been full Wolves for over a decade, and had no reason to get their hands dirty when someone barely out of puppyhood was around. Even less reason when their resident pup was an itinerant fuckup who'd unaccountably been given a second chance.

Grimacing, Hob crouched down next to the still man and pushed him over. His face was bloated horror, eyes gone, but she'd seen worse. Something niggled at her brain, the set of his jaw maybe, still visible in silhouette. She felt at the man's pockets and found a small wallet with some money in it. Gold flashed on his finger – a ring – and she lifted the hand up for a closer look, glad that she was wearing gloves.

She let go abruptly. "Shit..." she whispered.

Coyote's voice came tinny and thin from the speakers of her helmet, overturned on the sand nearby; apparently he preferred heat to stink. "What's wrong, Hob?"

Hob took up the man's hand again, this time much more reverently, inspecting the ring. "We know him." She'd seen the light play off etched geometric shapes time and again, helped lose it once and find it again in a much more innocent time.

"I had a bad feeling you might say that. Who is it?" Coyote asked.

"Uncle Phil." Philip Kushtrim wasn't her uncle by blood; she had no blood relatives on the entire planet, had jumped ship here over a decade ago from an interstellar cargo hauler. But he was Nick Ravani's older brother, and Nick was the closest thing to a father Hob had ever had – sad comment on her life that it was.

"*Fuck.*" It was Coyote's turn to curse. Not that

any word existed to encompass the sight, Hob knew. They'd all been friends with Phil, one way or another. "Old Nick's not going to be pleased."

"He's gonna spit blood over this." Dambala sucked at his teeth. "Someone else's blood."

Hob held Phil's hand between hers for a moment, fingers gently touching his knuckles as if that could urge him to un-die somehow, to erase the horrors of a body left for days in the sun. It was hard to imagine this blackened, bloated sack of rotting meat was all that remained of the man who had tried so hard to treat her like a second daughter despite all the stubborn resistance she'd shown as a gangly adolescent. He'd been so kind to her, and she'd repaid it all with anger, selfishness, and betrayal.

She rolled his body half over, running her hand lightly across his back, something twisting inside her chest. "There's at least four bullet holes, middle of his back. Maybe more. Hard to tell with all the pickin' the eagles have done already. But whoever done this must'a gunned him down, as he was running. I seen it before."

"We've all seen it before. The only question is if it was greenbellies or bandits," Coyote said grimly.

"Ain't much of a difference, is there." Nearly five years ago, Hob had found a gold tie tack shaped like a maple leaf on the corpse of a bandit – same kind the Mariposa greenbellies wore. Old Nick had just looked like he'd been sucking lemons when she handed it over to him, not a hair turned with surprise. It was a well-known, black-humored joke that Mariposa must actually be bad at guarding things, at the rate so-called bandits stole state-of-the-art guns from them.

"TransRift don't care who cleans off their blacklist. Dead's dead," Dambala said. Though the thought of Uncle Phil on the blacklist was inconceivable – he was, *had been*, a crew leader at the mine in Rouse. He was no company shill, but he was respected and liked by everyone, and had as much power as someone who wasn't a blue suit could.

Hob shook her head, put Phil on his back again, then tugged at his wedding ring – his wife, Irina, would want that back – but it wouldn't come from the bloated flesh. Nothing for it, then; she slid a knife from her sleeve. "Sorry. Not like you can feel this anyway."

She took his entire finger and slipped the ring from the severed stump, tucking it into her pocket. The remaining carrion she made to toss back onto the sand, but then thought better of it and pulled a handkerchief from another pocket. Trying not to think too hard about what she was doing, she rolled the severed finger up in the handkerchief and tucked it away.

"Girl, you did *not* just–"

"Shut up, Bala. I got my reasons. Ones you don't want to know about." Ones that Old Nick might understand, but no one else. She patted down the rest of Phil's pockets and came up with a little burlap bag, stamped with the TransRift logo and a sample number. One corner was stained with blood, but the rest was clean. She had to take off her leather gloves so she could pick the tight knot of the drawstring apart with her stubby fingernails.

Something glittered in the bag; she shook it out onto her bare palm, just one little grain. She had a second to register that it was bright, and glassy, and blue, a little bit of shiny nothing, and then it exploded out into a flashing ring of fire. Hob jumped back, her fist going tight around the bag so she wouldn't drop it. The flame stayed over her other hand, growling and moaning, licking at her fingers like a living thing. It didn't burn, though. Fire hadn't been able to burn her for years, since she'd survived her time in the desert and come out witchy.

Answering light flared in the sky. She looked up, the fire in her hand growing to a column, a beacon. Wings of fire unfolded across the blue, the three great eagles flapping clumsily away as an enormous bird of white-hot flame opened its beak in a soundless, defiant shriek.

"Phoenix," she whispered – the name of the rift ship that had brought her to Tanegawa's World, and the strange vision she'd seen after Nick had tricked her into the desert and left her to almost die. This was something that no one but her should be seeing. Old Nick had told her too many times that this needed to be secret, and she'd heard of too many townsfolk dead or disappeared under the suspicion of *witchiness*, removed by TransRift for being dangerous and contaminated. Hob took a deep breath and closed her fingers around the flame, drank in the fire. The light and heat drew down and disappeared under her skin. It was one of the few things Nick had ever taught her to do with the strange power they shared, because it was both useful and easy to hide. Her heart sounded loud in her ears, the empty socket she had in place of a left eye aching in memory of talons ripping and tearing flesh in exchange for her life and blood full of fire.

"What the hell is that?" Coyote shouted.

Hob sucked in a shaky, scorching breath. "Past catchin' up with me, mayhap."

"What?" Dambala asked.

She shook her head. "Nothin'."

"That was definitely *something*," Coyote said.

Hob uncurled the fingers of her other hand, the one that had held the fire. Her olive-toned skin was still unblemished... if you ignored all the old crisscrossing knife scars, the half-healed scrapes. "Don't know. But think I better find out." She closed up the little sample bag with a defiant jerk and stuffed it into another of the pockets in her brown leather trenchcoat. Sweat pooled around her armpits, on her back. "We best get movin' again, afore we cook." She hesitated, then added, "Did you two... did you see anythin' in the sky, just then?"

"Was too busy watchin' your hand afire to look anywhere else," Dambala said.

"I didn't notice anything," Coyote added. "Why?"

Hob shook her head. She'd only ever told one person about the phoenix that had spoken to her that day – Old Nick, who was missing the same eye as her. Funny coincidence, that. Old bastard had just smiled, said, *I knew you had some fire in your belly, girl. Best not go spreading the story around. This here's a company world, and we got no truck with witchiness, ya ken?* Without those words, she might have just convinced herself it was the hallucination of a brainpan turned to jerky by the sun. "Never you mind."

"We best get the Ravani the news quick," Dambala said, as they got back on their motorcycles.

"No shit." Hob allowed herself one last glance at Phil's body. He'd been as close as she ever had to an uncle for seven years, and then a stranger like everyone else for the last three. After Mag – *no* – after *Hob* had ruined it all. He deserved better than this, deserved to be burned with honor and have a hell of a wake. Hauling his body home was a luxury of weight they couldn't afford, not with their bikes already laden with the contraband from Primero, motorcycle parts, the delicate things like chips and relays that the Garagemaster Hati couldn't jury-rig or forge on his own "Fuck. I'll go to Rouse, tell Irina and… and Mag. You both get home and let the old man know."

"Now, hold on a minute." Coyote shook his head, the bright sun glancing off his visor making her wish for her helmet and its polarizers. "That isn't your decision to make, and I seem to recall we ought not be leaving you to your own devices."

That hurt like a slap coming from Coyote, who wasn't so much a loose cannon as a loose surface-to-air missile. Hob ignored him and pulled the four heavy saddlebags off her motorcycle to toss them over to Coyote and Dambala, who caught them rather than let them fall into the sand. "Trail's already at least a day and a half, mayhap two days cold. Don't want to let it get any colder. And out of the three of us, you know I'm the best tracker. He's gonna be breathin' fire as it is, and you know it. Your ugly damn faces might be a few degrees less charred if someone's already started askin' around, tryin' to find out who killed his brother and why."

Of all the reasons for getting busted back to a recruit, lack of skill had never been one of them. Redoing all her training had only honed her to a finer edge she could put to use and attempt to convince them all that she truly did belong.

With a certain amount of bad grace, Coyote started fitting the extra saddlebags. "Your logic is impeccable, I'll admit."

"Don't like leavin' you alone, though," Dambala said. "And that ain't meant as an insult."

She shoved her helmet on. Dambala's care felt good, though she'd never admit it. He'd been one of the few who hadn't had a hell of a good time making up rumors about her fall from Nick's good graces. "I been a real Wolf for months now, boys. No need to keep protectin' me like I'm a pup. I can care for myself." She'd prove it.

Dambala nodded. "Don't do nothin' stupid."

"Gonna hurt my feelings if you keep talkin' like that."

"And we all know how delicate your feelings are," Coyote drawled. "Like a hatchet in the back."

"That only happened the once." She flicked on her engine, goosed the throttle to spin the motorcycle in place in a halo of thrown sand, and headed off in the general direction she knew held Rouse. Once she was up to speed and on the flats, she reset the map on her HUD. Now that she was a full soldier, she had a real bike: twice the engine she'd had as a pup, computer in it as sophisticated as one could be without the strange magnetic fields of Tanegawa's World frying it. Which wasn't very sophisticated, and prone to malfunctioning and shorting out at random besides. Global positioning and comms satellites were things that happened to other, more normal planets, but anyone who wanted to survive more than five minutes learned how to read a map and track their course with velocity, heading, and time. Rouse now plotted as her destination, she flipped her intercom off so she wouldn't have to hear Coyote and Dambala going to static as the unsteady atmosphere gobbled up the radio waves.

Alone, with only the sound of wind whistling past her helmet and the hum of wheels on sand, she let the sadness and rage at seeing Phil shot in the back and abandoned to burn black on the sand well up inside her. It made her eye sting, but no more than that. Maybe because she hadn't seen him for anything but business in three years – though whose fault had *that* been, with her too ashamed to look anyone in the eye after what had happened with the preacher's boy?

Or maybe she just didn't have it in her to cry any more.

She hadn't seen Irina or Mag at all these past three years. First she'd been fighting just to convince herself she deserved to live, then to convince the others she still had a place among the Wolves. And by the time she was allowed back into Rouse, she'd found she was still torn up and angry at Mag for betraying her to Old Nick, even though she knew now it had needed to be done. No other way had been possible, but that didn't make it hurt any less when your best friend, your *sister*, turned on you. But she knew also that she owed it to Mag and to her mother to bring this message in person. Some small, horrible part of her was a little glad to have this excuse to see them again, to maybe wring a drop of something positive from a tragedy.

Maybe she'd forgive them.

Maybe they'd forgive her.

Except this chance to reach back to the pretty parts of her past had come at the cost of a good man's life, the only truly good man she'd ever known.

It wasn't worth it.

CHAPTER TWO

Then

The accident, the second in two weeks, started as a rumble in the ground, indistinguishable from normal blasting down in the mines. Only no blasting had been announced by the pit boss, and the sirens hadn't sounded the two-minute warning.

And the rumble continued, building. Windows and dishes rattled; pictures fell from walls.

Men and women hurried from their houses, turning their eyes toward the high mine shaft. Dust poured from it like the black rocks had become a smokestack.

Phil stood in the street with a napkin still tucked into his collar, a half-eaten sausage and cheese klobasnek in his hand. He'd taken the early lunch today, trading his normal spot with another crew leader so the man could leave work a little early and celebrate his anniversary with his wife. He watched the dust pouring from the mineshaft, his face gone grim and pale and his stomach gone hollow around his lunch, but made no move toward the mine, not yet.

Until a cave-in had finished, there was nothing to be done but wait.

Mag rushed from their house, took the napkin and half-eaten roll from him, handed him his hardhat. As Phil slipped the helmet on, its sweatband gone stiff and crackly with salt, the rumbling stopped.

Every able-bodied man and woman ran for the mines.

Even with sweat and fear thick in the air, the crowd was orderly. Everyone had a job for cave-ins and accidents, and disturbing that order would only claim more lives. First aid kits were grabbed, reinforced emergency pneumatic struts and timbers hauled up to the mine entrance, rope laid and belayed.

Phil was an experienced rope man, nimble and quick like a monkey despite his girth. He was the first in, his headlamp lighting automatically in the darkness. As he clipped on a harness, someone else handed him an oxygen mask and tank, and a lamp with a live flame and a special chimney that was far more reliable at detecting deadly gases on this world than any newer technology the freshest immigrants tended to brag about.

He looped six more ropes and harnesses through his belt and set off down into the dark. Behind him there was no shouting, just grim words and the jangling of harnesses, the shuffling of ropes as more rescuers got ready.

The main tunnels were still intact, but he noted warped and cracking timbers as he went deeper and marked them with hasty splashes of luminescent paint. The few places reinforcement plates had been melded on, corrosion turned the bright steel black, and pressure had the members warped and twisted.

He moved slowly and cautiously, listening always for the sound of more cracking, the sign that another cave-in was imminent. Dust was thick in the air, first white, then gray, then black.

At the bottom of the main shaft the dust took on a strange quality, glittering in the air like tiny blue sparks. He checked the lantern; the flame flickered in a strange way he'd never seen before. Not wanting to take chances, he pulled on his oxygen mask, and then took a small emergency light from one of the packs at his belt. He twisted the light to connect the battery and spiked it into the wall, leaving it there as a blinking red warning.

He peered down the branching paths of the secondary shafts, each cut to follow a separate vein of ore – Perida Type One, Skana, Norline Type Two, ores that had no off-world equivalent that any miner had ever discovered, with names that had no meaning beyond a suggestion of how best to break the rock. All were still active, but instinct turned him toward the newest. That was where the most activity had been, and where the other accident had happened a little over a week before: a wall collapsing to reveal a new vein that had the company men all but soiling themselves with glee. Something about purity, reactivity, a brittleness to it that also spelled danger.

Only a hundred feet into that shaft there was a shattered timber, warped shards of it half buried in rock. He held his breath, turning off his oxygen for a moment so he could just listen.

Sobbing. There was sobbing, coming from below

the timber.

He crouched down, peering into the darkness under the timber. "Can ya hear me?" he whispered.

The sobbing hitched, stumbled to a halt. A hand black with dirt thrust out from the rocks. He could make out the tattered remnants of a jacket, what might have been blue, and a filthy shirt cuff beneath; this was one of the company observers. "Help me," the man whispered, breath rattling.

"Got more coming, you just hold on," Phil said. No matter how he felt about TransRift, every man buried alive in a mine was his brother at that moment. He'd survived two collapses himself, and still woke with nightmares. "You know if anyone else is close behind you?" Carefully, he began to clear little rocks a few at time, testing each before moving it. The smallest thing could set off another chain reaction if he was too hasty.

"No. They were… still down at the vein. Found something big. Super told me to run it up… to the surface."

More to keep him talking than anything else – talk had a way of calming a man, particularly when it was work talk – Phil asked, "What kind of big thing?"

"Important. Real important. Got to get it to the lab." The man snorted, sniffled, then gasped. "It's in my coat pocket. Get it to the lab. Promise me."

"Promise I will. What's your name, friend?"

The man didn't answer. Phil tried again, then felt his wrist, searching for the flutter of a pulse. There was nothing. Even knowing that it was a corpse on the other side, he continued his painstaking task. Two more from the rescue crew joined him, and they started digging in earnest, unearthing the ruin of the man. His head was bloody, face obscured by a self-rescuer, not that the little air reservoir had been able to help him at all. One side of his chest was crushed, presumably from the roof collapsing. It was impossible to tell if he was young or old, what color he was, anything. Phil hauled the body out to the main shaft, carefully avoiding men carrying timbers. At the surface, he felt through the man's jacket pockets, remembering his promise. All he found was a little burlap bag, the sort company men used for assay samples – nothing that unusual. He didn't bother to open it, just stuffed it in his own pocket to deal with later.

The nameless company man wasn't the last corpse they hauled out from the cave-in.

They worked for hours, painstakingly digging and reinforcing as they went. They unearthed more dead men, miner after miner, and Phil took his turn at the grim work of escorting the corpses to the surface where their spouses and children waited to try to identify them. Some wailed, but the worst were the silent ones; Phil wished he could simply stay under the ground, do the work. It would hurt less.

Muffled shouts of excitement heralded them breaking through to an air pocket. Three people – two miners and the other company man – had huddled together in a little pyramid of space made by fallen timbers. They were all three unconscious, but alive, pulses faint but there. Phil carried out one of the miners, a young woman with dragonflies tattooed on both her arms. As soon as they broke into the afternoon sunlight, medics took her from him. A man, presumably her husband, screamed her name, "Martessa!"

Those were the only survivors. It was impossible to know if they would recover, how badly they were hurt. Phil stayed with the crews until they were certain that no one else lived, and then the rest of the recovery effort was given over to the next shift, to finish reinforcing the shaft so work could resume. TransRift accepted no work stoppages for less than catastrophic reasons, and they had quotas to fill if they didn't want their pay docked.

Phil left most of his gear with the replacement crew. His headlamp made a circle of light that led him back to his house in the darkness; all power in the town had been diverted to the mine, to run the few simple machines they could get working underground with electromagnetic shielding on full. He'd heard the pit boss complaining about the expense of repairing the machinery after even limited use, but getting the mine back online again outweighed that cost. That was the reason sweat and muscle dug the shafts, and most of the conveyers were powered by teams of oxen. Blood and sweat was cheaper than electricity and shielding and the maintenance on finicky mining equipment that worked just fine on every planet but this one. None of the miners complained about that fact; it meant they had steady if dangerous work that fed their families.

Mag and Irina both waited up for him even though they, too, were exhausted. They hadn't gone down into the mine, but they had helped keep the rescuers fed and watered, had helped the newly minted widows and widowers deal with the corpses of their loved ones, and had helped with first aid as well from the look of the stains on their skirts and sleeves. Mag took Phil's clothes to be washed – he needed them for tomorrow since he had only one safety jacket – while Irina assisted him into the bath, scrubbed his back for him and washed his hair.

When he insisted he could handle dressing himself, Irina went to fix them all something to eat before they crawled into bed. Phil always felt too heartsick to eat after an accident, but knew his stomach would be howling as soon as he clapped eyes on any food.

Mag waited at the bottom of the stairs as he came down. "Papa?"

"Hm?" When had she gotten so big? She was a solid girl, his Mag, a workhorse, as plump as he and Irina had been able to manage. She kept her dark brown hair in a long braid, a short fringe hanging over her earnest, hazel eyes and snub nose.

"I found this in your jacket." Mag held up the dirty little burlap bag. "What is it?"

"Sample bag, I think." Phil took it from her and opened the drawstring at the top, then spilled the contents onto both his hand and Mag's: shining blue crystals, ranging from the size of a penny down to little more than dust, half perfect crystal faces and half broken shards.

Mag let out a little wondering sigh at the sight of all that sparkle, her breath stirring the dust. "What is it? I've never seen anything like it."

"I haven't either. Guess they found this at the end

of the new shaft. One of the company men had it; said it was important, needed to go to the labs. Here, best put it all back."

"Most beautiful thing I've seen in a while…" Mag said. She tipped her hand; most of the crystals slid back into the bag, but the small ones clung to the fresh cuts and scrapes that decorated her palm and fingers, souvenirs of a hard day's labor. She scraped the dust off with her fingernails.

Phil had seen sample bags before, had seen new grades of ore picked out by company men sent back to the lab for processing. After Mag and Irina had gone to bed, he sat up thinking, rolling the little burlap bag in his hands.

Tiny sample bags like this carried more than scraps of rock. If what they contained was good news for TransRift, there'd be new shafts to be cut and higher quotas from them, more company men pushing for faster work and demanding longer hours and more miners to do it. If there were offworlders coming in soon, they'd get swallowed up into the mine right quick. But if that weren't enough bodies to meet the work demand, there'd be mandatory overtime, and even regular townsfolk pressed into service in the mine. He'd seen it before in Walsen, almost thirty years ago. Seen people who'd never been in a shaft brought in to work with paychecks held captive until they complied, had seen the sickness and accidents and deaths that followed. The mine hungered for able bodies and spat out everything it chewed up.

He had never seen a sample, a vein like this. With the company man – must have been a geologist, he supposed, but all the management types dressed alike – so bleeding sure that it was important that he spent his last breath on it, Phil had no doubt it would be cause for fresh shafts and longer hours at the least. Already, the pit boss pushed them too hard; two accidents in two weeks, a third not a month before. He didn't want to see Mag being finally brought down into the mines with the siren call of overtime wages. She'd been speaking about it lately, making jokes about not being useful for anything else, how she needed to start earning her keep. She was his daughter, blood, bone, and soul; if she put her mind to something, she wouldn't take no for an answer. And even if he could keep her out of the voluntary work call, if production fell behind things could get involuntary in a breathless hurry.

He'd told the company man that he'd hand the bag over, but it'd been comfort for a dying man. TransRift never kept its promises to the miners unless it suited; he didn't feel even a twinge at welching on one to them, for a few days at least.

Phil climbed down into his cellar and opened up a nearly empty flour barrel. It had a false bottom and he dug out several stacks of flexible plastic bills, a box of chits. He'd been saving to get the three of them passage on a ship off world, but there didn't seem to be more time to spend on waiting. Mag would have to just go ahead of them. He didn't want to see his daughter get worked to death in the mines, or die in a cave-in, and he knew from speaking with representatives from Blessid that life was really no easier nor safer in the farming towns.

He stacked the money on the kitchen table, and then spilled the little blue crystals from their burlap sack again, stirring them around on the wood with one blunt finger. It was hypnotizing, the way the light glittered on their surface, all spark and fire.

Like the spark and fire he'd seen dancing across his own brother's hands on occasion over the last thirty years, and that scared him more than anything else. He wasn't supposed to know about that, and pretended he didn't whenever anyone breathed a word about witchiness. Bad enough that Nick – though he hadn't been Nick then – had been blacklisted so many years ago. He wanted no more stain on their family that would draw the eye of the company men, always so alert for their *contamination* and *disease* and *criminal hazards*. But he knew also that Nick had wanted him to see that fire. Maybe so he'd know his little brother had gone and really hecked his life up, maybe because Nick wanted to see if there was one person in the world he couldn't scare the hell out of. You never knew with Nick.

Phil scooped the crystals back into the bag, coming to a second decision; he needed to show this to Nick, and see if he'd know what it might be, what it might do to the town if they started hauling the stuff to the surface. Nick knew a lot of things he wasn't supposed to know. And if Nick wanted to bring his pet Bone Collector in, well, all the better since the man was strangeness embodied. Just thinking about him sent a cold shiver down Phil's back.

Keeping the sample bag hidden would be easy enough; no one knew he had it. Probably safest of all to keep it with him, where it wouldn't be found by Irina or a nosy houseguest. If there was trouble, the blame should fall only on him and not on his family. He could wait until he had a day off and meet up quiet-like with Nick.

"Papa?"

He looked over his shoulder. Mag blinked sleepily, face pale in the light of dawn. "Go back to bed, Mag. You worked hard today. You can sleep in."

Mag sat down at the table, eyes straying over the sample bag. Phil tucked it into his coat pocket when it looked like she might reach for it. "Did you even go to sleep?"

"Not yet. I had some thinking to do."

She turned her attention to the money that also sat on the table. "What's all this for?"

"Passage off world. If I read the schedule right, there should be a ship by the end of the week. I want to send you away on it."

Her face went dead white. "Papa, no..."

"I want something better for you than this," Phil said. "Don't argue with me, Mag. And don't be too scared about it. There's almost enough money for a second fare. I'll work harder, take some extra shifts, to get a third. Your mother and I should be able to follow you in a year, maybe two. So think of yourself as the advance party. You got to find yourself some good work, get a place prepared for us."

She shook her head. "I don't want to go."

"This ain't no place for honest folk, Mag. Not with cave-ins and the blacklist always hangin' over our heads. Your Uncle Nick is what he is 'cause he was blacklisted, you know that?" Phil reached out, put his hands over hers.

"And other things," Mag whispered. She looked down at their clasped hands.

"And worse things," Phil agreed. "Will you do this for me, for your mother?"

Mag looked up, her eyes bright with tears. "I'll do it," she whispered. "I'll find work, I'll get a big house for the three of us."

Phil's eyes stung; he should be happy, he knew, but the thought of his only child, his daughter going so far away left him spitless. But the unknown had to be better than this. "That's my girl."

CHAPTER THREE

Hob rode like a bat out of hell for Rouse, but even at full throttle with the electric motor half screaming beneath her, it was long gone dark by the time she rolled up to the town. With the sun down, the temperature dropped profoundly; she was grateful for her heavy coat, since her sweat-damp shirt left her feeling chilled. She pulled right up to the massive gates set in the razor wiretopped walls of Rouse, knocked on one in the special pattern that identified the Wolves to the townspeople, hoping someone would be near enough to hear. If it was a Mariposa man, she might end up getting shot for her trouble.

The small inset door opened in the gate; she drifted through on her motorcycle, nodding politely to the man who had opened it for her. In the dark, his face blackened with mine dust, she had no way of knowing if she'd ever met him or not. And even if she had, it wasn't likely he'd recognize her after three years and enough growth spurts that she was now only a few centimeters shorter than Old Nick himself.

Even at night, the mine works dominated Rouse, washed bright as day with floodlights set up all around it. The mine was a lattice of metal and wood built up the side of the black rock spires that loomed over the town like tombstones. Elevators ran up and down, some taking miners high onto the spires, others deep into the ground. Teams of men and women with hybrid oxen moved enormous carts of ore to a set of conveyer belts, which took the ore to a waiting train car, its metal shine muted by a hefty coating of red dust.

Hob turned away from the mine works and idled down the three little side streets to Uncle Phil's house, following them like a long-cherished scar in her own skin. In the narrow alleyway between the beat-up walls of his house and the next, she parked her bike and pulled off her helmet, replaited her hair into two smooth tails, fussed with brushing the dust from her jacket.

There was only so much delaying a body could do. Helmet tucked under one arm, she walked up to the door and knocked.

Irina opened it. She looked like she'd aged more than just the three years since Hob had seen her, round face haggard and her normally ruddy brown complexion blanched gray. Her dark hair was shocked with white; surely there hadn't been more than a few stray strands three years ago. Dark circles shadowed her hazel eyes, red from weeping. Maybe, Hob thought, she already knew. Only how could that be, and Nick not already here like a cat with his tail afire?

Irina stared at her uncomprehendingly, a frown creeping over her thin lips. Then her eyes went wide and she smiled, of all damning, awful things. "Hob?

Hob Ravani? You haven't paid us a visit in ages."

She didn't know, couldn't know, Hob realized. So she'd been crying about something else. "Ma'am, I'm…" She licked her lips, tried again. "Is Mag here?"

Irina shook her head. "No, and not Phil neither. Hob, we… we decided to send Mag away, get her off world so she could start setting up a new place for our family. Maybe we should have… I didn't know if you'd want to say goodbye, but there just wasn't time."

Hob gave her head an abortive little shake, trying to wrap her mind around that. Mag gone, Mag getting sent away. "Why – no, don't worry about it. I haven't been 'round in years. When did they leave?" It wasn't fair, she wanted to scream. That they'd send Mag away and she might have never known. But she'd long since lost her right to complain on that count. And how could she think so selfishly when she had her burden of news to still tell?

"Phil took her on the train to Newcastle the day before yesterday." She frowned, worry creeping back into her expression, cutting the lines around her mouth deeper. "I expected him home yesterday, but no trains came in, so mayhap the track's got some emergency repairs or such." It wasn't an unusual situation, with the sands constantly shifting and the hardpan settling at seeming random.

Hob's face felt strange, frozen, her blood cold. Mag had gone with her papa. But they hadn't found a second body, hadn't seen the great eagles circling a second meal, and hadn't seen even signs of more blood. Did that mean she'd made it onto her ship, or...? It was the *or* that left her stomach sick and chilled. She didn't know which leg of the trip Phil had been killed on, though if Mag had been with him, wouldn't she have been killed too?

"Hob? What's wrong? You look ill..." Irina looked ill herself, and she knew now, she must know, a little worm of horror uncurling in her heart and showing as a shadow in her eyes, in the way she gripped the door frame with knuckles going white.

Hob dug into her pocket, took out the wallet that she'd pulled from Phil's pants. Irina's eyes went wide at the sight of it, and she covered her mouth with a shaking hand. Hob shook the wedding band from the wallet, held it out to Irina. "I'm sorry. Truly sorry. We found him today, in the dunes a few hours out of Primero. Been shot in the back at least four times."

Irina collapsed to her knees, a thin wail coming from her mouth, tears filling her eyes as she shook her head. "But the train... train's just late, ain't it?" Her eyes went wider, throat straining as if to scream, but she could only whisper, "What about Mag? Was my... Was my Maggy...?"

"She weren't with him. We would've seen her if she'd been anywhere nearby." There was nothing more than that she could say.

"She's– she's got away then. Away." Irina sagged, sobs tearing from her throat.

Hob crouched down so her head wasn't so far above Irina's; it felt wrong, to be standing over her like that. "I was with Dambala and Coyote, and they went to tell Nick. He'll be here soon as he can. Won't be much longer now." Irina grabbed the collar of Hob's jacket with her hands, half falling forward to press her face against Hob's shoulder. Hob sucked in a shaky breath, chest gone tight like she'd never breathe proper again. "And I swear to you, Irina. We'll figure out who done this, me an' Nick. And we'll make 'em *bleed*."

Irina only sobbed louder. Feeling wooden, Hob slid one arm around her, rubbing little circles on her back and making noises she hoped were soothing.

It took nearly an hour to calm Irina enough to get a coherent word from her, but Hob didn't begrudge her that time in the least. Sallow, still, calm Irina was somehow worse than screaming and crying Irina; she looked like all the blood had been drained from her, all life, all hope. Hob made them each a terrible cup of coffee, like tar, just so they had something to hold and warm their hands, and she asked Irina all the horrible questions that had to be asked. Where had they gone, how much money did they have, had Phil made any of the company men angry, had Mag, had Irina, had anyone been bothering them.

Irina had no answers for any of those questions, not even a reason for wanting to get Mag off world other than Phil had decided it was high time and they had saved enough money for her, if not for themselves. Hob couldn't comprehend how a woman could know so little about her own life, leave so many decisions in the hands of a man, even a good one like Phil. On that count, she held her tongue.

Last, Hob took the little burlap sample bag from her pocket, showed it to Irina, even poured a few of the little crystals onto the table top, careful not to touch them. To her eyes, they pulsed with threads of flame, beating in time with her heart. "Do you know what these are? Have you seen them before?"

Irina gently stirred the crystals with one finger: no reaction. "Never. Nor the sample bag. That's not the sort of thing... Phil... it wasn't his job. Only company men do that, the onsite geologists. They wouldn't give it to him."

"Damn." Hob used her handkerchief to brush the crystals back into the bag; seemed best to not have Irina touch them, just in case.

"Are those somethin' to do with what– with what happened?"

"Don't rightly know. But I've got a few ideas on who I could ask." Hob pulled her battered watch from her waistcoat and checked the time. "I hate to ask but... you mind if I catch a few hours of shuteye? I'll be off early to go huntin'. I suspect Nick'll be here late tomorrow morning, so you won't be alone long."

Irina shook her head. Her eyes were red, but dry now. "I... I'm so glad you're staying. I don't want to be in an empty house right now."

Hob dumped out their untouched coffee and then guided Irina to bed, where she tucked her in like she'd seen Irina and Phil tuck in Mag, back when she and Mag were girls, pulling up the quilt to her ears. The woman curled up around her husband's pillow, face buried in it. Hob turned out the light and left quickly; she couldn't eat any more of Irina's grief. It made her feel too goddamned helpless.

Rather than return to the kitchen and make more undrinkable coffee, Hob headed upstairs to Mag's room, telling herself that it was just to see if anything was untoward. It was neat as always, but barren, most of Mag's stuff no doubt packed away for her trip off world. Felt strange, to contemplate Mag hopping onto a rift ship like the one Hob herself had jumped off over a decade before. Would Mag be relegated to the hold too, or to the closet-like cabins that always smelled a bit like vomit, from so many passengers unable to handle the moment the ship fell through a rift to come out in another system?

Hob found a bit of torn flimsy and the stub of a grease pencil in Mag's desk drawer. She wrote out what little she did know in a note for Nick, and an explanation of what she planned to do on the morrow with the crystals. If they had anything to do with Phil's death or Mag's possible disappearance, she didn't want them near Irina a moment longer than necessary. Herself, she didn't care about. All the Wolves were already long since damned, most of them corpses who had walked from the desert into a new life.

Hob took off her black tie, shrugged off the black waistcoat she'd lifted from Old Nick's closet a couple of years ago, and then in her shirt sleeves laid down on Mag's bed, curling up so her feet didn't hang over the edge. The sheets smelled of the soap Mag liked, cinnamon and vanilla like her mother's cookies, and a little bit of sweat and dust. But it also smelled different from all those the times they had shared it as teenagers. There was a grownup smell, a hint of perfume, and something else. Made sense – Mag had been a few years younger than Hob, still in shouting distance of childhood when Hob had been a wild teenager and sowing her oats. After three years, Mag would almost be a woman full grown, and Hob had missed it all. For a stupid argument, because of a stupid boy, and the stupid had spread like blood in water. She'd about drowned in it before she was through.

"I'm sorry, Mag," Hob murmured to the pillow. "I'll make it up to you. I pay my debts."

Hob woke early, feeling like she hadn't slept at all. Her back ached, one arm gone numb and tingling. The sky outside the window was starting to lighten up; false dawn was as good a time as any to leave. It was a long journey ahead, and she preferred to get as much distance as possible before the sun really set things boiling.

Hob tucked the note she'd written for Nick under the coffee pot on the kitchen counter, then helped herself to a couple of slices of bread and a wedge of cheese, gobbling the food down as she walked the short distance to where she'd left her motorcycle. She finished the last mashedup mouthful while she filled up her canteens at the water tank that occupied a place of honor on the street, under its own little roof. The taste of cheese still thick on her tongue, she shoved her helmet on and rolled out of town.

This time it was a man from Mariposa security at the gate, his green uniform ill fitting, shirt tails untucked and poking out from his unbuttoned jacket. When he approached, Hob just shoved a handful of plastic chits at him, everything she had in her pocket. She wasn't in the mood to answer questions or even pick a fight. There was somewhere she needed to be.

The ruins of Pictou were north, just off due north, a location she'd had to mark on the map herself years ago since the town no longer existed and had been struck from the official maps. She kept an eye on her compass, the steady ticking of the chron as her course plotted on her HUD, and just relaxed into the ride, trying not to think too hard about Phil or Mag as the dunes spooled by. No tracks or way markers existed to keep her on course. The town had been abandoned for a half a century, destroyed in a single night by a crazed witch, according to TransRift. It was story numbers one, two, and three any company man would trot out as an example of why all witchiness should be reported before the contaminated individual grew too strong. Old Nick had never offered her an alternate explanation, something she still found disturbing. Pictou now sat at the middle of an area marked as a toxic disaster site, a circle thirty kilometers in diameter that warned of a deadly miasma of witchiness Hob had never noticed. Perhaps it wasn't visible to someone already "infected."

Close to boiling midday she arrived at what was left of Pictou. Anything soft had been stripped from the streets by the wind; there was no synthetic wood left in it, no plastic or scraps of fabric or signs of any life. Tumbledown stone walls sat in the shadow of the black rock spire that the miners of Pictou had once cut their way through. Here and there, rusted bolts were visible, the remnant of a piece of metal, like a flywheel, that was all that remained of the mine works. The only thing that had saved the town from being completely buried by traveling dunes was how far into the hardpan it was, how it was sheltered by the black buttes above from the worst of the winds. As it was, dust and sand had drifted up onto most of the ruined walls, filled in the gaping holes that had once been basements so that they looked soft and safe to walk on.

She parked her motorcycle in the deepest shade, where she'd be safe from the sun until the end of the day, took her helmet and jacket off, and waited. She gave the body of the machine a few desultory thumps to knock the thick caking of dust away, but the scratched and sandblasted paint beneath wasn't much prettier. Shiny, clean machines were things that happened to people who didn't ride them daily through an endless dustbowl, she reckoned. The engine was the important part anyway, and Hati the garage master kept it humming at a perfect pitch she knew like the sound of her own breath and heartbeat. She brushed another swath of dust off the battery stack and turned her attention back to the ruins.

The Bone Collector haunted this place like a ghost, Old Nick had said. Well, not so much told her as implied it in that smug bastard way of his, lips all screwed up like he was holding in laughter. She'd dropped messages and packages off here on errands, but she didn't know how to summon him. Nick just always seemed confident that he'd find the little packages he sent.

She passed the time sharpening her knives; she always carried six with her, distributed over her belt, boots, and wrists. They didn't really need tending, but she hated having her hands idle. Idle hands did nothing to keep her mind busy, when she'd rather be thinking of anything but what she'd already lost and might still lose. Nick had fished her up off the streets young and thrown her straight into training, but he'd never treated her special, no matter what the other two pups – Francis and George, they'd been called back then – claimed to the contrary. Hob was fair certain he'd been meaner to her, most spiteful, harder on her, if anything. But she'd stood up to him and spit in his eye and worked hard to learn how to fight and ride her motorcycle and do the hundred other things every fullgrown Wolf knew – though never how to use her witchiness. That was a secret Nick had sworn her to once and then left her to figure out on her own.

The reward she'd shared with Francis and George for all their hard work was trips into Rouse where they got dropped off on Phil's doorstep so he and Irina could give them some veneer of civilization. Neither of the boys had ever had much use for Mag, and she'd had even less use for them, but she and Hob had taken a liking to each other immediately and been thick as thieves. Felt like sisters, Hob thought, not that she'd ever had one properly, but that had to be what having a family was like in some kind of back-asswards way. It hadn't been an easy life even so, but she'd been happy and confident that she'd keep moving up in the world, keep being Mag's friend, keep having a family. Then she met the goddamn preacher's boy.

Oh, he'd been cute, and no one had thought anything of it at first, other than Nick giving her the stinkeye like he always did. Jeb fussed over her and told her how scared he was every time she went out with the big Wolves to carry their ammo boxes or watch the motorcycles while they did the real work. She'd always been tough as hell, mind, and proud of it, but a little fussing had felt perilously special, when the only special thing she had to her name was the witchiness she never dared talk about. And then they'd started kissing. And then they'd started fucking. And Old Nick pulled her off town detail. In retrospect, she could see it hadn't even been anything that personal. She'd been due for the next step in her apprenticeship, more responsibility, and that just meant guarding their base while everyone else was away. But she'd been thinking with her cunt instead of her brain, as Nick had accused her of later, and she took it a place beyond personal. She'd argued with Old Nick and got her ass grounded, of all humiliating things. And then she'd gone and done it proper stupid, and left the base while everyone was out on a job to go get her boy, bring him back, and then screw him there like it was the world's biggest *fuck you* to Nick Ravani for daring to think he could tell her what to do. The one rule he'd ever given her, and she'd shit all over it at the first opportunity because she was *mad*.

The night she'd gone to Rouse to get Jeb was the last she'd seen Mag. Her best friend and sometimes sister had tried to talk her out of it, and Hob should have listened. But Hob had never been that good at listening to anyone when she had her back up. Old Nick had told her later that it was Mag who ratted Hob out to him, and that was a tangle she still couldn't undo in her own brain. It had been the right thing to do, the *necessary* thing, because Old Nick had been right

– because somehow the dried-up sonofabitch always managed to be right – because the preacher's boy had just been using her to get to the Wolves, and she'd almost brought TransRift down around their ears with her stupidity. All the horror that had happened next and ended with Hob busted back to pup and starting fresh had been necessary too. But she couldn't divide what she knew intellectually to be true from the sight of blood spraying across a ceiling, and from the absolute hurt of knowing Mag, the person she trusted most in the world because only a damn idiot trusted Nick Ravani, had betrayed her. Even if it had been right and proper and necessary, it still hurt.

Well, right and proper and necessary was more important than her own long-nursed wounds. She'd been wrong to avoid Mag even when she was allowed to go back to Rouse. But she'd been so ashamed, and so afraid that Mag might look at her the way everyone else on base had for the last three years: like she was the biggest fuckup in the world. As if that could have hurt any worse than where she was now, sitting in the burning sand and trying to swallow guilt and fear with a dry mouth.

And to think, she'd been convinced that she was done fucking up after the last big mistake. But it just kept going and going, like the winds that never stopped pushing the dunes across the hardpan.

Eventually, Hob dozed fitfully in the heat, jerking awake every time the wind made even the softest sound. Her stomach grumbled, and she grudgingly ate half the emergency rations she'd brought, chewing on jerky softened with the smallest possible sips of water until she thought her teeth and jaw would crack.

Sunset painted the hardpan salmon pink and orange with reflected light. She sighed and looked up at the sky. "I ain't goin' anywhere till you come and talk to me. I'll wait all night if I have to, all day tomorrow too."

In a just world, that would have gotten her some sort of instant response. Instead, she watched the sunset colors on the sky, and napped again as the stars began to come out.

The cold woke her, and a soft noise, a whisper of sand moving against sand. She sat up, pulled on her coat, and slid a knife into one hand from the sheath at her wrist. The Bone Collector walked up from one of the abandoned cellars, digging his staff into the sand.

CHAPTER FOUR

Then

One day before they were set to leave for the landing field at Newcastle, Mag was alone in the house, taking care of last-minute laundry so that she could pack all of her clothes clean. Every little bit would help, wherever her fare ended up taking her. Papa was at the mine, already working the promised extra hours; Mama was up at the works too. She didn't have the lungs or the back for mining, but she earned extra money carrying water to the miners and tending to their little hurts.

Someone knocked on the front door.

Mag dropped the little bag of clothespins on the floor, the dry rattle echoing the shudder of fear up her spine. She barely dared to breathe. When the knock came again, she jerked like she'd been slapped.

Every instinct told her not to answer the door, to pretend to not be home. But it was a rare thing for it to be someone bad. Mostly it'd be a person looking for her parents, or a neighbor asking to borrow flour or a few eggs.

A third knock: it had to be something important.

Mag untangled her hands from her apron – how had the fabric gotten so twisted up in her fingers? – and went to answer the door.

The man on the doorstep was no neighbor, nor any of the miners. He wore a suit of company blue, his dark hair neat and slicked back. He might even have been handsome, sharp nose and all, if just the sight of his face didn't fill her with such dread. His dark eyes glittered and he smiled, showing all his teeth. "Ah, I knew you were home, Maggy-girl."

Her face felt stiff and wooden. "Mr Franklin, good afternoon."

"Go ahead, invite me inside. Saw your mama, she said she made some lemonade fresh this morning, I should try some."

"Of course. I didn't mean to be rude." She stepped aside, hiding her hands in her apron.

Mr Franklin was one of the company representatives that rode with the trains; he wasn't in town often, but he was always stopping by to say hello to her parents. He'd known them for years, friendly-like; he'd helped Papa get his promotion to crew leader. Mag hated him, feared him, more than she could bear.

He took himself to the kitchen; she followed behind. He pulled out a chair at the table as she turned to get a glass from the cupboard, but he didn't sit. Instead, he moved up behind her and leaned, pressed his body up against hers. She knocked the glass over in the cabinet; it took down the rest like dominoes, though none broke.

"Your mama also told me her little chickadee was flyin' the nest tomorrow," he breathed into her hair.

She closed her eyes tightly, as if not seeing would make the world less real, shut it all out of her head. "Yessir, going off to have an adventure." Her voice wobbled as she spoke.

"Sound sad enough to cry, you do. I'll put a smile on your face, Maggy-girl. I can't let you go off without saying a proper goodbye." His aftershave half choked her.

She had an inkling where that hiss of words might go, and her thoughts melted into a panicked scramble. Her first instinct was to scream, but she already knew that was the wrong one. Because someone might rush in, and fling themselves at Mr Franklin, and all too easily Mag could imagine that faceless rescuer getting thrown off a train. Because you didn't tell a company man no, not if you valued your job. She'd learned that just by watching and listening around town, ignored and overlooked because she was quiet and young.

One of the glasses rolled against her hand. She grabbed it and pretended to faint, then slammed it into the cabinet. The glass shattered into razor-sharp shards with a loud crack, and cut deep into the meaty part of her hand. There was nothing feigned about the cry of pain that tore out of her, but it wasn't a scream for help.

Mr Franklin jerked away from her like a shot, so fast that she had to grab the edge of the counter to keep herself from falling. "What are you up to, Maggy-girl?" he said. There was a look in his eyes – anger, confusion, and... fear? Had he imagined that glass cracking across his head for a moment?

"I'm sorry!" she gasped, leaning against the counter. She wasn't sorry at all, but she managed to *sound* it, with all that real pain screeching from her hand and up her arm. "I'm sorry, my hand slipped and… Oh. Oh God." That really was a lot of blood, she thought numbly, running off her palm and pattering down onto the counter top.

"Well, put it under the tap." He grabbed her by the wrist and jerked her over to the sink.

She yelped again, unabashedly. Mr Franklin kept calling her *girl*, talking to her like she was a child. And it made her sick, but fine, she could act like a child too. Being a child was safer than being a grown woman. Loudly, she began to cry. It felt strangely good, a way to let out some of that fear choking her that – she hoped – wouldn't make him mad. And more important, it was a way to make some noise. "Oh, it hurts! It hurts!"

"Quiet! Hush. It's just a scratch," Mr Franklin snapped. He turned on the water, which at its coldest still came out of the tap lukewarm. It seemed to multiply all that blood even more, washing it red down the sink.

Someone pounded on the kitchen door, then jangled the handle and let themselves in. "Everything all right– Mag? Mag what's wrong?" It was Lonny Hastert, their next-door neighbor – she normally worked the night shift. Mag felt a brief pang of guilt that she'd managed to be loud enough to wake the woman up. She obviously needed all the sleep she could get. Dark circles surrounded her narrow brown eyes, creases lined the red-brown skin of her face, pores darkened in with rock dust that could never fully be washed away. A brief glance at Mr Franklin's face, pale and gone a bit bug-eyed with barely suppressed rage, dried any guilt right up.

"She's fine," Mr Franklin said tightly. "Just broke a glass. Clumsiness."

Mag gave Lonny a wide-eyed look; the woman's expression was so blurred through her own tears that she couldn't read it. "My hand slipped. I was going to give Mr Franklin some lemonade, and my hand slipped." She gulped. "There's so much blood, Lonny!"

"Let me see." The miner moved in close and – "Excuse me, if you please, Mr Franklin, you wouldn't want to get blood on your fine suit" – shouldered the man out of the way, then took possession of Mag's wrist. Lonny pulled Mag's hand out from under the water and looked at the fresh flow of blood. "You got most of the glass out, so thank you, sir. But these're gonna need stitches for sure. I'd best take Mag to the doctor and let her mama know."

"I don't think that's–" Mr Franklin began.

Mag, still staring in fascination at the blood welling from her hand, deliberately burped. No one wanted to be around a person who was vomiting, particularly not someone as fussy as Mr Franklin. "I don't feel good."

"Head down, Mag. Head down," Lonny said, almost cheerfully. "Mr Franklin, the trashcan, if you please?"

Crouched down, Mag couldn't see the man any more, but she leaned against Lonny and stared into the brown potato peels that filled the trash bin, trying not to breathe in the stink. She might really throw up then.

"Give me that towel there, thank you." Lonny wrapped a dishtowel tightly around her hand. Mag whimpered again for good effect, though she couldn't help noticing how fast red spots started soaking through the fabric.

"I think I'd better go," Mr Franklin said.

"I'm sorry, Mr Franklin," Mag mumbled. "About the lemonade."

"Thank you, sir," Lonny said firmly. "I'm sure Phil will let you know how it all works out. Think you can stand now, Mag? I ain't carryin' you to the doctor."

"Think so," Mag said. She let Lonny hoist her up and direct her to the door. She heard Mr Franklin's footsteps follow them out, but he turned right when they turned left at the doorstep. The crunch of his fancy shoes faded away quickly.

"You all right for true?" Lonny asked. "I never known you to have a faint bone in your body."

Mag cast a covert glance behind them, waiting until Mr Franklin's dark blue back rounded the corner before she straightened up all the way. "I'm all right," she said. "Do I really need stitches?"

Lonny shrugged. "Maybe. Least some glue to get you to stop bleeding, but you got that in the house, don't ya?"

"Yeah," Mag said. She gripped Lonny's arm a little bit harder with her uninjured hand. "Thanks for comin' to help me."

"Anything I should know?" Lonny asked.

Mag shook her head. Because what could Lonny do? Punch Mr Franklin, and get in trouble herself? "No, ma'am."

Lonny gripped her shoulder tight and didn't ask anything else. Mag was glad for that, even as she hated it. She wished Lonny would push, would make the horrible fear and the disturbing *what if* that almost happened spill out so she could be rid of it. But it was another secret now, one she didn't want and certainly wouldn't treasure.

And it made her think of Hob, who was supposed to be her best friend, but who hadn't so much as spoken to her in three years. The Hob of three years ago *would* have done something. Hob lived outside the reach of the blacklist, like some old-fashioned hero that could bring justice where it could never be found. She carried knives, she knew how to shoot a gun – hell, the first time she'd met the preacher's boy she'd dropped him to the ground in one smooth move and pinned his arm tight because he'd been spying on them. Mag had tried to teach her how to sew, had told her every secret she knew because the thing Mag had always been best at was listening and that was all she could offer.

But after three years, Hob might as well be a goddamn fairy tale. And tomorrow, Mag would be on her own for true. There'd be no Mama, no Papa, no Lonny, just like there'd been no Hob for years.

Papa went with Mag to Newcastle the next day, sitting beside her on the train and helping keep an eye on her small trunk. It was baking day, and Mama had gotten several orders for pies, so she couldn't come with them. She was in tears about it that morning, but if their grand plan was to work, she needed to earn all the money that she could to help. So she'd kissed Mag goodbye, leaving a salty little mark on her cheek, and watched them from the train platform until she was out of sight.

It wasn't the most comfortable ride, just one car attached to the ore train right behind the engines, with hard plastic benches that magnified every rattle instead of seats. Mag curled up next to Papa and rested her head on his shoulder, doing her best to doze. Her hand rested curled in her lap, the cuts sewn and glued tight by the doctor the day before throbbing in time with her heartbeat and every little jolt of the train. She kept her eyes shut tight when she heard the voice of Mr Franklin. He stopped to talk with Papa, and even touched her hair, but she kept her face smooth and mimicked sleep.

She pretended to wake up after Mr Franklin had been gone for a good twenty minutes, and smiled when Papa told her that she'd missed their good "friend." It hurt to smile, but it had to be all right, she told herself. She'd be free of him in a few hours, and good riddance.

Papa handed her a kolache from the basket Mama had prepared for them. She ate it slowly, savoring the taste of homemade bread and sugared fruit. This she would miss, though, if all went well, only for a few years. As she ate, she looked out the window, watching red dunes rolling by, interrupted by pink and white flats of hardpan, and one mountain of black rock that the train went through by a tunnel. New workers that came off the rift ships always used words like *lonely*, *isolated*, when they saw the world stretch out around them like that. But Mag had been born here, just like Mama and Papa, children of the First Great Wave of immigrant workers. She had a hard time imagining how else a world could be. Claustrophobic, maybe. She'd find out.

On the other side of the tunnel, far too long for her to hold her breath through, the land changed. It was still all sand and dust, but there were spiky plants nailing the dunes down, and then stunted trees with dry, twisted branches. More green than she'd seen in her whole life.

Then the plants gave way to another long stretch of hardpan, shining so white in the sun that it nearly blinded her. She knew what that was, the great red-veined salt flat that was the foundation of Newcastle, the City. That was how everyone said it, city-with-a-capital-C, because it was the only proper city on the planet, impossibly big and shining. They said the salt that was Newcastle's foundation was four hundred meters thick and hard as synthcrete, the bones of an ancient ocean that had long since dried up. Where the water had gone no one seemed to know, since there weren't enough little lakes and rivers to make up for it, and no other oceans.

Mag craned her head to try to catch her first glimpse of Newcastle. All she got was the impression of light, mirrored glass shining so bright and fierce that it was impossible to make out the shapes, the glare spreading for kilometers in a ribbon, with spires striking up at the sky. She sat quickly back, rubbing at her eyes with her hand, and tried to comprehend the magnitude of it. She had never seen a place so huge, so bright. She couldn't imagine so much glass, and mirrored too – how did it stay so bright, against the sand and dust storms? She felt like she'd already jumped to a completely different world without ever being on a ship.

The train diverted around the maze of skyscrapers, toward an area surrounded by a high fence which only had a few small buildings tucked away in one corner. Still, those buildings were fancier than anything Mag had ever seen, spotless glass windows and stone facing. It looked of a piece with the other buildings she could see, sleek and foreign, rather than the more organic look of flimsy prefab housing that had been built out in different ways by the families living within. Most of the flat area was filled with a tower of shining metal with strange fins and antennas projecting from it, larger than she could really comprehend. "Papa, what is that?" she whispered, awed.

"That's your ticket off planet," he answered. "The rift ship. Big one like that is for hauling cargo, but it takes passengers too."

"You seen something like this before?"

"A time or two. Came down here with my papa to greet newcomers a time or two when he was crew master." Papa frowned. "Was a different time then."

"It's so big. How does it fly?" They didn't even have small ships like the military flew on other planets according to her history and civics lessons. The atmosphere on Tanegawa's World was too uncertain. She couldn't imagine something so enormous and ungainly launching itself up into the sky.

"I don't know, but it does, you can trust in that.

Every scrap of ore we sweat to the surface gets loaded on one of those and taken away."

The train pulled to a halt. The little box speaker in the car crackled into life, a sickeningly familiar voice announcing, "All passengers for the landing field to disembark, please. Good luck, Maggy-girl."

The few other passengers smiled at that, and a couple even clapped. Mag did her best to pretend that her face, suddenly gone dead and pale, and the shakes in her hands were because she was upset to be leaving home.

Papa stood, carrying her trunk to the door. "This is goodbye for now, Mags," he said, kissing her on the forehead, on the cheek, on the top of her head, and then pulling her in tight for a hug. "I've got to ride this train all the way to the station now, catch the next back. You be good, and you be careful, and you write to us every week, OK?" The pit boss had refused to give him more than a single day off, Mag knew; he couldn't even stay to see her off.

"Every day, I promise." Even if the letters would collect up for months before the next rift ship came to Tanegawa's World, she would give them a daily accounting of her life to read.

He pressed a purse into her hands. "Tuck this into your shirt now, don't take it out till you're at the ticket counter. I've counted it out, it's all there."

Mag nodded and tucked it away. Then Papa crushed her with another hug, the money digging into her belly hard enough to make a bruise.

"It'll just be a year or two," Papa whispered. "I promise."

"I'll find us a good place. And if I make any money extra, I promise I'll send it back."

The speaker made another noise, and there was that voice again. It near made her sick. "Final call for passengers to disembark."

Papa helped her lift the little trunk off the train. It wasn't that heavy; she could carry it easily enough on her own, but she knew it made him feel better. He gave her one last kiss, then stepped back into the train car so a man on the platform could shut the door.

Like Mama had back in Rouse, she stood on the platform and watched the train until it was gone, shielding her eyes with one hand as it wended into the shining buildings.

She sniffled, her throat tight, but no tears came as she picked up her trunk and walked it slowly to the building just off the platform. Heat radiated off the gray synthcrete and glass facing in waves, like it was a second sun. The salt hardpan heated her feet, even through the thick, new soles of her boots.

As soon as she crossed the threshold, stepping through a nested set of glass doors, the air turned cold enough to make her shiver. She looked around, feeling like a bumpkin, craning her neck to spot where the cold air came from as she took her place near the end of the line. The cold air dried her sweat, and she enjoyed the feel of it; it was never this chilly except in the dead of night, and only then outside of the town. Dozens of screens had been set into the wall, two large ones over the ticket window displaying endless scrolls of news, weather information, scheduling times. She'd never seen even one screen so fancy

– the few in Rouse were blocky, thick affairs with bad color and simplistic rather than photorealistic graphics, the images often jumping and stuttering with interference. These were smooth and bright. She almost wanted to touch them. It must be nice, she thought a bit sourly, to have so many fine things you could waste them on telling you that it was damned hot outside.

When it was her turn at the window, she pulled the purse from her shirt and handed it to the ticket clerk, a man in company blue with tiny round glasses perched on the end of his nose. He was going bald, what hair he had left iron gray and cut close to his skull. "What destination do you want?"

"Honest sir, I don't know where the ship's going. But it don't much matter. I'd like to go as far as that money will take me."

His eyebrows jumped a little, behind his tiny glasses, but he counted out all of the big chits and folded bills silently. "This will take you three stops, and you'll have a little left over." He consulted a screen. "The third stop will be Poseidon."

Mag licked her lips nervously. "What sort of place is it?" Maybe it would be better to take a closer stop, save the money and hope that'd get Mama and Papa off world sooner. But instinct told her to get as far away as she could, to use as much of the money as possible for its intended purpose.

The man pushed his glasses further up on his nose. "A very watery planet, I hear."

She tried to imagine that, and couldn't. It sounded far too exotic. "What sort of work is there?"

"Fishing, mostly. Other related industries." He frowned slightly.

She wanted to ask if the work was scarce, if it was all owned by TransRift like Tanegawa's World, a million other things. But she could tell that he was getting impatient. He was nice, and polite, but that didn't mean he was on her side. "I'd like the ticket for Poseidon, please. Thank you sir."

He named the price, counted a small pile of chits into her purse and handed it back to her. She tucked it carefully back into her shirt, so no one could try to steal it. He handed her a ticket next, explaining that it was all general boarding, that she was on the cheapest fare and would have to share communal quarters with everyone in steerage, that food was provided as legally required but only at base nutrition and anything fancier would be extra, and that the journey would take four weeks due to insystem flight speeds and loading times on world.

Mag did her best to listen, wishing that she'd thought to bring a flimsy to take notes, but then he handed her a little folder that he said contained the details of everything he'd just explained. He tucked a thin metal sheet into the booklet – her ticket. "Keep this safe and be ready to present it at any time. If you lose your boarding pass, I will be unable to provide you with another."

Mag nodded, tucking that into her shirt as well. "Sir, can I ask…"

He raised his eyebrows at her. He seemed a little impatient, but not unkind. "Yes?"

"What's it like? To fly in one of those things? I don't

even know why they call 'em rift ships and not space ships." She had vague recollections of history lessons, and remembered that the colonization of the myriad distant worlds had happened by way of space ships.

"They fly through space, but only enough to travel between rifts. And rifts…" The clerk frowned slightly. She couldn't tell if he wasn't certain of his answer, or just not certain how to explain it in a way she could understand. "The ship makes temporary holes in space itself and flies through them. What's on the other side is called the 'rift', and distance doesn't work the same as it does here. So a distance that would take centuries to travel like it used to can be crossed in a few hours."

"What's it like, in the rift space?" she asked, fascinated.

The clerk shook his head. "Nothing I can describe, little miss. You'll find out yourself, soon enough. Just don't go eating too soon before you're scheduled to cross the rift. It affects some people in a very bad way." He reached under the desk and brought out a little pamphlet, which he offered her. "This ought to cover a lot of your basic questions. Read the safety information first, it's the most important."

The reality of potential vomit made the thing seem even less like an adventure, though she took the pamphlet gratefully. A cartoon of a smiling man in a company blue suit waved at her from the front of the pamphlet, a little speech bubble saying: "Hi there! I'm Weatherman Bill. Ready to ride the rifts, little buddy?" Obviously intended for children to read, but she couldn't find it offensive, not when she knew nothing at all. Mag hazarded a glance behind her and noted several people there. She probably should stop taking up the man's time. "Thank you for all your help, sir. Where do I go now?"

He pointed off to the side. "Standard security and health screening, please. Once you've been screened, you will be directed to a waiting area. Boarding will begin in two hours."

Mag tucked the pamphlet in the pocket of her skirt. Trunk held between her hands, she joined the next line. There were little glass booths lined up there, and men in green Mariposa security uniforms; most of them were old and all of them looked bored. Passengers stood in the booths while scanners moved around them and security men watched. Other guards waved wands over their belongings.

Tongue stuck to the roof of her dry mouth, she waited her turn. It didn't look painful or indecent, but it was another hurdle to be crossed, and another thing she had never done in her life, more equipment she hadn't seen. The screening only took a minute for each passenger, and then the security men waved them out of the booths to pick up their belongings, then sent them down another hallway. No one seemed the least bothered by any of it.

They told her what to do every step of the way when it was her turn. Stand in the booth, hold up her arms. She answered questions about where she was from, swore that she had no animals or plants or seeds in her trunk, told them which vaccinations she'd had and which ones she'd missed. "Proceed down the hallway and enter the next room on your left," one of the guards told her.

"Is something wrong?" she asked, trying to smile cheerfully.

"Nothing at all." He didn't smile, didn't even look her in the eye, but that might not mean anything. She hadn't seen them smile at anyone, or look anyone in the eye. "You're missing two critical vaccinations. The doctor will give you the shots and then you'll be set to board."

It seemed so simple, enough that it made her knees a little weak with relief. So much for her paranoia. She took up her trunk and walked down the hall, just a short distance, and around the corner to a small room. There was no one waiting for her inside, but there was a little counter; maybe the doctor had just stepped out.

The door slammed shut behind her. She turned around, dropping her trunk. That was all she had time to do, because then there was a soft hiss, a scent both unnatural and sweet. Hands clutching at her nose and mouth, she collapsed to her knees.

She didn't try to yell for help.

CHAPTER FIVE

Hob had seen the Bone Collector only once, a decade ago. He'd started out as a statue in a wet cave that had no business being at the heart of one of the great sand seas, undeniably made of stone. He hadn't stayed a statue.

He also hadn't changed one bit in the intervening years. His staff was straight and smooth, made of a yellowed, impossibly long bone, with a wildcat skull affixed to the top and surrounded by feathers bleached pale and carved bone beads on leather cords. He left the staff standing up in the sand, like an unholy signpost. The Bone Collector looked like he was made of living bone himself, or maybe cream-colored limestone like the cave she'd first seen him in: skin pale like he never saw the sun, waist-length tail of hair almost white and his eyebrows near invisible. He was dressed like a vagrant, clothing and gray leather duster ragged. His white shirt was buttoned all the way to his throat; chains of knucklebones and lizard skulls were strung around his neck, hanging over his chest. Strings of talons, so large they could have come only from the great eagles, decorated the edge of his rain cape and hung from his buttons. His waistcoat was deep blue and embroidered with constellations of silver stars, the color jarring when everything else about him was so pale.

She remembered the pop of that color, too. That first time she'd seen him, he'd transformed from stone to flesh in an instant, after she and Freki and Geri – then still wearing their pup names Francis and George – had wet the underground lake with the blood of a company man who'd wanted to break the Bone Collector to pieces with a hammer. He'd scared the hell out of her, changing like that, and she'd tried to stab him in the side with her knife. The blade had shattered against him and he'd laughed of all things, kissed her forehead, and said, *I expected someone taller*.

Well, she wasn't some overhyped kid fresh off her first real knife fight now. "Took your time," she called to him, rising to her feet. And then, to prove she remembered and she wasn't scared, "Am I tall enough yet?"

He laughed, though he didn't speak until he came to a halt in front of her. "Your feet seem to reach the ground. Didn't Nick Ravani tell you the way to gain my attention?" He was her height, maybe even a mite shorter now, when he'd seemed to stretch for meters before. And slight, she realized; it was the duster and all the bones that gave him any sense of bulk.

"Nick Ravani don't tell no one a thing unless he thinks it's funny," she drawled. "So what way would that be?"

"Blood, Hob Ravani. Blood calls blood; just a few drops in the sand and I will find you."

Hearing her name come out of his mouth in that odd accent of his, those low tones, put a shiver down her back. She hid it with a shrug. "Or an eagle will show up."

"That too. But I don't think you'd have any trouble fending one off for an hour or two." He tilted his head slightly to one side. "This isn't a social call, I take it? It never is."

Did he sound disappointed? "Old Nick's brother's been killed. Gunned down in the back, out on the dunes."

"I don't know why you'd need to ask me about that. The answer is obvious."

Hob smiled grimly, because it was true. If there was another cause of people getting shot in the back in the middle of the desert, she'd yet to find it. Bandits didn't waste that many bullets – even those making good money under the table from Mariposa employers. "Yeah, the *who* is damned obvious. But I need to know *why*. His wife didn't even know he was dead till I told her. And Mag – his daughter – can you tell me if she's OK? If she made it off world?" She tried to keep steady as she spoke, pretending that this was just another job, but her voice cracked on the last word. She needed to be sure. "You can do that type of stuff, right?"

"Did you bring a bone for me?"

Hob reached into her pocket, pulled out the stained, stinking handkerchief-wrapped bundle. "It's Phil's. He's got no use for it anymore."

The Bone Collector unwrapped the handkerchief and looked at the finger, seeming to be caught between pleasure and disgust. "Three bones... and still wrapped in meat. It will do. This will make it easier to find out the answers you want."

"So you can do it."

"I can try. Would you like to come back later?"

"It's an awful long ride." She hesitated, sucking at her teeth. "What'll it cost?"

The Bone Collector shrugged, a small smile curving his lips. "For you... I would do it for free." The way he said that made something warm curl in her stomach; she wanted to like it and had long since learned to never trust such feelings or such men. "But since I know that would worry you, I will give you a price. All of the water you have brought with you."

Hob snorted. "You tellin' me that you're just coming up with a price to make me feel better ain't exactly havin' the desired effect."

"If you'd not mind skipping this part of the little dance, we are happily back to no price at all."

Exasperated, she said, "Why can't you just make this a normal fuckin' deal?"

"Normal." He said the word like it was a foreign curiosity. "Nick Ravani and I... how has he put it. We 'go way back.' As do you and I, if I recall correctly." The Bone Collector smiled.

"You could say that."

"Then you have your answer. I don't think any of us have too many friends."

It was Hob's turn to laugh, holding up her hands in surrender. "You've made your point. Friend." It seemed strange that the man – if he even was a man – thought of her like that after only one encounter where she'd ended it by trying to stab him, but she wasn't about to question it. She wasn't that rich. "Fine then. You do it for free and I don't bitch about it. You mind if I just wait around?"

He shrugged. "As long as you will be patient, and not interrupt me."

"Contrary to what Old Nick's been jawing, I got it in me to be patient." Hob pulled her cigarette case, a battered thing made of steel that she'd taken off a bandit a few years back, from her jacket. She drew a black cigarette out and tucked it between her lips. A little pulse of the heat that always waited in her blood and she snapped her fingers near the cigarette's end. A tongue of concentrated flame leapt, took, and then she sucked it into the end of the cigarette and turned it into a perfect, glowing cherry. That was one of Old Nick's favorite parlor tricks, and the first one she'd mastered, even when he kept telling her she was too young to smoke. A little hint of witchiness they could get away with showing off where others could see, since it was easily dismissed. "You want me to stand downwind?"

The Bone Collector watched each small movement with strange intensity; at the sight of the little flame spitting from her fingertips, he smiled. "I would appreciate it. Why you have chosen to acquire Nick's foulest habit, I cannot begin to guess." He moved to another sand-filled cellar.

"Mayhap we like how it tastes." Cigarettes were still the only thing that soothed the fire in her blood, kept it from burning her inside to out. So she smoked just as much as Old Nick, leaving chains of ash and burnt-out cigarette butts in her wake. She'd never asked, but she guessed he did it for the same reason. Hob followed the Bone Collector with long, easy strides, sand and dust puffing up around the toes of her boots. She paused when he turned and gave her a long, level look. "You want me to back off?"

"Not at all. I've just never had someone be so curious."

"I'm a curious sort."

He laughed, the sound pleasant and musical, and she hated herself a little for liking it. This was business, Uncle Phil was dead, and she needed to have her head in the game. She'd sworn to never have her head out of the game again.

At the cellar pit, he unrolled the severed finger from the handkerchief and plunged it into the sand, holding it under as if he expected it to come alive and struggle. His face creased with a frown for a moment, and then he pulled his hand back up. Three clean finger bones sat on his palm.

"Nice trick."

"I have many." The Bone Collector sat down on the remnants of a stone wall. He moved the bones around on his palm with a few gentle nudges, then nodded to himself. "You must be quiet now." He looked at her until she nodded in return, and then bowed his head, covering the bones up with his other hand.

At first, she thought it was a trick of the thin light coming from the moons; his face went pale, dead white, and that pallor spread, flowing up from the roots of his hair to the tips, moving down his neck and onto his jacket. And then she knew it wasn't just a trick of the light when his waistcoat turned pale as the rest of him.

She shuffled a little closer, peering at him, but didn't touch, didn't make a sound. The very texture of the man had changed, from fluid and living to smooth and unmoving. Even the stray threads of embroidery on his waistcoat had gone still.

Rock. He'd turned into rock. She'd always told herself that it must have been her imagination, though she hadn't been that imaginative of a child. You didn't really need to be imaginative when you'd had your eye ripped out by a phoenix and had a crazy old coot telling you with nods and winks that witches were real and that's what you both happened to be. But seeing it twice was believing.

She finished her cigarette, burning out the last of the paper in a flare of sparks between two fingers, then started on another. Only three cigarettes left in the case before she'd have to roll up some more. No talking, no pacing, no anything, all she had to do to keep herself entertained was stare at the stars and smoke. And think, about a spray of blood, about regret, about the hole she'd dug for herself, which she was still struggling to escape.

No wonder she always kept herself moving.

CHAPTER SIX

Then

Mag's head ached, her pulse pounding behind her eyes, and her mouth tasted terrible, like dust and plastic and bitter medicine. She sat up slowly; she'd been dumped on a hard bed that was actually just a shelf covered with a thin pad and a blanket. There was a shiny metal toilet in one corner of the room, a tiny sink next to it. That was it. Her trunk was nowhere to be seen. She checked the inside of her blouse; the remnants of her money was still there, as was the ticket. As she moved, the pocket of her skirt crinkled – they'd left her the pamphlet with smiling Weatherman Bill on the front.

Fat lot of good any of that would do for her now, least of all the ticket. She had no idea how long she'd been out, but from the cramping of her muscles, the ache in joints held in one position for too long, it had to be more than two hours. And if they'd locked her in a cell, well, they must not want her getting out. Either way, the rift ship was probably long gone, and with it her chance of escape.

Mag huddled in the corner, knees pulled up to

her chest, arms wrapped around them. She didn't call for help, didn't ask any questions of the empty air, swallowing again and again at the panic that fluttered in her chest. It was obvious enough that the Mariposa men had done something, likely at the behest of some TransRift rule she'd never heard of. There was no escaping, no help coming. She wracked her brain for where she'd slipped up. This couldn't be just about vaccinations, no matter what the guard had told her. Had Mr Franklin done something? Was this a punishment, aimed toward Papa somehow, even though he'd never done anything wrong?

She dozed a little, head nodding, then woke to the sound of a loud clang. A little window, about head height, slid open in the door. She could see part of the face of a person, just the eyes, blue as ice. She stood, trying to smooth out her blouse, look presentable.

Maybe it was all just a mistake.

"Magdala Kushtrim is your name, correct?" It was a man's voice, tone dry and disinterested.

"Yessir. Why am–"

"Your town of origin is Rouse."

"Yessir. Please–"

"Were you accompanied by anyone here?"

Mag hesitated, then stood up a little straighter. "Why should I tell you that, if you're just gonna hold me like I'm some kind of prisoner and not even tell me why?"

The man's eyes tilted slightly, as if he'd moved his head. "If you comply, we will be able to get you out of here sooner."

"But why am I in here to begin with?"

"We have detected some sort of contamination on you. You are not a prisoner, Miss Kushtrim. This is for your safety and that of everyone else. You'll be able to leave as soon as we've decontaminated you. A room is being prepared now."

Her stomach knotted in her chest, and she pressed her hands against her middle. "Contaminated with what?"

"We are uncertain. Did anyone accompany you to the landing field?"

Mag hesitated, but if there was some sort of contamination, something bad that would make her and everyone else sick, she needed to be honest. And where else could contamination have come from, except up out of the mine? All of Rouse might be in trouble. "My papa, Philip Kushtrim. We were on the ore train from Rouse. He's taking a different train back, though. But… sir, did I miss my flight? I don't have money to buy another fare."

"Your ticket has been deferred for now. You can use it at a later date. In the last few days, have you encountered any unusual substances or strange people?"

Mag shook her head. She thought about Mr Franklin, but he was a hateful bastard, not unusual at all from the rumors she'd heard, and he was one of *theirs*. The rest was a blur of work, cleaning up after the mine accidents and exhaustion. "No, no, nothing strange at all."

"Do your best to remember while you wait. If you think of anything, it could help us. Just speak your answer and we will hear."

She opened her mouth to ask another question, but the little window slid shut again. She ran to the door, banged on it with her fist a few times, but there was no response. "Hello?" she called. "Can I please have some food? And mayhap a book? Please?"

The silence of the room pressing in around her, she retreated to the shelf, curled herself into the corner again.

With nothing else to do, Mag eventually started reading over the pamphlet that the clerk had given her. She turned to the safety information and felt like crying. There would be no flight for her, so she certainly didn't need to know where the exits were, or the emergency air pods, or the proper procedure for deep space abandonment in case of reactor breach. She read it anyway, the friendly cartoon of Weatherman Bill explaining the various safety features blurring before her eyes.

The later pages of the pamphlet explained the history of TransRift, Inc in glowing terms. It was similar to what she'd learned in basic schooling, but told in a much cheerier way with colorful pictures: TransRift, Inc had been founded two hundred and forty-six Sol-standard years ago, after the discovery of faster-than-light travel – "That means rift space," Weatherman Bill added helpfully from the side of the page via speech bubble, "but we'll talk more about that later, promise!" Before then, humans had traveled out from the Sol system on generation ships and colonies, humanity spread out on lonely planets that couldn't really talk to each other because of the long transmission delays. The rift ships united the disparate worlds and turned one-way trips into commuter flights, the Federal Union of Systems got started, and the plucky settlers of Tanegawa's World welcomed the major investment that TransRift wanted to make in their little dust ball because all that raw material for making ships had to come from somewhere. They were all one big, happy TransRift family, the pamphlet assured her, working toward a common goal, greasing the wheels of progress with the sweat from their brows.

She laughed so hard at that last bit that she almost choked.

The next section showed a simple diagram of the rift ship Mag had almost gotten to fly on, with smiling people inside. The relentless cheer was really starting to get on her nerves. "It's time for me to tell you a little about myself," Weatherman Bill said on the page. "Now, you might be wondering why I'm called a Weatherman if I'm talking to you from space! Believe it or not, there's weather in space, only it's not wind and rain and snow – it's made of gravity, radiation, and even dark energy. Special people like me start training very early and very hard, from the time we're children, to understand that space weather and navigate those big rift ships. Not just anyone can do my job because it's so hard, but kids – if you think you have what it takes to be Weathermen, if you're good at math and seeing shapes in your head and you're really good at music, make sure to talk to the ship crew before you disembark for more information. Now, early immigrants to Tanegawa's

World called us Weathermen because they heard the crew talking about space weather, and the name stuck. Weathermen are just as important as the rift ships themselves for faster-than-light travel. Without us manning the helm, humanity would still be slow as slugs. But thanks to our understanding of space weather and its relationship to the rifts, humans can go anywhere, and the Federal Union spans system after system. Isn't that grand?"

Somehow, she doubted it was anything grand at all, from her little cell. When she'd finished reading the pamphlet, just hungry for the words, she tore it up and started playing chess with the disassembled bits.

A meal arrived. She ate it wondering what this contamination could be. The more she thought, the less likely it seemed to be what they said. She thought about Uncle Nick and his witchiness, and Hob the same. Maybe that was what "contamination" meant, but she couldn't do anything like they could, no matter how hard she strained. And she hadn't seen Hob in three years, Uncle Nick in over a month; she doubted either of them had passed something to her. Like witchiness was even some sort of disease you could catch. She was pretty sure it didn't work that way.

Then she remembered the little bag of blue crystals, something she'd never before seen in her life, just that glimpse after a long, exhausting night. Could that have been it? But they were just pretty rocks, nothing special at all. Papa brought pretty rocks up from the mine all the time. Maybe she should mention it anyway, but after so long, forgotten in this gray-on-gray oubliette, she didn't feel inclined to cooperate any more.

Mag tried calling out, experimentally, to the high ceiling and its sourceless light, asking if someone could hear her, if her papa was there.

Silence.

The door finally opened when she was halfway through another meal. Two men in green waited out in the hall. They didn't look nearly as friendly as the guards at the security check; both had guns and collapsible, spring-loaded batons swinging from their belts.

The taller of the two, a man with a crooked nose and gray shot through his dark hair, said, "Come with us, miss."

Mag put her tray down carefully on her bed and stood, smoothing her skirt. "What's this about?"

"We're still working on your case. But the Weatherman said he thinks he can help you. Come along."

"Weatherman? But…" Weren't they only on ships? There'd hardly be any of their special space weather on the surface of the planet. And hadn't the ship already left and taken its Weatherman with it?

"I'm sure he'll explain it to you. He's a busy man, though. Come along, miss." For all that he looked scary, he sounded nice. But Mag was well aware at this point that sound was just sound, and could lie easier than words. From the way the two stood, it was also plain that if she didn't want to come quietly, they'd be happy to help her. There didn't seem a point in making this into a fight, not when it was one she couldn't hope to win. The helpless feeling made her stomach clench around the lukewarm casserole she'd just eaten.

They bracketed her when she stepped out into the hall, pulled her along in their wake through a series of bare hallways. It was all synthcrete floors and walls, metal doors set in them, just like the door she'd come through. How many people did they have in these rooms? Mag clenched her hands in her skirts, gritted her teeth, and stared straight ahead. The gray floor beneath her feet was smooth to the point of slippery, polished by countless boots and so clean she probably could have eaten off it.

Around a corner waited a different door, one that was all glass, providing a window into a white room. It was different enough, brighter even, that she thought maybe they were finally going to let her go. But as the shorter guard opened the door, a smell washed out, something she could barely identify. Dry, slightly sweet, like a spider, a smell that touched deep at the back of her brain and whispered *danger*.

"Go on, then," the taller of the guards said. They didn't give her a chance to respond. Hands against her shoulders, they pushed her inside.

The door shut at her back with an anticlimactic, almost inaudible *click*.

There was a man in the room, sitting in a chair against one wall, his hands resting lightly on his knees. He looked ordinary enough at first glance, pale and wearing a company blue suit, his black hair just greasy enough to look like he needed a shower. But the little details screamed at Mag, like that smell, and his eyes. His irises were black, like holes floating in his head.

The man looked up at her and smiled, and those black eyes swallowed her up. She could hardly breathe, throat working uselessly as he stood and walked toward her, his gait odd and unsteady. This had to be the Weatherman, a sick parody of the friendly cartoon from the pamphlet – no, this was the reality, she realized. Weatherman Bill was just one more lie.

Mag pressed back against the glass wall even as he beckoned to her, and shook her head emphatically as if that would be some defense.

"Hmmm," he hummed, a light, not unmusical sound, and moved in closer. He breathed more soft notes as she scooted away from him until he had her caught in a corner.

He grabbed her face with long, pale hands, his fingers cold and hard as bone. Thin white scars crisscrossed his hairline, a strange detail to notice when the rest of her brain floated in sourceless terror. This was wrong, he was wrong, she didn't want him touching her. It was the same as Mr Franklin, worse than Mr Franklin, and he stared at her with unreadable eyes.

"What have we here…" he said in a little sing-song. It was a beautiful sound, and it didn't have a right to be. He let go of her face and grabbed her hand, the one wrapped in now-dirty bandages.

"Don't…" She didn't know what he was going to

do, but she didn't want it, didn't want any of it.

"Shh, shh." He unwound the bandage and dropped it to the floor negligently, then examined the angry, red-brown-crusted lines that crisscrossed her palm, the little black loops of stitches, the shiny patches of tissue glue. With one hand, he held hers steady in a grip she had no hope of escaping; not crushing, but it didn't need to be. With the other hand he lightly drew a fingernail along one of the cuts. Glue and stitches dissolved and her flesh parted again, bright red blood welling.

"No," she whimpered, through a throat gone sick with nausea and fear. She tugged uselessly at her hand.

"Shh," he repeated. He leaned down to sniff the blood and then slid his tongue over the wound.

Mag screamed.

The man looked up, his eyes gone black on black on black, and then the black was filling her nose, her mouth, her head, and she couldn't see or breathe, just feel the tugging at her blood that ran down her arm and into her spine, pulling at every nerve in her body.

Dimly, she heard her own heartbeat thundering, too fast, too fast. She felt cold lips on her palm, and faintly heard the words, "What have we here?"

Then the black swallowed her up.

CHAPTER SEVEN

After what was probably just an hour but felt far longer, the Bone Collector made a soft noise. Hob looked down to see him back to normal, opening eyes that were once again a startling blue. He made to stand, wavering on his feet. She lunged forward to grab him by the collar and pull him upright before he fell and knocked his fool head on the wall.

One hand still clutching the bones, he held on to the front of her black undertaker's coat with the other. It brought his face in far too close to hers. His breath smelled odd, like cinnamon and blood, something she could suddenly taste in her own mouth around the tobacco; his eyes were dark and unfocused. She felt the urge to press their foreheads together, as if that would give her some insight into what he was thinking. It was such a strange tug on her heart that she didn't welcome – she'd had enough of that bullshit to last three lifetimes and no good came of it. But fuck, she couldn't help but think of a hand sliding along her neck until he had his feet properly under himself.

He didn't seem interested in letting go of her jacket, even when she let go of his. "I'm sorry. I usually allow myself a little more time to recover," he said, not sounding at all apologetic.

"Must've come up with somethin' good, then." Hob disengaged his hand and took a deliberate step back. "What you got?"

The Bone Collector looked slightly disappointed for a moment, then smoothed back his hair with one hand, his smile taking a crooked tilt. "Has Old Nick told you much about me?"

"We talkin' about the same dried-up ol' asshole? 'Course not."

He laughed. "You could say that I see the future, though it's not set in stone. And I can see the past as well. That is part of what I do."

"Huh." Hob crossed her arms over her chest. Considering she could call fire out of thin air, she wasn't too quick to dismiss anyone else's claim to witchiness. Particularly not when they were as blatantly strange as the Bone Collector. "Can you see *my* future?"

"I could if I wanted, though indistinctly. Unless you'd like to give me a bone?"

It was her turn to laugh. "If it's all the same to you, no."

He shrugged. "Philip was thrown from his train by men in green. The train had stopped in between towns, very abruptly. After he'd gotten a little way from the tracks, there was a helicopter. They shot him from inside it."

Hob let out a low whistle. "Don't see those that far out all that often. He must've done pissed someone off."

"More than that, I cannot really say."

"What about Mag?"

"It's… difficult. She is his blood, but not. But I can tell you that she still lives. That she is far away."

"That could mean a lot of things." Far away could be good. Far away could mean *on a rift ship and flying the fuck out of this system*.

That hope died with his next words. "Still on this planet, but not nearby. I can also tell you with full certainty that she was not with him when he was thrown from the train."

She exhaled a long, smoky breath she hadn't even realized she was holding. "Still on the goddamn planet. Fuck."

"Is that not what you wanted to hear?" He tucked the finger bones into his pocket.

"Better'n being dead." But worse than escaped. A lot worse than escaped. "Can you get more specific about where she is?"

"Not as I sit here, unless you have one of her bones. Is that all?"

What, so he'd know more if he sat somewhere else? Hob knew better than to demand more help from him; the Bone Collector cared about only his own affairs, was what Nick had always told her. Coming from someone like Nick, that made it a fair miracle that she'd gotten any help at all. She could at least take the information back that Mag was still *here* to Nick, and they could figure out what to do next.

Except…

She snapped her fingers. "Right… wanted to show this to you as well, see if you seen 'em before." She handed him the little burlap sample bag. "It's these little crystals, all pretty and blue. When I touched one, damn near took my hand off. Well, tried. If I could get burned by fire, I wouldn't have been so happy."

He undid the strings holding the bag shut and peered into it, as if he could see without the benefit of light. When he looked back up at her, his eyes were wide. "Where did you get these?"

"Off Phil's body... he had it in his pocket. Dunno where he got 'em. You know what they are?"

He closed the bag back up and tucked it into his pocket. Looking at his face, Hob decided not to argue for now. "Do you recall that moment, when the claws of the phoenix sank into your eye?"

Just the mention of it had her touching the patch over her left eye. Even now, the empty socket below burned and throbbed. "Yeah." But how the hell did he know that? She'd never told him. She'd only ever told Nick Ravani the full story, and just because she hadn't been thinking so clear at the time. And while Old Nick might be friends with the Bone Collector – if *friends* were even a thing either of them did – she still couldn't imagine him running his mouth off about something so personal to both of them. The phoenix was too strange, too much a hallucination, too painful, too damn private. She would have dismissed it entirely, but for the fact that from that moment on, she'd had sparks of flame dancing off her fingertips, fire pounding in her blood.

"Like that."

"But they're crystals."

As if annoyed by her stating the obvious, he said, "Yes."

"That don't make a lick of sense."

"It doesn't have to." He held out his hand. "Come along."

"Excuse me?" The rapid back and forth turns of the conversation left her feeling dizzy.

"I want you to come with me. I... now have an interest in finding the dead man's daughter. And I may need your help."

Another sudden reversal, but this one was going in her direction. "Can I take my motorcycle?"

"It will be safe here. My way is faster."

Hob frowned, and then shrugged. This was the best information she had, the *only* information she had for helping Mag. Not much of a choice, really. "Let me write a note for Nick, since he might send someone to check here once he's gotten to Rouse."

"Of course."

The Bone Collector followed her over to the motorcycle, watched her write her note with more curiosity than the simple act really deserved. "You never seen handwriting or something?"

He smiled slightly. "Not any quite that terrible."

"Yeah, fuck you," Hob muttered. "Why you got this sudden interest in finding Mag, anyhow?"

"She may be... changed."

What the hell did that even mean? She took her best guess. "She's grown in three years, sure."

"No. Changed like you did, when Nick sent you out into the dunes." He reached out, pausing when she flinched, and then lightly laid his fingers beside her eye patch. "When you offered your eye to come home."

"You're gettin' a mite too friendly, there." The Bone Collector knowing this left her more spooked and off balance than if she'd just caught him peeping on her while she was bathing. Better to be angry, like she'd be for any other invasion of her privacy. "Don't remember *offering* anyone any damn thing," she muttered, and then shook her head. "Remember gettin' my fuckin' eye tore out by an eagle. That's why you care, huh?"

"My reasons are legion." He offered her his hand again; she took it, but then he shook his head and let go. "Take your gloves off."

"Why?"

"Do you ask questions every time someone tells you to do something?"

"Can't rightly do that back home, so I guess I got a powerful backlog to get out of my system now."

He laughed. "Remarkable. Take off your gloves so that I can touch your skin. Otherwise, I might lose you."

"Don't sound pleasant, the way you say it." Hob flicked away her half-finished cigarette, hitting it with a pulse of heat so that it burned to ash in the air. She pulled her gloves off, but hesitated before reaching for his hand again.

"You have another question?" A smile twitched at his lips.

For all she was used to Old Nick giving her looks like that all the time, Hob wanted to punch it right off the Bone Collector's face. Maybe Nick wasn't as handsome as this fellow, but at least he'd earned the right to look at her like she was a joke. "You got a name? Not supposed to go anywhere with strangers, y'know."

The Bone Collector laughed, but it was an odd, flat sort of sound. "I don't." The humor fell away from his face in an instant and he caught her hand before she could react. "Would you like to give me one?"

His skin was cool, dry, no calluses that she could detect. It made her feel very rough and scratched up in comparison, and put a strange tingle up her arm, like there was some kind of electricity radiating off him. She hadn't felt a thing like that in years, and maybe it felt good, but it set off every damn warning bell that she had in her brain. Dangerous. The sort of person who was bound to ask for things she shouldn't give but would fool herself into thinking she wanted to. Want was a mirage over ugly truths, ready to lead you astray in the desert.

Hob squeezed his fingers hard as she could and was rewarded with a dismayed flicker in his eyes. "Everyone's got a name. Don't fuck with me."

Hurt, emotional rather than physical, twisted at his mouth. "Not everyone."

She might have been all right, if she hadn't looked him in the eye. There was a world of pain on display there for a moment, so naked it made her want to cringe. Hob looked away first, loosening her grip. "Ain't gonna happen."

The Bone Collector didn't let go of her hand. "Let's not argue. We've more important concerns. Come along." He pulled her over the little sand drifts, and then down the slipping slope of a flow of red, into the cellar. The foundation still visible was stained with streaks of rust like dried blood. There he paused, surrounded on three sides by walls half buried in sand. "Whatever you do, don't let go."

She tightened her grip again until he gasped, but he didn't complain. "I think this is the craziest thing I've ever done." And she'd done some crazy shit, up to and including going out into the desert on Nick Ravani's say-so.

He smiled. "Yet."

At first the sand was solid beneath her feet, but then it flowed, first slow and plastic like taffy and then fast like water, crashing up and over them both. Hob opened her mouth to scream, had just enough time to hear the Bone Collector whisper into her ear, "It will be all right, dearest, I won't let you go," as sand filled her mouth and nose and eyes.

Things went strange.

Hob's brain froze with sheer terror, senses firing randomly because there was no input except *pressure* and *movement*. She focused on feeling the Bone Collector's hand clasped in hers, his cool skin hard like stone, and more stone all around her. No matter how tightly she held on, she felt like he was about to slip away, flesh going smooth and slick.

Her ears rang with his voice, stretched out infinitely. Her eyes filled with unseeing starbursts. She couldn't breathe, yet her lungs felt so full they might burst, her heart hammering against them fit to bruise. She didn't pass out. She wished she could pass out. Screaming also would have been nice, something to relieve that pressure as something far firmer than sand slid through her hair and tightened around her ribs and still he pulled her onward, faster and faster and *no don't let go of my hand–*

Fingers touched her cheek, feather light. Her eye flew open – when had she squeezed it so tightly shut, her eyelid felt scratchy – and she looked up into the Bone Collector's upside-down face. His blue eyes were filled with amusement and a little crack of pain.

"Let go of my hand now, please. Before you crush my bones."

She felt a pull on her arm; somehow afraid to move her head, in case she felt rock instead of air against it, she looked with just her eye. She still clung to his other hand, knuckles gone white. His fingers, visible around hers, had taken on an unhealthy red tinge of the blood trapped inside. Huh, so he did have blood in him, actual blood instead of dust. What a thought to have, floating up out of a brain too scrambled to do more than make inane observations. One finger at a time, she made herself let go.

"Thank you." He leaned over, his nose only a few centimeters from hers. "Try to breathe. In and out. It's merely air, you don't need to fear."

She did as he said, and marveled at the working of her own lungs.

"Very good. You know, you're taking this rather well."

She managed a dry, croaking laugh. "Am I now."

"You're not crying. Or screaming. Those are the two reactions I've seen most often." He smiled, his thumb moving lightly across her cheek.

She had to swallow hard, blink, and tried to refocus.

They weren't outside any more, that was for sure; there was a roof, more rock cut smoothly like butter, high overhead. And it was light, imagine that, steady and white, familiar enough to tell her it was a powered lamp like the kind the Ghost Wolves used. There was more rock under her back, but it was something far softer under her head; she was stretched out on his lap like some lovesick girl.

Hob sat up so abruptly that she nearly slammed her forehead into his chin; only a quick jerk back on his part saved him. He only seemed more amused. "Normally, I let people lay about and recover a bit longer."

"Guess I'm quicker'n most." She shook her head, grimacing, and then felt at her hair. Her braids were full of sand. A quick glance at the Bone Collector confirmed that he was neat as always, not a hair out of place. She undid the tails, jerking the knots out of her hair without regard, and roughly combed her fingers through to shake the worst of the sand out. The Bone Collector reached toward her – to help? touch? didn't matter – and she slapped his hand sharply away. No one messed with her hair; it was her one bit of flip, considering the few other women in the outfit had all cut their hair short or even shaved their heads like the men, because it made wearing helmets all the time more comfortable.

He wiggled his fingers to shake off the sting. "So it seems. With a little practice, you won't need a rest at all, I'm sure."

"That how it normally works?" Fingers slowing out of habit, she separated the strands and began replaiting her braids.

He smiled, and stood. The rock ceiling was low over his head, but not so much that he couldn't stand straight. Walls, ceiling, floor, it was all the same, dark gray with veins of pink and white, copper and gold, lit with yellow lamp light. "I can't think of anyone else who has gotten a second try. Can you stand?"

She was a little unsteady on her feet, but she'd be damned if she'd let herself cling to him. "Don't have time to waste, do we?"

He started walking down the tunnel; lamps were screwed into the walls at regular intervals, others in holders on old timbers – real wood, probably come in from the farming towns. There was little of that to be had on planet, and it all ended up in... "We're in a mine," she said, blinking stupidly.

"The Pictou mine, yes. I've blocked off the entrance at the surface, so it's a safe enough place to stay."

"Downright thrifty of you."

"The humans were no longer using it. And it is very... defensible. Too many ghosts."

There was a lot she could pull from what he'd said, and none of it sat well. Just the offhand mention of *humans*, like they really were two different species for all they looked the same, made her twist uncomfortably inside. "That's some sound strategy you got goin' there," she finally remarked.

"Nick Ravani has proven an invaluable resource."

Well, now it all made more sense. Nick Ravani was crazier than a shithouse rat, but when he was thinking about the long term she'd long since realized that he played his games of chess on levels no one could even see. Though it made her wonder how much of *that* was the Bone Collector's influence. How well did they actually know each other?

Hob took her cigarette case from her pocket by habit, tucked one between her lips. The look the Bone Collector shot her could have curdled milk. "We're inside."

"I noticed." She grimaced and put the cigarette away, wishing she had something to gnaw on while she thought. Too much, all at once, and all of it long past strange.

The Bone Collector took a left-hand branch, came into a much larger room that had been hollowed out. There was a bedroll spread out there, and a little stove with a coffee pot on top of it. "When the witch hunters take people into the big city, Newcastle, they go to one building. The largest of them, where the Weatherman is."

"There's a Weatherman *here*?" Hob asked. She'd never encountered a Weatherman before, not really. But she knew that Weathermen were the beating heart of the rift ships, revered and feared and never seen by ordinary crew rats like she'd been, and there were all sorts of theories about them being aliens, being monsters, being able to kill the unwary with a look. The thought that one had come to rest here and put his feet down on the ground felt wrong and terrifying to her remaining spacer superstitions.

There was a strange tightness to the Bone Collector's face. "There has always been a Weatherman here, as long as Weathermen have existed. Your friend will be with him."

"How do we get her out of there?" She had to swallow down the feeling of sickness along with all of her questions, telling herself to act like it was a job, just another job. Focus on that. "You ain't ever done this before, have you?"

"They have ways of keeping me out. But now, I have an idea," the Bone Collector said, his smile turning secretive.

CHAPTER EIGHT

Then

The next Mag knew, she opened her eyes to the featureless wall of her cell. Her head ached, still filled with the black and the horrible man's voice. The inside of her left wrist hurt sharply, burning and throbbing. Her hand felt like it weighed a thousand kilos as she lifted it up to see a series of parallel lines scored into her skin with black ink. Making a frantic little whimper in her throat, she tried to wipe it away with one thumb, and it just hurt. Worse, she felt something hard and round, embedded under her skin and topped with the thin, red line of a scar.

Mag rolled from the bed and crawled over to the toilet, vomited until there was nothing left in her stomach and she was shaking and raw.

For all that her left wrist hurt, her right hand didn't. Filled with dread, she checked her palm. The cuts had transformed to smooth scars, still angry and red, but healed like it had been weeks since she'd been cut instead of a couple of days. Maybe it had been. She flexed her fingers, then remembered the sensation of the man – no, he couldn't be a *man*, whatever a

Weatherman was, it was only man-shaped – licking her palm, and her stomach heaved again.

Mag curled up on the floor, knees hugged to her chest, and stared at the door with dry eyes. She had no reference for any of this but stories, novels, fairytales, the occasional vid. If she believed those, she should be brave and ready to sing and maybe even dance, no matter how miserable she was at being imprisoned. She had a feeling whoever had written those stories had never been in this position, hip and shoulder digging into a synthcrete floor, mouth sour with bile. And shouldn't she be rescued by now? Where was her knight? Maybe if Hob–

No. Hob really was a myth. Just like the friendly cartoon face in the pamphlet about rift ships, hiding the monster beneath. Weatherman Bill, her ass. She didn't know and couldn't begin to guess why the Weatherman was here, what he was doing to her. But when they came for her again, those guards with their fake courtesy, she would fight them. Fists and feet and teeth, she'd fight them, and if they knew what was good for them, they'd shoot her down.

With that resolve, the knot in her chest loosened and she could breathe again. Though when they slid the food tray through the slot in her door, she made no move to take it. The horrible, beautiful voice of the man-shaped thing still echoed in her head with more words she couldn't understand, filling her blood with sickness.

Four uncaten meals later, the door to her cell opened. Mag pretended to be obedient until she'd gotten out of the door. Then just as the thought sparked in her brain to punch the man on her right and her muscles began to tense, something like a mule kicked her in the back. Her muscles went rigid, and she smelled ozone and charred fabric.

The taller of the guards caught her as her legs gave way. She tried to struggle against him, twitching feebly.

The shorter of the two guards waggled a black baton in front of her face. "Predictable. They always fight, the second time," he said. "It's easier for us all this way, scum."

Mag tried to protest that she hadn't been going to fight – she wasn't going to bat an eyelash at lying now – but her mouth didn't want to work. A nonsensical mumble spilled out between her lips.

The taller guard hitched her over his shoulder like a sack, and they walked down the hall.

"Now, if you don't want this to happen again," the short guard said conversationally, "you play nice with the Weatherman. And the next time we come to pick you up, you offer us your wrists so we can cuff you properly." He tilted the box at her again. "Or I can stun you again. Don't care. You can think it over."

They dumped her in the white room again, hard enough that her head bounced against the floor. Pained stars danced in front of her eyes, and she couldn't do more than make vague, ineffective swimming motions with her arms as the monster – the Weatherman – walked over to her. His legs folded in a strange way as he knelt, too smooth, too wrong.

"Hello again," he crooned, taking up her hand. Beneath his finger, one of the scars opened, smooth as if he'd taken a razor to it, but there was no pain.

He leaned over as the blood welled again, his eyes gone to black holes. "Something's not quite right," he murmured.

She tried to tug her hand away and he simply set it down on the floor and pressed his knee over her wrist. Then he ran his finger over his own palm – it seemed wrong, somehow, that his blood was the same color as hers, it should have been like tar – and reached to press their hands together.

"No!" she managed, a coherent sound at last, for all the good it did. Ice flowed up her veins, from her hand, inexorably toward her heart, her brain. She kicked weakly, hating herself, hating the guards, but hating the Weatherman most of all.

"I'm going to make you better," the Weatherman said, giving her a wide, open smile. "Better than ever."

Another two days – or what she assumed was that from the number of meals – the lower meal slot in the door opened only a short while after she'd already eaten. A woman whispered through it, "Hello?"

Mag crept forward until she could press her ear against the slot. "Hello back," she whispered. The other woman's voice sounded oddly familiar, though it was hard to tell when it was only a whisper. Probably her own desperate imagination.

"You've been good so far," the woman whispered. "Don't give up now. You've got friends, and we're coming for you. Call for us when they next take you from your cell."

Mag opened her mouth to ask what friends, what any of this meant, but the slot snapped shut. She went back to her corner, hugging her knees to her chest again as she mulled those few words over in her head. She had no idea what friends she might have, but they had to be better than the company men that had put her here.

The next time she was due for a meal, the door opened. A man in a company blue suit stood there, two Mariposa guards with him. The company man's eyes were icy blue; his version of a friendly smile left her cold. "Miss Kushtrim, if you'll come with us, please. The doctors have designed a procedure to remove your contamination. You'll be free to go soon."

Mag wanted to resist on principle, but she remembered what the strange woman had told her – and she remembered the stun box too. Eyes locked with the familiar, shorter guard, she offered her wrists out and waited.

"Good girl," the guard said, as he wrapped a few thin strands of razor tanglewire around her wrists. Mag suppressed the urge to bite him.

Maybe it had been a company trick to make certain she'd go quietly. And, she admitted to herself, if something horrible was going to happen, better to go with dignity, on her own two feet. She'd have that small comfort, at least.

She stepped into the featureless hallway. Flanked by the guards, Mag followed the company man. As they turned a corner in the hallway, their footsteps crunched. That couldn't be right. Everything was clean and smooth, even her cell had been every time she was thrown back into it. There'd never been so much as a speck of dirt in the hallway before.

"I'm here," she whispered, not knowing who she might be calling to. She felt an answering tug, heard the far-off music that felt like someone shouting in her ear: *now now now now NOW*. It gave her the boldness to shout the next two words: "Help me!" She ducked away from the guards as they tried to grab her arms. Teeth bared, she aimed a clumsy kick at the shorter guard. By some miracle she connected, and the black stun box went flying.

The tiny grains of sand scattered across the hall ran together, like drops of water, around her, under her boot heels. Mag bit back a scream, her arms, still tied with the wire, whipping back and forth for balance as she skidded forward. The sand formed itself into a rust-red line across the floor, with her at its center.

An agonized crack like a gunshot echoed down the hall as the synthcrete broke open beneath her feet. A chasm yawned to swallow her whole.

CHAPTER NINE

It took four separate underground journeys to reach the outskirts of Newcastle. Coming up from the second, Hob threw up, then passed out. She woke with her head in the Bone Collector's lap again, the shrill ringing of her ears driven back by the sound of his voice as he crooned something like a lullaby. She didn't understand the words as federal trade standard, and couldn't place them as any other language she knew: not spacer lingo nor street-cha nor miner's Slovak.

After the third trip, she could stand on her own two feet, even before her senses had cleared.

And the fourth, she just kept her eyes shut tight and hummed to herself, the same tune she'd heard the Bone Collector singing, until she felt the pressure of sand and salt and rock go away. She opened her eyes to see mirrored buildings that reflected a sea of stars, gray synthcrete streets, train tracks snaking back and forth at all elevations like a shining lattice: Newcastle. She'd only ever been this close once before, the day the rift ship *Phoenix* had landed and she'd escaped onto the landing field, determined to make a name for herself somehow.

"We can't come up any closer," the Bone Collector said. "They've paved it quite thoroughly. But you can walk the rest of the way."

"I think that'd be mighty nice, actually," Hob said. She pulled off her trenchcoat and shoved it into the Bone Collector's arms. She had more than enough layers on under it, shirt and vest and coat, and if she did happen to steal a motorcycle in the city, she could still survive without it.

"Give me your handkerchief." The Bone Collector gave the disreputable piece of cloth she offered him a disapproving look, and then filled it with sand scooped from his pocket. He tied it securely and handed it back. "Be careful with it."

"Don't really want a pocket full of sand," Hob commented

"And you recall what to do with it?"

"Yeah, whether it makes sense or no." She shrugged. "Old Nick's primed me good and proper to do shit that don't make no sense."

The Bone Collector laughed. "I will be waiting and listening."

"Long as it works the way you say it will."

"Trust in me."

She felt like she should say something more to that, do something to interrupt the intent smile he offered her. That was precisely the reason she turned on her heel and started walking without another word.

Hob used the rest of the night to walk into the city, find an alley to hole up in while she planned her next move. Unlike the night-cold desert surrounding it, the roads and buildings radiated heat like an oven and left her sweating until she soaked her shirt through and into her black undertaker's coat. The synthcrete streets felt strange beneath her feet; too smooth, too solid, and there was something else she couldn't quantify, something that made her plain nervous. The surroundings made her feel like she'd stepped back into the belly of the rift ship that had brought her here, the *Phoenix*. Too much metal, too much glass, and display screens everywhere, showing strange, bright advertisements instead of cargo manifests and schedules. She spent five minutes nearly transfixed by an animated, dancing, bright pink potato that wanted her to check her car's power cells, trying to figure out how in the hell anyone had even come up with something that bizarre. Maybe she had wandered back onto the rift ship, a decade too late, and it had let her off on a completely different planet. There was nothing like this in the mining towns.

As the sun came up, people poured into the streets. Most were in company blue suits or Mariposa green, but there were a large enough number of ordinary people that Hob didn't stick out like too much of a sore thumb. Someone had to run the restaurants, bars, and shops, she supposed. Someone had to gather the garbage and sweep the streets, and even those people looked fat compared to the miners.

Hob made her way through the streets to the TransRift tower, and there she waited, for an entire day. It made her grind her teeth, and her leg muscles twitched with the helpless need to go somewhere and be doing something, but she kept herself still and out of the way and simply watched. Watch, wait, find a way into the building that will give you the element of surprise – that's what the Bone Collector had advised her.

She saw quickly that the employees had to swipe a card to get in, which meant she'd need more than just a uniform or a suit to enter the building. From there, she started watching for female employees that were close to her size and shape. It was no easy task; she was tall for a woman, and too thin from years of not really having enough to eat. At least the second problem she could fake with a little padding, but it was damn annoying all the same.

She found a likely candidate, a tall enough woman with her brown hair in a severe bun. The woman had a blue company suit on, a jacket and a skirt. As a bonus, she looked soft, a management type rather than the rougher sorts Hob was used to seeing out near the mines. She'd hopefully put up less of a fight, and there'd be less risk of her mussing her clothes in the struggle.

Hob stalked her like a dune wolf stalked lizards, following her as she went on her lunch break, always watching from a safe distance. She hunkered back down outside the building, ignoring the grumbling of her stomach – she wasn't willing to abandon her post to search out something cheap to eat – and waited for the woman to go home.

Though of course, the woman didn't head straight home from work. She went to get dinner, and drinks with her friends. She even went to a second bar, while Hob contemplated just taking her out in the bathroom so that she could have done with it and buy herself some damn food.

But patience. It was all about patience. It wasn't as if this woman knew she had a date with destiny. Or more accurately, a date with Hob's fist and the inside of her own closet.

She followed the now drunk woman onto a train – one different and much nicer than she'd ever been on herself, the ride smooth and quiet, the design inside all curving lines and polished metal, well-padded seats. Then she shadowed her to another tall building, hopefully full of apartments. The lobby was two stories tall, home to a long granite fountain that water just ran down endlessly, and lined with glass. That amount of water, just doing nothing, was enough to give Hob pause before she got her head back in the game. Vents along the lobby floor that made barely a whisper of sound gobbled up the few flecks of dust that floated off Hob's black coat. The woman barely acknowledged her presence as Hob slid into the elevator right before the doors shut; she just stood, swaying gently as they went up and up. She stared at the floor, at the ceiling, chewing on a stick of gum, anywhere but at Hob. Though Hob caught a few little flicking sideways glances, a little smug tilt at the corner of her mouth that just made her blood boil up.

"Are you going to select your floor?" the woman asked, words slurred. "All you do is push the button."

"We're going to the same floor. Real coincidence, there. My lucky day, someone pushed the goddamn button for me."

The woman laughed woodenly, then stared at the corner for the rest of the ride.

It made her angry, seeing how secure and safe that woman felt, in her little TransRift suit. Out in the mining towns, there might not have been too much crime that people talked about, but they constantly guarded their words, watched the security guards, wondered if today was when they'd end up dead in an accident or blacklisted for saying the wrong thing to the wrong person. They worried about if they'd be able to afford food, if they'd be able to afford new shoes, a thousand other things. And then this woman, looking at her like she was some kind of country moron, like she was surprised Hob even knew what a goddamn elevator was.

It wasn't fair, Hob thought grimly. It wasn't fair, even before she added Mag into the equation, a blameless person these sons of bitches had just kidnapped, like it was their right to do what they wanted with people already knuckled under by fear.

The woman didn't even look back when Hob followed her from the elevator, just stumbled down the thickly carpeted hallway in her impractical shoes, humming to herself as she fumbled in her little purse. Hob stalked behind her silently, just a soft swish of her coat, then the sound of metal brushing leather as she drew her pistol.

The woman stopped at one of the doors, trying to bring key to lock with an unsteady hand. Hob flipped her pistol in her hand and covered the last few steps at a run, arm whipping up. The woman opened her mouth, wad of pale green gum visible on her tongue, and then Hob slammed the pistol butt against her temple.

She grabbed the woman as she fell, balancing her on one bony hip. Not because she particularly cared if the company woman hit the carpet; she just didn't want the noise or the extra fight with gravity when it came time to pick her up. She scooped the keys off the floor one handed, and tried them until she found the one that opened the apartment door.

The apartment inside was almost bigger than Mag's entire house, and far finer than anything Hob had ever seen. The pale gray carpet made her feel off balance, it was so thick. All the furniture was white synthetic leather, polished wood and glass. Hob took care of business first: she dragged the woman back into her walk-in closet – a whole room, just for clothes! – and tied her up with a selection of neckties and pantyhose, making sure none of her restraints were too tight. It wasn't specifically this woman's fault that Mag had gotten snatched by her employers, or that she owned more pairs of shoes than any entire family Hob had ever known. Maybe if she kept reminding herself of that, she'd believe it at some point.

She took a fresh suit from the closet – since the woman had more than one – and the woman's purse, then shut the door securely. As drunk as the woman had been, Hob was hoping she'd just go from unconscious to stupor without making a pass at being awake.

Hob explored the apartment, ignoring most of the fancy technology that she'd never seen and didn't know what to do with. She turned on the wall-mounted vidplate – she knew what that was, even if they didn't get it out in the desert because

transmissions couldn't seem to make it through –
and paged through channels until she found a news
program. The announcers talked about the Federal
Union of Systems, about trade agreements between
colonies, and TransRift stock hitting the roof because
of it, all in voices filled with carefully measured
excitement. A lot of it didn't make sense to Hob; she
didn't understand much about economics, and the
names of most of the colonies were so much noise to
her. The Federal Union didn't ring many bells to her
either – government, she knew, but a toothless one
when it came to the only homes she'd ever known,
the rift ships and Tanegawa's World. Company policy
and the supervisor's word were the only laws in either
place. Vaguely, she recalled police on other planets
she'd been to before jumping ship, but they'd always
just ignored her, and had acted very much like the
security guards from Mariposa. There didn't seem to
be much of a difference.

She left the vid on for the novelty of it, accompanied
by the background noise as she ransacked the woman's
kitchen. She made herself three thick sandwiches,
drank half the beer in the fridge (some of it was pretty
good), and took the only bottle of whiskey for later.

Belly finally quieted, she turned her attention to
the woman's ID card; it was a swipe card, but with a
picture and name on it, fastened to a clip so it could
hang off a jacket. The picture looked enough like her
if she squinted, and she could probably make up the
difference with a little use of the extensive collection
of cosmetics she found in the bathroom. She'd never
been one for makeup, herself, but Mag had shown

her the basics using the little set she'd bought with hoarded birthday money. She could fake it well enough, she thought. She doubted that the security guards would pay that much attention, anyway. The eyepatch, she'd just have to come up with a good story for, something juicy and distracting. Her name, she discovered, would now be "Mary Riley."

Hob dozed a bit on the weirdly shaped sofa in front of the vid, and then woke up with the real Mary Riley kicking the closet door. She quieted nicely when Hob let her look down the barrel of her pistol. "Make noise again, and I'll be shootin' ya. Keep quiet until tomorrow, I'll let ya live."

Not another peep came from the closet, and Hob dozed off again until dawn turned the sky gray. One eye on the floor-to-ceiling windows, Hob pulled on the blue suit and grimaced all the while at how weird it felt, the fabric hugging curves she didn't quite have. It firmed her opinion that her habit of dressing like Nick was the right one. The makeup was even more of a struggle, left her feeling like she was trying to paint a picture with no skill and a broom, but after three false starts and a lot of face scrubbing she managed something passable. Then to her dismay she discovered that Mary had goddamn tiny feet – or maybe Hob's were just big – and nothing with a heel shorter than six centimeters, which seemed downright excessive considering how tall they both were already. She was bound to break her damn ankle, she was sure, or her toes. Maybe both. Her own clothes she folded up and stowed in a briefcase she found by the door, along with her small collection of weapons – throwing knives, combat knife, garrote, pistols – and the handkerchief full of sand. She even did her hair the same hairstyle as in the picture, an extremely tight bun, though it made her forehead feel stretched and her scalp scratchy.

It wasn't just her head but her whole skin that felt itchy, ready to crawl off her body at a moment's notice as she approached the tall building that stood at the heart of Newcastle, the main TransRift office tower. Fear turned her belly in slow circles, but she forced herself to keep her chin high and walk as comfortably as she could in Mary Riley's too-small black pumps. It was all about attitude, that was what would get her through this; she had to act like she belonged and hope she didn't run into any of Mary's close friends.

Even so early in the morning, there were employees streaming into the building. She tucked herself into the crowd and let them carry her into the huge, echoing lobby of glass and metal. Ahead was a curving desk occupied by a fat man in Mariposa green, and behind him two sets of fancy wooden doors inlaid with silver – more elevators. The employees all took a left turn past the security desk, though, heading for a plain glass door. A line had formed there, people swiping their ID cards – no problem there – and then pausing at some sort of scanner that shone light in their eyes. A dim memory, from years ago when she was still on the rift ship, reminded her that was a retinal scanner. Not good. But she'd gotten plenty of places on her own with a bluff, and seen Old Nick do the same.

Mouth dry, Hob sauntered over to the security desk. The security man looked supremely bored, leaning back in his chair, thumbs tucked in his suspenders. Hob gave him the sweetest smile she could and said in her best fancy accent the words she'd practiced all night just in case someone asked, "Got in a little accident last night, doctor says I have to keep my eye covered for a week or two." She flashed him her badge.

The man smirked. "Sometime you'll have to tell me what poked you in the eye."

Hob smirked back at him. "Maybe if you buy me a drink."

He laughed. "Got yourself a deal. Get in line, I'll buzz you through."

She gave him a flirtatious smile, since she still remembered what those felt like even if hers was rusty with intentional disuse, then got in line. She made idle chatter with the men and women in their blue suits until she reached the door – weather, talking about the weather was always safe. It felt weird after living her life on base, where idle chatter normally fell somewhere between target shooting bullshit stories and well-worn debates on the best way to sharpen a knife. She swiped her card, and then paused, forcing herself to breathe normally while the retinal scanner blinked and beeped urgently, demanding she lean forward into the beam. After a few seconds that felt like a damn eternity, a buzzer sounded and the lock clicked. Hob made sure to wave to the security guard and give him another painfully sweet smile, and then walked through into the hallway, her legs feeling half melted with relief.

That was, she tried to remind herself, the easy part.

Now time for the real challenge. The Bone Collector had only been able to give her a hazy idea of where to go: *down, to a place where everything is made of cold, dead synthcrete*. Not much of a help, since she'd wager the entire damn building was made of synthcrete everywhere it wasn't glass.

Shoulders tight, ready to hear a shout, someone asking her what she thought she was doing, Hob kept up the confident walk and pretended that she knew exactly where she was going. She found a building escape map posted on one of the walls, showing exit routes in case of fire. The map also showed the stairways, and only two went down below the ground floor.

There was a door at the bottom of those sets of stairs, made of metal, and a place to swipe a card next to it. Hob tried Mary's card, but the little light on the lock went red. She froze, waiting for the sound of an alarm, of running feet; nothing. She retreated into a corner of the stairwell, where she would be sheltered from the sight of someone going in or out of the door, and waited.

Her feet ached fiercely, but she couldn't afford to take off the shoes, put on her boots; they would be much too out of place. She chewed at her lip, counting the seconds as they passed by, and tried to stay calm.

This was a ridiculous idea. She never should have agreed to it. She should have thought of some other plan. Like knocking on the front door and asking nice, or riding in with guns blazing, or… From any angle she looked, it was all stupid.

The lock on the door snicked. She tensed, barely

daring to breathe. The door opened, and a short man with a white coat over his blue suit walked out. She tried to time her steps with his as he went up the stairs; he didn't look back as she caught the door and slipped inside. With one hand she held it just open as she double-checked that a card swipe wasn't going to be necessary to get out – no, there was no card reader. Just to get in, then.

As she let the door close, her ears popped. She yawned, making them pop again. The hallway in front of her was plain, just synthcrete walls, ceiling, and floor, lights in long strips along the top. But it felt odd, very dead, like sound could get no more than a few centimeters through the air.

There was a little prep room, first thing off the hall. Hob ducked inside and grabbed a white coat of her own, then set off down the hall, trying to act like she did this every day. She felt eyes boring into her back at every turn, though she was alone. The clack of her heels echoed.

The hallway branched several times; the first route took her to a dead end, more locked rooms. The doors were glass panes, which made no sense to her since she could just look inside. What was the point of even having doors, then? It was all computers and fancier gadgets that she couldn't hope to understand, screens that covered entire walls. She made a point of opening her briefcase, pulling out a stack of flimsies and flipping through, then turned back the way she'd come.

The next hallway: the locked doors were metal, and she could about smell despair seeping from under

them, the shape alone screaming *prison cell*. Each door
had two slots, one at waist height and one at face
height, and a tag bearing a name and number. A few
also had a sheaf of flimsies clipped next to the name
tag.

Mag's name was on the third door, along with a
number. Hob swallowed hard, fought to keep herself
calm. Her instinct was to attack, to try to batter the
door open. But the Bone Collector had a specific plan,
and at the time it had sounded good. Now, she wasn't
so sure, but she knew it had to be better than a crazy
charge in. She didn't want it to be Mag's blood sprayed
across the ceiling for her bullheaded mistakes.

She looked at the file clipped to the door. There
was a schedule, indicating Mag had some kind
of procedure scheduled for today. Hopefully that
meant her getting taken out of her room. The pages
of notes beneath didn't make much sense, but she
tried to memorize the words, on the off chance the
Bone Collector might know what they meant: *acute
manifestation* and *unknown biomarker*. One word did
stand out: *contamination*, company speak for *witchiness*.
How could that be possible? Mag had never walked out
into the desert. Reading further, she found a notation
that said Mag was "well behaved, but uncooperative
with questioning." That made Hob smile, a big, wolfy
grin that she quickly hid with one hand.

She checked furtively up and down the hallway,
then squatted awkwardly so she could open the meal
slot in the door and whisper through it. She hated
herself for it, but she did her best to hide her accent,
to speak softly so Mag wouldn't immediately know

who she was. There would be too many questions otherwise, and Mag might give something away by accident. None of them could afford that.

"You've been good so far," she whispered. "Don't give up now. You've got friends, and we're coming for you. Call for us when they next take you from your cell." She heard Mag suck in a breath to ask questions – that was what Mag did – and she quickly snapped the slot closed.

Hob walked to the far end of the hall, digging into the briefcase for the handful of red sand, letting it dribble from her handkerchief and onto the floor, the movement hidden. Then she went back the way she had come, leaving a trail of sand grains as she went, in case Mag's appointment was that way.

That was her task in its entirety: bring in a little sand, warn Mag something was coming, and get the hell out. The Bone Collector had said he needed something natural in there, something that could resonate with his blood. She'd swallowed that and let her questions fall away, because all they'd gotten was that damned floaty smile of his and no answers.

Hob had never been one for simply trusting, and didn't like the feeling of it now. Her hands itched, her head aching as she clenched her teeth against the desire to *do* something, see some kind of result. But she knew what happened when you ignored every warning, every bit of wisdom, and went off half cocked. She remembered melted silver buttons getting stuffed into her shirt pocket, the sound of Nick Ravani snarling in her ear, the hot spray of blood against her cheek. Never again. Stomach churning, she made herself turn and walk from the basement, the horrible shoes pinching at her feet with every step. Walking away was the hardest thing she'd ever done.

No one stopped her as she left the building; she waved to the security guard as she went by, gave him her best copy of the flirty smile from earlier. She changed into her real clothes in an alley between two restaurants that were doing brisk lunch business. Habit had her hair out of that tight, brain-aching knot and back into the two braids she normally kept. She stuffed the woman's blue suit into a dumpster, along with the stolen ID. No point in keeping that. Even if this worked once, she knew it would never work again so easily.

Melting into the crowd of ordinary folk, she shoved her hands in her pockets and walked down the sidewalks toward the outskirts, where the buildings and synthcrete gave way suddenly to hardpan. The first few steps with her feet flat on the ground were almost an orgasmic relief, and then they began to ache fiercely, the pain traveling up her calves and toward her back.

A few blocks away from the city's end, the crowd thinned to almost nothing between the warehouses and silos. They had to store everything the miners and farmers produced somewhere, she supposed, while they waited for the next rift ship to arrive. Then behind, she heard the soft hum of an electric motor, and glanced back to see a black saloon car, shining and fancy, skimming smoothly over the street on some kind of hover field. It was the same sort she'd seen when first arriving here, that had carried a Weatherman from the depths of first class on the rift ship and across the landing field. She still didn't know anything about Weathermen, only that Nick had called them the witchiest things of all.

And right now was *not* the time to find out.

Hob made her stride a little longer, trying to cover more ground without appearing to hurry. But the car pulled ahead of her and stopped, settled down against the sidewalk. The passenger door lifted up like a wing, and a man climbed out.

He looked ordinary enough, the sort that would be otherwise lost in the city. He wore the same blue suit as every TransRift employee. His hair was dark and a little greasy, his face pale, nose slightly crooked. But something was wrong with his face, his expression: his jaw just a little slack, his eyes too wide. Scars laced his hairline, dead white and old, fine as a razor.

And those eyes… all black, Hob saw in a glance, no difference between iris and pupil.

He stepped in front of her. It was stop or run into him, and more than anything in the world, Hob didn't want to touch him. Her skin crawled. There was something wrong, sick in the air like the outpouring of dust and bad gas from a mine collapse, or the sight of a broken bone bending a leg in half far from the joint.

The man smiled. His voice was light, his words oddly stilted. "You weren't easy to find. I've been looking since last night."

"Think you got the wrong person. Sir." Company men always liked being called *sir*.

The doors on the other side of the car opened: two

security men in green, their belts weighed down with pistol, baton, who knew what else.

The man smiled, shaking his head. "I've got it right, I've got it right. You will need to come with us now. Come with us. It will be all right. You belong with us."

Something in his voice was oddly compelling, whispering to Hob that yes, this was a thing that she needed to do. She felt strange, sleepy, and made the mistake of looking him in the eye. She felt like those eyes would swallow her, that they were actually real black holes that could warp time and make it slow to nothing.

"Lovely," he whispered.

Someone grabbed her arm.

She shook off the strange lethargy, twisting her arm to break free. The other security man made a grab for her, and she jammed her elbow into his gut. "Back the hell off," she hissed.

How often did this happen in the city, two guards showing up, overpowering someone, dragging them into the car? Probably more than she could know. There was a metallic hiss, a snap, as one of the men drew his baton and the springs snapped it to full length.

Hob yanked her revolver from its holster and didn't hesitate. Even as the first guard jerked up his hands, showing he was unarmed, she shot him. Without skipping a beat, she smoothly switched her aim to the other, shot him too, square in the chest. The baton rattled down onto the sidewalk.

Blood decorated the car in a messy spray, dotting the shining building next to them, turning the sidewalk into something much more organic. Both bodies hit the ground within a few seconds of each other, a wet *thump-thump*.

She looked at the strange man and he didn't even seem afraid. With a face spattered red he smiled, open and filled with wonder, and held out a hand to her. He opened his mouth, and what came out wasn't more words: it was music, strange and beautiful.

The sound flowed into her ears, rooted her to the ground, promised her things with no name and wrapped her in love. Her hand dropped to the side, fingers popping loose. She almost – almost – dropped the revolver, but something was left in her, enough fire and anger to tighten her muscles a little and hang on. She'd earned her damn gun; like hell she was letting it go.

She knew the music, somehow. It was the same song that the Bone Collector had sung to her on the way here, though this man was missing the words, and that note wasn't right, that one was sour...

Knowing the real thing, hearing what was wrong, broke the lethargy and gave her strength to raise her arm. Like she was drowning in ink and had gotten her head up to the air for one last time, she screamed, "No!" and leveled the gun. Her finger jerked, just enough to pull the trigger.

The bullet made a shockingly tiny hole in the front of his neck. Then his face went slack and he fell to the ground, head slamming into the synthcrete with a damp crack. His mouth opened and shut with a faint gurgling sound, like a fish taken from water. He seemed to be trying to form words, to speak to her again. She took a step forward to stand over him, leveled her gun at his heart – don't look in the eyes, she couldn't risk looking at those eyes again – and pulled the trigger. The wet sound of his breath mercifully stopped.

In death his face regained no humanity. His half-open eyes remained inky black, the strange slackness only worsened, like he was a mask of loose skin now abandoned. All that changed was the growing blood pool that spread over the sidewalk in a dark halo.

Hob wondered if eagles would smell the blood from this distance and come. Probably not. As she breathed like a bellows, she felt there should have been regret in her heart for shooting three men, but she searched and found none. The men in green had tried to grab her, drag her away. And the man in blue... was no man at all, just wrongness somehow man shaped.

The sound of more motors approached, a whining siren echoing between buildings. Hob lunged into a run, gun still clutched in her hand. The bright white of the hardpan ahead filled her vision, leaving her half blind. She threw herself from the sidewalk and out onto the salt crust with a scream of effort. As soon as her boots touched down, the ground flowed beneath her and she sank like a stone through water.

PART II

CHAPTER TEN

Hob surfaced like coming up for air. Hands pulled her from the ground by her shoulders, dragged her until she was flat. She stared up at the star-filled sky and gasped, trying to shake the feeling that she'd been drowning. Then the Bone Collector came into view, leaning over her with a hand planted on the ground either side of her face, his arms rising above her like pillars.

"You smell like blood," he whispered, his tone almost flirtatious.

She laughed at him, a sound that came all the way from her toes and felt like a cough. "My favorite perfume. Shot three men on the way out." A thought sparked in her brain, something important that had almost been lost in the confusion. "Mag?"

"Your friend is fine. Though a little worse for wear. This is the first time she's been underground." He sat back, pulling his hands away to rest in his lap.

Hob turned her head, not quite up to sitting. Mag was there, stretched out, her face gone a delicate green and her eyes shut tight. Hob grinned, just glad to see her alive and in one piece. "Did I look that pathetic?"

The Bone Collector laughed. "More."

Mag responded to the sound of her voice with a little whimper, all sound and no words. She reached toward Hob, eyes still shut tightly, hand flailing like she was drowning and searching for help. Hob caught her hand and squeezed it tight. "It's OK, Mag. We got you out of there."

Mag swallowed hard; her voice was soft, words slurred as she spoke through clenched teeth. "Thought I heard you, Hob."

It was like three years hadn't passed at all, and it was like a million years divided them. Their hands felt the same together, but when had Mag grown so much? When had she broadened out in the hips and shoulders while Hob had just stretched taller and taller? When had her hair gone from its childish, mousy blonde to brown? Hob could barely breathe around the lump in her throat. "Sorry to keep you waiting." *Sorry I was selfish. Sorry I was an idiot. Sorry for everything.*

Mag didn't say anything else, just squeezed her hand so tight that it made her fingers ache.

"What men did you shoot?" the Bone Collector asked. "Were they in the building?"

"No, in the street, near the edge of town. Two security guards and one other who… had eyes like… I don't even know. Like black pits. Ink." She covered her face with her free hand, squeezing her eye shut as she dragged her thoughts into line.

Mag made a horrible noise then, like she was choking almost. It took Hob a moment to realize she was laughing, or maybe crying, or both. "The Weatherman. You shot the Weatherman." Her hand went tighter around Hob's. "Didn't even give a day before you started slayin' dragons for me."

"That can't be so," Hob whispered, though she squeezed Mag's hand just as tightly. "Weathermen don't ever set foot on a planet." She'd never seen one in person before, but she knew as much about them as any common spacer did.

"Believe it," Mag said. "That's what they called him. And the things he did to me, Hob…" Her breath caught. "Lickin' blood off my hand and crawlin' into my head and– and–" She swallowed hard.

The Bone Collector went so absolutely still and silent that Hob lifted her head to look, then reached out and brushed her fingers against his knee, just to make sure he hadn't turned to stone. His eyes went a little wider at that contact, rolling down to stare at her, then flicking back to Mag. "You are certain he is dead?"

Hob let her hand fall back down to the sand. "Most folk I know don't recover too well from a round through the neck and another in the heart." She huffed out a breath, trying to remember; there'd been something else important to tell him. "After I shot the guards, he tried to get me to come quiet-like, by singin' at me. Kind of like you did, only you're a lot better at it."

His face tightened down in fury, a strange expression she'd never seen on him. He slapped her hand away when she tried to touch his knee again. "Monster," he hissed, then surged to his feet and stalked away.

"Why's he so mad?" Mag whispered after a moment of shocked silence.

"Guess he don't like Weathermen," Hob commented to the sky, shaking the sting from her fingers.

"When they tell you to do somethin', you want to do it," Mag said. She sounded a little stronger now, less like she was going to be sick. "They put me in a room with one. I thought I was gonna die when he touched me, but I couldn't even move a muscle to try to get away."

"Don't make no sense to me," Hob said, not because she disbelieved Mag – she'd seen the Weatherman herself; she'd believe just about anything after those few minutes – but because nothing made sense with what she'd already known. "They fly the rift ships. To spacers, they're practically holy, like little gods instead of men. You pray to 'em in the hopes you'll make it through the rift alive, and it ain't really a joke. Speak ill of one and it'll get you beat, in the cargo hold. But they just do mumbo jumbo with math and – and *spatial mechanics*." She pronounced the words like they were from a foreign language, and they might as well have been for all they made sense to her. "They don't go drinkin' blood or singin' or any of that nonsense."

"This one did."

"I believe you. I don't fuckin' understand it, but I believe you." Hob squeezed Mag's hand again. Trying to square the monstrous *thing* she'd shot – still made her sick to think about it – with what she'd always been told about these might-be superhuman navigators gave her a headache. She focused on the important facts for now. "Well, unless they got spares wanderin' around, that one's got two bullets through him and won't be botherin' you no more."

Mag laughed. "That's somethin', at least." Her

laughter turned into sobs; she curled into a ball on her side, one hand over her face, her other still tight around Hob's. "I didn't think you'd come for me. I didn't believe in you. I'm sorry, Hob."

"Hey, hey now." Careful, like she might break, Hob rubbed Mag's back. It hurt to see her so upset over doubting someone she had every damn right to doubt. "I ain't given you much reason to think I'd come. And I'm sorry too. I shoulda been there already. Shoulda never gone away to begin with. I just wasn't brave enough."

Mag laughed. "That don't even make sense."

Hob couldn't put it to words, didn't want to either, like that would make it all more real, bring up ghosts that she was still trying to escape. "Don't worry about it. Whether it makes sense or no, I'm here now, right?" She sat up, scooted across to Mag, and pulled the other woman into her lap.

She knew she should tell Mag that her father was dead, and maybe now was the best time, since she was already crying. But these tears seemed more like release than sadness, and she didn't want to stop Mag cold when she was just starting to feel alive and hopeful. It weighed heavy and burned in her throat, but it was a secret that could keep for a while longer. Phil was already dead; he wouldn't get any deader.

The Bone Collector returned, stopping a little away from them, hands clasped loosely behind his back. Hob only stole one look at him, and she didn't care for what she saw: he watched them like a scientist would watch a strange animal, taking in Mag's tears as another interesting result to be cataloged.

•••

They kept traveling until they reached the mine in Pictou, where the Bone Collector looped Mag's arm over his shoulders so he could lead her to the blankets and help her lay down. Hob at least was moving under her own power this time. "I'll make you both some coffee. That seems to make you feel better," he said. The inflection on *you* made her think of his casual mention of *humans* earlier. Not *you*, not *human*.

Coffee started, the Bone Collector sat down next to Mag. After four trips, she was far worse for wear than Hob. Without asking, he took up her right hand, curling her fingers around his and pressing her knuckles against his lips, eyes falling half shut. Mag looked away from him, fixing her eyes on Hob, her face gone pale.

"It's OK, Mag. He's passin' strange, but means well enough. I think." If she hadn't known any better, the gesture would have looked tender, but she was starting to think the man didn't even know the meaning of the word. Quiet and soft was easy to mistake for gentle when you'd seen precious little of either, but it seemed more a matter of constitution rather than an empathetic choice coming from him.

"He ain't gonna try to drink my blood?" Mag asked in a whisper.

"He tries and I got a knife with his name on it." Whatever odd history she might share with the Bone Collector, it was nothing compared to her and Mag.

"OK." Mag closed her eyes tightly for a moment. "I want to go home. But I was supposed to leave on the ship, you know that right? But they locked me up, and all our money's gone. And if I tried to leave again…" She shuddered.

"Your mama told me that." Her head felt clear, and she sat up, leaning against the stone wall of the mine. It would have been better for Mag to get away, go to a better planet and get her family moved. But a selfish, mean corner of Hob's heart was glad she was still there. "I don't think it'd be a good idea to send you home either, for other reasons."

"I don't–" Mag stopped, her eyes going a little wider. "Hob, he's gone all cold," she whispered.

Hob leaned in to take a look at the Bone Collector, and then thumped back on the wall. "He's turned to stone. Does that too, regular enough. Can't say I'm a hundred percent sure, but I reckon that means he's thinkin' real hard. He'll be all right in a minute."

Mag giggled, covering her mouth with her other hand as if to keep crazier laughter from escaping. "Turned to stone. Be right as rain in a minute. Oh, is that all." She shook her head. "But… wait, what do you mean, other reasons?"

It wasn't fair, to drop it on her like this, trapped in a mine with her hand held captive. Stall, she told herself, stall until Mag could at least move. "They know who you are. They know where to find you. Wouldn't be surprised if they went looking."

Mag swallowed hard. "What about Mama and Papa?"

"I don't know. We'll talk to the Ravani – your Uncle Nick – real soon. And see if he's got any ideas. Mayhap another of the mining towns would take you in, like over at Shimera." She fell silent, staring at the wall above Mag's head. The marks made from chisels and axes, the butt ends of drill holes for explosives made sharp shadows in the lantern light.

"There's more, isn't there," Mag whispered. "Hob, tell me." She tugged her hand, trying to pull it from the unyielding fingers of the Bone Collector.

"In a minute. I'll tell you everything when he lets you go."

That seemed to scare her even more. Hob wished she could just kick the damn statue, wake the man up that way. But after all he'd said when she'd brought him Phil's fingerbone, she was scared to do it.

Color rippled through him; Mag yanked her hand away and shoved herself upright. "Tell me!" she screamed at Hob.

"Your papa, Mag." Hob kept her words measured and calm as the Bone Collector stood and moved away, face tight. He disappeared down one of the shafts, leaving them alone with the weight of awful news waiting to be told. *Coward*. Unfair, maybe. It wasn't his burden. "I found him out in the dunes not far from Segundo. Shot in the back, from a helicopter."

It was like telling Mag's mama had been, but worse somehow, because Mag didn't scream. She just covered her face with her hands and sobbed, and when Hob tried to touch her she jerked away and choked out, "Leave me be."

Hob knew that when Mag wanted to be left alone, she damn well wanted to be left alone; she stood, headed the same way the Bone Collector had. He waited for her just up the tunnel. The sound of Mag's sobs echoed behind them.

"She cannot stay here," he said. "And she cannot

leave this planet. The voice of the world is in her blood. If she leaves, she will die."

Hob stared at him. "Voice of the world? The fuck you talkin' about?"

He smiled. "If any of us leave, those like me – and Nick – and you… we die. We changed to fit this place. We don't fit anywhere else any longer."

Not that she'd ever really entertained ideas of leaving, but the thought still made her feel a little trapped, claustrophobic. The dark stone walls surrounding them didn't help. Screaming about it now wouldn't make a difference, though. Punching him wouldn't, either, even if she was damn tempted. "Fine. So why can't you take her in?"

"She wouldn't be able to take care of herself. The way I must live out here is not something a human can survive."

There it was again: *human*. She'd never shied away from bluntness, and she was damn tired of all the mystery. "Define human."

He smiled at her. "Not *us*." From the intensity in his light eyes, staring right through her, Hob knew that she was included as one of "us."

She took a step toward him, so close their noses almost touched. "Then why don't you tell me, what makes the difference between us and them? You said Mag had changed too."

"She's different. She's…" He didn't back up even a centimeter, his breath washing over her lips. "I don't have words that can tell you. There's a war, in her blood. The world versus the other. I don't know which will win, but I *will not* have her here if the world loses."

"The world. You keep talking about the goddamn *world*. What's so special about this place?"

"Everything." He smiled, slowly reaching up to rest his hand on her left cheek, her blind side. She hated the wobble that put in her as he leaned forward to rest their heads lightly against each other. "There's a song in this world," he whispered, "like what I sang for you, but more, so much more. It is change, unmaking, remaking. It is the universe unraveled into the rifts."

"It's Weathermen navigate the rifts," Hob said. It was the only thing she felt she still knew for certain. *What are you*, sat on the tip of her tongue, but she'd asked him that before many a time, and he'd only ever laughed at her.

"Oh no," he said, shaking his head ever so slightly. He smoothed his thumb over her cheekbone and she couldn't stand it any more, because she liked it too much. Hob shoved him away, and he only smiled. "They are but a bit of twine to leash a wolf."

Mag had herself more together when Hob came back, leaving the Bone Collector and his damned mysterious smile behind in the tunnel. Eyes red and face pale, she had at least stopped crying. She had a cup of coffee clutched between her hands like a lifeline. Hob got a cup for herself – smelled better than anything she'd ever had on the base – and eased down to the floor.

"So it's not safe for me to go back to Rouse," Mag said, not looking up from her cup. "And I got nothin' but the clothes on my back."

Hob nodded. "I was thinkin' we could take you to

Ludlow or Shimera, get you set up there. The workers in both places know how to keep their damn mouths shut."

"What about Mama? If they killed Papa…"

Hob cursed; she hadn't even thought that far yet. "We can probably move her out to the same place as you. But we're gonna have to be smart about it. The Ravani will know how to do it. He's cunning as fuck, your uncle."

"OK." Mag took a gulp of coffee that probably should have scalded her, but she didn't seem to notice. "Just got to roll with it."

"Nick's got money, too. He's a stingy old fart, but I know he'd give you and your mama the shirt off his back if you needed it." It felt weird, talking about Nick Ravani as anything other than *Old Nick* after three years of him being just that, the monkey on her back and the devil on her shoulder. It was strange to be reminded that he came from somewhere, and, however briefly, he'd made her a part of that origin as well.

Mag nodded. "Then let's go. I… I need to see the sky. I feel like I'm still in a damn prison."

"The Ravani has sent two of your fellows here. I hear them at the surface," said the Bone Collector.

Out of the corner of her eye, Hob saw Mag jump, her head jerking around to look at the man. His sudden appearance was a shot up Hob's spine as well, but she'd be damned if she'd give him the satisfaction. She stood, offering her hand to Mag. She had to wiggle her fingers to get her friend's attention. "Then we shouldn't keep 'em waiting. As much as we appreciate your hospitality."

"Need you to do somethin' for me, Hob. Afore we go." Mag turned her wrist over, showed the black lines tattooed there. "And there's… under the skin…"

Hob reached out to feel the round, hard thing under Mag's skin, knowing what it was already: a little silver button, a transmitter, just the sort a clever boy could leave scattered along on the sand like a trail of bread crumbs. Short range, at least, because nothing long range worked out here. She felt sick, and sicker still knowing what Mag wanted her to do. "You sure?"

"Can't go to a town still marked like this." Mag's face was pale to the point of being green. "Quick, afore I change my mind."

She didn't want to do this, at all. Not when they'd only just gotten back into the same damn room again, when they'd been clinging to each other's hands. She felt like she'd cut Mag enough with words and actions. And yeah, it might be necessary now, it might be something that Mag wanted, needed her to do. But it would hurt. Pain was still pain.

"Please, Hob," Mag whispered.

It wasn't fair. But she was also just thinking about herself again, not what Mag wanted. "It's gonna hurt."

"I know."

"I can take away the pain," the Bone Collector said, in the same sort of tone he might use to remark about the weather.

Hob didn't question it. She wasn't going to question anything about the man for a good long while. "Will you let him?" she asked Mag.

The look Mag shot her was pure panic, for a moment. Then she bit her lip. "Yeah, that would be…

better. All right."

The Bone Collector knelt next to Mag as Hob heated one of her knives up in her hand, pouring fire into it until the blade glowed. Mag stared at him with wide eyes, and flinched back at first as he leaned in close, then slowly relaxed. He had his forehead resting lightly against the side of Mag's head, lips by her ear, first whispering words that Hob couldn't understand, and then singing softly to her – a different song from the one he'd sung to Hob.

Hob grabbed her wrist and cut the marked skin with her knife, sinking the tip in to pop the damn silver button out into her palm. The knife seared the flesh shut behind it, and Mag didn't so much as whimper. It was a small mercy, and she could be glad for it. She could be grateful to the man, even if it made her feel passing strange when, head still, he looked at her from the corner of his eye. Hob closed her fist around the transmitter and clumsily tried to focus more heat on it like she'd seen Nick do before, until she felt the casing warp and melt. She dropped the blackened, twisted thing on the floor and tried not to taste the combination of charred metal and her friend's burnt flesh in the back of her throat.

Coyote and Dambala were waiting at the surface. Coyote looked half ready to faint when Hob and Mag walked out of one of the cellars, his face sallow with the shock under his spiky black hair, though Dambala took it in his stride. He volunteered to ride ahead to Rouse, to let Old Nick know the plan and see what could be set in motion. Hob and Coyote took Mag to

Ludlow. Mag knew people there, the representatives that sometimes had come to Rouse to talk to Phil – even if she still wasn't entirely certain what they'd come to talk about.

One of the crew leaders, Clarence Vigil, met them at the gate. "My house is your house, long as you need. I owe your da more than you can know." He offered Mag a hand to help her off the back of Hob's motorcycle.

Mag had enough time for a bath, a change of clothes, and a cup of coffee before Old Nick showed up. He looked like he'd aged twenty years in just two days, his skin gray and sagging, his single eye bloodshot. Hob had never seen him look so old. Really *old*, not like crusty old fart old, like she always teased him about. It made her a little sick, made her wonder if maybe this was all some bad dream. He slid an arm around Mag's shoulders and just held on to her for a solid minute before they disappeared into Clarence's parlor together.

Hob didn't try to follow. For all she'd called Mag's papa *Uncle* Phil, the man hadn't been blood kin of hers. She headed outside to smoke and try to escape the oppressive atmosphere of grief, only to have Coyote grab her arm as soon as she crossed the threshold. Hob almost slapped his hand away – she didn't like anyone grabbing at her, least of all from her blind side – but the look on his face stopped her.

He looked scared, brown eyes wide and earnest above his sharp cheekbones. "The Ravani would kill me if he knew I was telling you this, but I think you ought to know." Coyote had been shorter than her ever since she'd had her last couple of growth spurts, but he seemed even smaller, somehow, wound in tight on himself with worry.

"What?"

"When Dambala and I returned to base to tell Nick what happened to Phil, he had an… episode." Coyote finally let go of her arm to smooth his hand over the stiff, black hair that bristled out from his head.

Hob dug her cigarettes out, from habit; it gave her fingers something to do, bought her a moment to think. "What do you mean?"

"He collapsed. Gave us quite a scare, but he was back up on his feet fairly quickly and made us swear to tell no one. But… he's been coughing lately, and I think there's blood."

Hob almost crushed the cigarette in her fingers. "Know what it could be?"

"There are several possibilities that spring to mind, and none of them are good."

Hob nodded. "Thanks for tellin' me. I'll figure out a way to 'find out' on my own."

"I trust you to get it done. He'll listen to you. He won't listen to any of us." He gave her a quick salute, which seemed strange since last she checked she was the low wolf of the pack, but Coyote did things she found strange all the damn time.

Hob shook her head. "Don't know where you been all this time. Man wouldn't even listen to me if I was tryin' to tell him piss ran downhill." She tucked the cigarette between her lips and lit it. "Fuck, like we didn't have enough shit pie on our plates."

CHAPTER ELEVEN

"Is Mama gonna be OK?" Mag asked Uncle Nick, as soon as the door closed.

"Your ma's a tough old bitch." Immediately, he winced, at his own words perhaps. But Mag had always known that Uncle Nick and Mama didn't get along; she just never figured out why. His hand rested awkwardly on his shoulder, a subtle tug, then a push, then a tug.

He wants to hug me again, Mag thought. But he didn't know how, maybe. Uncle Nick had also never really been one for affection like that, not like Papa. And how sad was it, as a man grown and more than old enough to have had children, that he didn't even know how to hug his own niece proper?

But did she even want to be hugged? She'd stayed calm, the whole journey. She'd already done her crying, she thought, but she could feel more tears just below the surface. She was so tired of crying. She *wanted* to be angry; Hob had always said angry was better than sad, and Mag was more than ready to believe her. So where was that anger that Hob always had seething in her like more fire?

"What am I going to do?" she asked, instead. This, she still had no idea about. She couldn't leave the planet, she couldn't go back home.

"Clarence said you can work here. Town's big enough and enough folk blow through that the company men won't notice if you keep your head down."

She frowned. "Papa didn't want me in the mines." But Papa hadn't wanted a lot of things to happen.

"Won't be down in the mines. Clarence promised that as well. Gonna get you workin' in the warehouse." He paused, squeezed her shoulder one more time, and then let go. His hand disappeared into his duster for a moment, and then came back out with a small silver pistol that he offered her.

Mag stared at the gun. "What's that for?"

"Hell, girl, didn't your papa ever teach you to shoot?"

She shook her head. It had never come up. And she wondered if that would have made a difference a few days ago. She imagined Mr Franklin, dead on the floor of the kitchen with a hole in his forehead, blood spreading out across the floorboards. There was a sick sort of satisfaction to the image, perhaps. She imagined the man with the black eyes, the guards, them all dead as well, before Hob ever got to them. Shouldn't that make her happy? She didn't feel much of anything at all.

And she also thought about Papa, dead in the desert with a cluster of bullet holes in his back. She should want to find the people that did it and shoot them in return, she was sure. Did it make her a bad daughter that the thought only made her ill? Did it mean she loved her papa any less?

"Take it," Uncle Nick said. When she made no move, he grabbed one of her hands, pressed the gun into it. His fingers shook, just slightly. She looked up at him, at his one muddy hazel eye, and saw how red it was. Did Uncle Nick cry? Could he? He couldn't give her papa back. All he could give her was a gun, heavy and hot from his hand.

She carefully stuck the gun in her skirt pocket. She didn't want it, but she didn't want to tell him no either. And because he couldn't, she wrapped her arms around his waist and pressed her face against his chest. Uncle Nick was stiff for a moment, and then he just collapsed down onto her, his face on her shoulder. He was shaking; his breath heaved, though he stayed quiet. But Mag felt her shoulder go hot and damp with tears soaking through her borrowed shirt.

Carefully, she rubbed his back between his shoulder blades, and listened to his heart thumping. She didn't shed a single tear, as she counted each beat and added them into minutes.

After dinner, Mag asked Hob to cut her hair, take her braids off with a knife in Clarence Vigil's kitchen. Uncle Nick had long since begged off, making grouchy noises about his age, about needing his goddamn beauty sleep, just look at him. Mag doubted that Hob was any more into fashion than she had been when they were girls – not at all, and plain allergic to skirts – but it didn't take talent to hack her hair down to something short and no-nonsense that would fit under a hardhat. Mag wanted to look like just another miner, even if she wouldn't be going underground. Then, Hob watching her keenly like this was some sort of mysterious black magic, she filled a bowl with store-bought dye that stank like a laboratory and looked like it ought to be smeared in the gearbox of an elevator. Grimacing, Mag pulled on a pair of plastic gloves and started slopping the mess into her hair. The box had claimed it would quick-dye to permanent black.

Hob had a cigarette between her fingers, rolling it back and forth like a nervous tic. But at least she hadn't lit it yet. Mag couldn't stand the smell and Clarence wouldn't take kindly to his kitchen being stunk up with tobacco. "You look like a ghost," Hob said.

Mag managed a wan smile, "I feel like one. Been dug up out of the ground enough that it don't seem so far from the truth."

"I could ask the Ravani again, 'bout money. Put the screws on him. You're his kin. He should provide for you."

Mag gave her head an abortive shake, then carefully raised her plastic-gloved hands to make certain her hair hadn't sprayed. "I wouldn't be much help on that base of yours. Your motorcycles scare me and I don't think I ever been mad enough to want to shoot anyone, even now. And I don't think it's the life my papa would have wanted for me neither."

"Don't have a lot of choices."

"I got plenty of choices." Mag felt her throat beginning to close up and gritted her teeth. "Just might not be the choices you'd make."

Hob stared at her for a long moment, still rolling that cigarette between her fingers. She laughed sharply. "Guess I deserve that."

"I didn't mean nothin' by it." She hadn't meant it like that at all; she was just thinking about Uncle Nick's gun, still weighing down her pocket. That was the kind of choice that Hob would make, and Mag wouldn't.

"No, I hear ya, Mag. But I promise I won't disappear again. I'll come by as much as I can."

"I'd like that." Mag shrugged. "But we both know that ain't all that much."

"It's up to the old man how much time he'll let me have and where he'll send me." Hob had said things like that before, though, and then had started spending more and more of her time with the preacher's boy, Jeb. Though at the time it hadn't seemed so bad; Mag had been happy for her, if a little jealous.

She'd never thought Hob was the sort to turn her back on family for anything. And it had gnawed at her. "Were you working all that time?" she asked quietly. She might never get a chance to ask that again.

"Think it was all my choice?"

"Yeah, I do. Uncle Nick said you didn't want to come 'round."

Hob sighed. "Asshole," she muttered. "No… yes. He was right. Was shamed, Mag. Powerful shamed. Ain't a thing to be proud of, what I done." Hob crushed the cigarette between her fingers, like punctuation. "But I was also mad."

"Mad about what?"

"You told the Ravani I'd taken Jeb back to the base."

Mag stared at Hob, open-mouthed as she tried to make sense of those words, which had nothing to do with reality. She'd seen Hob that night three years ago when she climbed in her window, tried to tell her not to do anything dumb, and of course she hadn't listened. But that was it. She'd never breathed a word of it to anyone, because that was what she did. Mag kept secrets. And for three years she'd been left wondering what had happened – something to do with the preacher's boy; it was obvious when he hadn't come back, though Father Lee had just claimed he'd run off – and not even able to ask Uncle Nick a question because it would have been too incriminating. And then Hob accused *her* of kicking the mess off?

Hob continued on, staring straight through her. "You were right. You were fuckin' right. I almost got us all hanged 'cause I was thinkin' with my cunt instead of my brain. But it still... it fuckin' hurt, Mag."

Mag finally found her tongue. "Never. I would never have told on you." She'd never even ratted out those little assholes – what were they called now, Freki and Geri? – when they'd done something bad. She'd always taken care of things herself, taught her own lessons with pranks.

Hob drew back as if slapped, but she looked to be listening now, keen and hard. "What do you mean?"

"I mean I didn't breathe a word to anyone! Not Papa, not Uncle Nick, not anyone! And no one asked. The very *idea* that I'd snitch on you–"

"If it wasn't you, then who was it?" Hob interrupted.

"How would I know?" Strange, she could be mad about this and still feel numb about her father's murder. But this was years past gone, and a safer way for all that anger to leak out, maybe. "You ain't talked to me for three years about it, and no one else did either. You might as well have fallen off the map and stopped existing, for all anyone said!"

"But–"

"But nothing! Do you know how much it hurt me, Hob Ravani, to not know if you were alive or dead or – or whatever?" She made herself take a deep breath. "If Jeb… if Jeb got you killed, it would've been just as much my fault 'cause I wouldn't have told. But I still kept that secret. I always keep your secrets."

Hob took a deep breath and let it out very slowly. "I'm sorry."

Well, it wasn't every day someone with the last name of *Ravani* said those words. It was plain startling, even past all the numbness. "I'm sorry too." She sighed. "I wanted… Hob, I wanted you to be happy. He made you happy. Even if it felt like you were leaving me behind and didn't need me no more."

Hob covered her face with her hand for a moment. Flakes of unburnt tobacco, shreds of paper fell to the floor. "Don't fuckin' say that, Mag. Just don't."

"We can't… We can't keep playin' *what if* about this, Hob. We just… we gotta let it go. Say we both made mistakes."

"I think I made more'n you."

Mag snorted, smiling in spite of herself. That was more like the Hob she'd always known. "This ain't a contest."

"Everythin's a contest, ain't it?" Hob shook her head, dropped her hands to her sides. "But if you didn't tell the old man – all this was for even more nothin' than I thought." She shut her eye tight for a moment, and then opened it narrowed. "Who the fuck told him, then?"

It was a question, and even without an answer, an easier one to contemplate than the rest of the ugly mess. "I don't know. Could ask him?"

"Might as well ask a crow what color the bottom of a rock is on Tuesday," Hob said. She bared her teeth in an expression only smile-like. "But I aim to try."

"Don't go doing anything dumb." Carefully, Mag reached out to take Hob's hand. "I already lost too much. Don't you go away again too."

Hob looked down at their joined hands, nodded. "It'll be different this time. I promise. I crawled belly-down through hell for three years just to get back to where I started. I ain't doing it again."

After so many days of unrelenting shadow and evil, was it wrong of her to smile, to feel a little hint of hope? That choked her throat more than sorrow had been able to over the last day. "I'm gonna hold you to it, Hob Ravani. Don't you make me come after you."

"I wouldn't dare, Mag. You'd eat me alive with no salt."

Mag laughed, and then Hob laughed, and that felt good. Not like old times, when they'd been giggling girls. Maybe like new times. "Neither of us want that. You're too damned stringy to eat."

CHAPTER TWELVE

"Vice President Gregson? Sir?" Female voice, fuzzed with static.

Leeroy grunted, cracked his eyes open into slits that showed him the familiar rippling shadows of his office's ceiling. Right. He'd sacked out on the couch, not wanting to go home until the current crisis had some kind of resolution. It was out of his hands, but he'd found his presence in the building tended to compel the white coats in the basement to stay at their stations instead of weaseling out.

"Sir?" More static, a few pops.

"Status report?" he said. His throat felt like gravel, his mouth tasted worse.

"They'd like to see you down in the basement, sir."

"All right. I'll be there in a few minutes." He levered his heavy frame to sitting, the faux-leather couch creaking beneath him. "Lights!"

Nothing.

Annoyed, he walked to the wall plate and tapped the lights on. Another damn maintenance ticket to put in. But as he headed to the little coffee nook past his desk – he had a whole, upper floor of the TransRift

tower to himself, since upper management tended
to be a literal thing – something seemed off. Coffee
would clear the fuzz out of his mouth and brain and
get him ready for dealing with a bunch of scientists
and doctors all trying to throw each other on top of
a live grenade. They could wait a few more minutes.

When he had his glass mug in hand filled with black
coffee so strong it threatened to eat the skin off his
tongue, he finally saw it – the liquid tilting, this way
and that, ever so gently. The tower was made to sway
in high winds, flexing without danger of breaking – an
architectural necessity of skyscrapers that the builders
back on Earth had figured out centuries ago. TransRift
had commissioned its tower to be able to withstand
the full fury of Tanegawa's World's desert winds.

But it hadn't known the full force of those winds,
not since before Leeroy had taken over. And the
lights of his office – a glitch, sure, taking out the voice
command module – were brightening and dimming
ever so subtly in an unknown pattern. And – that's
right, there'd been static on the intercom. There was
never static on the intercom. Power fluctuations.

None of these things were supposed to happen –
that was part of the point of having a pet Weatherman,
wasn't it? Sure, the majority of them were built to be
pilots, but one of Leeroy's long-ago predecessors had
discovered that they could also affect the stranger
phenomena found only on Tanegawa's World. The
damned lab-designed freaks were spooky as hell, but
they could calm the odd weather and the magnetic
anomalies somewhat and, more importantly, they
could detect and sometimes remove the planetary

contamination the idiot workers were encouraged to call *witchiness* and view with superstition. And then the current resident Weatherman, Mr Green, had been something of a special project, designed specifically to stay in Newcastle at Leeroy's request rather than be rotated in and out of piloting – most of the Weathermen did go a little odder if they were planetbound too long, creepily twitchy even for them. But since Mr Green's arrival, living in Newcastle had almost – *almost* – been like living on a normal planet, the effect he had was so profound. And now it seemed that effect was already draining away, which didn't bode well for the smooth running of Leeroy's division in the near future. Or for Mr Green's health, he supposed.

Leeroy set his unfinished cup of coffee down very carefully and headed for the elevator, quick walk. Not a run. Upper management didn't run. But he walked with purpose.

A gaggle of white coats waited at the elevator doors in the basement, and they all started talking at once the minute the doors opened.

"Quiet," Leeroy snarled. He scanned the anxious faces, sallow, pale, black, brown, and no one seemed to want to meet his eyes. He pointed a finger squarely at a middle-aged woman, her dark brown hair shot through with steel gray, a set of anti-splash glasses still perched on her nose and covering her green-flecked brown eyes. "You. Give me the report."

She took half a step back, then seemed to find her resolve. "It's not good, sir."

It had already been not good since this afternoon. "Who are you?"

"Larsa Kiyoder." At his raised eyebrow, she hurried to continue on, "Neurosurgeon. There was a lot of damage, sir. Heat, spinal fluid leakage – I stopped the neural disengagement before it could advance further, but…"

"But?" The answer was already plain on her face, but he wanted to hear her say it.

"I can't reverse it."

"You're supposed to be the top of your field," he said, accusingly.

"If he'd been human–" Kiyoder waved away a protesting hiss from one of her colleagues with an impatient gesture "–he wouldn't even have made it to my operating room. Maybe I could have done more, but with the generation of equipment I have? Not likely. If my upgrade request had been–"

"So what have you done with him?" he asked, cutting her off.

She glanced at one of the other white coats, plainly passing the responsibility bomb before it could explode. "Metabolic coma," another scientist said, a younger man with narrow eyes and a prominent nose. "Dr Nikhat."

"Didn't bother asking me first?" Leeroy growled. "And I don't care." This was his ass on the line, the disposition of perhaps the most expensive single asset he controlled.

"There wasn't time," the man said firmly. "I judged it best that no further damage was risked by a delay."

Leeroy weighed the desire to kick someone, *anyone* for this tangled mess, and the knowledge that yes, it was policy to reward good, quick thinking. The two thoughts ended their brief skirmish in a draw. "Show me."

Most of the scientists took their chance to make good their escape. Dr Kiyoder led Leeroy and those who remained down the hall. Overhead, the lights dimmed briefly.

"Isn't it a bit too early for that to be happening?" Leeroy growled.

"From my understanding of it, the Weatherman is in a continuous… ah… communication and feedback with the systems he's controlling. As soon as he's removed, things will start cycling back to native equilibrium."

He didn't like the sound of that at all. "How long's that going to take?"

"I don't know, sir. It depends on how far from the planetary equilibrium we are right now." She glanced at him. "But it could get a lot worse before it gets better."

"It might not go completely out of control," Dr Nikhat offered. "Metabolic stasis isn't the same as death, or even cryonic freezing."

"It's a static state," Dr Kiyoder disagreed.

"But the mechanism for what the Weathermen do is still poorly understood," Dr Nikhat said, his shoulders jerking in a shrug. "That's all I'm saying. It might not be as bad as it could be."

Leeroy pulled a memo pad from his breast pocket to note: *Get all nonessential systems offline, triage for the stable grid.* The stable power grid was extremely limited – half the benefit of the Weatherman had been not needing to expand it, the other half that he was far more reliable than the technology.

"Here we are." Dr Kiyoder stopped them in front of a clean room, this one full of equipment that surrounded an exam table. Something far too like a body bag for Leeroy's comfort, though translucent rather than matte black, sat on the table, shrouding the tall, thin, unhealthily pale form of the Weatherman. The monitors attached displayed steady enough lines; he had to assume those were as things should be.

"As you can see from the ongoing neural electrical activity, he's still mentally engaged with *something*," Dr Nikhat said. "Though not anywhere close to his normal operating capacity."

Leeroy didn't know why he'd needed to see this to believe it. Stupid on his part. But it highlighted to him that he didn't have many good choices. There was no way to avoid mentioning this goddamn fiasco to Corporate, because they needed a new custom-built Weatherman before things really spun off the rails. And they'd need to be put back in rotation for the pilot assignments until the new one was online.

What the hell had possessed the Weatherman to demand to leave the building? And what had possessed his handlers to *allow* him to do that? Weathermen weren't supposed to go out unattended. They weren't even supposed to be *seen* in public – it was as much PR as a safety issue, helping maintain the illusion of mysticism and infallibility. But Mr Green had seemed so relatively normal – or maybe he'd just grown too familiar to everyone – that he'd been given far too much leeway perhaps. It had kept him happy, but it had also resulted in *this*.

He'd need to sack the current handlers, Leeroy decided. Send them out to the mining towns, since they all liked being outside so much. And, in the future, keep the staff on a strict rotation so no one got too familiar with the Weatherman and started thinking he was some kind of– of *person*.

"I want your full report ready for transmission in two hours," he said. "Both of you. And Kiyoder, I want a precise plan of recommendations laid out. One that ends with Corporate needing to send us a new Weatherman rather than trying to repair this one on site."

"But sir–"

"No buts." The handlers were half the problem, and Mr Green's aberrant behavior the other. That could be officially blamed on the handlers and the scientific staff, he decided. Let them take the fall. It wasn't as if Leeroy had much direct contact with Mr Green. He avoided the Weatherman like the plague.

"Did they catch him, sir?" Dr Nikhat asked.

"Who?"

"The criminal who shot Mr Green."

Of course they knew. Another problem, Leeroy thought, information leaking out and causing who knew what explosion of rumors. He bit back the urge to deny there'd been a crime at all. It was painfully obvious. The Weatherman hadn't shot himself in the neck or the chest, let alone his two bodyguards. And how the hell would he spin that? Dangerous criminal who was about to singlehandedly shut down the bulk of TransRift's operations for the foreseeable future, on the loose after vanishing like a ghost into the desert?

He could *feel* his career flushing down the drain.

"Shot by the police," he said. "While trying to escape arrest." Another memo for himself – he'd better have the press office plant a story that would fall along those lines.

On the table, Mr Green's chest rose and fell slowly. Overhead, the lights flickered.

CHAPTER THIRTEEN

"The fuck do you want?" Old Nick growled over the top of a tumbler half-filled with amber-colored whiskey. He had taken up residence in Ludlow's little hotel while the rest of them were supposed to sleep out in one of the warehouses with the motorcycles. He'd got himself the nicest room besides, a wing chair with slightly stained upholstery and an end table to go with the double-wide bed. She wasn't sure if the bottle of whiskey had come with the room or in Nick's duster pocket, and it didn't really matter.

Hob shut the door quietly behind her. The old man looked like hell, she thought dispassionately, saggy in the face like an old, sun-cracked duster. "Got a thing or two to say."

He snorted into his glass and took a slug off the drink. "Give you one brief moment of competence and suddenly you're gettin' full of yourself like you ain't the bottom-of-the-pile fuckup no more."

"I know what I fucked up," she said through gritted teeth. "But now we're gonna have a talk about what you fucked up."

He stared at her. "I ain't fucked up a thing."

"You told me. You fuckin' *told* me that Mag ratted me out that day."

"She–"

"Don't you fuckin' lie to me again, Nick Ravani," she snarled. "'Cause me and Mag, we finally had us a talk 'bout a lot of things."

He took another pull of his whiskey and, of all things, settled back into his chair. "Glad you girls are gettin' along so nice again."

"That all you got to say for yourself?"

"I don't have to justify shit to the idiot girl that almost got all us killed 'cause she couldn't stand goin' a night without a cock to ride," Nick said.

Hob rocked back on her heels like she'd been slapped, but how long did he get to hold that over her? Forever maybe. She'd cost herself a lot with that mistake, and she'd never forget it. But she couldn't and wouldn't believe it justified this lie. "You're always sayin' family's the most important thing, you old bastard. Mag's my family as much as she's yours, and you took her away from me with your fuckin' lie."

"Nah. Just you bein' proud even when you got no reason to be ever again."

No one else in the damn world could hurt her like Nick Ravani. "I trusted you!"

"And I fuckin' trusted you." He bared his yellow teeth at her. "Don't know what you're whinin' about. Got your shit together in the end, didn't you?"

"And brought the last blood you got on this planet out of hell." She kept her voice even through an act of will.

"Expect me to be grateful?" he asked, mocking.

"I know better'n that." If she stayed here, she'd probably try to take his head off, she thought. She still didn't think she could win in a fair fight against Nick, and with him it was never a fair fight. She turned to go. "Fuck you."

"Mag ain't the only blood I got, anyway. Don't make her less special, but you want honest things, that's a fuckin' honest thing."

He always knew how to cut her off at the knees when she tried to talk away. Cursing herself, Hob turned back toward him. "You countin' all them little bastards you fucked out of whores?"

Nick laughed. "You got no fuckin' idea what I do." He curled the fingers of his unoccupied hand idly, yellow-orange flame licking over them. The fire crawled into the glass and lit up the whiskey, going from orange to cold blue.

Despite her frustration, she took a step back toward him. Her boot heels scuffed on the worn carpet. Other than the cigarette-lighting trick that she'd learned from him early on, he never showed his witchiness where other people could see, never talked about it. Hob had figured out nearly everything she knew for herself.

"You'n me are the same," Nick said. "Witchy ones gotta stick together. We ain't got no one but each other."

The only reason she even had this power that could get her killed or worse was because Old Nick had tricked her into almost dying in the desert. She still wondered at times why he'd done that – and what exactly it had done to her. He'd never had an answer for her, not that he ever answered anything unless he felt like it. "That like bein' blood, then?"

"Same and different, I reckon."

"What about them the company takes?" Hob asked quietly. "Like they took Mag."

Nick shrugged, and the flame went out like it had never been there. He downed the rest of the whiskey in a single gulp. His single eye had gone dark with an emotion she wasn't used to seeing there – regret? "Can't save everyone. I got the Wolves, and the blood of that covenant's thickest of all. Got to look out for your own first, and always."

Sounded like a coward's answer to her. "So who were you lookin' after, when you broke me'n Mag apart? Me, or her?" It hadn't done either of them any good.

Nick bared his teeth at her. "Get the fuck out of my room." Maybe she'd made her point. He stared at her until she turned to leave, but spoke again as she reached the door. "Bone Collector found me while I was scoutin' in the desert and told me."

Hob paused, gripping the door frame with one hand. Why did that thought hurt almost as much as her betrayer being Mag? "That another lie?"

Nick laughed. "You know it ain't."

Hob left a blackened handprint on the doorframe. She was still angry at Old Nick for his lie, but this truth was the closest she'd ever get to an apology from him. The Bone Collector didn't control her life, couldn't hurt her the way Nick could. It was safer to be mad at him.

She grabbed her motorcycle and headed right out of town, front wheel turned in the general direction of Pictou. An hour out from Rouse, she stopped between two low, scrubby dunes hardly worth the name. She didn't stop to think; she didn't want to. She drew one of her knives and cut across the fleshy part of her palm, then let the blood run onto the sand.

The stinging of that cut finally brought her to her senses. She wasn't anywhere near Pictou, and it was the middle of the night. She'd be needing to be up early in the morning to do whatever tasks Nick came up with just because he felt like being an asshole, to remind her that she owed him still and always for being a damn fool. Hob wiped her knife off on her sleeve and sheathed it, then pulled out her handkerchief to wrap around her hand.

Damn fool again. Her whole life was being a damn fool, and she'd get the Wolves all killed for it some day. Maybe she should just ride off into the desert and save them the trouble. The moment the thought formed, she already dismissed it. She'd survived as an abandoned child in the hold of a rift ship, survived the desert, survived having her eye torn out. She didn't know how to give up.

"I didn't expect to hear from you again so soon," a familiar voice, the Bone Collector, said behind her. "Though I could like this as a habit."

It didn't startle her, and maybe it should have. But, subconsciously, she'd felt some shift to the air, some weight that his presence brought. Hob turned to look at him, pale and smiling at her in the moonlight. He was beautiful. And she found she didn't much like him right now, or the way he looked at her. She took all that *damn tired*, of being mocked, of not being taken seriously, and packed it into her fist. It made a satisfying, meaty *crack* hitting his face, and she felt the shock all the way up to her shoulder.

The Bone Collector stumbled back, one hand coming up to clutch his nose. Bright red showed between his fingers. He caught himself with his staff and simply stared at her, eyes wide and shocked.

"Old Nick told me," Hob said, measuring the words around breath that wanted to come too fast. "Three years ago. You're the one who sent him to– to stop me."

The Bone Collector straightened. "Didn't you know?" His voice sounded odd, muffled by his hand.

Hob laughed sharply. "No one fuckin' tells me a goddamn thing. I'm tired of it." Maybe she ought to be grateful to him, because if he hadn't set things in motion all the Wolves including her probably would be long dead. She didn't much care at that moment. "You been following me or something?"

The Bone Collector speared his staff in the sand, and then came up with a handkerchief from his pocket to staunch the flow from his nose. "Or something."

"Because I'm witchy, ain't it."

"Blood calls to blood, and I hear it clearly." Even with his mouth hidden, she got the impression he smiled. "I watch all of the witchy ones."

"Not the way you watch me. Or Old Nick. What the fuck are we? What the fuck are *you*? No one'll give me a goddamn clear answer."

The Bone Collector shrugged. "You are tangles

of possibility, seeds beginning to flourish where all others are dormant. You are the voice of the world in flesh. I–"

Hob threw up her hands in frustration. If one more nonsense puzzle came out of his damn mouth, she'd hit him again. "Never fucking mind."

The Bone Collector pulled the handkerchief away from his nose and inspected it curiously, then folded it and tucked it away. "I think I might end up with a black eye."

"You lookin' for a sorry?"

"Not particularly."

Hob blew out a breath. She wasn't Old Nick. "Well, I am anyway. Sorry. Even if I'm still madder'n hell."

He seemed to consider this. "I am not sorry that I gave the message to Old Nick, three years ago. I need the both of you to live. Though I am sorry that he lied to you about it. I would have told you the truth, had you asked."

"Didn't exactly see you, to ask. Or know I should." Or expect an answer she could understand. Everyone who spoke plain seemed too spooked to ever come up with an answer, and the one person who was willing to talk was crazier than Old Nick, if a hell of a lot more eloquent. She'd scream in frustration if she didn't think someone would just laugh at her for it.

"That will change," he said, turning to leave. He gingerly touched his nose. "Though with less of this, I trust."

Hob smiled crookedly. "Depends on how fuckin' mysterious you gotta act."

CHAPTER FOURTEEN

Hob and Uncle Nick stayed another full day, and Mag was grateful for it, since it almost made them into a kind of family again. More like Hob and Uncle Nick were adopting her than the other way around. Then Dambala came to Ludlow to tell her that Irina didn't think it was safe to leave Rouse yet, because company men had already been looking for Mag, and Father Lee had come around three times already to see how Irina was bearing up. A visit in itself wasn't strange; Mama went to church plenty regular, which had always been a bone of contention between her and Uncle Nick, even if Mag wasn't quite sure why. But Father Lee had never quite warmed to her, maybe because she didn't drag her husband and daughter in on Sundays and she had admitted to getting salty at him when he pushed her on it. Church, in Mama's opinion, was a Personal Thing, about Personal Relationships, and she always said it like that too, like there were capital letters on the words.

Yet when Uncle Nick and Hob left with Dambala, lithe little Coyote bringing up the rear, Mag felt strangely relieved. She couldn't look at Uncle Nick without seeing the ghost of her father's face, and the guilt in his one eye threatened to eat her alive; she could almost hear him screaming in his head, *should have… should have…* She had enough *should have* and *what if* to last her a lifetime, without borrowing from anyone else.

That night, right after shift change, Clarence took her to one of the warehouses, filled with miners from the day shift. Several men hung around on the street, trying to look casual but keeping their heads moving back and forth, watching for something. She knew them for sentries, had seen similar things in Rouse when the company men were in their beds or off having dinner. Her papa had gone to a lot of meetings that hadn't existed. And she had followed him on more than one occasion, spying because she was curious and knew how to not be noticed.

Clarence tucked her away in the back of the room. "Gonna tell them what happened. Thought you should be here. But we're gonna keep your name quiet for now. If people guess, they guess, but there's too much company interest in you right now." He waited for her nod, and then went to the front of the room.

"A good man's dead, and we know who killed him, with no reason or mercy, no justice." That was how he started, flat, with no preamble. What followed were the bare details, Papa being thrown off the train, shot from the helicopter. Hearing it stated so cold, hard, and angry made Mag curl around her stomach. At the end of the too-short story, Clarence paused, and raised his arms for silence. "Philip Kushtrim deserves a wake, brothers and sisters. And mayhap the men who murdered him need a reminder that they own our labor, not our lives."

Mag swallowed carefully around the hot lump in her throat. Maybe she wasn't done crying after all.

"I say we throw our brother Phil a big party, in two days' time. Big enough that none of us are gonna be able to work, day shift or night shift. And we'll invite the miners in Rouse and Shimera, even Walsen if we can get a messenger that far, to join in. They can come to our party, or throw their own, but I say we got a right to remember our friend. Hands, who agrees with me?"

It looked like a forest of hands to Mag, rooted on taut, angry faces. There was no hesitation; some even seemed to punch the air, driving their fists toward the ceiling.

"Looks like the majority has spoken. Two days. Bring a pie, bring your beer, and bring your guns if you got 'em, 'cause it could get ugly."

The miners dispersed quickly, flowing from the warehouse in a grim tide. A few hung back to speak with Clarence; he dispatched them one by one to the surrounding towns with the news, gave them money so they could get onto the trains or get passage on a caravan, and noted their names so he could mark them as sick.

When the last of the men was gone, he turned to Mag. "Two days, we'll give your daddy a good sendoff."

Mag shook her head. It was more than that – it was a work stoppage, something that would make the pit bosses furious, something that would make a splash and cause trouble. "I don't think Papa would have wanted that," she whispered.

Clarence smiled. "I think there was a lot about your daddy you don't know yet, Mag."

"You could get a lot of people hurt. Or worse. I don't want anyone else losing their papa over what's happened to us."

"Ship just left a few days ago, Mag. Won't be another one for six months at the earliest. If they hurt us or blacklist us, they'll lose a lot more than one day's work in their mines. So long as we stick together and stand strong, ain't nothin' they can do to us."

Mag shivered. "Plenty they can do to you. Things that are way worse than bein' killed."

The night shift miners of Ludlow, their husbands and wives and children, filled the streets two days later right at lunch time. They dragged dining tables out of their houses, covered them with pies and pitchers of lemonade, any sort of food that people were willing to share. The whole thing felt like a festival more than a wake, but it was the sort of thing Papa would have liked. He'd never been a man to let people be sad; he always tried to crack jokes, get people to laugh even when there was reason enough to be grim.

From the works, all the dayshift miners came down the hill to cheers from the night crew. They were handed plates and cups, offered seats so they could rest. People ate fried protein with dirty fingers, wiped dust from their faces with the corners of checked tablecloths. The whistle blew again, and the miners stayed seated.

On the surface, it was all gaiety, people gossiping and telling jokes. But a deaf man could have heard the undercurrent of nervousness, and felt it tickling at the hairs on the back of his neck. There were people playing handball in one of the streets, but players missed passes because they were keeping an eye on the guard shack and the mine works, waiting for men in Mariposa green to come pouring out.

Mag took a slice of mince pie and slowly disassembled it on her plate. Her mouth tasted strange and the spices would have been welcome, but anything that passed her lips felt like glue and dust.

An hour and forty-five minutes into the street picnic, the pit boss came down the street, the full security contingent at his back. The guards were bulky, chests like barrels; they had to be wearing body armor under their uniforms. Batons and rifles were out and ready. Some guards showed grim faces, and others had a shine of excitement in their eyes that said they were itching for a fight, looking for a chance to use those company-issue guns for something other than taking potshots at passing eagles.

Further down the table, one miner handed another a fistful of chits; they must have been betting on how long it would take for security to come out.

"Clarence!" the pit boss called.

Clarence stood, a few seats down from Mag. "Bill. What can I do for you?"

"I got quite a few questions, Clarence, but maybe you can start by telling me what you're doing down here. Whistle's blown twice, and I'm not seeing anyone at work."

"Taking the day off, Bill. Funeral. We've all had a death in the family."

The pit boss made a big show of looking back and forth across the street. The crowd had gone silent, watching and waiting; the only sound was the breeze lapping at the tablecloths. "I find that hard to believe."

"Phil Kushtrim out of Rouse. He was brother to us all, and we're determined to give him a proper sendoff. I expect you understand. We got a right to funerals, a day off."

"I heard rumor of this, so I did a little checking. Philip Kushtrim's on the blacklist, Clarence. You can't expect me to approve time off for someone like *that*."

The sound of angry shouts was dim in Mag's ears, like everyone was yelling from down a tunnel. She drifted up to her feet, it felt like, pushing against the table with her hands, but somehow that sent her fork tumbling off onto the ground, made her coffee slop over onto the tablecloth. "You're a damn liar!" she shouted. "He weren't on the blacklist when you bastards shot him in the back!"

Silence again. Her hands trembled against the tablecloth, but it wasn't fear, it wasn't even grief: it was rage, pure and hot, so much fire in her blood that she wanted to leap onto the man and tear his eyes out. All eyes were on her, and she didn't even feel the weight. She just stared at the pit boss, something fierce itching in the back of her head, until he looked away.

"Well, I hardly see how that could be the case–" he started to say.

"Shame on you!" she shouted again, cutting him

off. "Shame for slanderin' a good man! Shame!"

Others picked up the word, a murmur that grew into a chant, up and down the street: "Shame! Shame! Shame!"

More miners surged to their feet, crowding up around her and hiding her from the company man. They pressed forward, a unified front until they were up against the security guards, still shouting, waving their fists in the air. The power of that crowd, like they melded into a giant beast, made her forget every misgiving she had, everything but the anger, the desire to just fight back.

A guard drove the butt of his rifle into the stomach of a miner. The man half fell, the people next to him catching his arm. Another miner lunged forward at the guard, and Clarence himself grabbed the man by the shirt collar, yanked him back.

Mag surged with the crowd. She wanted blood.

"We're supposed to be celebratin' a man's life," Clarence said, shouting to be heard. He repeated himself until people quieted down enough to listen. "I don't think you want this turnin' into a fight, Bill. Ain't no place for a riot at a funeral."

Bill's face was paste white. He reached over and grabbed the sleeve of the guard who'd hit the miner, jerking him to the side. "I don't think anyone wants to see that."

"Then why don't you go on back to your office, do some paperwork. We'll have us our party, and then we'll be back to work tomorrow, like nothing ever happened."

"The night shift—"

"Needs a chance to rest and do their own mourning. Today belongs to us."

"One day," Bill said. Each movement of his hand jerky, he adjusted his tie, smoothed it down. "You can have one day. But I don't give a shit if any of you are hung over, everyone's back at work tomorrow if you don't want your pay docked."

"We do appreciate it. See you tomorrow morning." Clarence crossed his arms over his chest and just stood, watching the company men until they turned and left. The street was silent until they'd gone back into the office building, and then there was cheering, even singing. Someone grabbed Mag's hands and swung her in a circle; a woman kissed her on the cheek.

It felt like a victory.

It felt less like a victory in the next days, when Clarence was at work and Mag took messages at his door for him: three blacklisted in Walsen, with most of the other miners too afraid to try the work stoppage, so there wasn't a group to protect them. A riot in Shimera, two miners beaten to death by security guards and the mine works smashed to pieces. That would be a longer stoppage than just a day, waiting for repairs.

And in Rouse there had been a successful wake, but two nights later Phil Kushtrim's house burned down, his widow trapped inside it.

Mag sat at Clarence's rough kitchen table, the note that had brought that news sitting in front of her. A cup of coffee cooled slowly between her hands as she tried to comprehend the words. The note was battered, the flimsy streaked with sweat and dirt, almost torn in half. The handwriting on it belonged to someone ill educated, half the words spelled wrong. But she couldn't pretend that bad spelling made anything less real in the heartlessly plain summary: house burned, Irina's remains found in the ashes, no one heard anything.

Maybe Mama had already been dead, heart attack or stroke or just plain grief. Maybe the fire had been an accident, and the smoke had gotten her. But Mag didn't believe those hollow excuses for one second, and with the timing of it, no one else would either.

And did it even matter? She felt numb. How much tragedy could one person truly understand in the space of a few days? Her papa murdered, her mama likely murdered, and all of the things that had happened to her; she didn't even want to walk through those memories, not now, probably not ever. Everything ached, her head heavy, her throat tight, her hands trembling against the coffee cup. She might have cried, but her face was numb; if there were tears she didn't feel them.

Maybe there weren't tears at all, maybe she'd already cried as much as she could ever cry when Papa had died, because she'd been so selfish about it and saved no tears for Mama.

Mag had once wished that she were tough and angry like Hob, that she had that sort of permanent chip on her shoulder. They'd never been alike in that respect; Hob's anger frightened her sometimes, and she knew she could never feel that sort of white-hot rage at the general injustice of the world. Like Uncle Nick – the two of them were bullets from the same mold, ready to go hot and spit blood. And maybe it meant Hob did stupid things, ill-advised things, but she did them fast and hard and with conviction. Maybe that made those stupid things a million times worse. And in the end, they'd both had their hearts broken equally, hadn't they?

Mag had always been the quiet one, who watched and waited and plotted. The one who everyone called a good girl, no one suspected when things went sideways because a rope was frayed or a button had come undone. She wasn't a good girl, had never been a good girl. A good girl wouldn't have been friends with Hob, wouldn't have loved an uncle like Nick with all her heart. And she spared a little corner of worry, for what Uncle Nick would do when he heard this news, what Hob would do as she got pulled in his wake. Their damn drama, their chest-beating and flash-hot anger. Damn them for making her worry when, for once, she wished she could worry after her own self.

Mag had been a good daughter, even if she'd never been a good girl. She'd been dutiful, and she'd loved her parents, and now she loved Hob and Uncle Nick as the last family she had left. Maybe she *could* do more than just sit and worry. Papa had been a quiet one too, a deep thinker, a plotter, as unlike his older brother as Mag was unlike Hob.

Clarence walked in the door, skin blackened with mine dust. He stank of sweat and black powder. "Evenin'…" he stopped, peering at her face. "You all right, Mag?"

She offered the note to him; her hand was steady now, as if she'd come to a decision in her heart already that her brain hadn't quite caught up with. She watched his expression as he read the short message, saw the sympathy in his eyes, all that empathy for a pain that he couldn't truly understand, because no one could. He reached for her, and she stood, walked away, dumped her coffee out in the sink and rinsed the cup.

She was tired of men touching her, even well-meaning ones. It seemed maybe Clarence wanted to be a father to her, wanted to take her in like a stray and treat her like his own. But he wasn't her papa, he could never be, and it made her a little sick to think of even a good man like him trying to step into her father's shoes.

"Mag? Anything... I'm sorry. I'm really sorry. Is there anythin' I can do?"

Mag turned, leaning back against the counter. The rough edge poked the fading bruises that Mr Franklin had driven in to her, but this time it was a pain she owned, a place she'd decided to stand. "I want to know everythin' my papa was doing with you. Everythin' you were plannin'. It's *mine* now."

He stared at her, looked her deep in the eye. Whatever he saw was enough to make him look away, and enough to make him start talking.

CHAPTER FIFTEEN

Nick laughed as he read the note Hati handed over to him, so loud it shut everyone in the little mess hall up. The sound ended in a wheezing cough that he cut short, the muscles of his throat working strangely as he stood and raised his beer mug. "Those crazy shaft-rats in Ludlow are gonna have a wake for my brother, an entire goddamn day of eatin' and drinkin'. And in Shimera, Walsen, and Rouse besides! I say we join 'em. We'll take tomorrow off and make it a big damn party!"

Everyone cheered, though to Freki's ear, well tuned by their childhood years together when he'd been Francis and hadn't yet earned his Wolf's name, Hob's was halfhearted at best. "You OK?" he asked in an undertone.

"Me? I'm fine. Never better. *He* seem OK to you?" she answered.

Freki shrugged, turning to look at his brother. Geri had always loved to talk, so it was easiest to just let him do it. It used to be that no one could tell him and his brother apart, except for how much Geri ran his mouth. But Hob had cut Geri a good one on the scalp with a broken bottle, during a particularly idiotic fight they'd had in a bar. Freki still wasn't sure why they'd always hated each other, and that left him as disturbed as his more laconic nature would allow. The scar was mostly hidden in Geri's hair, but a tuft of his tight black curls came in shocked white. Just meant that now they wore hats everywhere.

"Seems as OK as a man can get after his brother's been turned to eagle meat," Geri said. "But he's a tough old bastard, so what can you say?"

"Just dunno if I ever seen him cough, is all." Hob shrugged.

She made a good point. Thinking about it, Freki could never recall a time when Nick had the sniffles, even when a cold was raging through the barracks. Maybe it was the tobacco; burned out all the viruses. Man had never even been hungover properly that he could recall. But he let Geri make the answer: "You got somethin' to tell us?"

"Nah. Bein' a worrywart for no good reason, I guess."

Geri snorted. "Must be those motherin' instincts of yours."

Hob laughed. "Oh, you know. I got 'em in spades. Mothered you a time or two, good and proper."

Geri propped his arm up on the table. "Come on, let's see you wrestle me."

"Best muscle I got is my brain. Means I don't take sucker bets." Hob finished her beer, bolted down the rest of her potatoes as Nick headed out of the mess hall, shoulders hunched like a vulture. "Gonna make it an early night. You boys try to save some fun for the actual party." She slid off her seat on the rough bench and walked quickly away, plate in hand.

Geri barked a laugh. "Probably run off to see Old Nick."

Freki swirled the dregs of the beer in his glass. "Better not be thinkin' to add somethin' nasty to that, brother. You know it ain't a thing I like to hear." He was tired of Geri's sniping, and he'd always had a soft spot for Hob, even when they'd been boys and calling her *pinkbelly* for the way she always burned lobster red in the sun while they'd just tanned blacker and blacker. Though come to think of it, Hob hadn't spent that much time with her sunburns; they'd stopped about when she started smoking. Odd thing, that. Probably the witchiness he pretended he didn't know about.

"Ain't you supposed to be takin' my side?"

Freki smirked. "I'm your twin, not a total fuckin' moron."

"Coulda fooled me, the way you go moonin' around sometimes."

"You ain't gonna pick a fight with me neither. I don't got your burnin' desire to be the top wolf in every pile."

"Wolf always wins over a bitch."

Freki stood, waving Geri's comment idly off. "You know where to find me when you're ready to be a fuckin' adult." He tucked his thumbs in his belt and wandered out after Hob.

Hob followed Nick at a distance, pretending that she was just going to the barracks. Ready to escape at a moment's notice, she hunkered down just out of sight of his office and listened. Coughing, hacking and painful, filtered through the door. She grimaced, the sound making her chest itch in sympathy. She heard footsteps, the sound of Nick dropping into his chair. More coughing.

She didn't know what to do. It wasn't like him; the old bastard was too mean to get sick. Her pointing out a problem would buy her nothing but a week of shit jobs, likely why Coyote had told her instead of approaching Nick himself. Coyote was crazy, not stupid, and he loved to get other people to take the fall for him.

Wait, she decided. It wasn't impossible that he just had some bug he picked up in one of the mining towns. Give it a week, see if it was still happening and then she'd be worried. Grief worked weird on people; maybe Old Nick couldn't cry, so he coughed instead. Maybe the problem would go away on its own.

Hob crept back down the stairs, easing the door to the little office building shut. She turned around to come face to face with one of the twins, skin almost pitch black in the dim safety lighting. She jerked back, one hand resting on her pistol for a moment while her brain caught up to her reflexes and let her know that no, it was probably OK. She stared at him, then said, "Freki."

He nodded, the corner of his mouth twitching slightly.

"What d'ya want?"

He tilted his head up toward the closed window of Nick's office. "Somethin' wrong?"

"Ask me in a week. Mayhap I'll have it figured out

then. Good night." She took a couple of steps around him, and then stopped. "You ever wonder how I know which of you is which?"

He shrugged, but she could see that little spark of curiosity in his eyes.

"Ain't your hair. You're the one that don't look at me like I smell bad."

Freki laughed, covering his mouth with one hand so the sound didn't carry too far. "Don't take it personal. He's got a problem with women."

Hob stared; it was the most words she'd heard out of Freki at one time. "Guess I'm glad it ain't just me."

"Girl bit him when he was little. Never got over it."

Hob laughed as Freki walked away, not giving her a chance to ask anything else.

Later, Hob found out it was a miner from Rouse, his clothes still stinking of smoke, who brought the news. Middle of the night, and he'd still managed to find one of their in-town lookouts, gave them the message.

But all she knew was that someone hammered on her door with the butt of a gun, yanking her from a solid sleep. She rolled out of bed, scrambling to pull on her pants and button them while the banging just kept going. She jerked the door open before the man on the other side had a chance to knock it off its hinges.

Dambala, raccoon-eyed with exhaustion, his expression grim, said: "Full muster. Get downstairs."

"The hell exploded?"

He paused at the stairway, looking back at her. "Weren't an explosion."

Her blood felt cold in her veins as she pulled on the rest of her clothes and shoved her feet into her boots, not even bothering to lace them. Her fingers fumbled with the buckle on her gun belt as she thumped down the stairs.

Every last man of the outfit was out in the exercise yard, some of them standing a little sideways, leaning against their compatriots. Nick shouted at them to hurry, to smarten up, fall in.

Hob took her position at the back of the column, glancing at Geri next to her. He was too tired to give her a dirty look.

"That's all of 'em, Ravani," Makaya said, surveying the group. "Where we goin'?" She was Nick's second, and looked the same as the day Nick had brought Hob in off the dunes: a stringy brown woman barely over a meter and a half tall. She wore at least ten knives plainly; she had a lot more hidden in her clothes.

Nick crossed his arms over his chest. His face was pale, skin clinging to his skull like wet paper. "We're ridin' to Rouse. Bastards burned down Phil's house, and Irina in it. We're goin' for blood."

Hob glanced around at men nodding, their faces closing off in anger that they hadn't even shown at Phil's murder. Irina had been kind to each and every one of them at some point, had looked away when they stole her pies, and darned more socks than Hob cared to count.

Fire snarled through her blood, anger tight through her. Irina had been the closest thing she'd ever had to a mother, in the sense that she was Mag's mama, and she'd tolerated her daughter's wild friend. But Hob was so used to rage always cooking at her insides that she could think around it. "We goin' to war?"

Nick snapped around to face her. "We're goin' hunting."

"We go rolling in to Rouse, it'll be war. Company ain't just gonna sit by and let us string someone up as we please."

"If you're yellow, you can get the hell off my base. Get mounted up." He strode away, duster snapping behind him.

Hob looked at Geri again; for once, he wasn't trying to stare down his nose at someone taller than him. "Guess it's war," he said. "You comin'?"

She almost laughed, because it wasn't like she had a choice. It didn't matter if it was plain suicide Nick was asking; he'd saved her life, given her a second chance when she hadn't deserved one. She owed loyalty to Nick as the Ravani, and to Nick as the man that pulled her from the desert and gave her a name to call her own. "Wouldn't miss it for anythin'."

They rode in grim silence, twenty strong. There wasn't a sound but the wind and tires humming over the dunes. Rouse was a string of lights on the horizon, yellow sodium flares lining the top of the wall. Nick's voice became a whipcrack over the abnormally staticky radio channel. "Makaya, take care of the gate."

"Sir." Makaya peeled off the formation, motorcycle speeding over the dunes. The rest of them slowed, hanging back, giving her time to work.

Hob saw the black shadow of Makaya in the yellow

light at the gates. She knocked at the inset door, it opened a crack, and then wider to let her in. She disappeared for a moment, then her voice came over the radio, barely audible even at the short distance. "Gate guard's down. Going for the west side of the wall."

They sped back up, arrowing toward the town as a single unit. Ahead, the gate yawned wide.

A moment later, Makaya's voice came up again. "Neutralized. East side now."

They pulled up to the walls, flowed inside in a silent tide.

"East side neutralized. Where to now, boss?"

"We're goin' to get churched," Nick said.

They followed him through the streets like ghosts. The electric motors on the bikes made only a hushed hum, inaudible over the endless churn of the mine that made the town's sleepless black heart. Houses stood dark and quiet, no sign yet given that their presence had even been noticed. Hob's shoulders tensed up around her ears, waiting for the lights on the two guard towers to spring on. It was only a matter of time until an alarm was called.

The Wolves surrounded the church in a wall of metal. The simple sight of the building made a sick twist in Hob's stomach, even so many years later, a reminder of how she'd been used by Father Lee and his adopted boy. Nick stepped off his bike, pausing to take off his helmet and light a cigarette, the yellow flare showing a face empty of any humanity. Then he spread the front doors wide with his hands, framed by the candlelight inside.

Hob slipped off her own motorcycle, made to follow him. Dambala grabbed her sleeve, didn't let go when she gave it a warning shake.

"Leave off," Makaya hissed. "Hob's got a debt of her own to collect." On the base, they called Makaya the debt keeper; she never forgot who owed her blood.

Dambala let go and Hob followed Nick, drawing her pistol. Vengeance be damned, she wasn't going to leave the old bastard without someone to guard his back.

"Preacher!" Nick shouted. "Preacher, you get your goddamn flabby ass out here! We got you surrounded, so don't you even think of tryin' to run!"

The man emerged a few moments later through a door at the back, clad in a green dressing gown that looked nicer than any clothes Hob had ever owned. His face was pale, but he drew himself up, hands clutching at the front of his robe. "What have you need of, my... *son*?" The man almost bit the word off before he could say it.

Nick laughed, sharp and nasty, as he grabbed the man's collar. The preacher screamed as Nick dragged him over to the altar and threw him down on the ground. He drew one of his pistols, the bone butt the color of butter, and the preacher fell abruptly silent. Nick pulled the hammer back, barrel aimed unwavering, dead center on the preacher's forehead. "I know you got your finger in every goddamn pie in this town, you fuckin' spy. So you tell me now, you tell me who killed my sister-in-law."

"I don't–"

The barrel of the gun twitched down and Nick fired,

the retort deafening. The preacher screamed, tried to scramble back. Blood, almost black in the candlelight, ran from his leg, a long graze across his thigh. Nick grabbed his collar again, leaned down, pressed the gun barrel to the man's cheek. "Next time, I won't miss a-purpose. You tell me what I want to know!"

The preacher started babbling, words almost impossible to follow as they tumbled from his trembling jaw. "She told me all about sending her daughter away, she was a good woman – a God-fearing woman! I just told the foreman about it – and then there was the wake, and she was *glad* about it, but it got so many people muttering about worse, about more than one day. The foreman said they needed a little warning. I didn't know he meant a warning like this, I swear!"

"Give me a name!"

"S- Savrille. It must have been Savrille!"

"Good man," Nick crooned, a tone Hob had never heard him use. It sent shivers up her spine, made her want to crawl away. He smiled. "Which one's he?"

"Foreman for the night shift. I swear, that was my only part in it, I didn't know what they were going to do!"

"But you did. You knew that they'd do something. And you didn't say a goddamn word to anyone, when you could have warned her."

The stream of babbling dried up abruptly. Maybe looking death in the eye, knowing he'd never escape it, made him calm. "It's my job to maintain the order and keep them all safe. The very things devil-loving catamites like you *hate*."

"Rina burned. You know how painful that is?" Nick clenched his fist tighter, almost choking the man with his own robe. Sparks ran down his arm, collecting around his hand. "Got a little taste of Hell for ya."

The preacher's eyes went wide. He opened his mouth, screamed "Witch–!"

His head burst into flame like a torch.

After that, he just screamed, for what felt like an eternity but could have only been a few seconds with his brain cooking. As soon as he went silent, Nick let go. The body made a wet thump on the floor, and flames licking out, searching for wood.

The air was thick with cooked-meat smell. Hob swallowed back bile as Nick turned toward her. His face was pale, eye wild, and for a moment there was no recognition. "Where to now?" she asked.

Nick shuddered, giving his head a sharp shake, then stood tall. "We get Savrille. He'll be at the mine."

"So will all the night shift guards."

Nick paused on his way out, looked at her. "Guess that means they'll know it was us an' not the miners."

Hob paused at the door, looking back into the smoky church. This was where the plan had been hatched, to have Jeb take the tracking devices, find out where she and the Wolves lived. This was where company men and Father Lee had decided she ought to be used, because order was more important than honesty. This was the reason Jeb had ended up in her bedroom. He'd even *pushed her* to take him back to the base, a subtle manipulation she hadn't rightly realized before. Learned at the knee of Father Lee, perhaps. There was no knowing, now, how much of

Jeb had been a lie. And it didn't matter either.

She rested her hand on the back of a pew, letting the rage roar through her bones. Her vision went red, her heartbeat sang in her ears. When she lifted her hand away, there was a burned print, its interior red and smoldering. Flames licked up, caught, and began to move slowly across the top of the pew. "Just this building. No more than that."

The fire was a living thing. It protested, it matched its will against hers, and she snarled at it to behave.

Hob turned her back and followed Nick.

There was no reason to keep quiet now, not if they were going to drag the foreman out of the mine in the middle of his shift. Nick just about vibrated with rage on his motorcycle, but calmed himself enough for basic strategy: he sent four to hold the gate, another six to secure the flanks, Freki and Geri with them.

One shouted order from Nick and the remaining ten Wolves drew pistols or balanced rifles across their battery stacks, steering their motorcycles with one light hand and the power of body weight. Coyote had a pistol in each hand, grinning all the while; asshole always did like showing off. They flashed up the hill toward the works, into the floodlights. People started shouting. Hob caught a blur of green to one side, a guard standing up with a cigarette dangling from his mouth, fumbling for his rifle. She shot him twice as she passed by.

Behind them, the guard towers lit up. Gunfire cracked through the night.

A few seconds later they arrived at the mine works

– and the shacks at the top where most of the night shift guards holed up. As they halted, the doors flew open and guards piled out, half drunk and thoroughly confused. The Wolves sprayed the shacks and the bottlenecked guards with bullets. Men in green fell, or threw themselves to the ground for safety.

Then silence but for the creaking of synthetic wood and flexsteel, the clank of the overhead drive chain doing its endless journey into the mine.

"Savrille!" Nick shouted. "Send him out, boys! It's him I want!"

One of the guards raised his head, looking up at Nick. Hob pointed her pistol square at him. He pressed his forehead back down against the floor of the shack.

Miners flowed from the works, a sea of smudged blue coveralls and dirty faces, pale arms streaked with grime. A man Hob didn't recognize, a reflective stripe on his hardhat to indicate he was a crew leader, yelled to Nick, "What do you want him for?"

"You all know damn well that the fire Irina burned in weren't an accident," Nick shouted. "Well, I know who gave the word to have it done. I want Savrille, now!"

The crowd of miners murmured, still more coming up from the works. Some sounded angry, nodding their heads in agreement. A few others stepped back, hands raised, wanting no part.

"He ain't bad, for a company man," the crew leader said. "Treated us fair enough. You sure?"

Nick glanced behind him, then jerked his thumb over his shoulder. "See the fire I started? That's how sure I am. Evil men talk a pretty game."

More murmuring. "Fire?" "Is that the church?" "Jesus, what did he do?"

But the crew leader nodded, slowly. "Phil was a friend of mine, and so was Irina. But if you want Savrille, he ain't in the pit." He pointed at the second guard shack. "Hangs out in that one, plays cards with his friends all the time."

Nick threw down his kickstand, strode over to the shack. A guard tried to rise and Nick kicked him in the face. He disappeared into the building; a moment later he came out, dragging a much smaller man by the back of his blue jacket, the nose of his revolver pressed into his cheek.

Behind them, more gunfire, getting closer.

"We don't have time for your theatrics, Nick," Coyote said.

Nick didn't seem to hear. "You tell 'em what you done," he hissed. "You fuckin' tell 'em, or I'll do somethin' a hell of a lot worse than just shooting you."

The man shook, tears running down his face, snot bubbling out of his nose. He didn't look like a murderer, Hob thought, wasn't all hard edges like Old Nick. But probably it was a hell of a lot easier to just kill with an order than to go set the fire yourself, pull the trigger. "I ordered it," he whimpered.

"Ordered what?" Nick roared.

"Ordered that the house be burned. The man was blackli–"

Savrille's head blew apart into a spray of bone and brain. Bloody mist painted one side of Nick's jaw as he let the body drop. "You all heard it. I done justice because the fuckin' greenbellies never will look at one of their own."

Behind them, someone screamed through the sound of gunfire, high and thin.

Nick turned and ran to his motorcycle. "Fall back!" he shouted. He tried to yell another order, but choked on the word as he pulled on his helmet. Half a cough came over the radio channel before the transmission cut out.

Hob leaned hard, chain mesh on the wheels throwing sparks on the uneven ground as she whipped her motorcycle around. They went down the hill faster than they should have, toward the gate. She waited for someone to echo the order, but no call came to warn the other groups. Hob keyed her microphone on and, as calm as she could given the circumstance, said, "Fall back, all hands to the gate."

The sound of rifles was replaced by the bark of bigger guns, bullets raining down from the guard towers. Hob half twisted on her bike, trying to keep her weight steady and her path straight as she fired at the floodlights on the tower. Two went out in a shower of sparks. Then she ducked her head as the trail of tracers moved toward her, swerving out as wide as she could in the all-too narrow street. She ran up onto the boardwalk, ducking below several awnings and low-hanging signs. Synthetic wood shredded around her; glass cracked and shattered.

They made a tight turn to the gate. That team was intact, hiding behind their motorcycles, rifles propped up on them or coming from between the wheels as they returned fire. Hob hung back just a little, let the other seven get out ahead of her with Nick in the lead, then called, "Team one out!"

Then she gunned it, running off the hardpan and skidding into the dunes, not looking back. A moment later, Dambala's voice came over the radio: "Team two out. Gate team, fall back."

Hob had one short moment to think about the fact that it was Dambala, not Makaya, that spoke, even though her team had been covering the flanks. Then all she could do was concentrate on the wobbling beam of light that showed her path, trying to keep her proper spacing with the people next to her.

"Somethin's comin' in from the west," Geri said. From the corner of her eye, she saw him sit up, saw him dig something from his saddlebags and shove up his visor: binoculars. "It's a chopper. Coming fast."

Nick's voice was little more than a croak over the radio. "There's some canyons, a few kilometers in. We can hide there."

They made it to the flat-bottomed canyon system with the chopper still flying a search pattern behind them, and rocketed through the twists and turns, sticking to the bare rock where they'd leave no tracks. Half an hour in, Dambala called for a halt. The Wolves dove from their motorcycles, hid them behind little rock falls, in narrow gaps. Like she'd done it a thousand times, Hob dropped off her bike as soon as it came to a rest, pulled a camouflage net from her saddlebags and spread it over the machine, then ducked under it herself.

Only then, with everyone hunkered down and as

safe as they could be, did they sound off.

No Makaya – taken down by two guards, one of them shooting her through both legs, Dambala said – and no Skoll, no Hukka.

It could have been worse, Hob told herself, shivering under the camouflage net. The rocks still radiated heat, but the air had gone freezing without the sun. With nothing to do but wait, the adrenalin leached from her blood, left her shaking, thirsty, and strangely hungry. They'd only lost three from a force of twenty. But even one death hurt, like a wound in the chest. These were people she'd known the majority of her life. Three more were wounded, doctoring themselves as best they could with the bandages they carried in their packs. Two motorcycles were also so badly damaged that they wouldn't be safe to ride home. Even before the wounded were finished getting glued and sewn together, Hati the garagemaster crawled under the tarps concealing the damaged bikes and started rendering them to parts over the hissed protests of their riders. People healed. Motorcycles didn't, and even now they had to be practical.

They all fell still and turned off their radios as the sound of chopper rotors climbed over the breeze. The chopper hovered for what felt like an eternity, shining lights down on them. Once the sweeping lights paused right on Hob's hiding place, light leaking through the gaps in the camouflage net. She tried to not even breathe, specks dancing in front of her eye.

The chopper flew away. Hob breathed, but didn't relax. It would be back. They'd kicked over a bloodleaper nest, good and proper. She pulled off her helmet and bellycrawled out across the rocks, searching out the spot she'd seen Nick pull in. Someone hissed at her to go back, and she ignored him. She'd hear the chopper before they'd be able to see her.

Without asking for permission – it wasn't worth making the noise to just have her request denied – she crawled under his net. Nick lay curled up on his side, head pillowed on his helmet. It was hard to see how he looked in the dark, but his breath told tale enough – labored, rattling. Hob reached out, hesitantly put her hand on his shoulder.

He didn't jump, or move away, just covered her hand with one of his own. She scooted around the motorcycle, still mindful to keep her head ducked and not disturb the net, and pulled his head into her lap, the way she'd done with Mag.

His face was wet, the cheek with tears, the chin with blood. She said nothing, just wiped her fingers clean on her pants. But it was terrifying, to think that Nick had even a single tear left in his one eye, let alone that many. She didn't like it; his anger and affectionate abuse was the foundation she'd built everything on, because he was supposed to be that strong, that unchanging.

She didn't realize at first that he was talking; she had to lean down, so far it made her back and hamstrings ache with the strain, and one of her braids slipped from her shoulder and rested over his eyepatch.

"I forgot," he whispered. "I broke the only rule. I thought of myself first. Never do that. You always think of the Wolves first."

His hand suddenly went tight around hers, so hard that her bones ground together and she had to bite back a yelp.

"You promise me," he said, more strongly, though his voice was still almost worn to nothing, crackling with something wet in his chest. "You remember what I forgot. You always put your people first, before yourself. Promise."

"I promise," Hob said, to keep him happy. She wouldn't have to worry about that kind of promise, ever. She was the fuckup, the omega. "Don't give me any more of this bullshit talk, you crusty old fuck. I'm gonna take you home."

The sound of chopper rotors grew in the distance.

CHAPTER SIXTEEN

The sound of the rotors loud over Ludlow woke Mag from a sound sleep. Only she knew she must have heard them for far longer, with her dreams haunted by images of a helicopter blotting out the sun, making a long shadow over the dunes that followed the fleeing, tiny form of her father. There had been no gunfire, not yet, but it was the dread of it that had her heart in her throat as she opened her eyes, because she knew it was coming. It had already happened.

Choppers in the sky meant that something had gone beyond wrong. Helicopters didn't brave the unpredictable weather and the dust so far from Newcastle, didn't cut back and forth across the desert just to see the sights.

She peered out the window, trying to see where the helicopter was, then padded downstairs, out the front door and into the street in her bare feet. The machine was a ball of light in the sky, floodlights sweeping over the streets, raking Ludlow. She ducked back into the doorway, swallowing a gasp.

Clarence joined her a moment later, wearing pants and suspenders but no shirt, his hair a gray-flecked whirlwind around his head. "They say anything?"

She shook her head. "Nothin' over the PA. But they're lookin' for somethin'. Up and down the streets."

Engines started up, deeper in the town. It wasn't a sound Mag was used to, the deep rumble of liquid fuel-driven engines, far too low to be something fueled by sunfilled batteries like Uncle Nick's motorcycles.

"Trucks," Clarence said, one hand rasping at the stubble on his chin. "Those're the trucks Mariposa owns. Hardly ever use 'em. Those aren't things you want to be caught out in."

The sound of engines grew steadily louder. Two trucks, the beds covered with tarps strung over a curved frame, lumbered down the streets.

"Where do you think they're going?" Mag asked. Clarence looked more grim by the second.

"Don't rightly know, but it's somethin' big, and somethin' bad for all of us. If they're sending so much of our garrison out, it means trouble the company wants fixed, and fast."

"Bandits?"

"Mayhap. I've seen it before. But I also seen 'em roll out for times when the miners are causing trouble. And for that, they stir themselves a hell of a lot faster."

She looked at Clarence; his brow was set in an angry line, his eyes dark. "And that's what you think it is."

"I do. But question is, which town. And what happened. And what it'll do to us."

"And what it's done to them."

"That too. But got to think of your own first."

"Folk always say that," Mag said. "Maybe that's why we're so easy to divide."

By morning, they knew it was Rouse, and they knew it was ugly, though how ugly was lost in the spread of rumor after rumor. Mag slept only fitfully through the night, waking up immediately as people started knocking on the door, bringing tidbits of news. Most were things overheard from the guards, or maybe picked up on illegal radio receivers and pieced together through the static. No one had come from Rouse yet.

Mag gathered the bits of information in her mind, rearranging them over and over, trying to find a way they fit together that made sense. She knew now that there had been some kind of attack on Rouse: guards were dead, maybe the foreman. There was talk of a riot from the miners, but no word of what might have set it off – though deep in her heart, she knew that it had to be about Mama. And some small part of her was pleased, to know that she wasn't the only one raging at the injustice of it all, but she also knew Mama never would have wanted to see people hurt on her account. There'd been more fires, maybe one, maybe as many as four.

The fires didn't necessarily mean anything. Fires happened all the time in a dry town in a desert. Synthetic wood wasn't supposed to burn, but it went up in flame nicely after a couple of seasons of its flame retardants oxidizing in the sun. Fires didn't necessarily mean it was Hob and Uncle Nick. It couldn't be them, because she didn't want to think about what they'd do, what could have happened to them. She'd already lost too many people, in too short a time. One more might just kill her, a shot through a hollow heart.

Through the afternoon, miners came by, just one at a time, to talk to Clarence like it was a casual visit. Some were scared, some were angry, all of them plain worried about what might be happening, because of course they couldn't get a straight answer from the guards.

Mag sat herself down across the rough kitchen table from Clarence one of the times when he was alone. He had his pipe out, stem clenched between his teeth, but wasn't smoking it. He just worried at it like a dog with a bone, fingers tapping out a rhythm only he could follow on the tabletop.

"What is it?" Mag asked.

"Latest I've got is that it was your uncle and his people, couldn't be anyone but them, swept in an' attacked the town–"

"That ain't true, he'd never do that!"

Clarence cleared his throat, a flicker of annoyance crossing his face. "Never said it was. But that's what Mariposa's sayin'. So more likely that they come in and mayhap shot some company men."

Mag didn't even have to wonder what might have possessed her uncle, if that was the truth of what happened. She crossed her arms over her chest. "And?"

"They're makin' a fuss about catchin' 'em out on the desert last night."

"But if that was the case, what's the chopper still around for, all this morning?"

Clarence nodded. "Exactly. So they want us to think they got the Wolves, because they don't want us getting no funny ideas about things."

"Are you gettin' funny ideas?"

"Some folk are. If they had any help inside Rouse, those people will be out on the sands by tomorrow. And even if they didn't, company might take it as a chance to blacklist any troublemakers they been eyeballing, make an example."

"We gotta be quiet, then."

Clarence peered at her, his face unreadable. "That's your uncle out there."

"He's either safe and will live to fight another day, or he's already eagle meat and there's nothin' I can do about it." Mag licked her lips, swallowed down a feeling of sickness. She didn't want to think this way, but she needed to forget all of her love and hate and just *think*. No one else around here seemed inclined to do it. "Can't let everyone here get too het up, neither. I know you said Papa wanted us to get organized, but we ain't half ready for it. So we gotta keep everyone calm, make 'em be patient, because otherwise there'll be talk of a strike and it'll slip into some Mariposa ear and then we'll all be dead."

Clarence nodded, gave her a dry smile. "Glad we agree, then. Ain't gonna be the easiest to keep folks calmed, but easier than if it was somethin' that happened in our town. So what are you gonna do to get ready for when we got no choice?"

"Other mining towns are in the same boat as us. We can't count on them to help, not when they all might be fightin' their own battles at the same time.

Send someone out to Blessid." It was the nearest farming town to Ludlow, a long journey away, but something that could be managed with a little crafty train hopping. "See what kind of deal we might cut with them."

"You volunteerin' to go?"

She sat back, surprised. "Guess so."

"I'll give you some spendin' money, and some different clothes. Best we get workin' on this sooner rather than later."

Mag nodded. "First thing Papa ever taught me was, never pick a fight you know you can't win."

"But if we get a fight picked with us, ain't gonna do much good." Clarence tapped his pipe stem on his teeth. "Wish I knew what changed. Time was, they squeezed us, they were rough, but you could still make a living and look forward to gettin' the hell out with your hide intact. They never done what they done to you or your family before."

Mag stood and went to the sink to dump her mug even though she would have liked to drink more. She didn't want Clarence to see her face when she was about to lie. Let him assume she was crying again. "Wish I knew too." Maybe she didn't really know, but the memory of those little blue crystals from the tiny burlap bag, rolling around on her hands like gemstones, wouldn't leave her alone, and her instincts told her: *that. That's the thing that changed.* But she wasn't going to whisper it to a soul until she knew what it meant, not when the only people she truly trusted were in hiding or dead.

•••

She set out for Blessid the next day, by hiding in a boxcar filled with crates of nonperishable foodstuffs. Clarence distracted the guard with a question and she slipped into one of the cars, its doors open to allow ventilation during stops. Many people did their traveling that way, since it was expensive to buy train tickets on the salary most miners got.

Mag squeezed in between massive barrels of flour and hunkered down as best she could. The heat in the boxcar was near suffocating. She had two small canteens stashed under her skirt, but she'd need to make them last, just wetting her mouth as she went. She'd be thirsty, but alright when she made it to Blessid.

Sweat dripped from the ragged ends of her hair by the time a man in blue slid the train car doors shut. She moved out from behind the flour barrels, finding a few crates she could lay across to stay a little cooler as the train started moving. She didn't venture too far from her hiding place, in case there was an inspector on the line.

As she stretched out on the crates, she rolled a stray thread from her skirt between her fingers, thinking about her uncle and all of his people, hiding in the desert. It was part of why she'd agreed to go so readily. With her life upside-down, she wanted to cling to Ludlow. But if she stayed in Ludlow and marked time, she'd do nothing but worry her stomach into knots, make herself sick, mayhap even make herself crazy, with no answer ever in sight.

•••

The rhythm of the train was oddly soothing, and she dozed for most of the long journey, ears always listening for the smallest change in the sounds. At long last, the little slide back as they slowed, coming in to Blessid, woke her up. She scrambled back to her hiding place, hunkered down, and used up the last gulps of her water to unstick her tongue from the roof of her mouth.

The boxcar doors slid open, and she listened with all her might to the sound of footsteps and retreating voices. When they were probably a car or two away, she slipped from her hiding place and skittered to the door, poking her head out. There were two guards further down the train, but looking the other way. She scooted out and hurried away from the track, losing herself in the crowd that invariably formed when a train came in.

At first, Blessid didn't look too different from Rouse or Ludlow: synthwood buildings and boardwalks, everything scoured smooth and shining with sand, any glass or plastic windows clouded up. But there were differences all the same: massive water tanks surrounding the town instead of mine works; far wider streets, echoing with the calls of animals; the scent of manure, earthy and strangely sharp in the nose. It wasn't the rainy season, so there were no green fields to marvel at, though there was a small grove of fruit trees at the town's center. Even knowing her task, Mag had to detour to look at those, just to gape. She'd seen little plants here and there in the desert, spiky things that were meant to preserve water, but never anything like this. She had to touch the soft, faintly waxy leaves of the trees to convince herself that they were real, standing in the cool of their shadows.

In the saloon she asked around about the crew leaders of Blessid, pretending that she was looking for work. The men in the saloon looked at her worn clothes and cropped hair dismissively; it was plain she'd come from a mining town. One man sent her to Tavris Meeks, the work gang boss – and the pitying look he gave her when she asked for one of the crew leaders put her right on edge. Mining and farming towns didn't even share a common language.

A little boy with no shoes answered the door she'd been sent to, then ran to get his papa. Tavris was a small, lean man, not much taller than Mag and only a little heavier. His skin was dark brown, wrinkled and cracked from spending his days in the sun instead of underground.

He peered at her, squinting like he needed glasses. "Rains aren't coming for months more, girl. Got no work for a new mouth to feed." He started to close the door.

Mag stopped it with her foot. "Actually, that's not what I'm here to talk about."

His eyebrows, pale against his dark skin, crept up. "Then what is it you do want to talk about?"

"Mind invitin' me in? It's not somethin' we should be chattin' about, out on the street."

He hesitated, eyes searching her face, then nodded. "Come in, then. Richie, go tell your Ma to get us some lemonade."

The house wasn't much different from anything she'd seen in Rouse. Neat and clean, calico curtains that had been hemmed by hand, floors clean but for the grit of ever-present dust that no amount of sweeping could defeat. He took her into a little parlor room that was barely bigger than a closet and oven-hot besides, nothing fancier to fill it than two cushioned plastic chairs and a small, plain table.

Tavris pulled one of the chairs out for her, then pulled the other around so he could sit down opposite. He examined her for a moment, one forearm resting on the table between them. "Which town you from?"

"Ludlow. Was originally from Rouse, but... things have a way of happenin'."

"Both those towns got a real reputation."

"There's trouble aplenty, if that's your meanin'."

"We got our own troubles here, missy. We're not lookin' for more."

Mag licked her lips, tried to think of what she ought to say now that she was here. She should have known that a farmer wouldn't be eager to jump feet first into the problems of miners. Their worlds were very different. "We're... not lookin' to pull anyone in with us. But we're hopin' for maybe a business deal. If'n you ken."

"What sort of business you thinkin'?"

Mag opened her mouth to answer, but Tavris' son came in, a glass of lemonade in each hand. He set them down, then hurried out on a wave of his father's hand. It gave her a minute to consider her words, but that didn't really seem to help. She settled for the truth, because there was no lie in her head that sounded good enough and she was mighty tired of lies. "You all, you can at least eat and such, if say...

the trains stopped comin'. Hypothetical-like, say the tracks went out. Your town wouldn't just dry up and blow away."

"True enough. Can't say we could survive without the trains entire, but we could keep ourselves going well enough until track repair were to happen."

"Ludlow and Rouse, we don't got that. Everythin' has to come in to us, twice a week, food and even water if we're outside of the rains."

"That's how it is. I'm sure you've got some advantages over us."

"Mayhap. But we're lookin' to get a contingency plan. In case our train tracks go bad."

He sat back in his chair, eyes narrowing. "And say, if your tracks was to get buried in a rockfall or somethin', and help wasn't terribly forthcomin'... you're lookin' for a neighborly sort of hand?"

Mag nodded. "Just so folks don't die of thirst or starve or anythin' else from deprivation."

Tavris nodded. "And say... what if you were to lose your food and water from a different mishap. One not so natural. Would you be expectin' the same manner of help?"

Again, she nodded. "That would be the idea."

"And in the case of some... unnatural mishap, what'd keep similar misfortune from comin' to our door?"

That was the rub; she didn't have a good answer for it, because there was too much uncertainty about everything. "We'd stand by you, if trouble came to your door. If we all go together, makes us stronger than if we're alone. We got resources you don't."

He didn't look convinced, so she said it baldly: "Explosives. More guns than you do, I'd bet."

"You might be surprised." He shook his head. "You're askin' us to throw in our lot for nothin' that'll help us in the long run. What's the point of farmin' or minin' if you ain't got someone to sell it to?"

Mag sighed miserably. "Mayhap not livin' under someone's thumb might sound appealin'."

"Things are different here, miss, way different than in the mining towns. They let us keep to ourselves outside of harvest time."

"We're all here on company time."

"Mayhap," Tavris said, finally taking a sip of his lemonade. "But we all got to think of our own, first. Now you drink up and enjoy. I know you've come a long way and must be parched. Least I can do is see you back on the next train in good condition."

"Thank you," she said, the words bitter ashes in her mouth. She allowed herself a moment to hate this quiet, confident man and his logical selfishness. Because she knew that things were different out here, and in his place, she'd be saying the exact same things.

The return train was mostly empty, just a few crates in one corner that were stamped with dry goods symbols. Mag guessed that it was likely some handicrafts the people of Blessid had finished, then pooled their resources together to have sent to Newcastle in the hope of making a sale. That was something the farmers did, outside of the growing and harvest seasons. Miners tended to sneer about it, because they never had that sort of time to spare, couldn't imagine what sort of feckless people did.

Mag swung around the crates and came face to face with a dark young man, maybe a few years older than her. He had a black eye and a sullen expression on his face. "Car's already taken. Go away."

She ignored him and squatted down behind the crates. "Didn't see your name on it."

"I still got here first. You'll get me caught."

"I try to leave now and I'll get us both caught, since Tavris has probably moved on now."

He scratched at the back of his neck. "Tavris put you on here? You don't look like kin of his."

"I'm not. I was just here to talk with him."

He looked at her, lip curling up slightly, and snorted. "And?"

Mag laughed softly. "And he didn't much like hearin' what I had to say, so now I'm goin' home."

His mouth opened to guffaw, but he laughed silently, just little exhalations of air so he wouldn't draw attention. "Where's home?"

"Ludlow, now."

"Now?"

She shrugged. "Was somewhere else, once. What're you doin' here?"

He shrugged, expression closing up to nothing. "Felt like a change of scene. Ain't much of a farmer."

"So you gonna try your luck at bein' a miner?"

He looked wiry enough, but she wasn't sure if someone accustomed to open skies all the time would do well in the mines. "Mayhap. Or some other job. I was workin' for the veterinarian, doctorin' oxen and the like. Can probably learn to do the same on people."

"I could prolly introduce you to the doctor in Ludlow. Not the company one, he only comes about once a week to check up on things."

He smiled. "I'd appreciate that greatly."

She stuck her hand out toward him. "Maggy Vigil."

He took her hand readily enough. "Davey – I mean David Painter."

"Pleased to meet you." She looked him deep in the eye, taking that moment to try to read everything in him, listen to all the things that hung over his head that he wasn't willing to say. It was almost a tangible thing to her now, like her senses had been sharpened by all the grief, and she could almost – almost but not quite – hear solid words whispering off him in waves. She couldn't make out the details, but she knew one thing for certain – he was running from something, some sort of pain and anger that he'd never talk about no matter how many times she asked.

That gave them something in common. She shared her water with him and they chatted all the way to Ludlow. When it came time came to slip from the freight car, they were fast friends.

CHAPTER SEVENTEEN

With Makaya dead and the Wolves trapped in the canyon, Hob found herself in the strange position of going from being the disappointment, the pup that had been forced to redo her whole basic course, to Nick's right hand. No one wanted to bother him, probably because his temper when he was feeling off was legendary. Made her a good sacrifice, she supposed. Everyone asked her about plans, about rationing, about this idea or that regarding how they might get out of their predicament. Even Geri asked her things, listened to her when she told everyone to rearrange their layout of tarps to something that'd be harder to spot in the harsh light of day.

One day into their hiding, a dust storm blew up, to everyone's relief. They wouldn't be hearing the chopper rotors while the wind howled. They all hunkered with their backs to the wind, every square centimeter of skin covered so it wouldn't be scoured off. Hob scrambled to make sure everyone had coats and gloves, and checked everyone's neck to make sure they didn't have a gap between jacket and helmet.

It wasn't that everyone had gone stupid or

forgotten how to survive. It was more like every Wolf had gone into shock, all at once. Three dead, Nick maybe deadly ill, though no one was willing even to give voice to the fact that he wasn't healthy, that they were taking orders off a girl who couldn't be more than twenty because she was the closest thing Nick had to a mouthpiece.

They waited out the storm, keeping radio silence because no one had a damn thing to say. Hob wondered if they all felt like her, if they kept running the ride to Rouse, the fight, everything through their minds and trying to pick out the moment where they could have stepped in and changed things. The hell of it was, she could find no place to make it all better; anywhere she could have stepped in, could have tried to stop Nick, she knew it would have just led to her being put out on her ass and what followed unchanged. It was like trying to pick out a single pebble to prevent an avalanche: the events felt like fate, Nick crashing against the town of Rouse like rocks falling to the inexorable pull of gravity.

Something in Hob half expected and half hoped that the Bone Collector would blow in with the storm, ready to spout more incoherent messages. At least then there would be someone with more power and strength than her that she could look to, what with Nick refusing to meet her eyes. But he never did turn up when he was wanted.

The Wolves were gung-ho to break camp and get back to base as soon as the storm had ended; they were achingly thirsty, tired, and hungry. Hob put her foot down and made them bide. Running in the storm's wake was exactly the sort of move she'd expect from a bunch of dumb-as-shit bandits, and the company thought every miner and farmer was a proper idiot. She argued for that, not long and hard because she didn't want to make the noise, but in emphatic hisses at Dambala and Geri. "She's right, you know," Coyote had added now and again for emphasis, and Hob wasn't sure if that helped her or hurt her since no one was ever that inclined to heed him either. But she argued them into a standstill until an hour after the storm had died down – and then the sound of chopper rotors echoed down the canyon again.

They settled into another day of hunger, thirst, and boredom. A few of the men started betting over when the next chopper pass would be, though all they had to bet with was stones.

As the sun went down, Coyote bellycrawled under Hob's tarp. He'd aged about twenty years in two days, the lines in his face like they'd been cut with a chisel, but his accent was still as clipped and precise as always even with thirst thickening his tongue. "I think we need to run for it when night hits," he said without preamble.

"I think you're fuckin' crazy. They're still lookin' for us. We could run without lights, but it's too risky."

"Nothing is without risk. We're running out of rations. Half of us have no water left. I think some have been sneaking drinks when no one's watching."

Or maybe they'd just forgotten to refill their own canteens. Who knew. Hob couldn't watch everyone as they hid under their tarps. "One day without water won't be fun for anyone, but I think we got it in us.

We're layin' as low as can be."

"Maybe most people. But I'm..." He hesitated, voice dropping to an almost theatrical whisper, "I don't know about the Ravani. Whatever is wrong with him, all the heat and breathing in dust constantly is only going to make it worse. We need to go back now, while he's still strong enough to drive himself."

Hob wanted to deny what he said, but she'd spent more hours with Nick in this living hell than anyone else. The man looked worse with every passing hour; he needed to be in a clean bed, not curled up under a tarp in the middle of the dust bowl. "You sure he can still make it?"

"I think so. He'll at least be able to give it a good try. But we need to leave *now*."

Hob closed her eye tightly for a moment, rubbing at her face with her hand. "Why the hell are you askin' me this, Coyote? You should be talkin' to Dambala, or Akela, even Freki and Geri afore you talk to me. I'm green to the ears."

"You're the only one I trust to actually give me an answer I can work with," Coyote said flatly. "We like to play at being some sort of paramilitary mercenary company, Hob *Ravani*, but we're not by a long shot. I know what a real army is like. Whether we admit it or no, we're a family first."

She sat back hard. It was almost insulting, acting like they were just playing at their roles as soldiers, as if it was dress-up instead of deadly serious. Looking at Coyote, Hob realized that he didn't think it was a bad thing. She couldn't quite wrap her head around it. And how the hell did he know those things anyway?

She wanted to ask, but one of the few hard and fast social rules they had was that life began when you joined the Wolves; what happened before was no one's business.

"Good, I take from your silence that you've listened. Well done. What's it to be? Stay or go?"

The real choice was, try to save Nick and risk their lives, or play it safe and risk his. Hob knew the choice she *should* make, after Nick had made her promise to put the Wolves first. But she also knew that she wasn't the only one Nick had fished out of the dunes or given a second chance.

She couldn't live with herself if she made the smart decision instead of the right decision. "Tell everyone to pack it up. We're goin' home an hour after full dark. So long as the choppers don't come back by then."

Coyote nodded, foxy face neutral, not a flicker in his eyes betraying what he thought. "Aye, sir."

It was a long road home, made longer by the constant sound of Nick's labored breathing over the radio. Hob had turned his helmet mic to vox, because she wanted everyone to know in an instant if Nick took a turn for the worse. He was at the heart of their formation, him and the others that were injured. The two that were worst off rode with Dambala and Lobo, who had the biggest, heaviest motorcycles and were strong enough to hold them upright if they fainted.

It was a neverending nightmare. A ride that normally should have taken three hours at the most stretched out more than twice that long as they picked a course the injured could navigate, and that wouldn't get them killed in the dark when they couldn't afford running lights. The moons overhead only made the shadows trickier, casting everything in dim doubles. Dawn washed out the horizon when the base finally came into view, reassuringly quiet and dark.

She didn't have to give orders. Coyote and Dambala threw together a quick team to go inside and make certain everything was safe. Hob straddled her motorcycle and stayed next to Nick, one hand resting on the right grip of his bike to track every little shift of balance. He slumped over the battery stack, arms crossed and helmet pillowed against them.

It scared her that he didn't even seem to notice she was there, didn't snap at her for treating him like an invalid.

The sun oozed to a bloody sliver up over the horizon by the time Dambala signaled the all-clear. They were a sad dust and blood-flecked pack that rolled into the garage. As soon as Hob parked, she saw to Old Nick, pulling his helmet off and helping him off the bike. A thin thread of blood dangled from his overly large nose, vivid against his dead white skin. "Can't breathe in that fuckin' thing," he wheezed.

She slung one of his arms around her shoulder, and did her best to ignore just how much he leaned on her as she took him to the little ground-floor room that served as an infirmary. There were only two beds in it, and a couple of chairs; she settled him onto one of the beds, helped him pull off his coat and made sure he had a big glass of water to drink.

He took a few swallows then waved her away, laying back on the thin, stained pillows and closing his eyes. "You see to the others. I caused enough trouble already."

"Never thought I'd see a day when you were tired of bein' trouble," Hob joked.

He snorted, but that made him cough, and she regretted opening her mouth. "Stop hoverin' over me, girl. You'll smother me to death."

"I got a name, you know."

He cracked his one eye open, gave her a wan smile. "'Course I know. It's the name I gave you. But you're still my girl all the same."

She was too stunned to try to argue with him again. Maybe that had been his intention; she retreated in confusion, to get caught up in the fuss over the motorcycles.

Someone tapped her on the shoulder when she was halfway done with cleaning Nick's bike, clearing sand from one of the valves. She glanced up at Geri. He looked ready to fall over, deep circles around his eyes, too tired to even hate her. "My brother reminded me that you're a good hand with the needle." She half expected some crack about her being a girl, that being what girls did, anything, but he just continued on, "Need you to sew some folks up."

She swallowed hard, then offered her rag to Geri. "Can you finish with his bike?"

"Yeah, no problem." He squatted down next to her, peering into the engine. "And I'll get yours too, if you're not back by then."

"Thanks." She was too tired to hide her surprise.

A little of his old nastiness returned, but his tone was halfhearted at best, like he just felt he ought to say something and really didn't believe it himself. "But don't you dawdle."

Hob laughed, more like a bark than anything else. Her voice cracked from dryness; she might have given Nick some water, but hadn't thought about it for herself. "Wouldn't dream of it."

Any love for sewing she'd started to feel when Mag taught her died in the infirmary. Sewing flesh had its similarities to fabric, and Hob made neat enough work of the stitches just because she knew how thread was supposed to pull and move. But the pale, sweating faces, the blood, the voices worn down with thirst that squeezed out little whimpers, that she couldn't handle. She kept her lips tight and teeth clenched as she sewed and sewed, bullet wounds and gouges and long knife slashes. When the last was done, she scrubbed the worst of the blood off her hands, then went outside to get some fresh air.

It was for the best she hadn't eaten at all, or drunk much of anything yet. She dry heaved into Lobo's desiccated little kitchen garden, retching and shuddering in the bare shade of the mess hall. She didn't think the skeletal, dead plants would mind.

PART III

CHAPTER EIGHTEEN

The rift ship *Raiju* was named for a beast of myth, like every ship in the TransRift fleet, but looked like none that had ever graced the Newcastle landing field. The synthcrete expanse dwarfed the relatively tiny ship, its aerodynamic curves engineered for rapid atmospheric maneuvering shining blindingly in the noonday sun. Gossamer solar sails, folded away neatly for landing, had been extended like the wings of a great bird for the inspection of ground crews.

And instead of a river of humanity and cargo streaming through multiple exits, ordered and ranked by class, there was only one hatch on the ship's smooth side, obviously meant for the fast vessel's crew. Comms ships like the *Raiju*, made for relaying messages and undertaking emergency deployments, didn't come to places like this, and certainly didn't expose their highly trained crews to the atmosphere of a world under long-term Class B hazard quarantine – an internal corporate designation for the eyes of upper management only. Tanegawa's World was good enough for immigrants, but too dangerous for valued employees such as space captains or courier crews.

But a special, air-conditioned ramp was escorted to the ship by a squad of men and women in green, a black saloon car parked and waiting as close as safety allowed. One woman and one man exited the ramp, quickly covering the few steps to the car. Both wore the standard TransRift blue suit. The woman was tall and broad-shouldered, her iron-gray hair short and neat. The man, obviously the lower on the food chain, waited deferentially for the woman to get into the car first. He had neatly trimmed black hair framing narrow eyes; a wide, rounded nose; and was of medium height with a slight build that made him look delicate next to his boss.

They rode in silence to the TransRift tower, the hum of the car's tires against the synthcrete roadways barely audible. From the car they went directly into the elevator, and from there to the top floor of the building, the Vice President's office. The lights in the elevator dimmed and brightened as it hummed smoothly up the floors, something both passengers noted coolly.

The elevator doors opened to reveal a spacious floor with a fountain, decorative plants, a desk, a large conference table surrounded by leather-upholstered chairs, and a small coffee bar. The windows offered a panoramic view of the city and off into the bright wasteland that surrounded it.

Vice President Leeroy Gregson waited for them, standing in front of his desk, feet apart and shoulders stiff. He looked like a man anticipating a fight, short-cropped salt and pepper hair bristling. "Gentlemen, good afternoon. Can I interest either of you in a drink?" The words were companionable, the tone formal and cold.

The woman stepped forward, and offered her hand to be shaken. "Jennifer Meetchim. So good to meet you. Water would be lovely. This is my secretary, Mr Rolland." The man bowed his dark head.

"A pleasure to meet you both." He shook both their hands. "Please, have a seat. While I hope you both had a good trip – and I appreciate Corporate responding to my request this quickly – you're not who I expected."

"Not *what* you expected, you mean," Meetchim said. "If you please, Mr Gregson. Be mindful of security."

"Right, right." He moved to his desk and tapped a button, then frowned and pressed it again. When nothing happened, he moved to manually pull a set of dark blue curtains across the windows, rendering the office a velvety, dark cave. The lack of natural light only highlighted the seemingly random brightening and dimming of the overhead lights. "Damn curtains don't work half the time," Gregson said. "All the minor tech in the city is fucked."

"Your report indicated that was likely," Meetchim observed. "And I assume that's why your research and productivity numbers have fallen."

"It's not something I can control. Miracle I've got anything done at all in these conditions." Leeroy poured a glass of water for each of them, setting the tumblers down on the glass-topped conference table before sitting himself. "It's not going to taste like much. The water. We've got to distill it down to nothing before we can drink it. It's the only way to be safe."

Meetchim didn't touch her water, even as her associate drank. "I read the security briefing."

Gregson stared at her, or perhaps tried to stare her down. She remained still, expression cool and pleasantly bland. He finally continued, "I can't help but notice you don't have a Weatherman with you."

"Keenly observed." Meetchim reached into her jacket. Leeroy tensed, and then relaxed as she drew forth a folded set of flimsies rather than something more sinister. "I have new orders for you."

Leeroy snatched the flimsies up and began leafing through them, his hands slowing bit by bit, face going paler and paler. "What the hell is this?" he demanded. "I'm being replaced? And *audited*?"

"And I'm your replacement and chief auditor. Though you needn't worry about finding a new placement within the company. We have a position prepared for you back at headquarters."

Leeroy slapped the flimsies down on the table. "I've been getting good production out of this shit hole. Good luck if you think you'll do better."

"Really, I wouldn't have thought that you'd greet a transfer back to civilization as a punishment," she said, her tone mockingly sweet. "Even if it will come with fewer managerial responsibilities... and a proportionally smaller pay scale."

"We both know what this is," Gregson growled. "I kept production at an all-time high!"

"Yes, we do." Her voice was all ice, now. "And that is the only reason you still have a job at all. Enough of your posturing, Mr Gregson. My time is valuable. And your cooperation, or lack thereof, will be noted."

Down the table, Rolland took a small notepad computer from his jacket and activated the projected keyboard.

"You're better off using flimsies, or paper if you're feeling fancy," Leeroy said with bad grace, glancing at him. "Anything more sophisticated than a damn toaster isn't going to last long, not with Mr Green down. The planetary magnetic field is fucked to hell." He looked back at Meetchim. "So what are you *really* here for?"

"The break-in at the lab is concerning enough, even if Mr Green hadn't been injured in the process. A new strategy has been deemed necessary."

"That incident hasn't repeated."

The curve of Meetchim's eyebrow implied words politely withheld, likely to do with the current status of the Weatherman. "Corporate is well aware of that and is, of course, grateful that you have plugged that specific security hole. A pass over the history indicates unrest in the mining towns and the disruptive existence of non-employees from the wastelands, given free access. We fear it shows a pattern of disciplinary problems, exacerbated by those who have been allowed to go native."

Leeroy sat back in his chair. "Maybe you're right. I've been too lenient on the miners."

"They seem to have taken shameful advantage of your good will," Meetchim said, drily. "And forgotten who the real enemy is here."

That won her a grimace. "We're still trying to repair the structural damage to the floor of the lab. Taking longer than it should because the decent equipment shits itself half the time. One of the... natives... cracked the floor in half past the foundation. If you think you can handle that, more power to you."

"It has been nearly thirty-two years since the last planetwide witch hunt, Mr Gregson. Corporate believes that is likely why the situation has begun to spiral out of control. Our workers need to be reminded of the threat that hides amongst them and stirs such trouble. Humans really ought to stick together." Meetchim smiled thinly. "Of course, Corporate has an interest in furthering our research as well."

Leeroy rubbed his chin. If this was Corporate's angle of approach, it sounded like a golden opportunity to dodge responsibility for such messy business. Maybe he could land in a better spot back at headquarters. "You did hear the part where I said that one of *them* cracked the lab's floor in half? This new crop isn't the usual sort of freak."

"We'd gotten that impression. That is why, in addition to the repairs for Mr Green, I have brought an experimental enhancement."

"Experimental?"

Meetchim's smile offered nothing. "Highly."

Leeroy sat up a little in his chair. "Well, since you're taking over this viper pit, I've got some fresh information to share with you. In regards to production, not... the other matter."

"Please, go on." Meetchim gestured regally with one hand.

Leeroy went over to the desk that was so suddenly no longer his and pulled a small, burlap sample bag from his top drawer, as well as a plastic tray. He set the small tray down in front of Meetchim and emptied the bag onto it, a scattering of fine blue crystals like a little fall of rain. Some of the crystals were almost as big as his pinky nail. "The number seven shaft at Rouse had a cave-in about three months ago," he began.

"Rouse...?" Meetchim said.

"Rouse is the town that was attacked by bandits a few weeks ago, sir." Rolland didn't look up from his notepad.

"Ah, yes. Continue, please, Mr Gregson." She extracted a cloisonné pen from her breast pocket to stir the crystals, but carefully did not touch them.

"They just got the shaft reopened before town discipline went tits-up. It's mostly just a regular ore vein, but we found this as well."

"Interesting. Has the onsite lab found anything, or are they just pretty to look at?"

"At the pit, it might as well be stone knives and flint arrowheads. Our labs here aren't anything close to Earth standard on a good day, even with the Weatherman doing his job. Right now, they're practically paralyzed. The best the white coats could come up with was that it's not poisonous, it's not radioactive, and it's not anything they've ever seen. I've got sample bags prepared for the next cargo run, but—"

"The *Raiju* is holding for twenty-four hours for engineer inspection, as the atmosphere was extremely rough on the way in. The samples can accompany you and my initial assessment back to Corporate tomorrow. Are there other shafts that are workable at that mine?"

"Three right now, and we're sinking another."

Meetchim nodded. "We'll seal off number seven for now, then. Make note of it, Mr Rolland. Until we know what these little beauties are, I'd rather not have the common filth digging around and breathing them in." She carefully wiped her pen with a handkerchief – which she left on the table – and tucked it away again.

"Yes, sir," Rolland said.

"And now for Mr Green." Meetchim rose to her feet, Rolland following, after he'd finished the sentence he was writing. But as Gregson levered himself up, she held up one finger. "Mr Rolland, please stay here and help Mr Gregson clear out of my office."

"But–" Gregson began as Meetchim headed toward the elevator.

"Mr Gregson, you had best begin packing. The *Raiju* will not wait." She gave him a cool smile as the doors slid shut between them. "I am taking the Mr Green situation off your hands, if not in the way you wished."

She rode the elevator down to the sub-basement, noting the brightening and dimming of the lights. In the labs she knew precisely where to go; she'd studied the building layout during the journey.

The glass-walled observation room indicated as Mr Green's was a hive of activity, doctors and technicians in white isolation suits hurrying back and forth. One wheeled in the reinforced security case that Meetchim had brought with her on the *Raiju*. It was marked all over with biohazard symbols in a particular shade of bright, poison green. Mr Green had been partially unwrapped, the bag around him unzipped down to his navel. He looked like a corpse, eyes open and sightless, mouth hanging slack. Red lines carrying blood ran in and out from under his collarbones; they'd gone the direct route with blood oxygenation rather than depending on lungs that had been badly damaged at the time. His chest was a neat formation of red lines held together by temporary clamps. His heart had been replaced by a temporary pump; his new one, stored with the other spare parts at the Corporate laboratories, was also in the case.

Meetchim tapped the speaker output on the outside of the wall to hear the murmur. Mostly the sounds of a well-ordered team, laced with far more static than she liked, but then she caught a woman saying, "What's the security code for this? It's not in the manifest."

Meetchim activated the intercom. "It's a twelve-digit code. Stand by for it."

"Who are you?" the woman demanded. Meetchim noted her suit's tag said *Kiyoder*.

"Vice President Jennifer Meetchim. I brought the equipment for you."

There was a hiccup to the sound in the room, the noise of techs reshuffling their worldview made manifest. Then Dr Kiyoder said, "Thank you, sir. We will proceed."

Meetchim watched them unload the case: replacement heart in its static container; various syringes, tailored to the possibilities of what might have gone wrong with the Weatherman's internal neuro-wiring; and the experimental enhancements like a tangle of thin, squirming wires safely encased in glass. She observed with mild curiosity as Kiyoder and her assistants unzipped the Weatherman's chest and installed the new organ, redirecting the blood flow and starting his lungs working again over it. Then several of those syringes were injected, one right after the other, into the large catheters in both of the Weatherman's bone-thin arms.

The result was electrifying. Mr Green jolted on the table, eyes closing spasmodically and then opening, wider than ever. He screamed, high and thin and in registers that made bones and teeth itch.

"Hold him still!" Kiyoder shouted, barely audible over the burr and fuzz of the Weatherman's shriek. Several techs rushed to hold Mr Green steady, hard against the table. One of them collapsed without warning; their head bounced off the edge of the table going down.

Kiyoder took up the last syringe, the one filled with the sinister silver tangle, and with careful timing, drove the long, thin needle down through the orbit of Mr Green's right eye.

His scream cut off, his body went limp. Panting, Kiyoder triggered the injection, and carefully removed the needle. For a moment, Mr Green's eyes rolled wildly, a dot of overly-thick, silvery fluid flowing from his right eye. Then his gaze fixed on Meetchim, something she felt rather than saw in those black-on-black eyes, her figure reflected in their shining surface. His lips moved to form a single word, and then he lost focus and animation entirely.

"Success, Dr Kiyoder?" Meetchim asked.

The doctor cast around for the safety cap of the

syringe and slid it home with visibly shaking fingers. "We'll know in a couple of days. I want to keep him static until he's done rewiring."

Meetchim had seen the simulations before, the artificial neural connections growing dendritically throughout the brain, not quite biological and not quite machine. She had a feeling that the real process wasn't as neat or clean as branching lines of yellow and blue light in a holographic display. That really didn't matter, so long as it worked. "Very well. Call me immediately when he regains coherence. No matter what time of day it is."

As she rode the elevator back up to her office – that fool Gregson had better be gone by now – it seemed to her that the overhead lights had already begun to steady. She focused on that and the steady thrum of the elevator passing by floors, avoiding the mirrored walls. The reflection reminded her too keenly of the Weatherman's eyes – never look them in the eye, *never*, it was the first rule one learned – and the word he'd formed with his mouth, just two syllables: *Mother*.

Shige Rollins, known to everyone else at TransRift as James Rolland, made it his habit to work late. It made him appear industrious, which had helped him rise to such an ideal position, the secretary of an up-an-coming VP. More importantly, it meant that no one found it strange when he was in and out of his office at odd hours.

And working late was instrumental in being able to look at information he wasn't technically supposed to access. Better yet, Meetchim's files were generally far more detailed than anything he could ever find at the Corporate building – his boss was a very thorough woman.

Far into the night he finished organizing Meetchim's daily messages, then took out the files on the security breaches that had brought them to Tanegawa's World. The woman hadn't even bothered to lock the desk drawers; Shige had spent years crafting this identity and making himself trusted and indispensable so he would eventually have opportunities like this. That was the point of deep cover, so deep that the Federal Union agency he nominally worked for had long since forgotten he even existed. That was ideal, since TransRift had gotten its tendrils deep into the Bureau of Citizens' Rights Enforcement's directorship and rendered it unsafe for him to report officially. It only highlighted the necessity of his presence: TransRift's monopoly-driven stranglehold had to be broken, and that couldn't be done without good intelligence.

The file about the lab break-in had several security photographs of the likely perpetrator: a young woman, a patch obscuring her left eye, her brown hair pulled back severely. She wasn't pretty by any stretch of the imagination, but her face was quite memorable. Shige stared at her picture, fixing her into his mind as he took out a small, thumbnail-sized self injector. The taste of strawberries flooded his mouth as he pushed the needle into his neck, the chemical fixing the image into his memory with perfect clarity. There were a lot of interesting little biological quirks his parents had made certain to engineer into him, the sort that made him think Mother had intended him to be a deep cover spy even before his conception. Genetic enhancements didn't show up on electronics scans, after all, and for all its corporate abuses, TransRift still followed galactic law vaguely enough that it respected the right to genetic privacy.

Maybe it was a waste of a medication he had in only limited supply, but his instincts told him this woman was someone he wanted to find.

In the file about Rouse, there were a lot of conflicting reports, about how many had invaded, how well trained they were, everything. But everyone had agreed – they'd been led by an older man, his left eye covered by a patch.

Maybe it was coincidence. Considering that TransRift hadn't even allowed a single Federal Union safety inspection on this world during its century-long industrialized period, accidents that could destroy a worker's eye – or worse – were probably commonplace. On a planet where most of the population was kept starved for technology, half by design and half by necessity, he had no trouble believing that decent cybernetic replacements, let alone lab-grown organs, were in short supply. And yet.

Shige had learned long ago that in his line of work, one did not ignore apparent coincidences. Because it was those little, silly similarities, so easily dismissed by someone that was overworked and focused on a different goal, that could be the difference between a living, hopefully successful spy and a *We regret to inform you* letter to one's family.

His mouth still sweet with the taste of strawberries, he opened the next file, labeled: *Witch Hunts*.

CHAPTER NINETEEN

"Over a month and he ain't getting any better." Dambala's massive shoulders filled the doorway to Nick's office. Hob looked up from the stack of worn flimsies she was midway through sorting. Someone had needed to figure out what they had in the way of supplies, and what obligations were coming due. And then someone needed to figure out how to get them more food, more supplies, more jobs. No one else had volunteered. Hob privately thought they were all too damn scared to go into the old man's office without him.

"Then what do we do about it?" Hob turned from where she sat in front of Nick's desk, in one of the uncomfortable metal chairs that he kept there for anyone wanting to stop by for a talk. Made sure those talks were always as brief as possible.

"He needs a proper doctor."

"Can't take him into any of the towns around here. They all know who he is. And we can't take him further out." The far-off towns might already know the story as well – Mariposa had a way of spreading word when someone made them real angry – and she didn't think he'd last through that sort of trip anyway.

"Then we got to bring one here."

"You mean snatch one?" They'd always just doctored themselves as best they could, which wasn't too bad when it was all flesh wounds and broken bones and they could steal half-decent medical supplies.

Dambala shrugged, crossing his big arms over his chest. "Wouldn't have much of a choice but to look at him, that were the case."

Hob frowned, rubbing her cheek with one hand like she was Nick and expecting to rasp stubble. She didn't much like the thought of kidnapping someone – they'd always made a big fuss about how they weren't criminals to anyone but TransRift – but it wouldn't be permanent if they blindfolded any doctor they snatched up. As it was, why worry over giving Mariposa another reason to hunt them down? Almost being in open warfare brought with it a certain kind of freedom. "Probably would need some fancy medicine too, right? We got next to nothin' here."

"We need more bandages and pain meds and the like anyway. And some more of that brown antiseptic stuff. We're damn near out of everything."

She nodded. "You feelin' good enough to ride?"

"Cut in my back is still pullin' somethin' fierce. I could do it, but then you might have to sew me up all over again." His lips pulled up in an odd, secretive smile. "I want you to go for me."

"Me?"

"Ain't talkin' to the girl standin' behind you."

Hob snorted. She could see it clear. Any shit rolling downhill from Nick would stick on her, then, not

Dambala. She made a good scapegoat. Well, fuck it, she was tired of being cooped up on base anyway. "OK, fine. Who am I going with?"

"Coyote'll keep an eye on you."

"Are you–" She stopped herself. Dambala and Coyote were always thick as thieves. This was starting to smell like a scam. Like Coyote's work. "Send me with Lobo too."

"Now you're thinkin'." He flipped her something like a salute, but it didn't feel mocking. Hob shook her head and stood, stretching against the rusty ache in her back and legs. Things kept going like this, she might have to give in and use Nick's chair or risk being permanently crippled.

Lobo and Coyote were there already, but so were Freki and Geri. Freki gave her a silent shrug when she looked at him, but Geri said, "Heard tell you were inclined to do somethin' interestin'. Gettin' big for your britches, ain't ya?" He turned toward Coyote, as if expecting the man to agree.

Coyote shrugged. "Perhaps you ought to try being interesting sometime yourself."

"It's Bala's idea of interestin', not mine." Hob bit back a snort. But having Geri giving her that look made her want to own the idea all the more, just to annoy him. "Gonna see if Mag can point us at a doctor who won't be missed if we take him for a day or two. She's like to have the lay of the land by now."

"We're comin' with you," Geri said, jaw taking a stubborn set.

"Fine enough. If we're gonna be doin' some crime to get our medicine, couldn't hurt to have more. Get suited up."

Lobo caught her eye; his look eloquently asked just why the hell was he even here. Lobo was competent with a gun or a knife as any other man on the base, but he was also the oldest by at least a decade. People called Nick "Old Nick" because he had a decent amount of salt and pepper in his hair and beard and played it up extra cantankerous. But Lobo was *Grandpaw*, his leathery brown face deeply lined by laughter and frowns, his close-cropped hair and eyebrows iron gray. Only no one had the balls to call him Grandpaw to his face. He was old, and he had problems with his back that made him plain mean, which meant everyone was happier that he was just taking care of the base and cooking some damn fine meals because he was still fast as a striking snake when he had his temper up – and he kept his kitchen knives real sharp. Lobo also had a trike instead of a motorcycle to fit his bulk and help out his back; it had a special trailer so he could go off on supply runs.

Hob shrugged. "Figured you might like to get some sugar or sommat."

Lobo laughed. "Well ain't you a good, thoughtful girl. Maybe I'll make us all a cake when we get home with that sugar."

They stopped just out of sight of the Ludlow guard towers, where there was a bit of shade to be had at the feet of the rocks. Hob took off her helmet and replaced it with a hat; she looked ordinary enough, like someone that had hopped off a train or truck. She figured guards would be looking for Old Nick, and all the talk she'd overheard of the Wolves seemed ignorant of the fact there were any women in the group. Annoying, but maybe useful. "Head to the other gate, Lobo. Rest of you, stay cool here."

"You serious?" Geri asked, looking at Coyote. "When'd she get put in charge?"

"Shut up." Coyote grinned, pulling a pack of cards out of his pocket. "I can hear those chits rattling in your pockets like they're hot."

That certainly explained why Coyote had wanted to take the twins along, Hob thought as she strode across the sand flat to the walls. She knocked on the little door set into the gate. Sweat ran down her face and neck, pooled at the small of her back. The guard that opened it eyed her suspiciously. "Bit hot to be out, ain't it?"

"Just comin' to see my ma. She took sick. People I hitched with were in a hurry, didn't want to take me all the way." She grinned at him. "Not dyin' of thirst yet, but I might if you keep me standin' too long."

He didn't fall for the friendly act, demanding names and times and more details. She picked up quickly that he wasn't acquainted with everyone in Ludlow; mostly he was just trying to catch her in a lie. With enough names to drop, she bluffed her way through without bothering to feel worried.

Mag opened the door at Clarence Vigil's house. With a strangled yelp, she yanked Hob inside and into a tight hug that made her ribs about crack. "I heard... Hob, I heard so many awful things!" Mag gasped into her ear, sounding on the verge of crying.

Hob gave Mag a tight squeeze, then her arms went awkwardly loose with Mag still not letting go. "Lost some people. They lost more. But they ain't tracked us down yet."

Mag sniffled. "What about Uncle Nick? I heard…"

"Old Nick's the reason I'm here."

Mag finally released her, wiping at her eyes with one hand while the other clutched at her apron. "Is he…?"

"Not last I checked. But he ain't well, either. Man's taken sick, like I never seen in my life."

"Sick how?"

"He's coughin' up a storm, and he's weak as a kitten. There's blood, when he coughs. And we got no medic. Only one of us knew much about that stuff, and he got shot through the head in Rouse."

Mag shut her eyes tightly at the sound of that name. "Why'd you go?"

Hob shrugged. "He told us to follow, so we did." She patted at her pocket, then remembered that Mag didn't like the smell of cigarettes and Clarence probably wouldn't take kindly to it either.

Mag stared at the little square made by the cigarette case in the pocket of Hob's coat. "Don't know what could be givin' his lungs fits," she said, tone edged with sarcasm.

Hob laughed. "Gives the rest of us fits if we don't let him." She didn't want to have this fight, because she couldn't explain the compulsion that took her and Nick. "You know any doctors we could borrow a day or two without them being missed?"

"I might have somethin' better. One you can keep permanent-like." Mag smiled. "Come along."

Mag led Hob to one of the sheds where ore was

inspected before loading. In one corner of the huge, hot room, a young man worked to repair a broken mine cart. He looked sweaty and thoroughly miserable – he also had some of the darkest skin Hob had seen outside of Freki and Geri, too dark for him to be a miner.

"Davey Painter, this is Hob Ravani." Mag let them shake hands before continuing, "I know you ain't been real excited about the mining work. Well, Hob does somethin' else entirely, and she needs someone that can do a bit of doctorin'."

Hob regarded the young man suspiciously; she'd never seen a doctor look anything like him. She also told herself to give it a chance, since Mag had always been a good judge of character, and smart as a whip besides. "It ain't easy. But it's sure different from this."

"What sort of work?" Davey asked.

"We guard, hunt bandits, the like. The sort of stuff Mariposa don't stir themselves to do. Whatever folks'll pay us to do. It's a livin'. And not a bad one."

He inspected Hob closely, brows drawn together. "Don't look like it feeds you much."

Mag burst out laughing, covering her mouth with her hands. "Don't let that fool ya, Davey. She's just always looked scrawny like that. You should see some of her friends. Got arms as big around as my head, all beef and bark."

Davey didn't look entirely convinced, but he did crack a smile. "I ain't a real doctor, though. I was just learnin' to be a veterinarian."

"You think if we got you supplies, like real doctors got, you could make do?" Hob asked.

"Mayhap. And I know how to read just fine, so if you get me some books about people, I could learn."

It wasn't ideal, but Hob reminded herself that beggars couldn't be choosers. "If'n you're interested, we'll give you a try."

Davey nodded, but before he could say anything more, Mag interrupted. "I got another idea. You two bide a bit and talk. I'll be back."

Davey watched her go, frowning. "Don't know what she got all excited about."

Hob shrugged. "Means it'll be good. Look, we also got to get more medicine and the like. You know the names of good stuff, what kind of boxes it'd be in?" Hob started off by telling him what Dambala had said they were out of, then described to him what was wrong with Nick.

They'd moved on from medicine to Hob telling Davey stories about bandit hunting, her running the big gun with Freki and Geri as pups, when Mag came back. From under her apron, she produced two books and offered them to Davey.

He grinned, reading over the titles. "Well, if you want me to be a proper doctor, these'll be a start."

"Where'd you get those, Mag?" Hob asked.

"Can't rightly say." Mag smiled. "Might have looked something like the company doctor's office."

Hob grinned right back at her, but a corner of her mind wondered how the hell Mag had gotten in there and back out without a soul seeing, all while stealing something that hefty. "Thanks, Mag. But I got one more favor to ask."

"If it's somethin' I can give, you know I will."

"There'll be a supply train to Rouse tomorrow, right?"

Mag's smile faded, but she nodded. "They like it to be clockwork, and there ain't been any storms big enough to cause delays."

"Write down the schedule for me. You got that stuff memorized, right?"

"Not going to do somethin' foolish, are you?"

"Oh, you know me. Ain't got a foolish bone in my body."

The guard shift had changed by the time Hob took Davey out of the town. She just pretended they were a couple, sneaking away for a few minutes of canoodling in the shade of the walls during their break, even holding Davey's hand and pretending to be shy. The guard made a lot of nasty jokes, mostly about how much taller Hob was, but let them pass.

The Wolves had drifted around with the shadows, though as soon as he spotted her, Coyote gathered his cards back up, slapping the sand off them as he did. Nearby, Lobo's trike sat ready, loaded up with boxes and bags, all netted down to keep anything from moving even a squeak.

"This here's Davey, boys. Not quite a doctor, but we get to keep him so that oughta make up for it. You take him back to base so he can start workin' now, Lobo. Rest of us will be back tomorrow." Lobo's only answer was a nod, then he started getting his trike ready for a passenger to come with him, putting the books away in his saddlebags.

Geri opened his mouth to protest and got a fist in

the gut from Coyote. The short, brown man grinned. "Find a bit of fun for us while you were in town?"

Hob grinned right back at him, her confidence building. Coyote might be a slippery customer, but he was one hell of an ally to have. She pulled the slip Mag had given her from her pocket. "We got a train to catch."

CHAPTER TWENTY

The air in Primero stank of acrid fear thick enough that it made every swallow metallic. It was a bizarre counterpoint to the brass band, horns winking and flaring eye-gougingly bright in the sunlight, blatting away a cheery march in welcome. A red-faced, black-coated preacher stood on a crate nearby and attempted to bellow over the slightly out-of-tune music – hellfire and brimstone stuff, witchcraft and devilry. Shige Rollins kept his expression distant, neutral, pleasant, as if none of those things could touch him – even if he felt them keenly with biologically enhanced senses.

He was still rather surprised that Ms Meetchim had sent him to the first stop on the witch hunt by himself, as the liaison between Mr Green and the town – almost as surprised as he'd been by the series of inoculations he'd received in preparation, supposedly to protect against the contaminants found in the desert. It felt like some sort of test. The question was what constituted pass or fail.

"He just about ready, Mr Rolland?" the town's security chief asked.

"He's been ready," Shige answered. "Is your town?"

The security chief grimaced, eyeing the heaving, surging crowd that spilled out into the streets beyond the train station. A ring of green-uniformed security men, broken only by the presence of buildings, surrounded the crowd, hemmed them in: a none-too-gentle reminder that attendance was mandatory. "Still waiting for the final check signal. They're going building to building."

Shige offered him a friendly enough smile. "How distressing. I would have hoped your residents would understand that they've nothing to fear."

"People ain't out here in the wastes 'cause they were smart enough to do better for themselves," the chief growled. He waved his hand in a signal, and seemed satisfied with the reply. "We're ready."

"I'll fetch the Weatherman." He returned to the train car. The door sliding shut cut off the noise and heat as neatly as a knife blade slicing through butter, a relief destined to be short lived.

Mr Green waited inside, hunched over in his plush seat as he played with a bit of string, weaving it into intricate knots. He hummed to himself, though it sounded more like an angry cat growling than anything cheerful.

Mr Green didn't look like a man who had been close to dead a month ago. The spare parts and enhancements had done their work well, though his voice had remained a ruined, gravelly croak. They hadn't bothered to bring spare vocal cords. Speech wasn't necessary for what the Weathermen did and, according to Ms Meetchim, little they said ever made sense anyway.

But his recovery time had been well used. Guards had been drafted, specific guards who knew how to handle a Weatherman, who understood that little rules like never to look directly into his eyes existed for a reason, not just as useless etiquette. The route had to be planned, and campaigns of whispers set out across the locations. A witch hunt, Ms Meetchim had carefully explained as if Shige was a child who had never sniffed the underside of politics (good, it meant his cover was working nicely) was nothing without the tide of fear that carried it, reminding people that there were those who walked among them that were *different* and *other* and not the good kind like the Weathermen, who were special people who served humanity. Preachers had thundered from their pulpits about the guises of the devil, and how much like burning perdition Tanegawa's World had been before TransRift had brought along the first Weathermen to tame the storms. Personnel from Mariposa had whispered here and there, letting people overhear them talk about the freaks they found on the dunes, how in this town or that town, their cousin or former coworker had seen something terrible, a person made monstrous by the wilds eating the flesh of humans – anything guaranteed to both titillate and horrify.

This would be the test to see how well that groundwork had been laid, Shige supposed. This planet was unknown to him, and the situation. Could fear of the unknown and such bizarre superstition really run so deep? "Mr Green?"

The Weatherman looked up, and Shige carefully focused on the air just past his right ear. "Time?" he whispered hoarsely. His broad smile was visible even peripherally.

"They're ready for you. They've got quite a party waiting."

Mr Green stood like a spider unfolding its legs, coiling the string neatly in his palm as he did so. The loops he tucked into his breast pocket. "It's so nice to meet people," he breathed.

Shige opened the door and made to exit first. Mr Green's cool, bony fingers on his shoulder stopped him. He yielded without protest, allowing the Weatherman to plunge out into the hot sun and dust like he might dive into water.

The roar of voices cut off as Mr Green took his first step onto the station platform. The band continued gamely on, though one of the trumpet players seemed to lose track of the beat entirely. And the Weatherman stretched his arms up and up, reaching toward the sun for a moment, for all purposes like a man who'd just woken. Then he looked around the crowd, nostrils flaring as he sniffed. "Hello," he whispered. "What have we here?"

No one had been able – or willing – to tell Shige how the Weatherman would conduct such an exercise. And, perhaps unsurprisingly, there was no archival footage of the previous witch hunt, only written records that were a dry recitation of names, locations, classifications that he still didn't entirely understand. Shige took out his own metal-backed notepad and began to write his observations. He was known to be the secretary, after all. This was what he did. And it let him take a mental step away from what he did know would happen.

Mr Green moved through the crowd, people
bending and stepping to get out of his way; he walked
by most as if they weren't there at all. He let his hand
trail in the air over the hair and faces of the miners,
like a boy leaning from a boat to skim his fingers over
the surface of a pond.

Mr Green stopped short as his fingers passed near
the face of a young woman. "What have we here?"
he said, the words a barely audible growl. His fingers
shot forward, gripping the lower half of her face hard
enough to leave deep white dents in cheeks and chin.
Many people took steps back, though the girl's family
still hovered nearby. An older woman with iron-gray
hair cropped close to her skull – probably the girl's
mother – wrung her hands while a man close to her
age held tight to her sleeve.

Then, of all strange things, the Weatherman
reached his other hand around to take up her mousy
hair, comb it in half roughly with his fingers, and twist
the halves in an approximation of braids. "No, no, not
right," he said. Then he refocused on her, looking
into her wide, horrified eyes as silence peppered
with dismayed murmurs flowed outward through
the crowd. Mr Green smiled like the warping of half-
melted wax. "You can hear it, can't you?"

The girl's face went gray around the edges, but
she made a faint nod, the flesh of her face bunching
against Mr Green's fingertips. She stared unblinking
into the Weatherman's eyes, her own going from
clear white to strained and bloodshot.

"It's beautiful, but you mustn't be fooled." Mr
Green drew the girl forward until they were almost

nose to nose. "Tell me what you did. You can trust me."

"I heard the dust storm," she whispered. "It sang to me."

"And then you killed people with the storm. Very naughty of you," Mr Green said, sounding almost sad.

The young woman shook, her shoulders jittering, the tremors quickly running down her arms to her hands, clenched into white-knuckled fists. "No. That isn't what happened."

Mr Green shook his head and let go of her. "It's all right. I'm here to make you better." Two security men dragged the girl away; she went limp as they grabbed her, like a puppet with no strings. Then he continued forward into the crowd, as if she had vanished from his view entirely.

Shige knew the protocol for this. From his position, a few steps behind, he loudly announced the orders Ms Meetchim had given him: "Everyone she has touched as well. They are all contaminated. Family and close friends." It was important that the people hear this guideline as well.

It was easy enough for the guards to locate those people; the crowd cringed away from them. Most silently turned their backs. "I lost my brother to that storm," a woman hissed venomously, and gave the gray-haired woman a vicious shove toward the guards.

Into the train the young woman went, carried by men in green. More herded her family behind her, springloaded batons idly swinging in the hot air. Mr Green, smiling beatifically, continued to walk through the crowd.

He stopped abruptly, his head tilting as if he caught a sound beyond the normal range of hearing. The tip of his bright red tongue traced his lips in a quick flicker. Then he turned, looking over his shoulder as if he expected someone to be there. Another "witch" perhaps?

The few people brave enough to press in or unfortunate enough to be shoved to the fore by their neighbors backed away, looked down as his gaze skated over them.

Without a word, Mr Green strode back in that direction, spread-fingered hands clutching at his chest.

This, Shige decided, couldn't be normal at all. "Mr Green?" No acknowledgment. There was nothing to do but follow, the guards at his heels.

Mr Green walked in a straight line, even cutting through a house, scrambling over a dining table and sending dishes scattering to become shards on the floor. Shige skirted those delicately, not willing to quite close the distance between them. There was no knowing how the Weatherman would react.

At the town wall a little mewl of frustration escaped Mr Green's throat. He paused for a moment, scrabbling at the poured synthcrete with fingernails so short they were almost non-existent, then turned to follow the wall. His hands fluttered like papers on the breeze, searching for some gap through which to escape.

Visions of losing the Weatherman out into the desert now dancing in his head, Shige tried calling to him, "Mr Green! Mr Green, please stop. It isn't safe for you to stray from the train station. People will worry. Mr Green!"

Mr Green either did not hear him or did not care to respond, too taken with whatever had his attention. At the gates, he battered against the inset door with his fists, strange, bubbling growls coming from his throat.

"Sir…" a guard began.

Sedation, Shige thought. But did they have anything that would actually sedate the Weatherman? Had they even prepared for this contingency? Was this the reason they weren't allowed outside unsupervised? But all the reports he'd read of Mr Green before indicated that he had been outside Newcastle, had even been out into the dune sea in answer to his own curiosity, and nothing untoward had happened. So this was… interesting. A calculated risk. Maintain the safety of the shell of Mr Rolland, or risk and see what might come of it? He didn't know enough about the Weathermen – that was one of his major assignments. He made the decision in a split second: "Open the door before he hurts himself."

The door swung wide, revealing the expanse of hardpan outside of the town. At the crest of the closest dune that crept toward the walls, a pale man stood. The wind tugged at the hem of his gray duster, at the bones dangling from a skull that topped his staff. Mr Green took a few stumbling steps through the doorway and then stopped in his tracks, eyes fixed on the man.

The clear sky tasted of lightning. The guards at the gate backed up another step, covering their ears.

Something that was not a sound, but rather a vibration of the bones, a flutter of the heart, filled Shige's head. A strange, spicy scent filled his mouth, his nose. The wind whipped into a higher pitch, kicking a cloud of dust into the air.

Mr Green broke into a staggering lope that carried him into the sand. He ran with his arms outstretched, like he intended to wrap his arms around the pale man, pull him into an embrace. Shige followed, making no effort to close the distance. As he ran, he dug the pen-sized datcor out of his pocket; technology this sophisticated didn't generally work outside of Newcastle, but with Mr Green nearby, it was worth a shot. He set it to record as he caught a flash of wide blue eyes, pupils shrunk down to a pinpoint, and then the pale man shouted, flinging his hand at Mr Green. Dust spurted up between them. The man's staff darted through the dust cloud and struck Mr Green's hand with a sickening crack.

Mr Green screamed like a dying rabbit. At the sound, the guards scrambled away from the gate, pelting toward him, though their run was strange and drunken, rifle barrels waving unsteadily.

The wind cleared out the worst of the dust, revealing Mr Green, one hand shielding his eyes and the other clutched against his chest. Dust coated his hair, dulled the color of his suit to a muddy gray. His shoulders trembled, but he also smiled, wide and childlike. "You hide, then. I'll seek. And I'll find."

A *native* – he remembered Gregson's use of that phrase all too clearly, and with sudden clarity, he knew that was what he'd seen. A *native*, something that called the Weatherman to distraction, and could vanish beneath the sand in a heartbeat without a trace. Shige breathed out an unsteady sigh as the datcor sparked in his hand.

"And the guards found no sign of this... interloper after he had vanished?" Ms Meetchim asked, looking up at Shige from under her eyebrows as she turned the pages of his report.

"No, sir."

"And the decision to let Mr Green outside the walls was...?"

"Mine, sir." Shige had rehearsed this the entire train journey back to Newcastle. He'd also made the decision to postpone the finish of the witch hunt until Mr Green could be examined by his medical team. To his relief, the Weatherman had come out of that examination with nothing worse than a few plasters on his hand and a bright red lollipop. "I thought perhaps one of the so-called witches had gotten outside of the walls."

Ms Meetchim made a noncommittal noise, but he calculated that the answer satisfied her.

"I was able to recover a few images and clips of sound from the ruptured memory of my datcor," he offered, trying to inject the right note of hopeful eagerness into his voice. Let him be the underling striving to impress his boss, on a new world with fresh opportunities.

She looked up sharply. "Where?"

"I've put them in your secure file."

He observed her keenly as she moved the blotter

aside to access the display in the desk's top and bring up the images. Most of them were dataloss blurs, but there was one reasonably clear image of the pale man. He knew the moment she had reached it, because she sat back as if slapped. "You showed these to no one else?" she asked sharply.

Shige had spent his time with Ms Meetchim learning the subtleties of her expressions. She had an excellent poker face, but he'd had equally excellent training at his mother's knee, and it told him that she recognized the pale man, somehow. "Of course not. I assumed it would be for your eyes only."

"And you made no copies?"

He pulled his expression into one of sincere shock. "Of course not!"

"Good." She deleted the files with a sweep of her hand. Even more interesting. "For now, you will forget this incident. But if you encounter this... man again, pull Mr Green out immediately and call for backup. Understood?"

His own copies of the images and sounds were secure, soon to be moved off site. He'd have to wait an interminable time to get the images to a Federal Union contact who could run them through the recognition database, but that could wait. In the meantime, he had a new angle to approach his own subtle investigation into the TransRift files. Meekly, Shige bowed his head. "Of course, sir."

CHAPTER TWENTY-ONE

Through the evening and into the night Hob led her little party out toward Rouse, then swung wide before the rocks were more than a black line on the horizon. They picked up the train tracks that ran to the town and followed them for several hours out into the canyonlands and the sand sea that halfway filled them. Only when the horizon was just beginning to lighten did they divert to take shelter in the lee of a nearby butte.

Between dry bites of field rations, Hob laid out her thoughts. "We ride double, get two of us onto the train. Shouldn't be too much trouble, since a freight train won't be that fast near the canyons. And it won't have guards standing out on it, not during the day."

"'Cause ain't no one stupid enough to attack a train in the middle of the day," Geri said. "Gonna fry like bacon in the pan when you hop the car."

"Well, some might." Hob grinned. "We get dropped off and the riders hang in a blind spot while we check the cars until we find whichever one's got the medical stuff. We take what we want, toss it out along the tracks for pickin' up later. Once we're done, the riders come up beside the train and we do some fancy stunt jumpin'."

"By your use of 'we,' I assume you'll be one of the two," Coyote said. "And the other will be…?"

"You. We're the two lightest, so it'd be easiest for us to make the jump, I reckon, and Freki and Geri can muscle the bikes steady if it comes to that." She bared her teeth. "And you're a goddamn showoff."

Coyote held his hands up in a sign of surrender. She'd almost bet he was silently patting himself on the back, for all he tried to look dismayed.

"Why not just uncouple the car?" Freki asked.

"We might have to do this again, and for somethin' bigger," Hob said. "Why get 'em on the defensive now? If we do it right, they won't even know we were there until they check the manifest and find what's missing."

"And then they'll most likely assume that the theft was done at the last station," Coyote said.

"Ain't been anyone ballsy enough to do a train job in a while. Luck 'n' laziness will see us through." The skeleton of the plan seemed good enough. Together, the four of them fleshed out the details, then took turns napping in the shadows of the small butte when the sun came up.

Coyote shook her awake with a hand to the shoulder. He got Freki and Geri after her, and wasn't nearly as nice to them; both got nudged in the hip with the toe of his boot.

Hob stood and shook out her clothes, doing her best to ignore the sand that had found its way into her shirt and boots. "I don't hear nothin'." She eased over toward Freki's bike. Given the choice, she'd rather eat whole roaches out of the dunes than sit behind Geri.

"That's because I had my ear to the track. Sound of the train carries better at a distance like that. It's coming." The shrill, breathy sound of a whistle rolled across the dunes, bouncing off the little butte that had sheltered them. Coyote grinned. "As I said."

"Then we'd better get goin'." Hob jammed her helmet on her head, waited for Freki to get on his bike, then climbed on the back after him. Her knees near poked into his armpits; she'd outgrown riding on the back after her first growth spurt. Freki didn't complain, just told her to hold on tight as they whipped out from the shadow of the butte.

The train was a silver snake in the distance, metal skin blinding bright even with the helmet's polarizers switched on. It started off small enough that she could have blocked it out with one finger, but grew rapidly, sleek and dangerous and unnatural as it cut through the sand. The engine was shrouded in a dust cloud, fountains of particles spewing up on either side, plowed out of the way by the blade mounted on the front.

"You want to jump first, Coyote, or you want me to do it?" she asked over the radio channel – sound was clearer these days, less static. The garagemaster must have finally gotten the upgrades done that he'd been jawing about for ages.

"You go ahead first. That way you can catch me up in those long arms of yours if I miss."

Hob laughed. "Have it your way."

The air took on the rumble of metal on metal, the train towering up as high as a house as they swept in. The feel of the tires went from soft to firm as they hit a patch of hardpan. Hob clutched at Freki's jacket as he whipped the bike into a hard turn, putting them parallel with the rails. He eased back on the throttle, letting the train creep past until they were even with the last car.

Maybe it would've been smarter to start in the middle and work cars in both directions, but broken bones sounded better to Hob than getting turned into ground meat between wheels and rails.

"Good as it's gonna get," Freki said.

"Sounded like a much better idea afore we got here," Hob muttered. She set her feet firmly on the pegs, fisted the shoulders of Freki's coat in her hands, and stood. The motorcycle went a little wobbly, but Freki wrestled it back under control, hands gone tight on the grips. She narrowed her field of view to the ladder on the car's side, thought herself through jumping, catching hold of it, getting her boots jammed into the rungs. She refused to see the ground whizzing by below. Being scared would only get her killed. "OK, jumpin' in three… two… one!"

She jumped.

If she'd ever felt graceful for a moment in her life, it was this one, stretching out between the motorcycle and the train car. Then one hand closed over the ladder, the other over air, and her heart nearly stopped in her chest as she slammed into the side of the car, helmet making a loud *crack* as it hit one of the ladder rungs. She hung on with every ounce of strength, boots scrabbling against the smooth metal side, hand feeling for the ladder. For one frozen moment she felt herself slipping, the metal rung twisting from her fingers.

Her boots caught and she surged up onto the ladder, clinging to it like a lifeline.

"Are you going to make room for me, or should I give you two a moment alone?" Coyote drawled into her ear.

Hob laughed, the sound a little more high pitched than she was used to. "Give me a second." She scrambled up the ladder to the top, then got herself turned around, locking her legs in so her arms were free. "Come and get it."

Geri was ballsy enough to get closer to the train than his brother had as Coyote, balancing on the pegs with enough aplomb that he made it look good, and easy to boot, counted down. He stuck the landing better than Hob had, gripping firm with both hands. Still, she bent double and grabbed his wrists as he felt for the rungs with his feet.

"Good to go," Coyote said, sounding somewhere between unsteady and elated. "Get the top hatch dealt with while I climb up, all right?"

Hob scrambled onto the roof, not bothering to be quiet. If there was anyone inside – unlikely to begin with – they would already know that something was going on. One hand feeling in her pocket for the bolt cutters, wind slapping her coat against her legs, she squatted in front of the hatch.

Only it wasn't a padlock, like she'd expected. There was just a box and a little glowing light, like the electronic locks on the doors in Newcastle. "Well shit."

"Well shit what?" Geri asked.

"It's a fuckin' electronic lock. Opens with a code or sommat."

"Melt it," Freki said. There was enough tone difference between their voices for Hob to tell him apart.

"But…" Well, of course the boys knew she had that witchiness in her. She'd burned her handprint into Freki's forearm when he'd still just been Francis and had been trying to drag her somewhere by her hair. But they'd never really talked about it again after that.

"If that trained freakshow shit bothered any of us, you think we'd be following Nick Ravani?" Geri asked.

Hob laughed. Put in that light, it seemed damn dumb. Like everyone was pretending just to keep the old man happy. "Ain't rightly sure how."

Coyote tugged the bolt cutters from her hand. "You burn your cigarettes all the time," he said. "Figure it out."

That seemed a little unfair. She burned paper and tobacco and had even got a good blaze going in the wooden interior of the church, but all of those things desperately wanted to burn already in a place this dry and hot. And she could drink in heat and fire, sure. She'd figured that out early on when she was tired of getting sunburnt. Just gave her headaches sometimes, made her sick if she drank in too much. But metal? Melting *metal*.

Staring at it wasn't going to do a damn thing, she

knew that for sure. Had to be the same principle as burning anything else, right? She just needed more heat. It was worth a try at least, because otherwise they were on top of the damn train for nothing. Hob pulled off her gloves and tucked them under the toe of her boot, then covered the lock with her hands. The metal was already damn hot from the sun, and more sunlight, more heat beat down on her head and shoulders. She drank it into her blood until her head practically swam, then shoved it all back out, focused down onto the much smaller point of the lock. She pushed so hard she couldn't breathe for a moment and her vision whited out.

Coyote grabbed her by the arm when she started to list to the side. But she felt metal sag under her fingertips, saw it turning to blackened slag. She panted into the confines of her helmet to try to get her breath back. After giving her arm a little shake to make sure she was steady enough, Coyote tugged the hatch open.

Hob laughed a little giddily and pulled on her gloves. "Bet they'll think it was just a little too much sun."

Coyote snorted. "Well, when the other option is believing your train got invaded by a fire-breathing witch, I suppose so."

They dropped down onto a stack of crates, pulling out small handcranked flashlights; nothing helpful in the tail-end car. There was a door they could use to get between the cars, normally for guards and engineers, and it wasn't even locked. A little more cautious now, they moved up through the train.

At the fourth car up, they found the medical supply candy store, everything that Davey had told Hob to look for and more. Like they were shopping instead of stealing, they picked through, taking just a box here and a bag there, carefully calculating and weighing to make sure they weren't taking too much to carry in their saddlebags. They grabbed medicine and bandages, as well as a couple of fancier bits of technology that Hob had never seen and felt dubious about, but Coyote insisted were a good idea. Coyote climbed up to the roof and Hob handed him the boxes to pitch off after they warned Freki and Geri that supplies were coming.

Hob shimmied back up the stack of crates, glancing behind to make sure there were no obvious bootprints. Coyote shut the hatch behind her as she climbed back onto the roof, laughing when she cussed, fumbling for the polarizer switch. "How about you go down there first this time," she told Coyote. "You can show me how it's done, since you made it look so damn pretty."

"I'll get nervous if you watch me too intently." There was a shit-eating grin in his voice. Coyote climbed down the ladder, wind whipping the tail of his coat. "Get as close as you can, Geri." The motorcycle moved in. "Closer. Closer. A little closer…"

"Any closer, and I'm gonna crash," Geri said.

"You'll be fine. Hold it steady." Coyote let go with one hand and foot, the wind blowing him around like a kite. He made an odd yelping noise, then pulled himself back around, reached out his foot and got it onto the back of Geri's bike. Then he just stepped across, grabbing Geri's shoulders and dropping down so fast that the motorcycle bounced. But Geri got it away, moving out from the train. "Think you can do that?"

Hob gritted her teeth. "Bet it'll be easier for me, since I ain't got little stubby legs like you." She waited for Freki to get up as close as he could, maybe even a little closer than Geri had, like he was trying to make up for his twin showing him up before. She was ready for the wind trying to yank at her, didn't almost get blown off the ladder like Coyote. She stepped across and stood on the seat, hands grabbing Freki's jacket so hard that her fingers ached, then settled down more slowly, not wanting to knock him off balance.

"Now who's trying to look pretty?" Coyote said.

And then they were off, curving back and away from the train, aiming toward the butte where the other two bikes waited. Only then did she let herself laugh, and whoop, but that was all right. The men were yelling their damn fool heads off too, a mix of shouts and "Did you see that? Did you fuckin' see that?"

Felt like they'd done more than just a little robbery.

"The hell were you thinkin', girl?" Old Nick's voice was painful to hear, all raw crackles and gravel.

Hob hid a flinch in her shrug, dropping the stack of flimsies she held on the rickety bedside table. "What'd I do this time, you old bastard?"

Nick struggled up a little higher against the pillows. "I'm sick. I ain't gone stupid. And watch your goddamn mouth."

Hob stared right in to his evil, yellowed eye,

crossing her arms over her chest. "Thought we were bein' casual, seeing as you're callin' me girl again."

The old man's thin, pale lips curled up in a snarl, his eye narrowing. But he blinked first. "Fine. The hell were you thinkin', *Hob*?"

It should have felt like victory. Instead, it just made her feel small and mean, watching his shoulders heave every time he sucked in a breath. "I was thinkin' money's thin and bills are big, and there were things we were needin'." Considering the bottle of medicine that sat next to those flimsies, still in its pretty TransRift wrappings, she wasn't going to waste any more of his time by pretending not to know what he was asking about.

"So it was you." Nick covered his face with one pale, spidery hand.

"Who else would it be?"

"They fuckin' listened to *you*? I was hopin' Coyote, maybe. Man's a fountain of stupid ideas."

Hob snorted, not bothering to feel insulted. "This idea weren't stupid, and was all mine. Mayhap I finally done redeemed myself." Enough smart, competent ideas to outweigh the big stupid only her and Nick knew. It still wasn't enough, but if she saved each Wolf's life a thousand times by thinking clear, maybe it would be. She pointed at the flimsies, hoping to get him off the track. "Brought all the stuff you need to look at and sign. It's mostly bills. People ain't so eager to hire us right now. Imagine that."

"And turning thief ain't gonna help that neither."

"We still got to eat. Need medicine for people. Not just you."

"I'm still in charge here!" Nick drew himself up as much as he could, shoulders shaking as he muffled a cough with his hands. He continued on, a smear of bright red on his lips that he didn't even seem to notice. "Whether I'm ridin' around with you meat sacks or sittin' pretty in this room. You get any other bright fuckin' ideas, you run 'em by me."

She wanted to snarl at him, and shout, but that bead of blood on his lips had her transfixed. "I'll be sure to do that." He wasn't angry, not really; she knew what angry looked like on the man. No, the emotion written in the lines of his face was something else entirely: *fear*.

"Now get the hell out of here afore you piss me off again. You tryin' to kill me? Man in my delicate condition…" He grinned.

Only it didn't seem like such a joke. "Fine. When you're done with that stack of flimsies, you just have someone tell me." Hob turned to go.

"Take my guns with you. They need cleanin'."

Hob glanced at him, but his face was unreadable as always. He probably meant it as a punishment, some little shit job to get back at her for doing something he disliked in the most petty way possible. But it felt more like a treat than anything. Those pistols were heavy with history, art that could kill a man easy as breathing. "Yessir. I'll get right on it." She injected enough sarcasm into her tone to keep him happy if punishment was his aim.

Gun belt rolled and tucked in one arm, she let herself out of the room. Coyote leaned next to the door. At her glance, he pushed off the wall and followed her, instead of going in to see Nick like she'd expected.

"Ain't even bein' subtle about your eavesdroppin' these days," she commented.

"You make it sound so ugly when you put it like that." He grinned. "I expected there to be a lot more yelling, though. I had to press my ear against the door to hear anything at all."

"Think if he'd tried to yell more, it'd kill him." Hob thumped down the stairs, Coyote on her heels, and he stuck there like her shadow as she crossed the exercise yard, headed up to Old Nick's office. "What ya want, Coyote? Ain't got time for games."

Coyote stopped in the doorway of the office, leaning there with studied casualness. "We've got nothing but time. Which seems a shame. We find a whole new set of useful skills, and he wants us to keep them under wraps."

Hob watched the man carefully, trying to get a read on his game. Coyote had always been a good poker player, though, just smiling idly away like he didn't have a care in the world and he'd just mentioned wasn't the weather so lovely today? His narrow brown eyes gave away nothing. "World went tits up in a single night. Old man's scared. Lot of people are."

"But you're not."

"And neither are you, but that's 'cause you're bugshit crazy." Hob set Nick's gun belt on his desk. The yellowed bone of the butts stood out against the dark leather and blackened wood. She gave the metal chair she'd finally dragged behind the desk a nasty look, then gave up and sat on it.

He laughed, touching the brim of his hat with one finger. "Once upon a time – a week ago – so was Nick Ravani. Scared isn't a good way to get fed."

"But it's sure a good way of stayin' alive."

"Until you starve."

She leaned forward, elbows on her knees. "You heard what he said. You askin' me to disobey him? You gone fucking mental for real?"

Coyote shrugged one shoulder. "I can have the bright ideas if you'd rather not."

"Never knew you to be a goddamn lawyer. What are you trying to pull?"

"Making certain you understand your possibilities. I've still no idea what you did, three years ago, to put the Ravani in such a rage. But think carefully on the fact that as much as he's worked to grind you into paste, he worked just as hard to not throw you away." He touched the brim of his hat, his voice taking on a mimicked twang. "Thank you kindly, sir."

Hob stared at him and said the only thing that came to mind: "Get the fuck outta my office." Except she should have said *Nick*'s office. Coyote laughed and sauntered away.

PART IV

CHAPTER TWENTY-TWO

Nick was not a man on the mend, but neither was he a man at death's door. He hung for weeks in a strange sort of limbo, too sick to be anything but terminal, but too damn mean to give up. Every day, he swallowed down a handful of pills at the insistence of Davey Painter, the vet who would be a doctor. And he smoked constantly, on his own insistence.

He wasn't able to walk much any more, let alone ride, but he still worked. He had all the files brought to the infirmary. There were bills to pay and mouths to feed, though the sorts of jobs that could provide money for those were getting more and more scarce.

When you knocked over a town like you had more balls than sense, the things people wanted you to do were a similar level of dangerous and ballsy. Being in the bad graces of the company, being known murderers and thieves, made it hard to get legitimate work. They weren't just flying under company radar now, offering to do things Mariposa wouldn't. They stained everything they touched with that criminal element, and there was a price on Nick's head at least, big enough that people not wearing TransRift blue might be personally interested in his death. The reward offer on information about the Wolves wasn't a comforting number either, though them who knew much would keep their mouths shut.

If he'd been a braver man, Nick might have said fuck it, thrown himself right into that spiral down to hell and seen how high they could get that price to go. Fuck the company, fuck this world, fuck it proper. The Wolves would follow him, with varying amounts of glee. Most of them had no use for the damn world and the small-minded towns that spat them out into the desert.

But looking death in the eye had a way of changing a man. Knowing that his brother and sister-in-law had been murdered by the company he'd already angered made him cautious, reminded him that no one was safe. Maybe that should have made him angrier, but he was too tired for that now, too tired and too damn old, outliving his parents and a brother twelve years his junior, coming within a hair's breadth of outliving his niece in the process, his own damn adopted daughter too.

Those thoughts bounced in his head as his cigarette burned down to the filter and he stared uncomprehendingly at a letter from Clarence Vigil. The message was half progress report on Mag's wellbeing, half veiled labor talk, all implication and secretive phrases about maybe needing a hand from the Wolves, like they could even put a scratch in an endless army of empty blue suits.

"Nick?" Dambala said.

He looked up, ash falling from his cigarette and onto

the letter, obscuring Clarence's terrible chicken-scratch handwriting. Dambala stood as his second now that Makaya was gone, and that was his fault as well. Dambala was a good man, but he didn't have the fire, didn't have the spine to stand up to Nick when he needed it. That was something Makaya had been so very good at. She'd always challenged him and told him where to stick his orders when she thought they were stupid.

Well, she had almost every time. Every time but the last, most important one.

"What?" he asked, fatigue dulling his voice.

"Message for you. Another one." Dambala offered him a flimsy folded to be an envelope. "Was at one of the drop points, so I can leave your answer back there if you like."

Nick grunted, unfolding the flap of the envelope. A sliver of bone rolled out onto his lap. He froze, staring at the ivory stark against the dark brown blanket over his legs. "Never you mind. I'll handle this."

"Nick…?"

"You didn't see nothin'. Just get out." He waited until Dambala had shut the door, then got out of bed and dressed himself. He had to keep pausing to lean against the chair or sit and listen to his breath rattle in his chest. His clothes were looser than he remembered them being, his coat hanging off his shoulders, and his belt tightened down to the last hole and still not quite enough. Still, he was sufficiently quick on his feet as he dodged out of the infirmary and let himself through a trapdoor, down into one of the escape tunnels. No one saw him, though that wasn't so much speed as cunning. Cunning was always worth a damn sight more anyway.

The Bone Collector waited for him in the gulch where the escape tunnel let out. Nick barely had to step from behind the camouflage tarp and the man was right there, standing straight and silent, his staff planted firm against the stony ground. Angry red welts stood out on his face, like a vivid slap across his cheek. His normally calm expression was gone; the bones on his staff rattled as he trembled.

"The hell happened to you?" Nick asked.

"A new witch hunt has begun. They've brought out one of their... *Weathermen*." The Bone Collector's lip curled as if just the word alone tasted foul.

Nick fumbled for his cigarette case. He'd left it behind. "We've already gone to ground. Best we stay that way and not get noticed. Suggest you do the same, just slide beneath the radar and don't come back up till they done fucked back off 'cause they're bored."

"And what about those still in the towns?"

"Can't do anythin' for them. If there's a hunt started, it's already too late. You know this. You know how the last one went."

The Bone Collector's eyes narrowed. "There was a time when I never thought I'd hear you say that something was too late, or a problem too large for you to handle."

"I grew up." Nick laughed humorlessly. "Killed a lot of good people figurin' it out."

"You cannot turn your back on these people. Or on me."

"Why the fuck not? What'd they ever fuckin' do for me? For *us*? Threw us some scraps if we went and fuckin' bled for them. I don't owe them jack shit." He curled his lip. "And say I do decide I want to be a hero, at my advanced age? What are the chances of survival then? Tell me what the future holds, since you always seem to know. Am I gonna just waste more Wolves on a problem that we can't handle? I owe *them* better than that."

The Bone Collector shook his head. "There are too many possibilities."

"I'm startin' to think that's your speak for, 'yeah, it's gonna be bad.'"

"Nothing of the sort. It's too complicated to see through. There are too many things that I don't know."

"If we stick together, we'll be safer than apart."

The Bone Collector looked away. "That's no longer good enough." One hand ghosted over his pocket. "The townsfolk are in this as well, whether they know it or not."

"Tough shit for them. I gave all I got to give. I gotta think of me and mine first."

"I believe you when you say that." The Bone Collector sighed, shoulders bowing. "Goodbye, my friend. I don't think we will meet again."

"Wait…" Nick croaked. The words caught in his throat as the pale man walked away, and he didn't have the strength to chase him – not that it was possible to catch the Bone Collector if he didn't want to be caught. It was a punch to the gut, the look he'd seen in that man's eyes: worse disappointment than he'd ever seen on Phil's face, and Nick had been a powerful disappointment at times.

•••

The Bone Collector had him spooked enough that as soon as he'd settled back into his bed like he never left, he sent for the young Wolves. Couldn't even really tell himself why, maybe he just needed the reassurance that those precious idiots were still in one piece.

Hob came in like one of those rare seasonal storms, about to spit lightning and soak everything around her with acid piss.

"There you are, girl. Took you damn long enough," he said.

"You can't stay abed forever. I'm tired of playing secretary for you."

"Leadin' a group of roughnecks into battle's a dangerous job, girly. But look at me. I'm going to be the first Ravani to die in bed in three hundred years." Nick grinned. "I mean to enjoy it."

"It's always one damn joke after another with you."

"Where are Freki and Geri? I sent for them, too."

"They're out to town, looking for a dice game most like. Bored out of their damn skulls, just like everyone else," Hob growled.

"Right." He smiled. Yeah, that was her through and through, damn little hellcat he'd hauled out of a drift of sand a decade ago. Best mistake he'd ever made in his life. She was too damn like him. "Where're your guns? Shouldn't get caught naked, you know."

"Your office. I was cleaning 'em. Didn't come here aimin' to shoot you."

"Ah, I see." Nick reached over one hand so thin he barely recognized it as his own and patted his gun belt, hanging over the chair next to him. "Take mine and clean 'em too, while you're at it."

"Never get tired of this game, do ya." Still, she took them up just as reverently as the first time he'd given that order weeks ago. "Shouldn't keep letting these out of your sight, should ya?" A time or two she'd let slip silently by, since it was probably just Nick being a bastard. But this was turning into a habit, now.

"I don't expect to get haunted over it," Old Nick said calmly. They were important, those pistols, more than she guessed, even. A straight line back to the first man who'd ever worn the Ravani name, passed from one to another like father to son, only it was a closer bond than just shared blood. "Never figured you for the superstitious type."

"I come by it honestly," she snapped.

"But it was fun, wasn't it," he said, breathing the words out like a sigh. He sank a bit lower against the pillows. He'd messed with her good and proper, growing up. Taught her not to trust anything, not even him. "Had some laughs."

"You spend your whole damn life laughing at me."

"Why you in such a pissy mood, girl? You on the rag?"

Hob bared her teeth. "Best hope I'm not." Pistols held gingerly, she went back to the window. "You seen to me bein' restless, with your damn files."

He chuckled. "Ain't fun, but it needs to be done. I trust you with it more'n the boys." She was the only one who *could* do it. Who could do half of what he'd done. She had the fire in her belly, the hunger, like he'd had more than forty years ago when another wicked old man had torn his scraggly ass out of the dunes.

She gave him a sharp glance over her shoulder. "Thanks, old man."

"Keep callin' me that, and I ain't so sick that I can't come up to clip your ears."

"I'm countin' on it. And countin' that I can still run faster scared."

Old Nick grinned. "Age wins, girl. When you're old, you know how to wait."

She said the words like they were a slip, a thing she hadn't meant to speak aloud. "Just don't you go waitin' too long."

"What would you do in my shoes, girl? Shit's gotten downright deadly out there."

"You want a real answer?"

"Grace me with it, please." He didn't bother disguising the sarcasm in his voice. Needling her was the only fun he got any more. No one else fought back half as much, not with Makaya gone.

"Times're changin'. We gotta change with 'em if we want to survive." She crossed her arms, pistols cradled in one elbow. "I seen all the flimsies comin' in. Don't know what the company's up to, but people are gettin' scared. We can ride it, or we can get mowed down by it. So get your ass out of that bed, and get us ridin'."

Old Nick stared at her for a long time, then coughed, loud and theatrical. "Ain't a half bad answer, but there you go, tirin' me out. Get. I expect to see my reflection in those pistols when you're done."

"Yeah, yeah. I'll bring 'em back presently." She headed for the door.

"Oh, Hob?"

"Yeah?"

"Have 'em send up another book and some whiskey. Just about done with this one."

"Yeah, will do," Hob said. She shut the door behind her, not nearly as hard as he expected.

Nick remained thoughtful and quiet long after she'd left. One of the low men in the pack – Conall, that was right, decent shot and a quiet sort, always staring off like he was daydreaming – brought him a bottle of whiskey and some battered novel with a plain cover, which he accepted with only a grunt. Out of habit, he cracked the book open to reveal crooked printing on crinkled, reused plastic flimsies – probably one of Hati's hobbyist efforts from the overblown title, *The Murder That Shook the Canyonlands to Gravel*. He poured three fingers of whiskey into a glass and took a sniff, but didn't drink.

The girl was right, he thought, then: *she ain't "the girl" any more, ain't been for a while*. Hob had grown into her name; he might not have paid attention at the time to how she handled herself during the escape from Rouse, but Coyote had made it his business to fill Nick's ears with the story over and over again, in that pointed, prissy little accent of his. Hob was also right: things were changing. He'd kicked the change off two months ago, thrown them in a direction they couldn't backtrack with his temper. But the more he thought about it, the more he wondered if their invasion of Rouse was really the trigger, or if it was part of something so big he'd never have the full shape of it, a fault line that ran through the entire world.

It was too damn complicated, and he was too damn

old and sick with black fibers of drug-resistant, alien cancer strangling his lungs – a little gift from his time in the mines before he'd been put on the blacklist.

It'd be better to give Hob her head. Any direction she'd go would likely be better than sitting in place too scared to move, if she could scam the rest into following her – and he had no doubt she could. But she wouldn't be able to do it with him hanging over her shoulder like a rook of doom. Everyone would be looking at him, waiting for him to caw and flap his wings and tell them what he thought, instead of looking at Hob. And Hob would be looking over her shoulder too.

The thing that had struck him about her, right from the start, was the way that angry little girl had marched off into the desert without so much as a backward glance. She'd had enough of a chip on her shoulder for five men, and he'd pushed to turn her hard instead of cruel, because that was the only way he knew to survive. Phil had always said he was too tough on her, that it was no way to treat a girl that might as well be his daughter, Phil's niece. Maybe he'd been right. But from where he sat, listening to the unsteady beat of his heart and the wheeze of his own lungs, he thought he'd done all right. He'd pushed her and pushed her, and she hadn't broken; even when the blood had run and she'd ripped out her own heart rather than turn traitor, she'd gone hard and strong and straight in the back, and she'd earned her damn name ten times over even if part of the game was him never admitting it out loud: Hob Ravani.

The Ghost Wolves were a pack first and foremost, and that made them a family, for all their bellyaching and squabbles. And the head of that family had always, always, from the first days been named *Ravani*. Even then he'd known, when that ratty little girl had threatened to bite him if he didn't let go of her hand, the hand she'd been trying to pick his pocket with, right fucking now. Even then, he'd known, when she wanted fire of her own more than she wanted safety.

He sighed, and dug a little tin from his pocket, shaking out its entire load of pills. Before he had a chance to change his mind, he threw the bitter handful into his mouth and washed it down with the whiskey. Then he quickly poured another measure. He might as well enjoy as much of the bottle as he could before he finally drifted off.

He smiled and raised his glass, silently toasting the Bone Collector. He probably should have told the girl what he'd said, about the witch hunt, but it was too late now. No doubt she'd go to him soon enough on her own anyway, and find out then. Or the Bone Collector would find her. The two of them had kept crashing into each other in the most eerie way through the years, and there hadn't been a damn thing he'd been able to do to stop it.

He finished the glass, rolling the smoky flavor across a tongue beginning to go strange. Unsteadily, he poured himself another refill, and sank lower in the pillows.

First Ravani to die abed in centuries indeed.

The Bone Collector was older, far older than he looked, perhaps because he spent so many years asleep as living stone. He'd seen the previous witch hunt and the one before, the proto-witch hunt that had come with the industrial development of the planet just a hundred years ago. They'd come with their sparking, dying equipment, with their factories, then with their endless stream of workers – because blood and sweat could do what frail machines could not on his beautiful world – and they'd tried to excise everyone who could *hear* like a cancer.

He had been just as helpless every time because what he could do wasn't enough, or wasn't the right sort of power. Futures and stone and tunneling through the ground was nothing that could stand against Weathermen who got stronger with each generation.

Even that abomination was not the true issue. If it were only one entity, he could move around it, find other ways to fight it that didn't require direct conflict. But these hunts were all the same, planned by the company for a specific purpose: in the first few towns, they would find those that had evolved into something better, and they would round them up and take their families besides. After those few examples, in the outlying towns people would turn on their own, preferring to burn them cleanly instead of risking themselves in a purge.

He'd seen it three times. He had no stomach to see it a fourth. But there was little he could do if he couldn't even withstand the touch of an unnatural thing that had been brought from off world.

In the mine near Pictou, the Bone Collector dug his hand into the stone of one wall and drew out the little burlap sample bag that Hob had given him, so many weeks ago.

He'd always shared a special sort of bond, a resonance with the world that had given him birth, sounding for his ears alone like unending music. The Bone Collector held the bag up to his ear, eyes half closed. The tiny crystals sang as well, but there was something clearer to that song, purer; beautiful in a way that ached at the back of his throat. Perhaps it meant nothing. But it might mean everything, might be a path to something stronger, a deeper connection.

Not knowing anything more about the crystals, he couldn't even begin to see the possibilities. Strength, nothing, or death: those were the major branches. The one thing he could see clearly was that if he did nothing, he would eventually die at the hands of the Weatherman, and not a clean death. The monster would suck out his heart through his mouth, taking in everything that made him whole.

Nick Ravani had proven unhelpful, unexpectedly so. Perhaps he should have watched the futures more closely, but Nick had seemed a constant, a rock of his own sort. A rock that had inexplicably crumbled at the worst possible moment. He had few options left, now.

One of those potential paths had led him to plant the seed of an idea in Nick Ravani. Part of him hoped that it took, because it provided the best possible path from this tangle, the branch that provided the most options to the future. Yet part of him in opposition hoped that Nick would ignore him, would make good with his words and take his people to ground. Because for all his frustrations, Nick had been his friend first and always, since the day he'd found him crazed with thirst in the desert.

Sacrifices had to be made. Friendship was a fitting thing to lay bloody at the feet of fate.

The Bone Collector passed one hand in front of his eyes, and then sat down cross-legged on the floor. He drew a short, bone-handled knife from the sheath at his waist and made a deep cut from his wrist halfway to his elbow. Blood came, hot and immediate.

He dropped the knife on the ground and took up the little sample bag, carefully pouring the crystals onto the blood that covered his arm. When the bag was empty, he used his other hand to press them in more deeply, into the raw flesh, the vein he had severed.

Something beyond melody, beyond music, beyond all description burst through his mind as the crystals melted into his blood. He felt the world breathe, felt her heart beat, and knew her to be alive. He fell to his side, arms jerking, head whipping back and forth. The last sound that came from his mouth was a cry of exultation, because for these few breaths he could hear something far more powerful than the rumble of rock and sand, calling out to him, beckoning him on, her voice echoing from a great distance.

The sound froze into his throat as his skin flowed in to stone.

CHAPTER TWENTY-THREE

Hob's shoulders were tense fit to snap and her eyes burned from deciphering Old Nick's chicken scratchings by the time the paperwork was done. Still, she smiled and hummed to herself as she picked up the ancient pistols – her self-promised reward – and started cleaning them. She couldn't help but imagine the history, the battles, all the stories of the men bearing the Ravani name for more than two hundred years, before TransRift, before the mining towns were even camps. Old Nick didn't talk about the stories too much, but give Lobo a couple of shots of something with teeth and he wouldn't ever shut up.

Absorbed in her own thoughts, she didn't notice the commotion at first, noise drifting in through the open window. It was all normal base chatter, men laughing and the soft hum of well-tuned engines. The alarm bell sounding jerked her back to the present as chattering turned to shouting.

Hob lunged away from the desk to the window. "The hell's going on?" she bellowed.

The courtyard was full of men, with more tumbling in by the second. A cluster of dusty motorcycles stood at the center of the confusion; Freki and Geri, back from town, the towering figures of Dambala and Akela next to them, one-eared Bhima close behind, more joining them. "Hob!" Geri shouted up. "Old Nick's dead!"

Her hands went white-knuckled on the windowsill as shock stole her breath. That had to be impossible; she'd just been talking to him. He couldn't be dead, not in a quiet instant.

"Someone said you got his pistols. You bring 'em on down. We got a decision to make."

She felt lightheaded, unreal, but her voice was steady as she called down, "Be there in a moment." She put the pistols back together with hands that shook, holstered them, and left the office with the belt pooled loosely in her hands.

Everyone on base crowded into the square exercise yard. They parted ahead of her like water, making a path straight to where the twins stood. Geri's foot jiggled impatiently against the ground. For a crazy moment, she wanted to drop the pistols, turn and run. All that stopped her was the men closing in behind, driving her forward.

Geri smiled as she halted in front of him. "Hand 'em over, girl," he said, one dark hand held out.

"Don't be gettin' too ahead o' yourself," Dambala rumbled. His arms were crossed over his chest; Hob knew he didn't want to step into Nick's shoes. But others did.

"We'll decide," Bhima said. "Men'll pick who we follow."

It felt like her feet were a thousand kilometers away

as she looked down at that hand. It was simple; give them over, let the others decide, and spend the rest of her life being called "girl" like Old Nick had done every day since he'd named her. Keep being the ass-end of the pack, dismissed and constantly questioned, keep reliving her mistake and doing her penance for a crime only a dead man knew. Dead or not, she could hear the old bastard laughing in the back of her head fit to choke on it. Like this was his last, grandest trick. *What's it gonna be, girl? Done rolling in ashes? You finally ready to fight?*

She shifted her grip on the belt and, smooth as butter, like it fit in her hand, drew one of the pistols. She flashed it up to rest the tip of the barrel lightly against Geri's forehead. His eyes, fixed on her own, went wide.

"Guess you forgot. Mayhap all of you did." Her voice sounded hoarse to her own ears. "I got a name. It's Ravani."

Freki lunged toward her. The other pistol came to her hand without even a thought, the leather gun belt falling unnoticed to the ground. He froze in his tracks with the barrel resting against his cheek.

"You be calm," Hob said. "Ain't no one been shot yet. I'm wantin' to keep it that way." She thought about Coyote telling her that they weren't a military unit, not really, they were a family. She had never truly felt it until now, as certainty welled up in her chest. "Ravani he called me, and that's damnwell what I am."

"He never out and said you were to follow him," Geri snarled, eyes burning.

"I been followin' him my whole life." She glanced at Dambala, Akela, the few older Wolves left. "This ain't ever been a democracy. I'm his kin, like he was kin to the Ravani afore him. Anyone got a problem with that, I can send you to argue with Old Nick."

Geri stared at her, through her, like he was calculating if she really could pull the trigger. She didn't know the answer herself, and didn't want to know.

Uncertainty showed in Geri's eyes, then he looked at the ground. "What's it to be, Ravani?" Freki said nothing. He didn't have to. There was a faint smile on his lips, like a flitting trick of the light.

"We got a funeral to see to. And a wake. And then we got jobs." Her hands dropped to her sides. The pistols radiated the heat of the sun into her legs. "Get movin', all o' ya," she said, loud enough to reach every man around them. "We got an old wolf to burn."

There were murmurs and mutters, but none from the two men closest to her. Geri looked her in the eye once, nodded, and turned to go. She picked the belt up off the ground and put it on properly, holstered the pistols as the men filtered away to grab what passed for funeral finery and their best liquor.

"Gettin' bitched by a woman," Bhima muttered behind her. When he was younger, he'd gotten himself busted right and proper a time or two by Makaya and had choked on it. "Ain't natural at all."

Silently, she asked the ghost of Old Nick that she could just about feel at her shoulder, smirking into her ear, what she should do. There was no answer, not even of the useless, enigmatic variety that he loved so well. He was gone, she realized, and he never would have faced such words himself anyway.

She turned on her heel. With one hand she grabbed the man's jacket, yanked him around to face her. He was as tall as her, twice as wide, at least ten years older. "Now listen good," she snarled. "Just 'cause I got nothin' dangling between my legs don't mean I'm deaf. You want to fight me, then you do it to my face." She held her hand in front of his eyes. Flames flared up over her fingers, flickering in time with the adrenaline-fired beat of her heart. Old Nick had always wanted it secret, even from those who might as well have been his kin. She was done with that, she decided. Done with the secrets and the silences and the never getting a straight goddamn answer about anything. "This ain't natural either. I got something you don't. I'm something you ain't. Follow or leave, I don't give a fuck, but I hear you dropping shit from your mouth again and I'll burn you to dust.

"Coyote!" she snapped. She knew he was there and close, as sure as she could see Bhima's heartbeat fluttering at his neck. Coyote had been waiting in her shadow since she'd come down to the training yard. "Take care of this discipline problem. I got better things to do."

Coyote stepped out from around Dambala. It seemed natural, right, that suddenly he was the person she'd go to, just like Makaya and then Dambala had been Nick's choice. His hand replaced hers on the man's jacket. "Oh, Bhima, Bhima, Bhima. We are going to have such *fun* today, you and I."

And from where he stood, Dambala caught her eye

and nodded slowly, a smile tugging at his lips.

A test, she realized. It had been a test from him, from the other oldsters like Akela and Coyote, to see if she'd stand for herself and out-piss them all. Hob swallowed hard against her churning stomach. She kept her steps slow, steady, as she walked back to the office – it really was *her* office now, *her* ugly desk. She set the pistols among the files but didn't sit, instead leaning against the window frame. The intense afternoon sun fell across her shoulder and arm.

She took a cigarette from the crumpled foil packet in her pocket, then lit it with a snap of her fingers. "It's a joke, ain't it. Your last stupid joke, on everyone." A stupider, meaner joke than sending a girl out into the desert to survive or die, and then taking her home and giving her his name. She took in a long, shaky drag of smoke. The small breeze that was the only breath of such a hot day felt cool on her damp cheeks. "I still hate you, you old bastard. But I'll do you proud. See if I don't."

CHAPTER TWENTY-FOUR

Mag felt like her eyes were about to roll out of her skull. She'd been staring at the coded numbers in Clarence's ledger so long that they swam in front of her, rearranged themselves, danced in mocking little lines. So much water, so many shares of food, so much spare cash – never enough of that, never – and eight different requests over three different towns from miners who'd gotten hurt or taken sick or gotten disciplined and needed help.

They'd have to pass the hat around again, she decided. That was the only way to make any of this work. And they needed more people, to reach out to more mining towns since the farmers had sent her packing, find better ways of communicating, and–

She felt a hot breath pass over her shoulder, like someone's hand resting there, if a hand could be so hot or made of nothing but air. She still felt the weight of it, a palpable thing, the tug of fingers in a strong grip, squeezing. Something acrid and sweet caught at the back of her throat, just a hint of that smell Mama had always hated, the kind that came from those long black cigarettes. Mag turned her head, half expecting to see – "Uncle Nick?"

Ridiculous. He was sick, hadn't left his base in weeks, though he wrote to her regular enough. Mind was playing tricks on her.

The sound of someone knocking at the door was a relief, calling her out of that strange fancy. She went to answer, pulling her hat on out of habit. She'd gotten good at ducking under the brim, keeping her face out of view.

A woman dressed in blackened miner's togs waited on the other side. Mag didn't recognize her immediately, strange, since she knew all Clarence's regular visitors and conspirators on sight by now. "Can I–"

"Clarence here?" the woman interrupted.

"He's on shift. What do you need him for?"

"You a relative of his?"

"Sister," Mag said. Safe enough answer, even though she and Clarence looked nothing alike. But it had another significance. After watching the woman's expression, tense like she was fit to snap, Mag listened to the instinct that whispered in her, *this is one of yours*. "Got kicked out by my ma and pa."

The woman nodded sharply. "Then I need your help."

"Come on in. You want coffee, or lemonade?" Different kind of ritual, that, and just as important. Mag got them both glasses of lemonade and settled them in the kitchen, though she still took care to close the account book. "You look like you come a long way," she remarked.

"I come out of Segundo."

"Longer than a long way," Mag said, surprised. Segundo was the second closest town to Newcastle, almost as tightly in the company's grip as Primero. They tended to get the better equipment, the less angry supervisors. "What happened?"

"Somethin' big's comin'," the woman said. "Some kind of... they call it a witch hunt, like anyone but the preacher men believes in that nonsense any more. But they got us building a platform on the train station all special, been pulling double shifts to get it done to their satisfaction. Daughter's been helping me." She glanced at Mag. "Few years younger'n you, I reckon. There been all these special trains comin' in, and the engineer that come with 'em, he–"

She slammed her glass down on the table, lemonade slopping over the sides. "He hurt my little girl. Not just once. And I told the supervisor, I fuckin' *told* him, and the pit boss, and anyone who'd goddamn let me get in a word, even the preacher – and they put a fuckin' disciplinary letter on me, said I was lyin' and makin' trouble and my girl was lyin', and we had no evidence since it was just our word against his, and we better not spread our *slander*. Told me I could buy off the letter with money, but I ain't got money for that. One strike, said if I get another I'm out of work, and..."

Mag swallowed convulsively, feeling sick. She was glad she hadn't tried her own drink; she'd probably throw up. Might drop the glass too. Clear as day, she remembered the sound of a glass shattering to shard, of glass slicing through her palm–

"There ain't nothin' else I can do," the woman said. It was the defeated, hopeless note of her voice that caught Mag's mind out of the hold it had fallen into. Not anger, but despair. "And he'll just keep comin' back. My daughter ain't the only girl in town."

Mag licked her lips with a tongue that felt like leather. Her voice croaked when she tried it, like she'd been screaming even though she hadn't made a sound. "Mr Franklin, right?" she asked.

The woman gave Mag a long, assessing look. "Yeah, that's his name."

Breathe, she had to remind herself to breathe. She was still terrified of him, and hated him all the more for it. This only affirmed the fears she'd had that had kept her silent about her discomfort around him, the threat always hanging over her parents, because blue suits protected their own before anything else.

"Visitor from Rouse heard me making a stink. Told me if anyone could help me, it'd be Clarence Vigil." The woman looked at her levelly. "Ain't no one can take back what he done to my daughter, and no one can fix the black mark against me. But Mr Franklin needs to be stopped."

"What are you looking to do?" Mag asked, trying to think of something, anything. It had seemed so impossible to her, when she'd faced this.

"I want Clarence to get me a gun. No one's gonna sell or give me one in Segundo. But I'm walkin' half dead already if they think I'm a troublemaker. So get me a gun, and I'll take care of it myself."

The thought revolted her, even as Uncle Nick pressing that gun into her hand the night after she'd been rescued from Newcastle had revolted her. She was tired of blood and killing and death. But she also knew that there was no other recourse available. She had nothing but contempt for the company and what it had done to her, to everyone like her.

There was no other recourse but the gun. In a flash of understanding, though, she knew what gun in particular it should be. "Your daughter still needs you," Mag said. "And if you're half as fierce about protectin' your brothers and sisters, we need you too. So I ain't gonna give you a gun."

"But–" the woman started.

Mag held up her hand. "We can't afford their justice. But we can buy our own. Give what you can. I'll cover the rest." She'd eavesdropped on Uncle Nick enough as a girl to know what the price would be, and she'd figure it out. She'd needed to pass the hat anyway, and inventories were simple to fiddle if you were clever enough. "Tell me when the next train of his is coming in, so I can tell 'em. And you need to not be in town that day, you or your daughter. Take a day off, go to Primero for the theater. Somethin'. But make sure people know you're gone so they can't pin nothin' on you."

The woman looked slightly stunned. "Who you gonna buy?"

"Ghosts," Mag said. "A whole pack of 'em."

CHAPTER TWENTY-FIVE

Hob did her part to send Old Nick off when it was time. She drank whiskey mixed with Tabasco and gunpowder because that was the way he'd liked it. Her stomach felt like it was on fire, her tongue slack in her mouth. They made a bonfire out in the desert, far enough from the base that it wouldn't betray their location if someone noticed the light and smoke.

Drunk and shouting, they circled the bonfire, dancing with their arms to the sky to the sound of drum and guitar and concertina, only stopping to drink more, to gasp out whatever ridiculous stories they knew about Nick. Half of them sounded made up, but Hob was beyond caring. It didn't matter what reality had been; Nick was legend now.

Hob stared deep into the heart of the fire as it sparked, swaying as the men sang another drinking song about beautiful women and randy old Wolves. The fire roared and spat and at its heart wings unfurled, the phoenix raising its head to give a soundless cry. Flame burst into the air, a hot white flash that left everyone momentarily blinded and laughing drunkenly about the gunpowder in Nick's bones. Hob raised her gaze, wobbling with burned-in shadows, to the night sky and watched the phoenix circle once, bright as a comet, before streaking out into the horizon.

She sucked in a breath and blinked her eye hard, squinting against the flames as she strode in close. And while Coyote shouted something that sounded like encouragement, she plunged her hand into the fire and found Nick's hand, now with the flesh all burnt away. She pulled out one of his skeletal fingers, cradling the bones in her palm until she'd sucked all the heat from them, so much that yellow-white cinders bled from her skin. The men cheered for her, called her the Ravani, slapping her so broadly on the back that she almost dropped the bones. She curled her fingers around them tight until she had a chance to wrap them up in a handkerchief, like she'd done not long ago for the same bones belonging to Old Nick's little brother.

The Bone Collector should have this, since he and Nick had been so cozy, and she would have questions for him when she handed it over. Though at this hour and with this much whiskey in her blood, she had no idea what those questions might be.

To Hob's bleary, aching, hungover eyes, the pathetically short stack of job offers still looked like an insurmountable mountain. And the cup of coffee Coyote, looking disgustingly chirpy, set down next to it sounded like a gunshot against the wood.

"Bala's making bacon sandwiches," he offered. "Figured I'll grab you one."

"Don't talk to me about food."

"Grease'll do you good." He nudged the coffee cup a little closer. "Drink up, go through the stack, and I'll hand out the assignments."

"You're a fuckin' monster." She picked up the cup two-handed and scalded her tongue and throat on it. But coming out the other side, she did feel a little less like death. Even if she ended the cup with a dangerous belch.

The job offers were slim pickings, some of it stuff she wouldn't touch with a dead man's hand, stealing from the townsfolk instead of the company. That was a road to hell she had no intention of walking. But there was a little escort job they could do, even if the offered pay wasn't too good, a small pack of bandits that needed to be wiped out, and–

Hob looked dumbly at the familiar handwriting, the soft loops like a smile.

"Boss?" Coyote said.

She waved him off and opened it, read what was inside. "Huh."

"What?"

She offered the letter to him, the terms in black and white and very readable thanks to Mag's neat handwriting. "Mag thinks we should try our hand at policing."

Coyote scanned over the letter. "Policing doesn't seem to pay much," he observed.

Hob curled her lip. "Truth. But it ain't a half bad thought. Because if it gets known we take jobs like this, they'll come in more regular than anyone'll like to think, I reckon."

"Mmm. The fun will be getting in and out of the towns." And the way he said *fun*, all smiles, made it clear he meant *hazard*. "We're going to have to keep a roster of fresh faces that no one knows. Or find better ways of disguising ourselves."

"Or better ways of trackin' people down when they ain't in town. Smart things."

"It's going to escalate."

"It's already fuckin' escalated," Hob said. "Ain't gonna get any less goddamn escalated after Nick murdered a fuckin' pit boss in front of God and everyone."

Coyote shrugged.

Hob gave him a suspicious look. "Ain't you supposed to be tellin' me my crazy ideas are pure gold?"

"Oh no. My job is to disagree with you enough that you think your crazy through to the end," Coyote said. "And suggest a bit more if you're not going far enough. Lucky for both of us I'm so flexible."

"I ain't had enough coffee for this." She rubbed her forehead. "Take Freki and Geri. You run this one. I got other shit to do. And get me my fuckin' bacon sandwich."

He threw a parody of a salute her way and turned to leave.

"Wait."

"Yes?"

She squinted at him again. "When you do this job... get a couple of the wolf head coins. Leave 'em over his eyes."

"Ooh, dramatic. I like it."

She snorted. "If we're gonna declare we're open for

the justice business, we better make it clear when it's that kind of job we're doing."

For a moment, something serious shadowed his already dark eyes. "You'd better be certain, if you're going to make this sort of move and start calling it justice."

"Yeah," she agreed. "But when it's coming from Mag, *that* I'll trust."

"So Mag's the judge and you're the executioner," Coyote mused. "I always did think you were both cute as two buttons."

"Sandwich. Now."

Sandwich and a pot's worth of coffee later, Hob felt dangerously close to human. All but alone at the base, she took the time to do one more thing she'd been avoiding – sorting through Nick's things. Most would go to Mag as his last living blood relative, and that was a whole other visit that she wasn't looking forward to. His files for the Wolves, Hob would be keeping, but there were some diaries that should be passed along. Hob had to resist the urge to crack them open and look them over, but it didn't feel quite right. Nick had never told her that shit out of his own choice; she knew all she needed to about him. His clothes, she decided to keep. Nick had been skinny as a rail and only a few centimeters taller than her; they actually fit pretty well. There weren't enough alterations that could be done to let his suits fit Mag's shorter, plumper frame, even if she'd want to wear men's clothes. Mag had always been one for skirts. So it wasn't selfishness that had her keeping those, and his fine array of weapons. Knives and garrotes also weren't Mag's style. But a few pieces of jewelry, his books, a chess set – those she packed up to be taken to Ludlow.

Old Nick's blackened fingerbones still sat in the middle of the scarred desktop, mocking and profane. Hob took the smooth bones up and rolled them between her fingers, taking in the scent of char. For a moment, she imagined there was some beat of fire still left there, a remnant of the old man, but it was too childish. She shook a handkerchief from her pocket and tucked the bones away.

Before heading out, she stuck her head in the kitchen. "Gonna run an errand, Lobo."

The cook grinned at her, head tilted to point his good ear her way. "More like Nick every day, you are."

She perked up one eyebrow. "He go off on his own little errands much?"

"All the time, once everyone was out. Just atween you and me."

"Yeah, just atween you 'n' me." Hob touched the brim of her hat, but hesitated before going out the door. "You and Old Nick, you got a lot of stuff just atween the two of you?"

"If I told you, wouldn't just be atween me and him, would it?"

Hob parked the motorcycle in the lee of the ruined works at Pictou, sticking to the long shadow. It gave her an odd, ghosty feeling, wondering if Old Nick had done this same thing regular before, come to chat with the Bone Collector and taken these same steps. She wasn't sure if she liked him haunting her because she wasn't ready to let him go, or if she wished he'd go away for good.

Hob pricked one finger with a knife, squeezed out a few bright drops onto the low drift of a dune. The sand drank the blood in quick, leaving nothing but a sticky, rusty spot behind. Blood or no, the Bone Collector didn't rise from the ruined basements like magic. Hob hunkered down in the shade to wait.

Drawn by the barest scent of blood – and thus moisture – a great eagle cut across the sunlight, slowly circling the area, trying to find the source of the smell. It made a hole in the sky, shadow trailing along on the ground, rippling up and down the dunes. Hob drew one of her pistols and watched it warily; if the eagle went into a dive, she'd only have a second or two before it would hit her. But with a cut that small and her a dot in the shade, the eagle couldn't seem to get a fix on her. It just circled and circled, waiting alone.

Hours passed, the eagle's circling making her dizzy. She didn't dare even go for a sip of water, not with the bird close enough to smell it. Blood, he'd said. Blood would call. And it had before, out by Ludlow when she'd punched him one. Maybe that was why he didn't want to come now. After six hours, she gave up, caught between anger and worry, and headed back to base. Nothing could happen to him, though, right? He turned to stone, indestructible.

She tried not to think of men with sledgehammers.

CHAPTER TWENTY-SIX

"You sure you don't want a different beer, sweetie? You been nursing that one an awful long time," the waitress said. While the words were outwardly friendly, Coyote could hear the impatience beneath them easily enough.

He smiled. "Please, yes. It's gone a bit flat. Or do you have a sarsaparilla instead?" A drink was the last thing he wanted. The very last thing. He might start crying yellow tears at any moment.

"Yeah, we do." She whisked the glass off the table. "Decided what you're gonna eat yet?"

"My friends will be here soon, I promise." He gave her his most charming smile. Where *were* Freki and Geri? He'd expected them over an hour ago – hence the waitress's not unjustified irritation. It wasn't as if he'd given them the difficult part of the spying. He'd been trailing their target, while he'd set them on plotting the escape route and giving the town a quick look over. He really shouldn't have been sitting here, slowly drinking his way through the petty cash they'd been allotted.

The doors to the restaurant opened and at last the dark bulk of the twins came into view. Coyote waved them over, making a point of shooting the waitress a bright smile, to which in answer she only rolled her eyes.

He waited just long enough for them to sit and order drinks before he hurried off to take the mightiest piss he'd ever had in his life. Then, back at the table, fresh drink untouched and two smirking pups in front of him, Coyote drawled, "I do hope you were both having fun."

He was rewarded by Geri sitting back a little in his chair. Geri at least knew not to cross a man who smiled all the time. "Busted my ass," he said. "But I got the route plotted out. Three of 'em, just in case you fuck things up. Stashed some chemical lights as well, 'cause one of 'em is completely unlit at night."

"How good of you." Coyote glanced at Freki. "And you?"

"Don't think we should leave in the night," Freki said. "Not if we don't have to."

"Explain your reasoning." The plan had been simple enough: Coyote found out what hotel their target liked to stay in at night, got them a nearby room, and he'd do the deed with the two younger Wolves acting as lookouts. After, off all three of them would go, toddling off to pick up their motorcycles from wherever Geri had found to stash them, then into the night with no one the wiser.

"Something going on here in the morning," Freki said. "Some big company frou-fra."

"All the more reason to be quick about it and out long before daylight."

"They're callin' it a witch hunt. And it's the reason they built the special platform on the train station."

Freki shrugged. "Sounds like the kind of thing the boss'd want to know about."

Coyote sucked at his teeth for a moment, thinking. He hadn't heard of anything like that, not since he'd come to Tanegawa's World eighteen years ago as a refugee from his own family. But he knew what the so-called *witchiness* was, or as much as anyone did. It was impossible to not know about it, being friends with Old Nick and then Hob. "How time dependent are the escape routes?" he asked Geri.

Geri held one hand flat, let it see-saw back and forth. "One of 'em is solid. Other two... I could go do a little more leg work."

It was a calculated risk. If there was some sort of company-wide event, then that was a very likely time for their target's absence to be noted. On the other hand, with the distraction, it would also probably be relatively simple for them to slip out before the net got too tight. Coyote hadn't ended up where he was because he tended to caution. The thrill of risk was its own reward. That this one might come with useful information was a bonus. "Do it." He slid a room key for the hotel across the table. "Head back once you're done. I'll keep shadowing our dear friend." He wiggled a finger, indicating the low TransRift building across the street. Thankfully, in all the time he'd been waiting for the twins, Mr Franklin had followed his reported work schedule and stayed inside.

"Get to sit and drink beer while we sweat," Geri grumbled.

"You wouldn't be so envious if you had to piss as badly as I did before you showed up."

•••

Coyote trailed Mr Franklin all over town, huddling in an alley and entertaining himself with a deck of cards while the man had a nice dinner, keeping an eye on him across two bars where he seemed to be having business meetings. Disappointingly, he didn't come out of either drunk.

When Mr Franklin at last went back to the hotel, Freki and Geri had thankfully gotten there first. They gave him time to settle, and then Geri took position in the hallway near the man's room. Freki boosted Coyote across the balcony, and he quietly broke the lock and let himself into the room.

If he'd been expecting to interrupt some scene of depravity – possible, considering the crime for which this execution was to be carried out – he'd have been sorely disappointed. Mr Franklin was utterly banal as targets went, which made him a bit creepier in Coyote's opinion. He stood at the washstand, dressed in crisp boxers and an undershirt, carefully flossing his teeth as he listened to some rather staticky recorded music.

As intent as Mr Franklin was on his dental hygiene, it was trivially easy for Coyote to slip the garrote over his head and cut off protest and struggle with a practiced twist of the hands and a knee to the back. It was a move he'd learned and perfected by grace of being one of the shortest men on base, so of course Old Nick had thought it was hilarious to send him after the biggest fellows that could be found. He shoved the man hard against the edge of the counter and let him flail uselessly, scrabble at the mirror, and knock over the soap and other toiletries. The mix of

mint and floral scents that brought up was an odd
one, but it could have been a lot worse. Then it was
all over but for the gurgling, flopping, and twitching,
which had never been Coyote's favorite part.

Dead, Mr Franklin drooled crimson blood and
white toothpaste foam onto the hotel carpet. Coyote
dragged him over to the bed and lay him out neatly
– the boss *had* wanted theatrical – and covered his
sightless eyes with the two coins. He'd initially offered
to scrawl the man's crime across his chest with ink –
or blood, if they wanted to get *really* theatrical – but
had that idea vetoed because it too closely fingered his
victims. Fair enough. They'd know the justice was for
them, or they'd just be relieved that Mr Franklin was
dead, and it didn't really matter either way to Coyote.

And then, because no one had told him not to and
he'd wasted a lot of company money on drinks and
food, he carefully relieved the man of every bit of
spare cash, though after a moment of consideration,
he left the jewelry alone. He cleaned up all the traces
of himself, rinsed his garrote in the sink, pocketed it,
and let himself into the hallway. After he shut the
door behind himself, he stripped his gloves and gave
Geri a nod. They paused just long enough to collect
Freki, then ghosted down the short stairwell, into the
service hallways, and out the kitchen.

"Your show now," Coyote told Geri.

Geri led them along a quiet route through back
streets and the occasional warehouse. Rather than
head for the gates, however, they came to rest by the
train station.

"Close as we're gonna get," Geri said, letting them

through the side door of a machine shop. The air was heavy with the smell of oil and metal. "But I checked the sightings, we got a good, straight line to the platform."

"We're spying, not blowing off heads."

Geri shrugged. "Good view either way."

Coyote broke out his deck of cards and proceeded to clean the boys out of all their pocket money. At some point, he thought idly, he really ought to teach them how to spot when someone was cheating at cards.

Activity at the station started up before dawn, a security sweep going over the immediate area. Coyote watched it all through a scope. "Don't think they'll be coming out this far," he commented. "But you got the route out, just in case?"

"Yeah, it's good," Geri growled.

"I'll keep an eye on it," Freki said, moving off.

Coyote hummed an acknowledgment, eyes fixed on the show. Green-uniformed guards put out crowd control barriers, and– "Hah. Actual red carpet. How fancy."

"Must be some VIP."

As the sun rose, townspeople and miners still black with pit dust filled up the space around the concrete platform, spilling out into the streets beyond. It wasn't a large enough area for all of them, but they seemed determined to try to fit. Or rather, the Mariposa men seemed dedicated to making them all get in.

"Looks like they got guards going through the buildings," Geri said from his windows.

"Is our position compromised?" Coyote asked, still

watching the platform.

"Not yet," Freki said, after a moment of hesitation. "I'll keep watch."

At the station, the smooth, bullet-like shape of a train slid in. It wasn't one of the massive long-distance freight engines with its unending line of cars, but rather a sleek, low-slung model obviously built for speed, only pulling three passenger cars. "Think it's about to get interesting," Coyote murmured.

Not nearly as quickly as he would have liked, more guards coming out of the rear two cars. His patience was rewarded when the door of the first opened and a man in a blue suit followed the inevitable wave of green-uniformed security.

Coyote frowned, squinting down the scope like that would somehow give him a better look. The man looked really familiar, but that was impossible – right? Not the face, so much, but the way he walked... nah, it had been years. Things changed too much in eighteen years.

Those thoughts were swept away by the next man out, tall and thin and walking like all his limbs weren't quite jointed the right way. "Oh *fuck*," Coyote breathed.

"What?" Geri demanded.

"They've brought their fucking Weatherman out here." May it not occur to them to ask how he knew what a Weatherman looked like.

"Didn't the boss say she shot him?" Geri said. Coyote felt him try to grab the scope, and slapped his hands away.

"Either they brought a new one in record time, or

he wasn't as dead as she thought." He focused on the Weatherman, scanning over the crowd, then indicating someone. A plump young woman was brought forward, her hair in two plaits. As soon as the Weatherman got a better look at her, he waved her away. He grabbed a man, hand over his face, and swayed almost like they were dancing. Then the unfortunate bastard collapsed, and guards moved forward to drag him off to be stowed in one of the cars. His family followed, chivvied along. Coyote's stomach twisted. Whatever was happening, it wasn't good.

He liked it even less when the Weatherman had a second woman dragged out of the crowd, one with mousy brown hair in two braids. Coyote had never really believed in coincidence, not when it was in the middle of some job; he'd learned that one on his mother's knee.

"You seen enough?" Freki asked from the other side of the room.

"Why?"

"Our window's getting pretty narrow."

Coyote grimaced as the Weatherman returned to moving through the crowd. "Then we'd better go." There might be more to the spectacle to see, but it wouldn't do them much good if they were pinched while witnessing it. He stuffed the scope in his pocket.

Freki took them into a narrow alley between the machine shop and a warehouse. He stopped at the corner and frantically waved Coyote and Geri back into the shop, following a moment later himself.

"What's the situation?" Coyote asked.

"Whole crowd of greenbellies out in the street.

Hanging out in the shadow of our building, that's why I couldn't see 'em from the window."

Elsewhere in the building a metal door banged open. "Guess they're getting around to this shop," Geri muttered.

Coyote held up one hand, trying to think. The warehouse next door was doubtless for storing parts used in the shop. There had to be some way rigged to transport the parts more efficiently than walking them back and forth on a dolly, particularly on the second floor of the shop. He'd never gone wrong counting on the habit of engineers and mechanics to spend a lot of effort building their way out of a minor annoyance. "Upstairs. There should be some kind of conveyer to the warehouse next door. Find it."

Below them, a voice called, "Attendance for the celebration is mandatory. Come out now, and you will not be fined."

Geri shot Coyote a look, but he only shrugged. "If they knew we were in here, they'd be coming directly for us," he whispered.

The three of them spread out across the second floor with quick efficiency, searching the outer walls. Coyote had just broken the lock to get himself into the office space – stupid place for a conveyor, but you never knew – when Freki caught his sleeve. The big man jerked his chin back the way he'd come.

Feet clanged on the stairs coming toward them.

Geri had a plastic flap over a rubber conveyer belt pulled aside. Hot air flowed from the darkness within. Coyote grimaced as he stepped onto the belt and kept going, bent almost double.

"Really fuckin' small in there," Geri muttered.

"Your shoulders will fit. The rest of you can make it." Coyote kept going. It was hot in the metal tube, bad enough that sweat immediately started rolling off his nose even though it was only seven meters long at most. He slid out the other side and held the matching plastic curtain for the two younger men, who'd had to crawl through on their hands and knees. Freki dealt with it stoically enough, but Geri swore a blue streak under his breath as he tumbled to the synthcrete floor on the other side.

They hurried down to the street. "Access panel to the maintenance tunnels should be one building over from here," Geri said. The old settlers had taken to digging tunnels to get away from the dust storms, a habit the company hadn't quite managed to break when it built its first few towns.

They had to slide into the next alley as a bored guard standing nearby turned his head, but no one else stood between them and the square trapdoor. Geri grunted as he hauled it up. Coyote grabbed the flashlight out of his pocket and twisted it on, clamping it between his teeth before he headed down the ladder bolted to the side of the tunnel.

It was cool down there, strangely so after the familiar heat of the morning. He let his light play over the smooth walls. "You know where we're going?" he said. No need to whisper now, either.

"Yeah. I got a map." Geri closed the trapdoor slowly after his brother. "And Freki, watch–"

Thump

"–your head," Geri finished. "Low ceilings."

"Noticed," his brother growled.

It wasn't an unpleasant walk to the motorcycles, which Geri had hidden in a vehicle yard. They headed for one of the small gates in the walls, opposite the train station. The gates were always manned, but usually only just for form's sake. For safety, Coyote decided that he'd go up to talk to the guard alone – this wasn't a usual day.

"Turn right back around," the guard, a young man with a peeling nose, said as he rolled up. "Wall's locked down until the celebration's done."

"Celebration?" Coyote cocked his head quizzically. He fell into his best impression of miner talk. "Didn't get invited to no celebration."

"At the train station," the guard said. "Everyone's to report there."

"But I ain't from here. Was just visitin' my auntie, she took sick."

"Doesn't matter. Report to the train station."

Coyote sighed, pretending defeat. "All right. All right. I'll just…" He turned his motorcycle around and started away, looking over his shoulder. "It won't be too much–" He let the motorcycle fall over, apparently pinning him. "Shit! Oh shit, my leg!"

The guard seemed caught between annoyance and alarm. "You're fine," he said.

"Oh God, I think – I felt the bone snap," Coyote wailed.

Concern finally won its battle in the guard, and he came forward to lever the motorcycle off Coyote. Past his shoulder, Coyote saw Freki and Geri rolled silently by to the gate.

"Oh thank you – oh God, is that blood?" Coyote asked.

The guard rolled his eyes. "You're *fine*. Now, I can call for the doctor, but you're still going to have to go to the station. You get me?"

Coyote blinked away the few tears he'd managed to coax to his eyes. "Got no choice, if you're gonna help me... Hey, how come they get to leave and I didn't?" He pointed toward the gate.

"What–?" The guard spun, just in time to see Freki's rear wheel cross the threshold of the now-open gate. "Son of a bitch – you stay right here!"

"Couldn't go anywhere, not with my poor leg danglin' by a thread." Coyote almost sang the words.

The guard raced out the gate, fumbling for his pistol and shouting, "You two – get back here!"

Coyote flipped the motorcycle vertical with only a little grunt of effort and hopped back on. He revved the electric motor and spun out the gate behind the guard, reaching out to slap the man on the back as he passed. "Thanks, buddy!"

The wild shots that rang out after him just made him laugh all the harder.

Shige couldn't quite escape the vague feeling of disappointment that this third trip out with the Weatherman hadn't been nearly so interesting as the first, though none of that thought showed on his face. He should be concerned enough by the new set of people Mr Green sent off to occupy the holding pens in the third train car. He tucked his notepad away, prepared to take his last, formal leave of the town's security head when a new guard in green came running up, his face pale.

"Sir? There's been an incident."

The senior security man cast a wary eye in Shige's direction, and received only a bland smile in return. "What kind of incident?" he asked.

"We found a body in the Watercourse Hotel." The guard cast his own nervous look at Shige. "Company man. And... definitely murdered."

"If you'll excuse me, Mr Rollins..." the security head started.

"Since I am here, why don't I come with you," Shige said smoothly. "I'm certain Vice President Meetchim would be concerned by this. While it's not necessarily connected to Mr Green's visit, the timing is a bit suspicious."

The senior man didn't look happy, but also knew he didn't have a choice. "Just stay out of the way," he growled.

"Of course," Shige said. "I'm here only to help."

He'd seen far more violent death scenes than the one in the hotel room, though he made a good act of blanching and pretending to be shocked at the sight of such violence. It was convincing enough that it earned him a few covertly contemptuous looks from the security men; all the better. But the state of the body was definitely of interest, neatly arranged on the bed though the man had plainly been murdered elsewhere in the room, and his eyes covered with coins. Blood had dried dark and tacky in a ring around his neck – he'd been killed with some sort of thin wire, a garrote, Shige read it to be. Not the most common murder weapon around here.

"Have you identified this man?" he asked.

"Company ID was left in his wallet. Emmett Franklin, conductor for the regular passenger runs to the outer towns. Though he stopped into Segundo regular enough, and was pulling extra shifts here to help us get ready for you."

Shige lifted one of the silver coins and inspected the wolf's head stamped on both sides. "Not company issued," he said, to state the obvious. It was a hook thrown out, inviting information.

"Illegal scrip," the security head said. "Some of the towns get cute about this stuff. We stamp it out wherever we find it."

"And some of the bandit outfits," the more junior guard murmured. His superior shot him a withering look.

Shige concluded it was probably one of those "bandit" outfits, then. "I wonder why someone would want so badly to kill one of our model employees."

"Mine rats have filed some spurious complaints," the security head growled. "We'll be checking them first."

Shige set the coin back down with care over the dead man's half-open eye, fixing the lines of it in his mind. He'd never been one to believe in coincidence in the middle of an operation – his mother had seen to that.

CHAPTER TWENTY-SEVEN

Coyote's party was well past due, and Hob didn't like it one bit. She kept an eye on the front gates out the window of Nick's – *her* – well-placed office. She'd never realized what a good window it was into observing the rest of the base. Let her feel downright godlike – probably how the old bastard had seemed to know everything that was going on.

She saw the minute the gate opened and the three motorcycles rolled in. A knot of tension she hadn't even consciously felt eased off her shoulders. The day would come, probably soon, when someone wouldn't come back and she'd have to face that it was in part her doing. But today wasn't going to be that day. She waited until she saw them emerge from the garage, then headed into the exercise yard to meet them halfway.

"You're late," she greeted Coyote.

"And we have a story to tell." Coyote glanced at Freki and Geri. "You mind if we tell it while these two bottomless pits are feeding their faces? I've been hearing their stomachs growl for the last six hours, and it's about driven me spare."

Hob waved them toward the kitchen. "Could use a bite to eat, myself."

Lobo greeted the small crowd of people in his kitchen with no more than a grumble. He threw some sandwiches together for them to start, and got some tortillas cooking on the grill for the next round as Freki, Geri, and Coyote tore in.

"The job went fine," Coyote said. "Message left, and it ought to be spreading through the town rumor mill like fire by now."

"Then why so late?" Hob asked.

"Freki noticed unusual activity at the train station, so we decided to stay the night and observe. They had a special train come in from Newcastle at first light."

"Go ahead, you got my attention." She pulled Nick's cigarette case – now hers – from her pocket and pulled one out, lit it with a snap of her fingers.

"They brought the Weatherman to Segundo and had him work the crowd like nothing I've ever seen."

She almost dropped her cigarette. "Can't be. I killed him."

Coyote shrugged. "Either it's the same one – and from how you described him he sure fits the bill – or they brought one in on a special ship."

"You sure?"

He ripped a bite off his sandwich and gave her one of the stinkiest looks she'd ever been hit with, Old Nick's included. "Do you think you could ever mistake a Weatherman for a normal person?"

Hob grimaced. "No."

"So we'll assume that the impossible has happened." Coyote continued on, describing what he'd seen in

Segundo as Hob listened grimly. He finished with: "It gets even better. I think he was looking for you."

Her blood felt fit to freeze in her veins. "The hell you mean?"

"He was pulling every woman with brown hair in braids out of the crowd."

"Fuck," she breathed.

"So yes, I think it's the same one. And I think he hasn't forgotten you." Coyote said, and shook his head. "I've been here almost as long as the three of you have been alive, and I've never heard of anything like this happening."

Lobo cleared his throat. "Might know a thing, myself."

"Well, spit it out," Hob said.

"'Bout thirty years ago, they sent a Weatherman through to find everyone with witchiness and take 'em out. Called it a witch hunt, even. They only picked up a few people in Primero and Segundo before it had folks so scared that they plain murdered the witchy ones in their towns themselves."

"Why the hell they doin' this now?" Hob asked.

"Back then, they said there was a madman in the desert who tore a train in half with his bare hands and witchiness, if you believe that kind of bullshit story." Lobo shrugged. "Oldsters said there was a witch hunt years afore that too. Happened right around when Pictou got tore down."

Hob opened her mouth to protest, to say nothing big and flashy had happened recently —only it had. And it'd been them. She glanced at Coyote, who had his head tilted, eyebrows up as if to say, *no shit*. "If they're at Segundo, they gonna keep movin' further out?"

"Went through to all the towns before, though they weren't in no hurry. By the time they got to the farm towns like Harmony and Blessid, weren't no one left for them to take."

Hob pinched off her half-finished cigarette. All she could think about now was Mag, and whatever had happened to her while TransRift had her locked in that damn lab, whatever that "war in her blood" was the Bone Collector had mentioned. What if someone in Ludlow decided she was a bit strange and put a bullet in her brain? "Fuck this. I'm goin' to Ludlow. Any of you boys want to come?"

Hob rode to Ludlow like she expected a massacre, hunkered down over her motorcycle at full throttle, Freki and Geri behind her. It almost felt like an insult that the town was humming along, busy as could be, without even the smallest sign of trouble. The guard at the gate even waved to them when he let them in.

They parked their motorcycles out behind a warehouse, and then hurried over to Clarence Vigil's home. Mag answered the door. She still looked strange to Hob's eyes with her hair short and black.

"Hob? What are–" Mag peered around her, eyes going wide as she saw Freki and Geri. "There some trouble with the job I sent you?" Hob had nearly forgotten about it.

"That's well and done," Geri said, from behind her.

"Invite us in for lemonade, Mag," Hob said. "We got other bad news aplenty."

It was iced tea instead of lemonade, but Mag saw them to the parlor and gave them each a glass properly before sitting down herself in a threadbare armchair. No one seemed interested in drinking. Hob stayed perched on the edge of her seat and waved Geri on to give Mag the brief report on the task in Segundo.

Mag nodded grimly as Geri spoke, though her eyes were fixed on Hob. When he finished, she said: "You're wearin' my uncle's pistols, Hob. I saw 'em at the door. He's dead, ain't he."

"That's the first bad news," Hob said. She nudged the saddlebag she'd brought with her. "Figured you'd want some of his things. You can go through 'em later, toss what doesn't suit."

Mag nodded, swallowing hard, but there were no tears, just a pinched, tired look on her face. "I had a feeling, last week. Like he was standing over my shoulder. Thought it was just my mind playing tricks on me, but I guess not."

Part of her was relieved that Mag seemed disinclined to cry, but there was something far more disturbing about those dry, tired eyes. "Bad news don't stop there, though."

"Just out with it. I've had so much bad lately, bit more ain't gonna add to the load."

Geri recounted what his team had seen in Segundo, and Hob repeated what Lobo had said about the witch hunts. "So we come for you. I don't know when the Weatherman's gonna get here, but you don't want to be here when he does. So we come to take you back to the base."

Mag pushed away her untouched glass of tea with

care. "No, thank you, I'm gonna stay right here. But I thank you for lettin' me know you got my job done."

"Were you not listenin'?" Hob surged to her feet and started pacing. "They're gonna come here, and soon. And when they do, you know for damn sure they're gonna take you. They sure wanted you before. And before that, for all we fuckin' know, folks are gonna go crazy around here and might just do the job themselves."

"I heard you just fine." Mag's face was pale and set, an angle to her chin that reminded Hob of Nick when he had his back up. She'd always thought it was because he was a stubborn old goat, but maybe it ran in the family. "I'm done running. I got things to do here. And I don't think they'll turn on me. I'm in deep."

"Fear does funny things to folk."

Mag continued calmly as if she hadn't even heard Hob. "And if the Weatherman does come here and I can't find a way to hide, I'll put a bullet in my own brain first."

"You lost your fuckin' mind, Mag?"

Mag's jaw set in an all-too-familiar way. Her expression had been reminiscent before, but now it was damned eerie, down to the way her lips thinned out. "You ain't leavin' me to twist this time, Hob. I just don't want to be rescued."

"Fine," Hob snarled. "Guess if I ever needed proof crazy runs in your fuckin' family, this here is it. But if you change your mind, you know where our drop boxes are around here. We'll come for you."

"I know that." Mag smiled. "And it means a lot to me."

Freki and Geri followed Hob out of the house, moving out to one at each shoulder as they walked into the street. "Didn't much like that," Freki said.

Hob snorted. "I didn't much like it either."

"We gonna just let it go?" Geri asked.

"Hell no." Hob waited until they were around the corner, then turned to them. "I want a good listen around the town. See if we can find out when the Weatherman might be comin'. Then we plan for when we're gonna snatch Mag. She might not like it, but we're all a hell of a lot bigger'n her. I don't mind addin' kidnapping to our list of crimes one bit if it's her."

Geri laughed. "Take her back to the base like that, she'll like as kill you in your bed."

Hob grinned at him. "Good thing I got some strong arms at my back."

CHAPTER TWENTY-EIGHT

The death of Mr Franklin – whom Shige confirmed to his own satisfaction had soundly earned such an ignominious end once he had a chance to do a deep dive into the personnel files – became quite the opportunity. Ms Meetchim, it turned out, also did not believe in coincidences. And for that reason she chose to delay the witch hunt schedule by a week, to give security a chance to find solid leads on the man's death and make certain it wouldn't prove a threat to the continued events. Shige adroitly parlayed that into an opportunity to take a spa weekend, which was to say, a personal weekend for him to do a bit of spying for his own pet project.

He hadn't found any solid answers about the wolf's head coin, but he had found several mentions of a particularly annoying group of bandits that called themselves Ghost Wolves – how melodramatic – and frequented the outer mining towns, particularly Rouse, Shimera, and Ludlow. That alone caught his interest, considering the recent events in Rouse. With judicious use of a fake ID, he booked himself a cheap passenger ticket out to Rouse, then to Ludlow. He could ape the local accent well enough to pass muster and do a bit of nosing around.

The first day in Ludlow, he managed to get a drunk man in one of the saloons talking about the Ghost Wolves without too much prompting, though what he said didn't sound at all like bandits – more like a mercenary company. Not surprising, in Shige's opinion. Everything the company recorded was through the lens of their continued desire for control. Just as everything through the Federal Union had its own flavor, with conflicts labeled as *insurgencies* when outlying worlds didn't understand the wisdom of sheltering under the protective umbrella of the interstellar government. And these days they did love labeling TransRift as a government partner rather than a troublesome corporation that thought itself above all regulation.

From what his drinking companion said, it also sounded as if the Ghost Wolves were connected to the mess in Rouse – unless there were a lot of one-eyed mercenaries running around. Possible, but not likely.

The next day, as he headed to do another round through the public houses in search of a gossip eager to talk, Shige caught sight of a shockingly familiar face. The synthetic taste of strawberries flooded his mouth, another sense-memory reminder: the one-eyed woman who had been involved in the near death of Mr Green and the infiltration of the labs. He paused nearby for a moment as she talked to a large, dark man, likely some flavor of fighter from the way he carried himself. Then he continued on, not wanting to draw attention. He could circle back and try to pick up a tail on her again, now that he knew she was there.

He realized with a secondary shock of alarm, quickly suppressed, that she recognized him on some level as well. She followed him as he headed down the street, her gait casual in a very studied way, her thumbs tucked in her pockets.

Best to get this over with, perhaps, and try to craft it into an informative opportunity. He turned into a side street and felt no real surprise as she closed the distance with long strides. He was less pleased with the sensation of a pistol barrel pressed in the vicinity of his left kidney.

"You got a lot of interest in the private conversations of other people," she said.

Shige raised his hands from his sides enough to show that they were empty, but not enough to make it obvious she had a gun on him. "I'm unarmed."

"Good to know. Guess you can already tell, but I'm not. You see that little alley over there? Why don't we go have us a little chat." She stayed up close to his back – probably to keep the gun hidden from general view.

In the alley, he asked, "May I put my hands down?"

"In a minute." The one-eyed woman patted through his coat, feeling the pockets and sleeves. It was an impressively thorough search – she even checked under his hat and combed her fingers through his hair. She also found no weapons, because he'd specifically come unarmed. While he'd been given standard operative combat training, and was very good at it, having to resort to violence would be far too likely to destroy his cover. She pulled out his wallet from his pocket, took a look at the IDs inside and the large collection of cash. She read, "Now, I'm gonna guess you ain't actually Thomas Dunwell, class C miner, not with your pockets this heavy and your pores that clean. So... James Rolland, executive secretary employed by TransRift, Inc." She said that last sentence with a passable imitation of a central Earth accent, which was curious. She didn't seem the sort to mingle with the executive staff enough to have picked it up. Maybe she merely had a good ear. The one-eyed woman flipped his wallet closed, pressing the barrel of her revolver a little deeper. "I've half a mind to put a hole in your back just for that, 'cept I admit to some curiosity as to why you're dressed like a mine rat, and so far afield."

"I would prefer to not have this conversation facing a wall," Shige said.

"Go ahead and turn around." The moment he complied, she slammed him against the wall, one arm half across his throat and shoulder, the barrel of her revolver denting in the soft underside of his chin. "So, Mr Rolland, what brings you out to Ludlow this fine day?" She stared at him squarely. Her one eye was too blue to be gray, too gray to be really blue, and moved as she scanned over his face, like she was trying to puzzle something out.

"I was looking for you, actually."

She laughed. "What, I haven't pissed enough people off, all I rate is a secretary?"

"I'm not here to kill you."

"Sure hope not, the way you come armed."

Shige considered his possible lines of attack. She seemed the straightforward sort. "If you would look in my wallet again, please bring out the bank card and allow me to touch it." The woman did so, pulling the card with one hand and letting the wallet drop into the dust at their feet while she held the revolver steady with the other. She tucked the bank card into his hand. Shige drew his code symbol over the card, slow enough that it could read his fingerprint at each turn. The card obediently shifted, color flowing over in a wave and turning it to a white ID with the gold Federal Union seal, his picture, and his real name on it. "My real ID, if you would care to check."

She took the card back with her free hand, squinted at it. "Agent of the Federal Union of Systems… I don't even know what that means."

"It means I'm here from the government." He didn't find her response surprising. Federal Union presence was still extremely weak on these backwater planets, even the ones that weren't interdicted by the only source of interstellar travel. The government was still relatively young, after all – there hadn't been a point to an interstellar government until the advent of interstellar travel, and they were still seeking out the scattered, stray colonies of Earth. Too many records lost, too many splinter groups trying very hard to make certain they'd never be found again.

She laughed again. "Ain't no government here but the company."

"You're right, and it's been like that far too long. That's why I'm here. Now, may I please lower my hands?"

She let the revolver drop, spinning it and sliding it back into its holster in one smooth, practiced motion. "Since you asked so pretty."

Shige lowered his hands slowly. "There have been a lot of… rumors about this world, but nothing we've been able to substantiate. I suppose you're aware that TransRift controls all interstellar routes, and no one else has the necessary technology?" He waited for her grudging nod. "Consider the difficulty of investigating a planet when the company can simply refuse to bring us here, and threaten our contracts if we become too insistent. The Federal Union can only lease from them, ships and navigators both. Too much proprietary technology; no one else has made a successful ship design, or even properly navigated a ship into the rifts without a TransRift navigator."

"Got you by the balls," she commented.

"Put simply: yes. I was already in the company's employ under cover, so I was the ideal choice to come and… take a look around."

"Huh." The woman crossed her arms over her chest. "So what do you think?"

"I think this…" Shige indicated the town around them, the mine works, with a sweeping motion of one hand "…violates every labor regulation on the law books. And that is but a start."

She snorted rudely. "When you gonna get to the point about why I should give a fuck about any of this?"

Shige offered her a thin smile. "Think of me as… the first scout. What I am interested in is why TransRift wants to keep us away from here."

"If they're breakin' your law so much, seems like that answers your question."

"There's far more to it than that. I'm curious about the Weathermen now. You have the home office in quite a tizzy even if they have no idea who you are; you're the first person who has ever come so close to killing one of them. Thus, I wanted to have a chat."

"So he is still alive." She finally looked truly taken aback at that. "And how the fuck did you know that?"

"Yes, though he was badly injured. And I know because there was security footage from the laboratory you broke into. We see your face, then evidence of a breakout, and then the former Weatherman insisting on being taken out into the streets immediately to go looking for someone. Less than an hour later, he and his guard are dead, all shot with the same gun." The linkages between all of those things seemed very clear to him. "You were the foreign factor in the city, the locus of trouble. I find myself very curious as to why you were down in that lab, and how exactly you effected the escape that occurred after you had left."

Her jaw went tighter with each word. "I may just change my mind about shootin' ya."

Shige held up his hands again, giving her a disarming smile. "I want your help and information, not to make an enemy of you."

"Then back off."

"We could very well be on the same side here."

"Sharin' an enemy isn't the same thing as sharin' a side." The woman took a cigarette out from her case. "But I take your point. You wanna know about the Weathermen. So do I. Shootin' one in the neck ain't the same thing as knowin' about 'em unless you're interested in the particulars of how they bleed. You know about this witch hunt thing?"

"I was at the ones in Primero and Segundo, yes." He had an inkling, now, that things were far more than they seemed. One couldn't be around Mr Green for any length of time without recognizing that. But he wanted to see her reaction.

"Callin' it witchy is superstitious. But it ain't superstitious to say some of us ain't like the rest." With great deliberation, she lit the cigarette with a snap of her fingers, letting him see flame play across her hand for a moment. It was a surprise, and he let her see that, but it also fell in line with a few things he'd read recently, and with what he'd seen Mr Green do. "So they're huntin' down people like me, usin' the Weatherman. Why do you think that is?"

He paused, recalling the files he had been able to access. He could see the hunger in her eyes, understand it because it was one he shared. They both wanted information. Offering what he knew would cost him little and set him up as an ally to her, which could be useful. "Information about the Weatherman is far above the classification level I can access. What I can tell you is that TransRift considers people like you to have... *gone native*. You have been biologically altered by a poorly understood alien contaminant that exists only on this planet."

She snorted. "Fancy way of telling me what I already know."

"Ah, but it's an alteration that the Weatherman you almost killed – his name is Mr Green, by the way

– was specifically designed to combat." The words the document had actually used were *consume* and *control*, which he still wasn't certain how to interpret in the context of what he'd seen Mr Green do already. Though perhaps the control portion had to do with the Weatherman's supposed ability to keep the technology in Newcastle running properly, which he wasn't certain he believed.

She stared at him. "Designed. As in–"

"The Weathermen are, as best I've been able to find out, beings created by significant alteration in a laboratory."

"Ain't that illegal?"

"Evidence that will stand in court is harder to come by than you'd think."

"Shit," she breathed. "So I'm fuckin' contaminated by some – some unknown *thing*. How?"

He shrugged. "The main theory seems to be that the contaminant is airborne, due to how widespread it is. Everyone is contaminated, but only some of you develop this so-called *witchiness*. The reason for that seems to be as yet unknown."

"Hold the fuck up. *Everyone*?"

"Everyone who doesn't reside in Newcastle." Or wasn't given the inoculation he'd received himself after being given the witch hunt assignment, though he decided to not mention it if the woman didn't ask. He raised his eyebrows. "Did you think that any of you were actually allowed to leave?"

She rocked back on her heels, face going pale, then shoved him hard against the wall. "You got proof of that?"

He tapped his temple. "Only what's in here." It was too risky to physically remove or copy the records yet; maintaining his cover was far more important in the long term.

"How am I supposed to fuckin' trust that?"

"Do you think I am more or less trustworthy than TransRift?"

She looked like she'd just smelled something bad. "Friendship ain't built in a day, Rollins. You want my trust, you better act really fuckin' trustworthy."

It wouldn't hurt to let a bit of wry humor show. "I don't suppose I can appeal to a sense of patriotism?"

She laughed out puffs of smoke. "I like a jokin' man."

But he had her on the hook, he could feel it. A little more data to establish trust, and she could be a valuable contact when it came to the long-term goal of ending TransRift's monopoly. "Let me offer this to you, then. In three days, Mr Green will be in Tercio. Next will be Harmony, then Shimera, then Ludlow. The schedule after is still being set."

She repeated the names of the towns to herself. "I do appreciate it."

"I will likely be at these stops." He regarded her steadily. "So you understand the trust I have placed in you." He smiled slightly. "And without even knowing your name."

The woman only gave him a smug smile and touched the brim of her hat. "I'll remember it." She turned to go.

"And if I have more information for you, or you for me?" He was just planting the seed, he reminded himself. He'd dealt with paranoid types before, and cultivating those contacts required a careful hand.

She glanced over her shoulder. "Come to any of the second circle mining towns, and tell a crew leader that ain't in a bluebelly's pocket you need to get a message to the Ravani. They'll know how to do it." Out into the street, she stepped into the flow of people without a backward look.

Shige nosed around in Ludlow for another day before he took his seat on the afternoon train back to Newcastle. After his earlier stop in Rouse he had a few theories, and Ludlow had seemed a probable place for Magdala Kushtrim to end up, considering the ties between workers in the two towns. He'd memorized her face from her intake picture at the lab, but that would only help him if he personally saw her. Waving about the intake picture or a sketch would be too suspicious; asking after her by name at least gave him the defense of rumor. Everyone was still speaking of the Kushtrims, after all. And nearly everyone seemed certain that Magdala had been killed by TransRift, just as her parents had been. The undercurrent of cold, aching rage with which the workers spoke of the incident indicated much older anger that gathered under the surface and grew like the magma chamber of a volcano, waiting for the rupture of one small fault line to set off an eruption. This he made careful note of, as something that would interest his superiors greatly. That much energy waiting for an outlet made for a powerful potential weapon, one that just needed the smallest of nudges.

He also asked around to find out who this "Ravani" was: the name seemed more a title, belonging to whoever led a group of misfits and blacklistees that operated as mercenaries. More interesting, most people seemed to think the "Ravani" was an old man with one eye – called Old Nick – though a few thought it was a young woman, also with only one eye: Hob. From the description, the latter was obviously the person he had met. The former was another question, and certainly sounded like the perpetrator of the attack at Rouse.

He spent the long, hot train ride sorting the data out in his mind, compartmentalizing everything neatly so he'd be able to recall it as needed, as he'd been trained to do at his mother's knee. Civil service ran in the blood, after all – well, mostly. Most interesting was Hob Ravani's show of witchiness, for he thought it was most likely genuine – what good would it do for her to pretend to have such a stigmatized ability? And it meant that there was something far beyond the genetic damage or potential disease implied to be caused by the so-called contamination in the reports he'd read on the sly. What a difference, if the *contaminated* were in some way powerful, even potentially superhuman. The need to keep their numbers small and controlled rather than waiting for the damaged to die off was obvious from that perspective. There were other company resource worlds, some of which did belong to TransRift, but all the rest had at least a token federal inspector brought in to be wined and dined while well-fed workers were trotted out. Seeing with his own eyes, and what he'd observed during the witch hunt, also made more sense of the absolute quarantine of Tanegawa's World, when coupled with his growing hypothesis that the entire key to the interstellar travel monopoly resided *here*. He needed to worm his way further into the corporate hierarchy until he reached a level where there would be more answers than questions.

CHAPTER TWENTY-NINE

The Bone Collector occupied a confluence of relative perception. Centuries were the blink of an eye to a stone. Species lived and died in the time it took the steady drip of water to wear a surface smooth. Yet to a human, a single day could be an eternity, the passage of seconds like years. He was stone and not-stone. He was human, and very much not-human. He dreamed and didn't dream. In the human blink of an eye, he saw the stretch of history backwards, the winding paths of probability forward, could walk each to its conclusion.

But now he occupied all points at once and could not think around the sheer clamor of voice and color. Not just one person, one confluence, but an entire planet, tens of thousands of people. The crystals in his blood melted to blue water that carried him down the gravity well of the world and joined a dendritic network of more blue streams.

He floated in a cerulean vein greater than a river and saw himself reflected in it, only it was wrong, it had to be wrong, every mote of dust in him screamed at the sight of the pale face, the black-on-black eyes, the scalp crisscrossed with scars that he felt biting into his own skin. Worse, he heard the discord and mockery of the music that was not music.

He screamed out a note to shatter stone and drove his fists into the reflection, battering it and twisting it until it broke apart. He tried to reform the pieces into something that had harmony, but there discord spun every atom.

He tore at the abomination, becoming increasingly exhausted until he drank in more of the blue flow around him. It filled him with cool energy and gave him the strength to take the broken pieces to their component atoms and let them drift away. The last few glittering hydrogens and oxygens left fingers that began to unweave themselves in a more gentle dissolution. He had taken too much in, diluted himself down too much, he thought muzzily, as he flowed away.

He spread through the reservoirs of rock like blood vessels of the body, down to the thinnest capillaries that almost touched the surface. They were organic nerves of an inorganic lifeform. And then he discorporated completely into the flow, carried through the system again and again to a rhythm he couldn't comprehend, the massive beat of countercycling vortices in a core that was part liquid and part *other*.

Molecule by molecule, he caught himself in that fiery heart and listened to it sing, rebuilding his perception until he was close to whole, but the alien, impossible metal of that core flowed into his cracks and bonded him into something slightly different, a new form. He caught himself in that blue, crystalline vortex– one moment cooled and formed into an infinite lattice, the next broken apart with heat and light and sound and vibration – and looked up and up and up.

There is a hole through the world. I stand at the bottom of the well.

Through the outwash of light, he made out stars, and they were not the stars in any night sky Tanegawa's World had ever known, and the single moon that passed overhead was not either of the planet's moons. He watched the stars wheel in fascination, season after season, and they did not behave as stars should in a universe where gravity was the law and mass was conserved. Air whispered down into the bottom of that well, a few molecules carried in molten threads of magma that glittered with planetsong in harmony with the one he had simply awoken one day knowing.

Too much. He began to disintegrate again, and he did not think he would find himself a second time. He retreated from the light and sound, to a distance where he could begin to think again and try on the concept of *who am I* for size. He rolled the idea of self over his fingers like knuckle bones and tested each configuration until one made sense to his addled perception.

The Bone Collector. That was right.

Through an unknown distance of time, over multiple branching paths, he smelled familiar blood, so much of it. Perhaps now, perhaps in the future, the two were indistinguishable to a mind filled with blue and light. He longed to lick it from the lucky grains of sand, even as the quantity of it filled the remnants of his human heart with unease.

He should wake up. Would wake up. Soon.

A soon of relative time.

CHAPTER THIRTY

Coyote knocked on Hob's office door and let himself in without waiting for her to say anything. Dust streaked his coat and fuzzed his black hair gray.

"You always do that?" she asked, looking up from the scuffed ceramic dinner plate on her desk. Twists of ash and melted bits of metal sat on it; she'd been practicing calling up fires and putting them out, making heat without flame. She had a notion to figure more out about her own witchiness, without Old Nick riding her ass. Damn, but she wished he would have let her pick his brain about it. He'd always had tricks up his sleeve for everything.

He shut the door, a slightly amused smile on his face. "Never bothered Old Nick."

"I ain't Old Nick."

"I see that. Doing a bit of the…?" He wiggled his fingers at her, like a stage magician.

She snorted and shoved the plate onto a corner of her desk. "How'd the job go?"

"Smooth and easy. We… liberated the equipment. I also found a box of processors, thought we might see about upgrading the computers in the motorcycles a little."

"Think they'll be able to handle the heat and everything?"

"I handed them over to Hati and he said he'd get it all tested out before he sticks anything into a motorcycle that's headed for combat. But the company doesn't tend to send things out of Newcastle if they don't think they can take a little rough handling."

Hob nodded. "Good work."

Instead of taking that as the signal to get going, Coyote sat down in the chair in front of the desk, stretching his legs out with a sigh. "You look pensive, boss."

"Nice word for it." She stubbed her cigarette out in the overflowing scrap of twisted metal Nick had always used as an ashtray, already flicking open the silver case with her other hand. The words of the government spy, Rollins, still haunted her: *contaminated*. She didn't trust him, but she found herself believing that. It fit too many other things she'd seen from the company, and heard from the Bone Collector. Maybe *voice of the world* was a desert looneyman's way of saying *contaminated*. "Yeah. I feel pretty damn pensive."

"Want to tell me why? I think that's the sort of thing I ought to know, if you're going to saddle me with this second-in-command job."

"Didn't hear you complain at the time."

"It would have been a stupid idea to question your authority just then. You looked liable to shoot someone." He gave her a wide-eyed look, the light catching the odd green flecks in his eyes – which brought to mind other eyes she'd seen lately, brown with the same green flecks, under black hair. Though the man's face hadn't looked anything alike.

"You got any brothers?" she asked, leaning back on the chair.

Coyote's face went dark, his expression closing off in an instant. "Rude."

"I don't mean to pry just for the sake of bein' nosy. Just saw someone when I was out and about yesterday, looked an awful lot like you."

Coyote shrugged. "I don't come from Tanegawa's World. If I did have any siblings, for the sake of argument, I don't think you'd be likely to see any of them here."

"Fair enough."

"Is that what's bothering you?" His gaze flicked to the ash tray. "You seem to be… thinking quite a bit."

"Ha, no, was just a point of curiosity." She lit her new cigarette with a snap of her fingers, took a long drag as she leaned back. "You comin' from off world, though… folk out there even heard of this place? Give two shits about it?"

Coyote shrugged. "It cropped up in the more… yellow news from time to time, all sorts of conspiracy nonsense, particularly since it's a company world and connected to the wealthiest corporation the galaxy's ever known. But you get stories like that every other week in the tabloids, this or that lost colony world, only in this *new* one we've exclusively found, all the humans have evolved in the last centuries to be part lizard and they all have tails, isn't it startling. It's all bollocks. Why?"

Hob shook her head. "Still rollin' it around in my

brainpan." If there were hundreds of other worlds like this one, they probably had all the same problems. Maybe there were government spies crawling through all of them, asking snippy questions, but she somehow doubted it. "Found out the next several places the witch hunt's goin', and I've a mind to poke my nose in at the next town they're set to hit. Tercio."

Coyote gave her a look of disbelief. "Considering you're pretty damn witchy yourself, that strikes me as a bad idea."

"Company won't be there in force for three days." When his eyebrow went up, she shrugged one shoulder. "I got sources."

"Good for you. Taking after Old Nick already, I see." The sarcasm in his tone was thick enough to paint a wall. "Is there a job to be had?"

Hob sighed. "Not somethin' that would bring in money. I feel like I should go, see if there are witchy folks around, and get them the hell out." It still gnawed at her, the way Nick had tried to call witchy folk kin of a sort, then in the next breath say they couldn't be helped. She'd seen a pile of regret on his shoulders she didn't intend to pick up along with his old coat. She had enough regrets of her own already. Maybe some day, she'd have to draw the line between an *us* and *them*, but if Rollins was right and everyone was contaminated, there wasn't much *them* left except for TransRift.

"And where would you take them, once you have them out?"

"Different town. Or maybe take 'em by Pictou, see if the Bone Collector has a place for them first." But if he was gone… no, she told herself, asleep. Thinking anything darker made her stomach ache.

"I don't know much about the Bone Collector, so I'll just have to assume that would work. But how do you propose to find these people? No one advertises this. It's too dangerous."

"I don't know. Again. People in Tercio have heard of us. I thought mayhap if we showed our faces, some might come and find us in the hopes of savin' their own hides."

"It's possible, I suppose."

"But."

"Which 'but' in particular are you thinking about?" He laughed. "There's so many to choose from."

"It's not a job. It ain't for money."

Coyote sat up, leaning forward. "I'll let you in on a secret, Hob. As long as there is pay when the end of the week rolls in, you send us to do whatever you think needs to be done and no one needs to be the wiser."

She frowned. "Don't seem all that honest."

"We work for *you*. Just like we worked for Old Nick, when all was said and done. This isn't only a job. We live where we work. We have to keep it a place that we want to call home."

And have to be able to look themselves in the mirror in the morning. Some of the men probably weren't overly burdened with conscience, but she planned to hold on fiercely to what shreds she had. She'd suffered too much and too personally at the hands of such men to want to become like them. "There's money enough for now. I've got another job I can send a crew on tomorrow that'll bring in a big payout. Escort across the hardpan, black market. Small crew to Tercio ain't but a drop in the bucket."

"Then pick your men and get going. It's a long ride."

"You gonna come?"

"You call the shots."

She pinched her cigarette off. "Me, you, Freki, Geri. Four-man crew ought to be more'n enough. Don't want anyone thinkin' we're rollin' in to invade or nothin'. Go let 'em know?"

"Want me to tell them what it's about?"

"Do it. Freki and Geri grew up with me. They got no problem with witchiness."

Coyote smiled. "We all served under Old Nick, you realize. And I don't think a man among us missed your little display when you stepped into his place, if he'd somehow managed to ignore every other bloody time one of you played with fire. Perhaps we deserve more credit than you give us."

"I got a naturally suspicious mind, I guess." Habit ingrained by the paranoias of Old Nick. How much of his paranoia had been similarly ingrained, and how much of it learned? She'd never know. "You're right. I ain't bein' fair."

He held his hands heavenward for a moment. "It must be the end times. A Ravani just admitted to being fallible."

Hob snorted. "Get the fuck out of my office."

"That's more like it."

It was a long ride to Tercio, one that required they stop for lunch in a dune field. Then they were off into a stretch of canyons floored with hardpan, steep walls on either side and long flats that stretched straight for kilometers. Tercio was built into the wall of one wide, dry canyon, some buildings carved into the rock, others sprawled out around it to take best advantage of the shade. It made the town strangely linear, long but narrow. Tercio was an older town, at least three times bigger than Rouse.

Early evening shadows engulfed Tercio as they came to the gate. No guard hailed them. That alone had Hob's shoulders singing with tension as Freki went around to one of the side doors and jiggered it open so he could let them in.

The streets just inside the gate were empty. Geri started to say something, but Hob pulled her helmet off and signaled the others to do the same. The mine works were silent, not even the normal rattle and clank of the chain drive for the cars. The air sang with tension, the sound of a gathered crowd thunder in the distance. Hob tilted her head, listening, and then pointed south, away from the mine, toward the church steeple tipped with a frilly iron cross.

People filled the street near the church, too numerous to fit in the square. The Wolves drifted in as close as they could on their bikes, better for a quick getaway, but parked before the crush got too tight.

A scaffold rose above the crowd, nooses hanging from it. The sight made Hob's blood run cold. People in the towns weren't supposed to have guns; that was for the security men. So when they wanted to execute someone without involving Mariposa directly, they tended to get downright old-fashioned about it.

Hob scanned the crowd, signaling the three men

to fall in behind her. She didn't like leaving the motorcycles unguarded, but as tense as the crowd was, she wanted her men watching her back. She caught a glimpse of the conductors of this mob over the heads of the mostly shorter people: on the steps of the church, the town's preacher with his mouth open and angry, and a man with a crew leader's stripe on his shirt sleeve.

She saw a little clear area not far from the scaffold, three people surrounded by some burly miners, and forged that way, applying elbows and knees as needed. There wasn't a swatch of green Mariposa uniform to be seen; they'd probably retreated to the guard shack as soon as they smelled the crowd turn ugly. And if this was to do with the witch hunt, they probably had orders to not interfere with such things.

Closer now, she made out the preacher's words over the rumble of displeased talk, things about not suffering a witch to live. Some in the crowd nodded along, but most looked grim, unhappy, like this was a thing that had to happen, but they didn't like it one bit. Good. Grim could be reasoned with, if she talked fast enough.

"Oh, I don't like the look of this," Coyote murmured.

"You ain't the only one," she said back.

"Play it smart, boss. We don't have a big enough gun to punch a decent hole in this crowd."

Two of the three people in the circle were miners: a young man with floppy brown hair barely more than a boy, and a grizzled oldster that had a scar puckering his chin. The third was a brown-skinned young woman with black hair and dark eyes, her frame ill

fed and ragged. More important was the fact that her
tattered clothes looked like something out of a farming
town – if you dragged them through the desert for a
week – so she probably wasn't from Tercio.

Hob shouted, "There you are!" and pointed at the
young woman. "I been lookin' all over for you." She
tried to shove past one of the guards, then got shoved
back in return.

Geri caught her like it was just part of the plan,
pushed her upright, and then grabbed the miner by
the shirt. "You watch who you're gettin' rough with,"
he snarled.

"That's my cousin you got there," Hob shouted.
"The fuck you people doin' to her?"

Silence spread through the crowd as soon as the
commotion started. The preacher man paused on the
church steps, glancing at the crew leader, who yelled
at Hob, "The hell do you think you're doin'?"

She turned to face him. "I come to your damn town
to pick up my cousin, and you got her all trussed up like
some kind of criminal. The fuck is wrong with you?"

"She don't look much like you."

"An' I'm sure all your goddamn cousins are your
spittin' image," Hob retorted.

The preacher interjected, his tones all smooth and
round, "The woman has been accused and found
guilty of witchcraft. She hasn't said a word in her
defense."

Hob glanced at the young woman. Her eyes
were huge, her expression confused. But subtly she
pointed to her throat, gave a little shake of her head.
Hob looked back at the preacher, "That's 'cause she's

fuckin' mute, ya moron!" Someone near her laughed; she took it as a good sign.

"She has still been convicted–"

"Of what? You seen her turn someone into a frog? Light a thing on fire with the power of her mind? Fly through the air? What'd you see?"

"She has an unnatural air to her," the preacher said, drawing himself up.

"An unnatural air? Are you fuckin' serious?" Hob laughed. "You just want to fuckin' hang her 'cause she's a stranger, right? You think she's an easy target 'cause she got no kin here?"

There was a hurried, whispered conversation between the preacher and the crew leader. Then the crew leader yelled, "Let her go with her cousin. But you better get her the hell out of my town, right now."

One of the miners grabbed the woman and all but threw her at Hob, then scrubbed his hands on his pants like he was wiping away dirt. Hob caught her; the woman was shaking like a leaf, her face gone so pale her skin looked almost yellow. "You go with Freki now," Hob murmured to her. "Nice and slow. He'll keep you safe." She nodded to Freki, and then looked back up toward the preacher. From the corner of her eye she could see Freki hustling the girl through the crush, shouldering anyone out of his way who didn't move smart enough. "We'll be out of here in short order, don't you worry one bit. So much for the goddamn hospitality in Tercio. We'll be lettin' the whole damn world know."

A miner nearby frowned. "Hey, it ain't like that. Times are hard."

"Times aren't ever that hard," Coyote, still at her shoulder, remarked.

Hob pointed back at the two men still being held. "And what'd they do, by the way? They got an *unnatural air* about 'em too?"

"Ellis stands accused of lighting fires. Harding brought down lightning on the town."

"So what, Harding here was walkin' around when some lightnin' struck? Ellis been around a couple of fires 'cause he's careless with his cigars?"

"We don't have to answer to you!" the preacher shouted.

"No, you gotta answer to your god, and I hear he's got a warm place for liars!" she shouted back. Someone grabbed her by the collar. In a flash she had her revolver pressed under the stubbly chin of a man much brawnier than her. "You better think real hard about the way you want the next five seconds to go," she said to him.

He let her go and Geri shoved him away, but she kept her revolver out, let the people around her see the bone butt on it. "In case you ain't figured it out yet, I'm the new Ravani. And you know that means I ain't gonna stand by and let a couple of innocent folk dance at the end of a rope just 'cause you're scared of your own damn paymasters." It was one hell of a line to draw, and Old Nick was probably spinning in his grave. Or who knew, maybe he was smiling up from hell because she'd been goaded into doing a thing he'd never had the guts to do himself.

"The Weatherman is coming in the next few days. More than just those two will die if we don't take care of them first," the crew leader said. "Father Matthew could tell they were the ones the Weatherman would take. God guided him. We don't have a choice."

"You got a choice. You always got a fuckin' *choice*. Give 'em to me. I ain't scared of the Weatherman."

"They contaminate everything they touch with their sin," the preacher said.

"If you believed that, it wouldn't just be them waitin' to hang. It'd be every person the Weathermen would be takin' too, every one of their kin and every one of their friends, their coworkers." She tilted her head slightly. "Or mayhap you believe that, preacher, but I'm thinkin' these fine folks don't, cause they ain't offerin' themselves up to be the next sacrificial lamb."

There was a lot of ugly still left in the crowd, even if she had it confused for now. Near her two people were praying, hands folded and heads bowed. Barely daring to breathe, keeping her shoulders square and her chin up, she turned back to the miners that guarded the two men. "If you boys please, we'll take 'em out of here." She met the eyes of the man who had shoved her back before. There was uncertainty there. "Preacher man wants to hang 'em, but you don't want to see that. Them two, they're your neighbors. You don't want to have a hand in them dyin'."

The man licked his lips. "But he said death cleanses the taint."

"Think about it real hard, logic it out in your head and decide if that makes sense." She glanced over her shoulder. The crew leader and preacher were having another whispered conversation. She had a feeling the crew leader was on her side, was all for just getting the men the hell out of his town before the trouble started. "Ain't no reason anyone's got to die today."

He nodded and stepped aside.

Ellis and Harding walked haltingly to her, their shoulders hunched as if they expected perdition to rain down on them at any moment. "Slow and easy, boys. Don't startle anyone." She put them in front of her, Geri and Coyote helping cut through the crowd as they made their way back toward the street. Now that they had the "tainted" people with her, everyone made it their business to get out of her way.

"Ravani!" the crew leader shouted. "Don't you ever come back to my town again!"

"Not till the day it's you beggin' us to come back and save your asses." It wasn't the smartest thing to say, but she couldn't bring herself to let someone that downright cowardly have the last word.

At the edge of the crowd, she saw someone lunge out of the corner of her eye. She turned, hand snapping up to aim square at a dark-skinned woman throwing herself at the younger man – she still wasn't sure which was Ellis and which was Harding – with tears in her eyes. Coyote grabbed Hob's wrist and shoved her arm up even as her finger squeezed the trigger; her shot went wild.

The crowd nearest them hit the deck. Someone screamed. Hob cursed, grabbed the older man by the arm and shoved him ahead of her, shouted at the young guy to run. She jumped up on her motorcycle; the oldster got up behind her without any prompting. Behind them more screams, and there was another gunshot – there were some illegal firearms in the crowd after all, even if no one had been volunteering to play executioner. Geri threw the woman over his battery stack even as she screamed, and Coyote did the same to the young man. They peeled out as quick as they could, the sound of chaos growing behind them. Hob jammed her helmet on her head one-handed, just to cut off the sound of it.

"Goddamn stupid fuckin' *idiots*," she cursed into the channel.

"That could have gone better," Coyote observed.

"What the fuck happened?" Freki asked. He'd already gone back out the gates with the female prisoner.

"Stupid happened," Geri growled. "Entire square full of fuckin' scared and stupid."

They stopped a safe distance from Tercio to rearrange everyone more comfortably on the motorcycles. Harding turned out to be the older man, and Ellis the younger. The woman was Ellis' wife Amanda, who'd been locked in the basement of her parents' house until she escaped by breaking open the cellar doors. Her dark hands were covered with bleeding gouges, her eyes red and voice gone to nothing from screaming. Coyote bandaged up her hands as best he could, but they couldn't pause long. As they mounted back up, the dark shape of a great eagle cut across the sun, the bird no doubt smelling out the fresh blood.

The sun had sunk behind the dunes long before they made it to Ludlow, heading straight for Clarence Vigil's house. He was asleep, but Mag answered the door, listened quietly to Hob's explanation of the situation. "Ellis, I can set you and Amanda up in the guest room, I think. You can talk to Clarence tomorrow and ask about a job. He's the day crew leader."

Ellis stumbled into the house like a man in a daze; it was Amanda that stayed behind on the steps, looking up at Hob. "What do we owe you?" she asked, voice a ragged whisper. "Can't ever rightly repay you, but I've heard of the Wolves. You always got a price."

They'd been playing hero, but heroes still needed to eat, and she had to think of that ugly truth as well. She hadn't been doing it for the money today, but she didn't want people thinking they could just throw their troubles on the Wolves for free. She owed her people better than that, even if part of her did want to swoop up all the witches she could find and carry them off. The woman had a gold chain around her neck, so she pointed at that. "Whatever bit of shiny you got. We'll take it all."

Amanda's hand went to her breast, clutching at the necklace half-hidden there. But she gave her head a sharp shake, pulled it off and held it out. The necklace was nothing fancy, but fine enough jewelry for a miner's wife. "And this," Amanda whispered. She dug into her pocket and brought out a wedding band, setting it in Hob's hand. She tugged the other from her finger. The gold finish was clouded with blood. "They gave me Ellis' ring when they was fixin' to hang him. Considerin' they were blessed by that goddamn preacher, I ain't feelin' so attached at the moment."

Hob closed her hand around the rings, tucked them away into her pocket. She touched the brim of her hat. "Handsome payment indeed, ma'am."

"Thank you," Amanda whispered. Her spine bowed and her eyes went shining and soft with tears. Mag led her away, then, to Hob's immense relief.

The less normal cases were still to be dealt with: Harding, and the woman with no voice. Hob dug around in her pockets and brought out a scrap of flimsy and a grease pencil stub and held them out to the latter of the two. "Now that we ain't runnin', how about you write down your name."

Harding cleared his throat. "What if there was some truth to what we was accused of?"

"So what if there was?" Hob shrugged. She took the scrap back from the young woman. It read: *Anabi*. "Well, Anabi, my friend Mag'll take good care of ya. She's been my best friend since we was kids, I trust her with my life."

"I mean, Ellis was just on the block 'cause Amanda's parents didn't much like him, and… it's a long story. He ain't done a damn thing wrong, 'cept bein' a little careless with his cigarettes. But me…"

Hob held up a finger, and handed the flimsy back to Anabi since she was reaching for it, fingers opening and closing impatiently. "I know there's people around here that're different. They're people just like everyone else."

"But the witch hunt is gonna come here eventually."

"If it does, you know what's comin' now. Start plannin'."

"Don't s'pose you could use an old man like me in your company. I heard about the Ravani, and the Ghost Wolves."

"Depends, Harding." Hob took the flimsy scrap back from Anabi. It read, in tiny, cramped handwriting: *I didn't deserve to die for being a stranger in town. Thank you.* It made her blood boil, knowing she'd been right about it, folk turning on a girl just because she was a new face and had no voice. "How good a shot are you?"

CHAPTER THIRTY-ONE

"You got a second, Mag?"

She glanced up from the coffee pot to see Hob leaning in the doorway like a long shadow. Her friend looked and sounded more like Uncle Nick every time she saw her. "Another one?"

Hob snorted. "Got something you oughta know."

"I'll be right back." Mag handed off cups of weak coffee to the three new problems Hob had dropped in her lap, hoping a warm drink would help them calm their nerves. Then she followed Hob into Clarence's parlor, shutting the door behind her. "What is it now? You got another stray in your pocket you're gonna pull out?"

"Didn't know where else to take 'em." Hob had the grace to look abashed, at least. She sprawled out on a chair.

Mag sighed. She knew she had a better chance of setting these people up with something than Hob; she knew what crew leaders to talk to, what resources they had in their shallow pool that she could call on to help strays. "I know, Hob. We both got our own skills. What's the news?"

"Don't rightly know what it means yet, but you got a better head for such things than me. Had someone tell me that TransRift don't let no one off the planet, they just pretend to. Because for all that only a few of us are out-and-out witches, every last soul on this fuckin' planet is *contaminated*."

With each word, Mag felt herself go colder, stiller. Her mouth suddenly dry, she said, "Who might this someone be?"

Hob wrinkled her nose. "You know that ain't how it works, even atween you and me. I don't know if I trust 'em further than I can throw 'em, but my gut says they weren't lyin' even if they weren't tellin' the whole truth. And Mag, if it is true…"

In a small, awful way, it made her feel slightly better about what had happened. She hadn't done anything wrong, to have lost her one chance of escape. But shock and cold fury swept that minor relief aside. If this was true, it had become the biggest lie the company had ever told: a false division between the workers that made them turn on each other, and a false promise of a better future on a kinder world if they only worked hard enough. "But we got no proof."

"Not yet, though I asked for it," Hob said grimly. "But you know as well as I do that it is the truth. 'Cause you're lookin' like you're fit to be sick, same as I feel."

"Fit to eat steel and spit nails." Already she turned it over in her mind, thinking how best to use this piece of information. She looked solidly at her friend, wondering now *why* Hob had told her, what she expected to come of it. "What's your aim on this, Hob?"

"Same as always: surviving. Keeping my people alive."

"But who are your people?"

The corner of Hob's lips pulled up into a crooked smile. "Still figurin' that out." She stood and put her hat on. "But you know, Mag? You always had better aim than me."

Hob and the Wolves headed out while Mag was still trying to settle Amanda and Ellis, leaving mute Anabi huddled in the kitchen, staring into a cup of tea like it might bite her. Mag looked through closets until she found the little piece of slate and bit of chalk Clarence's children had once used to practice their lessons.

"Sleep first, or a bath?" she asked.

Bath, please.

Mag took Anabi up to her room, hauled up a little copper half tub and filled it for her, then helped Anabi get undressed. The young woman's body was a maze of bruises and cuts. "Didn't treat you too nice, did they."

Anabi shook her head.

"I think your clothes are a loss. You can wear some of mine for now, and then we'll get you something that fits better in a day or two." Mag began washing the young woman's hair. It would have been beautiful, all black, heavy curls, if it'd been washed or brushed in recent memory. "I think you'd do about as well in the mines as me. Can you sew? That's how I make my money right now."

I can embroider well. I'll earn my keep however I can. Hesitation, then she scratched out. *You don't have to do this for me.*

"People were kind to me when I needed it most. I'm not so mean I won't pass that favor along." She got that sense from the young woman, as if she'd been running for a long, long time. "You can bide a while and be safe here, I promise."

Underneath all of the cuts and bruises there were scars, lashed across the Anabi's back. She gently touched one, finger tracing the thin weal. "Where'd you come from?"

Anabi shook her head.

"I come from Rouse. They burnt my house down around my mama there, and shot my papa in the back, out in the desert. I can't ever go back. 'Cause they'd be lookin' for me."

Anabi stared at her for a long time, like she was trying to read the details off Mag's face. With a dripping hand, she wrote, *Harmony. That's where I came from.*

"Not such a nice place, is it."

They don't welcome strangeness, or strangers. Anabi wiped the writing away with one thumb. *I don't want to put you in danger.*

"I promise, you can't get me deeper in trouble than I already am. We strangers got to stick together." Following an impulse that drifted up like a bubble in her throat, Mag took Anabi's hand and pressed her lips against the back of it, felt the flutter of her pulse. Perhaps it was a strange thing to do, but of all the strangeness in her life, this didn't feel like a wound about to tear open. "You've had a long day. Let's get you put to bed, and you can tell me everything you want in the morning. But don't worry about it until then."

Anabi nodded, her dark eyes wide, looking at Mag as if she might try to swallow her up.

For once, Mag found herself not minding that look. She didn't know what to do about it, not yet, but she knew she didn't mind at all.

With Anabi asleep in her bed, blankets tucked up to her chin, Mag checked the clock and let herself out of the house. The reason she'd been awake late enough to greet Hob was that she was supposed to meet with the nightshift crew leader, Odalia Vigil – no relation to Clarence despite their shared last name. She let herself into the warehouse, the sudden hush like a physical thing as she opened the door on people who realized they had nowhere to hide.

"Sorry that I'm late. The Ravani brought me a few fugitives. So you'll have a couple of new hands in the mine in the next couple of days."

Odalia sighed, pursing her lips. Three men stood in the room, one from Rouse and two from Shimera. Mag had never asked their names. It was better not to know. "We seem to get a lot of lostlings these days."

The man from Rouse said, "Wolves used to bring them all to Rouse for Phil to take in, but they can't exactly show their faces around any more." At the mention of her papa's name, one of the men crossed himself like a nervous tic.

Odalia shook her head. "We'll figure it out. Mag, I wanted you to tell these men what Tavris Meeks said in Blessid. Better it come in your words."

Mag sat down, smoothing her skirts over her knees, and told the story. "He didn't see a reason to throw in his lot with us, because we've never done anything to throw our lot in with them. We're two different worlds."

"So we need to find some common ground," Odalia said.

"Don't see why. Farmers like bein' under TransRift's thumb? Fuck 'em," one of the men from Shimera said.

Mag shook her head. "We need 'em. If we ever get cut off from supplies on the train lines, they'll be our source of water and food. We can't keep relying on TransRift for anything, not if it means they can press their boot down harder on our necks. Mayhap we could even hide folk out there, if we can get things worked out."

"Big if."

"What about this witch hunt that's been going around?" the man from Rouse said. "That common enough? Far as I know, they'll be hitting the farm towns same as the mining towns."

"Things are gettin' dicey in Shimera already. Farm towns've probably hunted out all their own witches and hanged or burned them already," the other man from Shimera said. "They always been more thunder and lightning about their religion. That really the place we want to make our stand, for a bunch of sand-addled freaks?"

"If you have witchy people in your town, they been living and working beside you without hurting a soul so far," Mag said, keeping her words measured and patient. She thought, then, about what Hob had told her a few hours before.

"Yeah, but when it turns into us or them, we're

gonna have to go with us."

Mag shook her head. "And don't you see? That's exactly the same thing that's keepin' the farmers from helpin' *us* out. We always let the company divide us up. The only us and them is us…" she circled a hand wide to indicate the miners, their towns, and the farmers "…and the bosses in Newcastle."

"I don't think it's quite the same thing, Mag," Odalia said. "If someone's witchy, they ain't really human, are they? They're…" *Unbalanced, dangerous, destructive.* Mag already knew how those sentences ended.

"You ever know anyone, left the planet?" she asked, pleased to see all of them look a little off-balance at the shift in topic.

"What's that got to do with anything?" Odalia returned with asperity.

"News I got today, from someone I trust." Even if it had come from someone Hob wasn't certain she trusted, now seemed the time to put it to use. "Said company don't let any of us leave, not really. Company takes their money and gives them the same kind of treatment I got. Because we're all *contaminated* by this planet." She raked them with her eyes. "Contaminated sounds like a nice company way of sayin' witchy, don't it."

One of the men from Shimera shook his head. "Now hold on a damn minute. That's one hell of a wild accusation. You got any proof?"

"Ain't I proof enough?"

The other man from Shimera looked equally unconvinced. "We're powerful sorry about what happened to you, but that ain't ever happened before."

"You so sure about that?" Mag asked quietly. "Or is it just I'm the first one had a friend paranoid enough in the brain to come lookin' for her? You tell me. Any of you ever heard of someone who left Tanegawa's World writing back home to tell us how it is, where they gone?"

That made them all look distinctly uncomfortable.

"You think about it, good and hard. You go ask in your towns, if anyone's ever known a soul that got off world alive. And you think about why the company's so hot to hunt down the witches, too. If you got people around who can do witchy things, don't you think that's something that could only help us? We ain't supposed to have guns, so what kind of power do you think it'd give us, if we had someone could call lightning or fire right out of the air? And then the Weatherman comes around and scares us into killin' them first." She sat back, taking a moment to look each in the eye until they blinked and looked away. "So don't you give me none of that nonsense. The only *them* on this planet is the bluebellies, and we *do not* give our own over to the company."

No one outright agreed with her, but they didn't have to. Mag saw in them that they'd go back to their towns, and they'd ask around to see if there was truth to her words. It was a start, a line she'd scratched out in the sand and dared them to cross in front of her.

The man from Rouse gave her a tight smile as he slipped from the warehouse. "Every day, I think I see more of your daddy in you, Mag."

Mag laughed. "I do appreciate it. So long as you don't tell no one."

But it wasn't Phil that had been talking through her mouth just then, she knew that in her heart. It was her mama, gentle Irina, who'd made the best pies in Rouse and loved every miner whether they smelled of witch or no. But not Uncle Nick nor the devil had been brave enough to cross her when she drew a line.

CHAPTER THIRTY-TWO

Re-groomed back into perfection by a brief trip to the spa at which he'd supposedly spent his three days of vacation, Shige took the long elevator ride to the top floor of the building long before most people in the city were up. He carefully sorted through all of the correspondence that had piled up, did the other little tasks that his persona as an executive secretary demanded. By the time Ms Meetchim entered her office at precisely nine o'clock, everything was in perfect order and Shige stood by the elevator door, glass mug of amaretto coffee with a precisely measured amount of sugar at the ready.

Meetchim accepted the coffee without glancing up from her newsreader, "Good morning, Mr Rolland. I trust you enjoyed your vacation."

"Very much, Ms Meetchim. The spa here is lovely. Is there anything on which you wish me to focus my attentions this morning?"

"Not in particular, thank you."

Shige returned to his desk, keeping an eye on Meetchim as she took up her regular work. An hour into the morning the office intercom rang, displaying an internal building number. "Vice President Meetchim's office, how may I help you?"

"Please let the vice president know that we are ready for her down in the lab."

"I will, thank you." Interesting and unexpected: Ms Meetchim rarely deigned to leave the comfortable lair of her office during the day; normally, representatives were sent up, and Shige was asked to work elsewhere while the meeting happened. He picked up his steno pad and filed two pens away in his pocket, then crossed the floor to the massive glass and metal desk. "Ms Meetchim, the lab just called. They said that they are ready for you." He kept his back straight, expression smooth and disinterested.

"I see." Meetchim stood, then looked at him searchingly. "Yes?"

"Will you be wanting notes taken, sir?"

Meetchim frowned slightly, then said, "You've expressed an interest in promotion to management in the past, haven't you, Mr Rolland?"

"It's a career goal of mine. Though I of course have no complaints about my current position."

"Of course not." Meetchim nodded, seemingly to herself. "Come along, then."

Shige maintained his carefully neutral and disinterested expression as he followed Meetchim into the elevator. There was no reason to get excited yet, though the fact that he had been so carefully kept from the lab until now made him suspect interesting things were happening there.

It also suggested that he was in a great deal of danger if he didn't tread very, very carefully. But this was what he'd been trained for, even if the intent had been to send him against an insurrectionist planetary government rather than a supposedly friendly corporation.

The long elevator ride down to the subbasement was silent. One of the scientists, white coat over her blue suit, greeted Meetchim at the door. Her ID card read: *Kiyoder*. She gave Shige a nervous look, but when the Vice President didn't even bother to introduce them, she took it in stride.

The woman led them to an observation room, with several uncomfortable metal chairs arranged in front of a glass wall. On the other side, Mr Green sat in a similar chair, hands folded lightly in his lap, a half smile curving his lips.

"We've finished processing the first group," Dr Kiyoder said. "Of the twenty-three, four showed signs of contaminant alteration."

"The rest?"

"I released them to the western section chief from Mariposa. He said he would see to their return at an appropriate location." Mentally, Shige translated that to *they'll be turned loose in the desert, and shot if the section chief decides his men need target practice*. He wondered if Kiyoder was aware of this fact, or if she held to the sanitized lie of it to protect her own sense of moral rectitude. The section chief, he'd discovered, considered the miners to be vermin who turned against the only force of good and order in their lives at the drop of a hat.

"Excellent." Meetchim sat in one of the chairs. "Please, have a seat, Mr Rolland. It will be easier for you to take notes if you don't have to stand."

"I appreciate it, sir." He sat to the woman's left.

"We'll send the first of the four in now," Dr Kiyoder said, as she left the room.

"Have you been around Weathermen often?" Meetchim asked.

"No sir. Mr Green is the first one I've met."

"It is important for you to understand now that our Weathermen are not what one could consider strictly... human." Meetchim leaned back lightly in her seat, crossing her legs. "So we cannot expect him to interact with us as if he is. Modern navigators are grown rather than born."

"I am not certain of your meaning, I'm afraid." Better to pretend ignorance, even if he was filing away the very important fact that the Weathermen were lab-created life forms rather than humans altered post-birth. While artificial birth was no stigma in this day and age, there were strict laws against the corporate production of citizens – which had in the precolonial past been a method to rob them of their citizenship – not to mention experimentation on humans in such a fashion. The next report he filed would make very interesting reading for his superior, though how they'd gather the concrete evidence for prosecution was another question entirely. Perhaps a stint at Corporate headquarters would be the next step, if he could arrange it.

"Grown to order in our corporate labs," Meetchim said. "All modern navigators are male because the base modifications are carried on the Y chromosome."

A little curiosity was probably expected. "But not

the… previous ones?"

"Gene therapies and primitive neural overlays. Not well understood… or well controlled." Meetchim rested one finger against her lips, then pointed toward the window. "The other important factor you must understand is that the workers whom Mr Green has apprehended are not in any sense human either. Not any longer."

Shige remained silent; Meetchim had ordered him to simply watch, as loud as if she'd shouted the words. His stomach twisted with tension. Any time someone made claim of the lack of humanity of another, it sounded like a warning klaxon in his mind. His mother had made a point at a very early age of telling him how illegal the genetic alterations done to him had been. He'd spent years as a child terrified that people could look at him and see he was somehow not like them. And there were certainly those who wouldn't consider *him* human because of what had been done.

In the white-on-white room on the other side of the window, a door opened. A man with his wrists in handcuffs stumbled in as if propelled by a heavy shove. He fell to his knees, sliding along a few centimeters on the slick tiling. His head was bowed, slightly greasy brown hair hanging down toward his eyes.

Mr Green remained in his chair, though he sat up a little straighter, his pale, long-fingered hands moving to rest on his knees. "Good morning," he said, voice a gravelly croak from his scarred throat. The sound came through clearly into the observation room with a slight pop and crackle from transmission.

The man pushed himself to his feet and backed away until he hit the wall. He shook his head, keeping his face down toward the floor. "No. No. I'm not going to."

"It won't hurt, I promise. I'll make you all better." Mr Green went from croak to whisper, a more comfortable mode of speaking for him, Shige had learned. When the man didn't move, Mr Green began a song, a simple tune with no words, just tones strung together in a way that seemed oddly compelling. Slowly, the handcuffed man edged one foot forward, then the other. A little at a time, muscles shaking as he fought, he walked to Mr Green. Only when he was right in front of the Weatherman did Mr Green stand; he wrapped his arms around the man and kissed him lightly on the cheek.

The man screamed.

Shige turned his eyes to Meetchim, who didn't seem in the least bit concerned. "No longer human, Mr Rolland. Irrevocably contaminated by the Tanegawa factor and subsequently altered. If allowed to roam freely, they eventually go mad and tend to flame out in a very large splash of blood. You should not take it as hyperbole when I say that we have saved this planet from an influx of monsters on more than one occasion, a fact that the workers are inclined to forget the moment they don't get the brand of protein they like in the company stores. They tell themselves it is a myth because they do not want to believe that monsters are real and no one but us will save them."

Drops of water began to pour from the captive man's fingers, pooling onto the floor. The little puddle rippled and spread, pulsing like a living thing, a strange sheen of blue and purple running across its surface. If he hadn't seen fire running along the hands of the Ravani a few days ago, he might have dismissed it offhand as a trick, as an illusion caused by some vagary of his own mind. Now he found himself staring, his heart sounding loud in his ears. It was wrong, impossible, and happening.

When no more water fell, Mr Green held his own hand, palm down, over the puddle. The water streamed upward, wrapping around his fingers in shimmering threads. He drank it while all the while the man continued to scream, voice hoarse and dying. Red crept from under his eyelids, the corners of his mouth.

The screams cut off as the last drop disappeared between Mr Green's too-red lips. The man's head lolled back and he went limp. Though the Weatherman seemed delicate, almost spidery, he held the much heavier man up with no trouble. Tracks of blood streaked the man's cheeks and neck. Mr Green lapped at them with the vivid pink tip of his tongue.

Shige swallowed hard against the urge to retch.

Meetchim leaned forward and pressed a button next to the window; a curtain slid across. "It only gets messier from here, I'm afraid to say, so we needn't watch something unpleasant." A soft slurp came from the speaker before the sound cut off with a pop. "He'll be ready to process the next one shortly."

Shige was well trained enough that he stayed in character, kept his tone right for the persona he had labored so hard to build. He could regard this clinically; he'd observed far more brutal things in the past, the things that humans did to each other with sharp implements or drugs or electrodes. He'd been trained to withstand such things himself. Perhaps the reason this left him feeling at all off balance, was so difficult to stow back in a mental compartment, was because it was so *alien*. "Process, sir?"

Meetchim looked at him as if he was possibly a little dim. "The worst of the contamination is found in the blood and nerve tissues, which all Weathermen have some capacity to remove – though Mr Green is very special. He was created specifically for this purpose." She smiled thinly. "He is our sin eater, Mr Rolland."

"I see." He carefully took down notes, using the act of writing to separate himself from what he had witnessed, and what he tried not to imagine going on behind the curtain. "Though I had heard he was tasked with controlling the atmospheric anomalies, somehow."

"He does that as well, which is something all Weathermen can do. But that is a topic for another time. One cannot and should not learn everything in a day, Mr Rolland."

"Of course, sir. I was merely curious."

Meetchim leaned forward and pressed the button for the curtain. "Ambition is a laudable quality in our business, Mr Rolland. Curiosity, not as much."

Mr Green was back in his chair, not a drop of blood visible on him, though there was an odd flush to his cheeks now. The man – or the strangely pale collection of meat that had once been a man – lay in a heap at his feet. As Rollins watched, the door to the room opened and two guards used a long hook to catch the dead man's handcuffs and then drag him from the room. A moment later, another subject – this time a young woman – stumbled inside.

"Good morning," Mr Green rasped.

After the fourth time Meetchim pressed the button on the curtain to hide Mr Green, she took Shige's notepad and tore out the pages that he'd used. Shige bowed his head and didn't protest. The act of writing would fix the information, even the details, in his mind well enough until he got back to his apartment.

The gruesome deaths of four people had taken less than two hours; they were done long before Ms Meetchim's catered lunch arrived at her office. Shige spent the rest of the day at work, making Ms Meetchim coffee whenever she asked as if nothing untoward had happened. He stayed at his desk until after his superior had gone home, as was his daily habit, then closed down the rooms and headed for the elevator.

The doors opened to reveal Mr Green, waiting, his hands folded in front of him.

Shige forced himself to keep walking despite the shock, through an act of sheer will. His alarm showed as only the slightest hitch in his step. "Mr Green," he said by way of greeting. Where were the Weatherman's handlers? He was certain the man wasn't supposed to be wandering about the corporate office on his own.

Mr Green smiled brightly at him. As the doors slid shut, he reached out, fingers wrapping around Shige's jaw with a grip inescapable but not yet painful. He pulled Shige close, and a corner of his mind noted that the Weatherman's breath smelled like blood and cinnamon.

"Mr Green?" He kept his voice light, though the words sounded awkward through an unmoving jaw. Shige's mind raced, recalling the soft crunch and slurp he'd heard repeatedly that morning. One hand slid to where he kept his emergency weapon, a microinjector filled with neurotoxin – though knowing what he did about the Weatherman's alteration, would it even work?

Mr Green moved his face closer and inhaled. "I thought I smelled you," he whispered hoarsely. "You've been outside. Don't want you to get sick." His lips closed over Shige's, his black eyes swallowing up everything he could see. *Don't look them in the eye, never look them in the eye* – but how could he look anywhere else?

Shige brought the microinjector up toward Mr Green's neck with a hand that felt like it was weighted with lead as his vision whited out. It was like no kiss he'd ever experienced before, a sensation that shot strangely down his nerves with both pleasure and pain, enough of both that his hand dropped nervelessly back to his side. The microinjector clattered on the elevator floor like a dropped pebble, terribly distant to his ear.

It lasted only a moment, and then Mr Green pushed him lightly back and let go of his jaw. He licked his lips. "All better now."

Shige resisted the urge to mirror that gesture, or wipe his mouth with the back of his hand. He felt his fingers tremble. "Thank you, Mr Green," he made himself say. "This... This will be our little secret, yes?"

Mr Green smiled, open delight on his face. "Of course. I like secrets."

The elevator reached the lobby and the doors opened. Mr Green made no move to exit. After a second of hesitation, Shige propelled his legs in the right direction, though he took care to step on the dark speck of the microinjector and crush it. Stumbling a little drunkenly, he walked into the lobby. To his profound relief, Mr Green didn't follow – he glanced over his shoulder to see the Weatherman still smiling as the doors slid shut in front of him.

He kept himself together long enough to return to his spare apartment, where he put notes into an encrypted recorder, typing them in short bursts that a listener could easily take for correspondence. When the recorder was once more hidden away in his kitchen, he took out a bottle of whiskey that came with the apartment, and proceeded to get drunk for the very first time in his life.

CHAPTER THIRTY-THREE

Hob had no interest in showing her face in Tercio again, not after the mess she'd seen there. Seemed important, though, to find out what happened when the Weatherman arrived, and after he left. Knowing things was like an addiction; having even little bits of information dancing at her fingertips was a pleasant sensation all its own.

The day after the Weatherman visited Tercio, according to the spy Rollins, she sent Dambala off to sniff around. Davey Painter rode out with him, since the pup – it was weird to be thinking of him as just a pup, he was probably only five years younger than her at most, but all the new responsibility made her feel three times her actual age – needed some airing out. Davey could look wide-eyed and innocent when he felt like it, and had a good pair of ears on him.

The news they brought back wasn't good. The Weatherman had picked two people from the crowd, and greenbellies took in their families as well. The day crew leader was part of one of those families, and Tercio didn't take that meekly. Two miners got shot before the crowd was cowed enough to back down.

Hob listened to the report in grim silence, as did Coyote, perched on the edge of her desk. "Hope they learned that nothin' is gonna make them safe." She curled her lip. "And that the preacher got no fuckin' idea what he's talking about."

"Folks get scared. And when they get scared, they don't think right. They just think about their own hides." Dambala looked at Davey, made a little gesture as if prompting him.

"You got somethin' to add?" Hob asked.

Davey cleared his throat. "We stopped at Shimera on the way back. I know it wasn't orders, but folk in Tercio were sayin' that was the next stop for the Weatherman, and it was on the way and all..."

"I like people followin' orders, but I also like you usin' your damn brains. Go on, report it proper."

"Shimera got notice they're to be gatherin' at the train station in two weeks' time, to greet the Weatherman. And that it's mandatory if people want to keep their jobs."

Hob idly took a fresh cigarette from her case, offering it to Davey and Dambala next. Dambala snorted. "Not for us, ma'am–"

"You call me sir like every other Ravani."

"Sir." Dambala grinned. "You're like Nick. You smoke enough for ten of us, so we don't got to."

"Just don't want you folk to start missin' him too bad. Keep goin', Davey."

Davey nodded. "Woman killed herself there, in Shimera, the night they got the news. She was a witchy sort, doctored folk, and did a good job of it. Had a note in her hands, said she didn't want to get anyone taken in by Mariposa, 'cause she was friend and kin to too many, so she did it to save 'em. They buried her proper while we was there."

Hob shook her head. "Christ."

"Preacher's all hellfire and brimstone on the pulpit," Dambala said. "But I talked to some of the folk, an' he's tryin' to get people like her out on the sly. He's just beatin' the drum loud in the square 'cause the pit boss is in his house every damn morning. We can probably get people out as long as we do it soon."

Hob frowned. The words tasted bad in her mouth, but she said them anyway, out of a sense of obligation: "Y'all keep remindin' me that's just puttin' off the date of execution."

Coyote finally spoke. "We can hardly sit on our hands. Not after what we saw in Tercio."

"We very well could," Hob said. "That's what Old Nick would've done, I bet. We hunker down and don't draw fire on ourselves." She glanced askance at Coyote; he'd always been one of the biggest advocates of saving his own hide first; this was quite a change from him.

He smiled. "But you're not him. And you look like it nearly killed you to say that."

"Ludlow's gonna be under the gun soon, but if we can get some folk out of Shimera, take 'em there. But we got to think of another place to take the ones from Ludlow when it's their turn."

"Could we just bring 'em here?" Davey asked.

Hob shook her head, hating the calculation she had to make. But she was already doing far more than Old Nick would have stirred himself to do, and the more people they brought out to their little camouflaged base, the more likely they were to be discovered, and then it would be all their necks. "Can't have that many people here. We're already stickin' our necks out a lot, and if people know where we live... anyone'll talk if you do 'em enough pain."

"How many you want me to take, boss?" Dambala asked.

"However many you think you need. And however many you think you can trust to ferry witchy people across the sands."

Dambala laughed. "Plenty'd do it with a song in their hearts just knowin' it'll piss off the company. You don't got nothin' to worry about with the witchiness."

"Take a price for it. We're makin' this a job proper. Don't want folk thinkin' we gone soft and started doin' charity." If people thought the Wolves were doing things just because they had an ax to grind, that would make getting proper pay harder for other jobs.

"What kind of price did you have in mind?"

"Whatever they're willin' to pay. Change out of their pocket. Their damn wedding rings. As long as it's somethin', so we can say people was buyin' passage from us."

"You said there was another place they'd be hitting before Shimera, correct?" Coyote asked.

"That's what my source said. Harmony."

He whistled, long and low. "That's a hell of a ways away."

"Glad you even know where it is. I had to look it up on the goddamn map."

Coyote shrugged. "Send me. I'll see what I can see

before the Weatherman shows up."

"Doin' the drive on a bike? I thought you didn't like campin' out."

"I don't. But I thought I'd hitch a ride on a train, since I've developed such a good relationship with them lately."

Hob laughed. "You do that, then." Anyone that got out of Harmony, he'd also be able to bring back on the train. "See all of you boys soon enough."

She watched out the window as Dambala formed up his squad for Shimera and Coyote prepared to go on his lonesome way. When they were all gone, she took a motorcycle out on her own and made the long ride to Pictou, parking in that familiar long shadow of the extinct mine works.

Hob took her knife from her sleeve and pricked her thumb, then squeezed three drops of blood into the sand. This time she waited for twelve hours, a lone eagle circling overhead until the sun went down.

Answer enough: they were on their own.

CHAPTER THIRTY-FOUR

Mag wasn't surprised when someone knocked at the door during dinner. Clarence got visitors at all hours of the night, some of them legitimate, some of them secretive. Mag stood, giving dinner the sort of look normally reserved for departing lovers. Anabi had made shredded chicken-flavored protein and dumplings, the best she'd had in a long time.

Dambala and Davey waited on the doorstep. Mag peered past them, trying to spot the lanky form of Hob in the shadows, but they seemed to be alone. "Can I help you boys?"

"We brought you some more strays." Dambala gave her a sheepish smile.

"I'll let Clarence know. But... you realize, we're gonna get our own visit, in three weeks. Got informed of it proper today. This ain't a safe place."

"It's a week safer than Shimera."

Mag leaned against the doorframe for a moment, her forehead against her hand. Just saying those words – three weeks – made it feel more real, more urgent, a sudden twist of fear turning the dumplings to stones in her belly. "You boys got to go back tonight?"

Dambala scratched at his head under the band of his hat. "Don't think we have to, if you need us for somethin'."

"Yeah, I'll get Clarence to hand you the messages to run in the morning. You'll get 'em where they need to go faster than our regular fellow. You'll have to sleep in the shed, but we'll feed you proper. Where did you leave your strays?"

"They're with the motorcycles, behind warehouse six."

Mag nodded and fetched Clarence; he didn't look thrilled, but he took it as duty to bring new people properly into the town. He'd taken better to her drawing the line about witchiness than the men from Shimera and Rouse.

Dambala and Davey each got a helping of dinner in the house, and a proper introduction to Anabi. It didn't escape Mag's notice how the young woman shied away from even touching them. She did her best to indicate that they were good folk, ones that she'd known for a long time, but the wounded-animal look in Anabi's eyes was far too familiar. Then there was the bad news out of Tercio, the happenings in Shimera to be discussed. Anabi sat with her head bowed the entire time.

Anabi waited for her in Mag's room after dinner, a tattered flimsy clutched in her hands. She thrust it at Mag, who silently read: *I got thrown out of Harmony before we even knew that the Weatherman was coming. For other reasons. But in Tercio, they were going to hang me because of him. If he's coming here, they'll take me.*

"I'm sorry." The flimsy crumpled in her hand.

When the Weatherman came to Ludlow, she'd be in the same situation. She'd already decided she wasn't going to run again. "I got a revolver, in my dresser. I was thinkin' to just shoot myself if it comes to that."

Anabi shook her head, took the flimsy back and scribbled another sentence: *That can't be the answer.*

"You can run if you like, if there's a place you can run to and stay ahead of him. But I'm done running. Once was enough for me."

Anabi looked close to tears: *Is there any way to stop him?*

Mag laughed bitterly. "Not unless you got an army in your pocket. I barely got the reps from Shimera to agree that hangin' people weren't any kind of answer. Can't count on anyone sticking their neck out."

And yet. Mag frowned, as an idea uncurled itself in her mind.

Anabi reached out and gently shook her shoulder, head tilted to one side.

"You go on to sleep. I'll be gone a while." Mag smiled at Anabi, covered the woman's hand with hers for a moment, and then hurried from the room.

"We talked about this not four days ago, Mag," Odalia said. She glanced at Clarence, who looked ready to fall asleep at any moment. "Knowin' what happened in Tercio don't make much of a difference. We can't pick this kind of fight, not right now, and not for a few people half of us think ought to be dead anyway."

Mag leaned forward where she sat on an empty crate, elbows on her knees. "But what if we weren't the ones pickin' the fight?"

"Mayhap it's 'cause I'm sleepy, Mag, but could you explain yourself?"

"We don't got the guts or guns to do it ourselves. But the Ghost Wolves do, I wager. We hire 'em, have them do the deed before the bastard gets to Ludlow."

That woke Clarence up proper. "They're bandit busters, Mag, nothin' more than that. Ain't near enough of 'em."

"Old Nick wouldn't've done it. But he ain't in charge any more, remember? I know Hob, from way back. And they got no reason to lay that low, not after what happened in Rouse. We get a good enough payment together, I wager anything that they'll take the job." Hob had already been nibbling at the edges of it, after all, saving the witchy ones and calling it work by taking their cash. She'd as much as said she wanted Mag to aim her. Well, this was one hell of a target.

Odalia shook her head. "You can't kill a Weatherman."

"Hob almost did this one. Shot 'im in the neck. You heard talk about him only talkin' like a croakin' lizard."

"I don't believe it," Odalia snapped, but there was doubt in her eyes. "They ain't like us."

"They'll take a bullet and bleed from it like any other man. And what bleeds can die."

Clarence looked thoughtful, smoothing his mustache with one hand. "Think the Ravani can manage to shoot him in the head this time?"

Odalia shook her head. "You're talkin' a price that we don't even know the size of to protect a few people the preachers flat out want us to burn."

"Not all the preachers. And it ain't just them. It's their family and friends. Have you heard about any of *them* makin' it back to their towns after they been taken? And what about the two that got shot in Tercio, all because someone didn't want to see an innocent person get put on that damn train?"

"If we pay them, it'll hang on us."

Mag shook her head, gritting her teeth around her desire to shout. She had to be reasonable, logical. "People pay the Wolves to do things all the time, and you'd never know. Just short everyone's water ration a bit each week and send that to them. Little things like that, no one'll notice if you don't tell 'em. They'll take just anythin' they can get, since they got no supply train bringin' stuff to them. Broke machines with salvageable wiring, things like that even."

"You've gone crooked in the brainpan, girl."

"Mayhap." Mag stood, no longer able to hold in the anger that burned in her stomach. "But tell you what I am, both of you. I'm damn tired of running. You keep sayin' tomorrow, tomorrow, we ain't ready yet. Tomorrow ain't ever gonna come, Odalia Vigil. You keep sayin' it's just a few people. Well, *we're* just a few people on the face of this goddamn planet, and we're all of us together whether you want to admit it or not. If we won't stand for our brothers and sisters, who the hell's gonna stand for us?" She slapped her hand down on a crate, so hard her palm went numb, and it just made her madder. "We ain't ever gonna stand for anythin' if we ain't got a spine!"

Odalia looked stunned, like Mag had hit her with

a shovel instead of just words. Clarence listened, face
still sleepy but his eyes alert and glittering.

Well before dawn, she had an offer to send with
Dambala and Davey to go with the messenger bag.

Hob stared at Mag's familiar handwriting, reading the
offer through a second time. She hadn't been joking,
quite, when she'd told Mag she had the better aim.
But goddamn, she'd never imagined aiming this high.

"I think they were serious," Davey offered, when
she said nothing.

"Oh, I know they are. Mag don't do a thing that
ain't serious as a heart attack." She set the flimsy
down. She knew what Old Nick would have said
to something like this – too dangerous, not enough
payout, too splashy. But she wasn't Old Nick, and even
if she wanted to protect his legacy, being him wasn't
the way to do it. He'd tried to teach her self-respect in
his own fucked-up way, but had never quite realized
the contradiction of hiding their witchiness even from
those close as kin like it was a thing of shame instead
of a mark of survival – or what a hypocrisy it was to
turn his back on the other witches when they were
in need.

There wasn't really a choice here, not if she wanted
to be able to look herself in the mirror ever again.
The Wolves needed a job that paid, and she needed it
to be a job that meant something. And if they killed
the Weatherman – *if they killed the Weatherman* – they
removed TransRift's greatest weapon against the
witches.

She looked up at Dambala. From the steady gaze

he offered back, he already knew the answer and approved. "We're gonna kill us a Weatherman," she said.

"Shit," Davey breathed. Dambala simply nodded in answer.

Her hand felt far steadier than it had any right to when she put her pen on that contract offer, considering she might be signing all their death warrants. But Coyote had always said none of them were here looking to live a long and safe life. Maybe she owed it to the Wolves as well, to not second guess herself into stasis, the way Old Nick had at the end.

She folded the flimsies up and handed them back to Dambala. "You get these back to Mag."

He took them and hid them away in his jacket. "Heard anythin' from Coyote yet?"

"Nah, not yet. Harmony's a full day away if he caught the right train, more if he didn't." She pulled a small calendar book out of her desk, a present Mag had given to Nick that still had a heartbreaking number of pages left in it. Hob had written the witch hunt days down in it so she couldn't miscount them. "I want us at Shimera when the Weatherman's there, so we can see the dog and pony show ourselves, from start to finish. I wager he'll be back before then."

Dambala glanced at the calendar and nodded. "Wouldn't want him to miss the fun."

CHAPTER THIRTY-FIVE

Fun was the last thing on Coyote's mind. Stupid was foremost, with a healthy helping of regret. He should have known better than to ride a train so far afield, when it meant no easy avenue of escape; damn his dislike of camping anyway. He should have thought of a lot of things, but no, he'd started believing in his own legend, in the invincibility of Coyote, who could talk himself out of anything.

Coyote squirmed carefully, trying to find a more comfortable position for his back against the dirt wall of the root cellar. The skin of his shoulder and arm stretched tight, angry and red, his entire body throbbing in time with his heartbeat. He was full of birdshot and pus.

It had gone wrong from the start, but he still couldn't define exactly how wrong, or why. Days in advance, Harmony had been preparing for the arrival of the Weatherman like he was the second coming, had the brass band practicing and everything, flowers and decorations and an air of fierce righteousness. He'd stuck out like a sore thumb in that, expecting the same kind of attitudes that were normal in the mining towns near Rouse, which had been a stupid assumption to make. The people of Harmony already didn't like strangers. He'd done his best to just be neighborly, hang out in the saloon and listen, but then that farmer had shown up, the one that'd looked a lot like Anabi, and he hadn't been quick enough to hide that little prickle of recognition, hadn't been glib enough about changing the subject…

Well, the Coyote of legend had always talked himself *into* trouble first.

The shotgun came out then, and things had gone painful and confused. Since then, it'd been just a dark cellar and stinking pain, and he hadn't figured a way out of it yet. Escape seemed less likely with each passing hour, since the more his shoulder ached and flowed cloudy, stinking fluid, the less clear his thoughts became.

Coyote heard voices muffled through the cellar doors and didn't stir. The few times he'd heard anyone get that close, it'd just been so they could pry a board back from the door and throw down a hunk of bread to him before hammering it securely back into place.

This time, though, the cellar doors opened fully. He shielded his eyes with the hand he could move, squinting into the bright white light.

"This is the one," a man's voice said. "Came around askin' some funny questions. Didn't seem right to us. We think he's some sort of… agitator. Here to pour poison in the ears of good folk."

"You were right to bring this to my attention, thank you." The other speaker was also a man, his voice smoothed and polished, the accent screaming *offworlder* and *upper class*. Something else about the voice was eerily familiar, but Coyote cut off that impossible train of thought before it took him to a really idiotic place. "You, down there. Step into the light."

"Yeah, step into the light," the farmer said. "Don't make me come down there and get ya."

"A moment, if you please." Coyote struggled to stand on stiff, cramped legs. He should have kept himself moving around, but the cellar wasn't even tall enough for him, and after three days of high fever he was too damn tired to do much of anything. Still shielding his eyes with one hand, he stumbled into the light. "It's all a mistake, I swear. I think I got off the train at the wrong stop."

"Looks a bit of a mess, doesn't he…"

Coyote found himself peering into a face that was unfamiliar around eyes that he'd recognize anywhere. Eyes he looked at every time he hazarded a glance at the mirror. Eyes far too like his – *their* – father's. It felt like ten lifetimes ago, but he could still remember the old man clearly, the cold look in his eyes when he'd shipped his oldest son – and the black sheep of the family – off to military boarding school and Jeuno Prime. And now, somehow, those eyes belonged to someone wearing a company blue suit.

The company man's arms whipped out too fast for Coyote to track. There was a twist, a crack like the popping of a joint, and the farmer dropped. The company man turned back to Coyote, adjusted his tie, and said, "Killed while you escaped, I assume. I'm surprised to see you alive, Kazuhiro, and here, of all places. Though I suppose I shouldn't be. We've always been survivors."

"It's Coyote now. I haven't been Kazu for something like sixteen years." Coyote smiled miserably at his youngest brother – Shigehiko, the exuberant prince, the one designed from the ground up because the other kids had been such disappointments. Fuck their parents anyway. And fuck whoever had done the face sculpt on him, he almost wouldn't have known. "Can't say I'm impressed by the company you're keeping, Shige. How does mother feel about it?"

Shige laughed softly. "It's more complicated than you'd think. Let's just say that I've gone into the family business, since you had no interest in doing so. Now, what's this nonsense about your name?"

"Coyote," he repeated. "My name's Coyote now."

"How… charming. I never thought you looked like much of a Kazuhiro, though I'm not certain how much Coyote really suits either."

"It's served me well enough."

"What sort of crowd are you running around with these days? You never struck me as the sort to go farmer. Or miner, for that matter. You're not nearly responsible enough."

He grinned crazily at his brother. He guessed that was supposed to sting, that casually thrown little barb. But he was well acquainted with his own faults; they kept him warm at night. "Mercenary outfit's probably the closest to it. We get by well enough."

Shige's eyes narrowed slightly. "Don't tell me you're associated with that mad Ravani woman."

"She's my boss."

Shige snorted. "Well, that makes things easier, I suppose. I've got some information for her if you'd like to pass it along."

"Shoot." He wondered how Shige had found Hob; that probably made him her new source that she'd been so smug about. That also explained the sudden question about him having family around. He'd have to warn her about this, even if it meant coming clean on the ugliness of his own history. This was not a level of politics she'd want to get involved in, the arcane kind where people in suits worth an entire year of mining wages sipped cocktails and casually talked about the overthrow of entire planets.

"The schedule's being moved up. Mr Green – the Weatherman – is feeling quite a bit stronger lately, so he's decided to visit a town every three days instead of once a week. The date for Shimera hasn't changed, since they probably won't have the pad around the train station constructed in time otherwise, but Ludlow will be three days after. And after Ludlow, Delagua and Pryor."

Coyote repeated the information back to his brother; it was a little trick they'd all learned on their mother's knee. "Surprised you're being so free with information. What's the catch?"

"No catch." Shige smiled at the disbelieving look Coyote gave him. "Not as of yet. There's a larger game afoot, and I think your... boss... could prove useful. Unless you'd care to take up the responsibilities you so callously left behind."

Coyote laughed. "Not a chance in hell." He had every intention of running back to the den and telling

Hob to steer clear of his brother. She probably already had the right idea; she was a paranoid customer by nature. But if intelligence agencies from the Union were starting to take an interest in Tanegawa's World, it was time to batten down the hatches and lay low.

Shige checked his watch. "I'd love to chat more and catch up, but they might send someone to look for me if I don't return soon. I assume you'll be able to get yourself out of here?"

It didn't really matter if he could or not, Coyote knew. Loyalty to the Union first, family second. Shige wouldn't piss on him if he was on fire, not if it meant compromising his cover. "I'll figure something out."

"Good. Because I'd rather no one else see us together. We look a little too much alike. It's probably the eyes."

"The damn Rollins eyes from Father. Even if it looks like you've lost the Tsukui nose."

Shige smirked. "Take care, brother. I'll find you again at some point soon, since you might know something useful."

Coyote waited until his brother was out of sight before muttering, "Not a chance in hell, you little shit." He staggered up the few steps to the surface and dropped to his knees next to the crumpled body of the farmer. One-armed, he rifled through the man's pockets until he came up with something useful – keys. Two of which might be for vehicles.

At least this area of the town was deserted; everyone was out at the train station, to be viewed by the Weatherman. Coyote took his time, went through the farmer's house and got himself all the water he could drink and carry, wolfed down what food he could find, grabbed the farmer's shotgun and his revolver. Farmers got to have guns, how nice for them. To shoot at any native or introduced species that sought to bother their crops, he supposed. Then he made his way out to the shed where the vehicles would be kept. He had to stop twice on the way and just breathe until his vision cleared.

There was a solar-powered harvester in the shed, and a tractor. Neither of them were desirable as a getaway vehicle. Coyote sighed and picked the tractor, since it was lighter and had a better chance of making it somewhere if he stuck to hardpan.

He roared out of the back end of Harmony at a majestic thirty-five kilometers per hour, engine humming away just under the red line. It was frustrating, but, he kept reminding himself, it was better than walking. He gauged a course by the sun and tried to remember where the hell Harmony was on the map relative to anything else. It was on the wrong side of Newcastle, far from any town that he knew.

The solar panels fixed on the tractor meant he didn't have to worry about running out of fuel. It was just a question of if he'd get somewhere before the sand in the dune fields destroyed the tractor's drive.

The ride was shockingly green at first, kilometers and kilometers of carefully irrigated fields before he climbed a steep hill and out of the protected valley, into the hot wind and sparse plants of the desert plain. Even that was all right going, though he had to slow down a bit to get through some of the deeper dust bowls. After that was a track of kilometers and kilometers of hardpan.

Too soon, the hardpan gave way to dunes. He picked his way as gingerly as possible, but less than an hour in, the tractor finally stuck immovably, and that was the end of the road. He stayed in the shaded cabin, running the tractor's little fan until the sun went down. Then he set out on the dunes, keeping his feet to the west using the stars.

He shivered into the cool night, his mouth sucked dry by fever. The tractor far out of sight behind him, his knees gave way and he tumbled down the slip face of the dune, laying out in the sand at the bottom. "Can't talk my way out of this one," he mumbled, fingers curling in the sand. "'Cause sand's a shitty listener."

Then silence, and the far off, yipping howl of a species that had never set foot on Tanegawa's world: coyote.

CHAPTER THIRTY-SIX

Midway through the week, and still no sign of Coyote. Hob sent Dambala out by motorcycle, Akela and Maheegan to back him up, round trip and camping be damned. Motorcycles meant they could go armed as heavy as they liked, and make a quick escape if necessary – and that they could keep their eyes peeled for circling eagles. She didn't say that, but they were all thinking it.

Hob brooded mightily about why she'd been so damn stupid as to send a Wolf out alone. If Old Nick had still been around, he would have thought of all these things, cleared his throat and reminded her what needed to be done in that special tone that implied she was an idiot. Except if he was still alive, it wouldn't be her outfit to run, her Wolves to get killed, either.

She couldn't help but wonder, maybe, if that would be for the best. And the person who gave her little pep talks, who cajoled her along when she was teetering and feeling like a shitty leader, was the one who was missing. Now that was some irony there.

She pulled the stained envelope across her desk,

direct from Ludlow and set down by Dambala himself five minutes before she'd turned around and sent him back out to go searching. Inside waited the little handwritten contract, signed and countersigned. The simple flimsy felt heavy in her hands: it was probably the largest job the Wolves had ever had in their history. This was no den of bandits that needed to be wiped off the map; this was a planned and calculated attack against a heavily armed security force. Doubts didn't matter now, because they were committed; the stark signature in black and white made that a certainty. The only mortal sin a Wolf could commit, Old Nick had told her, was to welch on a contract.

She tucked the flimsy away, and pulled out the roster of the Wolves that remained – nineteen strong now, with the new recruits. Only eighteen without Coyote, but she lied to herself, pretended she was sure Dambala would find him and bring him home.

Shooting the Weatherman before hadn't been *easy*. It had been an accident, a gut reaction, her hand moving before her brain could catch up. Right place and right time weren't going to just happen again. They had to be created.

Shimera was the Weatherman's next stop, and the last chance before Ludlow. Time enough to suss out the situation, count the guns and see the security setup so they could cut a plan in the intervening week.

Hob pulled a small party together to go to Shimera: herself, Freki, Geri, Conall, Raff. They left the base when the night was deep and cold, guiding their motorcycles through the dunes and box canyons between with hands that felt half-frozen in the wind.

They broke from the dune sea that surrounded Shimera before the sun had even begun to rise. The Weatherman would be coming in not long after breakfast if the train didn't have to plow through too many dunes, and Hob wanted to be in place and watching well before that.

They moved up and down the surrounding area, circling dunes until Geri made a joke about getting seasick, before they found a good path up onto a nearby butte. The top was flat, covered with reddish dust and black rocks, dotted with scrub. The sides facing Shimera were near vertical. Hob had Freki walk the top of the butte, binoculars fixed over his eyes, his brother spotting him with a hand on his belt to keep him from getting too close to the edge. He found a good spot where they could settle and see down into the town – more importantly, get a good view of the train station.

"Geri, you and Conall go into town. Hang around in the crowd. Don't think anyone will recognize you two." She rubbed the bridge of her nose with one finger. "You should be fine so long as neither of you has a witchy little secret. And if you do, out with it now or forever hold your peace." The two men looked at each other. Conall shrugged; Geri rolled his eyes. "Get goin', then. When all the pomp and circumstance is done, we meet up at the bottom of that little trail."

As the sun came up, Freki and Raff set up a makeshift blind with camouflage tarp, positioned so the sun would be to their backs. No use having light glinting directly off metal or glass; that was amateur stuff.

394   HUNGER MAKES THE WOLF

It was already stinking hot in the blind when they all crawled in. The men had binoculars, Hob had a scope that she'd pulled from the armory. Attaching it to a rifle was damned tempting, to take a shot at the Weatherman. But none of them were good enough shots to guarantee a kill with a single bullet at that distance. She'd sent their one good sniper, Maheegan, off with Dambala.

Raff pulled a dusty deck from his pocket with scarred brown hands, surprisingly delicate fingers knobbly knuckled from some long ago accident or fight he didn't talk about. The cards scraped and scratched as he shuffled and dealt them each five. They bet using pebbles and a few dried-up beetles, ones with shells that glimmered with iridescence like an oil slick. Hob tracked time on her pocket watch, the minutes crawling by in the heat.

The sound of a train whistle had Raff scrambling the cards back into his pocket. Hob lifted her scope to her eye, tracking across the ground until she found the train, coming from a canyon. Sand burst up around the engine in a wave as it plowed through a small dune. The train was sleek and silver, its skin blinding in the morning light, curved to a graceful wedge in the front.

"Don't think I ever seen one quite like that," Hob said, looking down at the passenger cars. There were only three, and the shape of them was unmistakable, though they had no windows.

"Me neither," Raff agreed.

"Bet it's armored."

"I don't take sucker bets."

"Took enough of 'em off Freki just now." The shape of the train, everything about it, made their normal robbery style impossible. The thing looked like it had been poured from molten metal; there wasn't a handhold or a hatch to be seen. "I think if we want on that thing before it gets to the station, we're gonna just have to find a way of stoppin' it. Take a good look at the wheels." Most trains dealt well with track disruptions; they had to in a place where tracks could be easily buried.

"Thing's probably magnetic."

Hob huffed out a sound of agreement. "Anyone could get that shit to work here, it'd be with a Weatherman aboard."

The train pulled into the station, the squeal of the brakes echoing. It didn't matter how clean and sleek something looked; dust got into everything. The doors slid smoothly back, releasing a flood of men in green Mariposa uniforms, each armed with a rifle. Hob scanned the outer edge of the crowd to find uniforms there too, probably from the town's garrison.

"That's a lot of greenbellies," Raff muttered.

"As expected." She tracked movement within the town: another man in green, herding a couple ahead of him toward the square. Probably picking up stragglers for the Weatherman's little viewing. "Hell of a lot, but not more'n we can handle if we take the big guns out and get 'em parked somewhere useful. Element of surprise, bottleneck 'em, I think we can take away the number advantage. But we gotta hit this thing far out of town. Don't need the Ludlow garrison breathin' down our neck too, and in-town fighting's what fucked us before." Too much uncontrolled territory, too many noncombatants, no way to make an effective trap. She'd learned that lesson well.

"Weatherman's comin' out," Freki said.

Hob dragged her field of view back up to see the thin, reedy man exit the train car. Just the sight of him made her feel a little sick. Her free hand found its way to her revolver, guided by instinct that screamed *it's unnatural, kill it, kill it.* "That's him, all right," she said with a mouth suddenly dry as the sand around them. That was the one she'd shot before. Damn. She forced her hand to her cigarettes instead, slipping one out. A quick glance at Freki and Raff told her neither seemed more than curious.

"If we could do more'n stop the train, mayhap if we could damage it, derail it or somethin', that'd take some of the greenbellies out before we ever had to fight 'em," Raff commented.

"Tryin' to derail that thing'll be a bitch, but we got time to work the problem. Freki, you'n your brother's good with numbers and the like. Figure out a way to do it."

Freki grunted in response. Hob focused on the Weatherman again; he moved through the crowd. She shuddered, lips curling back in revulsion at the sight of those spidery hands. He picked out a young woman; the guards grabbed her, shoved her toward the train. "Bastard. Anyway... you can go make nice with some o' the engineers in Ludlow. Find out what you can about the explosives they use for minin'."

"No one's gonna sell us explosives," Freki said.

"Guarded too close."

"Bet they ain't guarded that close on the trains. Get us the specs, and if Coyote's supply train timetables hold true…" Down in the town, the guards separated more people out from the crowd, probably the woman's family. "Once we got the stuff, don't matter none if they know it's missing. By the time they figure out who's got it, we'll have 'em." She tucked the cigarette between her lips. At this distance, no one in town would be able to see the smoke or the glow, and she needed something to calm her nerves, the unending beat of fury that just looking at the goddamn Weatherman had lit in her. She snapped her fingers. "We got a week, some town oughta be gettin' in some charges atween now and then…"

Down in the town far below, the Weatherman froze, spine going ramrod stiff, straining as if he was a hound that had just caught a scent. She wondered what unfortunate bastard was about to get pulled from the crowd–

He turned and looked at her, down the barrel of the scope, straight into her brain. Unseen claws dug into her head, all around her face, yanking her toward the edge of the cliff. Hob dropped the scope, one hand swiping at her eye, because without the scope he was still there, mouth moving and whispering.

"Good morning." The sound, so soft and innocuous, filled her ears, echoed and re-echoed until she could hear nothing else, so loud that it split her head open.

Hob fell like a rag doll and jerked against the dusty ground, slamming her head against a rock. Freki cursed and threw himself on top of her as she rolled toward the cliff edge. The barrel of her revolver made a burning line into his side. She slammed her head into a rock again, a small scream escaping her mouth before Raff clapped his hand over the sound. Raff cursed a bare second later, yanking his hand away, smeared with blood.

"Hob? Hob!" Freki hissed. He caught one look into her eye, gone wide and wild and bestial, and knew that she wasn't going to answer. Freki slapped his hand over Hob's mouth to hold in the next scream, and he didn't do more than grimace as her teeth sank deep into the flesh at the base of his thumb. He kept his hand there, pinched her nose shut with his thumb and just held on as she jerked against him, movements becoming more and more sluggish.

When she went still, he pulled his hand free, leaning down to make sure she still breathed. Air tickled past his ear: good enough. "Check what's goin' on in the town," he snarled at Raff, then crawled away from the edge, dragging Hob behind him.

Blood welled from under her eyelid, flowed from both her ears, from the cut on the back of her head. He crawled a good distance from the edge of the butte, dragging her one-armed, and then picked her up, slinging her over his shoulder like she weighed nothing.

"Somethin's goin' on, Freki. Like a fuckin' anthill down there."

"No fuckin' shit. We're goin'. Throw the net over your bike. Take mine, it's better." He didn't wait to see Raff follow the order; he ran over to Hob's motorcycle, the best out of the bunch, stuck her on in front of him. She was way too tall to be manhandled that way, floppy arms and legs everywhere they didn't need to be. Cursing a blue streak, he got her propped over the battery stack, arms folded up enough that he could hold her in place, then revved the engine and burned ass for the trail down. He pointed them for the nearest canyon; it was in the wrong direction, but that'd be a place to lose anyone who might try to follow, leaving no tracks.

A steady trail of blood ran down from Hob's head, dripping slowly off the battery stack as they went.

CHAPTER THIRTY-SEVEN

Back in the airconditioned comfort of the train car, Shige sat with Mr Green, who rocked slowly back and forth, humming a quiet tune to himself with his ruined voice. The Weatherman seemed quite satisfied: two "witchy" people had been captured in Shimera, and a search party sent up to a nearby butte at his near-hysterical insistence. Mr Green had wanted to go himself, but the security supervisor who had come with them put his foot down. The Weatherman was not to leave the confines of the synthcrete pad, not with unknown risks out in the sands.

The search party was the reason they were still in Shimera, minutes clicking steadily by as they fell further and further behind schedule. Shige read over his notes, trying to think if there was any detail he'd missed. Ms Meetchim would want to hear all about the incident in her morning briefing.

The door slid open, revealing the security supervisor, now red faced and sporting a sheen of sweat. Shige rose to his feet. "Had any luck?"

"We didn't find anyone, but someone *was* there all right. Our dog found blood."

Shige nodded. "Probably a refugee or two from Shimera, trying to hide from the hunt. Even if they've escaped for now, I don't think they'll do that well in the desert."

"I've ordered the town shut in for a day, so no one can go try to help them out on the sly." The train car shuddered, and the supervisor caught himself lightly on the doorframe as they pulled from the station. "Don't know if it was just miners trying to pull a fast one, though. There was a motorcycle abandoned at the top of the butte, and tracks for two more, headed straight for the nearest stretch of hardpan. Found this, too." He pulled a scope, the sort that came off a high-powered rifle, from his pocket and handed it to Shige.

Shige held it up to his eye; one lens was cracked, and he could tell the others in the scope were out of alignment. "It's broken."

"Broken or not, I don't see why a miner would be running around with it."

Shige rolled the scope in his fingers. He found a rough spot on the side and inspected it more closely. "Something has been filed off here. It could be stolen company property."

The supervisor took the scope back. "Ah, I see it now. Might not be stolen property in that case. When we send our boys out to infiltrate with bandits, we remove the identifying marks ourselves." He tucked the scope away again. "I'll check and see if we've had people in that area lately. Sure as hell makes more sense than those townies growing some balls."

"Let me know what you find. I'll need to include it in my report to the vice president." Shige nodded when the supervisor saluted, and headed into the next car. He found it amusing that the supervisor was so eager to pick out the most innocuous explanation. Prejudices worked strangely that way. Personally, he doubted just as much that it had been someone from Shimera. He had his own working theories.

Mr Green smiled beatifically at him when he sat, pausing in his singing and rocking to ask, "Did they find the fire, Mr Rolland?"

"I'm afraid not, Mr Green. It had already gone out by the time they got to the butte. But well done today. You think quite quickly." Shige looked down at his notes, at his own notation about fire. Indeed, he had his own theories, ones involving that mad Ravani woman, and those would most definitely not be included in his report.

Freki waited for his brother in Hob's office when Geri and Conall came rolling in twenty-four hours late, irritatingly well rested and well fed. Freki had taken up station behind her desk, supply lists, flimsy sheets covered with neat lines of calculations, and maps surrounding him. He fixed Geri with bloodshot eyes. "Where the fuck've you been?"

"They locked down the town for a full twenty-four hours after the Weatherman left." Geri sat on the hard metal chair in front of the desk. "The fuck happened with you guys? Saw a bunch of guards burnin' ass to the gates and heading toward the butte, but weren't nothin' we could do."

"Weatherman did somethin' to Hob. Dunno what. Had some kind of fuckin' seizure and ain't come out of it yet."

Geri whistled low. "Who's been in charge, then?"

Freki frowned, not liking how fast that question came out. "Me. Worked out how much blast we'll need to derail the train. Sent men out to Rouse and Ludlow, see what's what with their shipments."

"What if she don't wake up?"

"Closed topic."

"You better start thinkin' on it, though. If she's been out for a day…"

Freki slammed his pencil down. "You my brother, or an eagle?"

Geri folded his hands over his belly. "You know I got a point."

"Yeah, I know." Freki sighed, scrubbing at his eyes with one hand. "If she's still out when Dambala gets back with Coyote, gonna see what they think of the situation."

"Dambala an' Coyote ain't interested in leadin'."

"And you're too damn interested in it for anyone's good."

Geri's face twisted a little. "What the hell do you know?"

He smiled. "About you? More'n I ought." That got Geri to laugh at least, then someone knocked on the office door. Freki stared at the door, lips closing firm out of habit.

After a pause, another knock, Geri answered: "Enter." He rolled his eyes at Freki. "See, this is why this job ain't for you. You don't like talkin' to anyone but me."

Freki snorted, fitting *sometimes I don't even fucking*

like talking to you into the sound neatly.

Davey poked his head in. "Someone's here. Wants to talk to Hob."

"Someone?" Geri tilted his head to the side. "Ain't any someones that should even know where to find us."

"Didn't give no name. Just this." He held out a scrap of cloth. Geri passed it to Freki with a nasty little grin. Freki unrolled the cloth, revealing a knuckle bone.

"Shit," Geri muttered.

"Let him in. Give him whatever he wants," Freki said.

As soon as Davey closed the door, Geri leaned forward in his chair. "You don't think it's that same guy. You can't."

They'd both been with Hob a decade ago when they'd gone to see the supposed statue in the cave, the one that had turned into a living breathing man. They'd both seen him, clear as day, walk out across the dunes and vanish when they'd been trying to bury the company man and preacher they'd killed to protect him – a damn statue. Freki stood, looked out the window. He twitched the curtain aside so his brother could see the pale man coming in through the gate, looking like he hadn't aged a day. "Don't rightly matter what I think."

CHAPTER THIRTY-EIGHT

Then

As she turns the corner on the second floor, someone reaches from the darkened hall, long arm wrapping around her throat. A thin hand covered with a worn, familiar glove catches her wrist, fingers pressing bruises into her skin as she tries to whip up the knife that comes to her hand.

"Quiet now, girly," Nick whispers into her ear. "Or I might just gut you with your own knife."

His tone chills her blood, prickles all the hair up on her skin. He will kill her if she struggles. She freezes.

Nick twists the knife from her hand and lets go. She throws herself back, running her shoulders into the wall, pressing her hands against it.

"I gave you two rules," he says his quiet words venomous. "Two simple goddamn rules, and you agreed to them, you lying little bitch."

She feels lightheaded, frozen, unable to speak or move. It's a nightmare, a hallucination. How is Nick home and no one else?

As if he read her mind, he says, "Got news of what you done, and I come home early. And god help me if he exists, 'cause I left everyone else to do the job. I wanted to give you a fuckin' chance."

"I don't know what you mean," she whispers. She's afraid to raise her voice more than that, in case Jeb, waiting in her room and naked as the day he was born, hears, in case Nick takes it as reason to slit her throat.

"You brung someone here. Even after I told you not to," he hisses. "And you want to know why? Lookin' at me with those goddamn innocent eyes of yours, you fuckin' idiot?" He opens his hand; there are five little silver buttons on his palm, all blackened and twisted.

"What are those?"

"Short range transmitters. And all of them in a trail from Rouse to our fuckin' doorstep."

She shakes her head. "Can't be true."

"You goin' to be stupid along with bein' a damned liar?"

Everything hurts: her eyes, her throat, her heart, her brain. "He loves me," she whispers.

"Mayhap he's an idiot too." Nick stuffs the transmitters into her breast pocket, then grabs her hand and shoves the knife back in it, wrapping her fingers around the hilt. He squeezes hard, twice, before she can make her fingers work.

She shakes her head, trying to push the knife back at him, because it's impossible, it's impossible, she's bleeding out without a cut in her skin.

"You done this. If you'd just fuckin' listened to me, you could've had your little boy toy, and kept him at a safe distance until you got bored with him, or really fuckin' lost your shit and married him. But you chose this road. This is your mistake. And you're gonna damn well fix it." He grabs her shoulder with a bruising grip, shaking her. "Look at me, goddammit!"

She tries, but his face is a pale blur, an unsteady wash of color that won't hold still. A strange, low moan comes from her throat.

"Don't you put this decision on me." Suddenly he just sounds tired and old, talking though a throat gone rusty. "I already killed too much of what I loved."

There is a horrible, ageless truth in his voice. Jeb will die no matter what tonight. She has no illusions that she'll be able to fight Old Nick, and no desire to even try on account of someone who has betrayed her. Because she believes Nick. He's a liar, and a cheat, and a nasty piece of work, but he's never betrayed her. Even when everyone else has.

The choice is horrible, and simple, and she made it long ago even if she hadn't known at the time.

Hob forces herself to suck in two breaths, and nods. Head light and far away, she turns and walks back up the stairs, feet not making a sound even on the creaky boards. Some memory from Makaya's thorough training has her holding the knife angled behind her back, so Jeb, her beautiful, dark-haired boy, won't see it until it's too late.

She pushes the door of her room open.

Jeb sits up in bed, gives her a broad smile. The expression fades away to nothing as he takes in her pale face, the way her shoulders shake. "You all right, Hob? You look like you've seen a ghost…"

She reaches into her pocket and pulls out one of the

transmitters, holds it up to the light. It would be easier, if he'd beg or rage or try to tell her his innocence. But in his wide, dark eyes, she finds only guilt and resignation, like he's a thief who's been caught with his hand in someone's pocket.

She walks over to him, runs her hand through his hair. His eyelids flutter, his face relaxing like he takes it as a sign that everything was all right, and he opens his mouth to tell her that he loves her.

Her hands know what Makaya the Debt Keeper taught her, the one tightening to iron in his curly hair, yanking his head back. And with the other she cuts off those words, those lies, before they make it out of his throat.

And the blood sprays a hot line, sprays and sprays and sprayspraysprays

Until the roof tears off her little attic room and she looks up, up into the endless blue. It's a blur with the tears streaming from her eye. Distractedly, she wipes her cheek with a hot, wet hand, leaves behind a smear something far thicker than water.

The sky bursts with fire, arcs stretching, feathering, flying. Phoenix. The phoenix, her phoenix. It opens its beak, and she opens her arms to it. Because if it's to be more fire, maybe this time she'll just burn.

Instead, feathers touch her cheeks like a caress and the phoenix whispers in a surprisingly gentle voice, "The past is the past, dear one. *Return. Wake. Live.*"

She tried to open her eye, but it was gummed shut. Her head pounded in time with her heartbeat; it felt like someone opened up the back of her skull with a hammer and no chisel. Cool lines against her cheeks – soft skin, fingers, and she felt breath brush against her lips, could almost feel those lips hovering over hers. And she wanted it. For one aching, horrible moment she wanted to wrap her fingers in his shirt – well-worn cotton, bone buttons, she could feel it, knew it, smelled him – and pull him closer, lose all that pain in a different way, in happiness at that son of a bitch being alive, or her being alive too.

But she remembered the heated spray of blood across her face, going tacky on her fingers, and swallowed back a retch. Her hand found the smooth butt of one revolver. She pulled it quietly from the holster, and pressed the muzzle against the side of the man leaning over her.

"Gettin' a little too close for comfort," she growled. Her throat felt scratchy and ached with each word.

"You needn't be so touchy, dearest."

She kept the firm pressure up on the revolver until she felt him move back, his fingers slipping away from her face. Then she used her other hand to rub at her eye until her lashes unstuck and she could blink. Remnants of gummy black blood crumbled between her fingers.

And there stood the Bone Collector, exactly the same as when she'd last seen him. She rubbed lightly at her cheek and sat up. The room was familiar; the sick room at the base. She was in the same bed Old Nick had died in, like a cosmic joke. She felt too damned rotten to be dead. "What're you doin' here?"

"You called me with blood."

She snorted, then gently probed at the back of

her head with one hand. Her fingers found stitches. "Didn't work the last two times I tried to do that."

"You used a lot more blood this time." He looked pointedly down at the gun still pressed against his side.

"You should be more careful about how you wake a body up. Some folk get mighty sensitive about it." She tucked the revolver away. "You been sick?" She swung her legs around, planted her feet on the floor. She wasn't ready to stand, not yet, with her head feeling so wobbly, but just having her feet firm made her feel better.

"There was something I needed to do."

"Hope it was worth it. 'Cause while you were gone, company's gone through four towns." She pressed the heel of her hand against her eye for a moment. "Five, even. Thought you woulda cared about that, the way you talk such a big game." She reached over to slap at his arm, noticed too late how his expression had frozen.

Then he had her by the shirt, fabric balled up in his fist, and yanked her from the bed like she weighed nothing, pinned her against the wall. "Have a care what you say," he hissed, eyes blazing. "I am not your *flunky*."

Fear surged into her throat, made her mouth sour. One hand went for her revolver again, instinct moving her fingers, but she tensed, stopped herself before she drew. Shooting wasn't going to do anything but cause anger and regrets. A flash of blue, peeking from his shirt cuff, caught her eye. She pushed his sleeve back to reveal blue in a fine line up his arm as far as she could see, hard under her fingertips. That line, like a vein turned to diamond, hummed when she touched it, made the fire roar up in her blood just like–

"What the hell did you do to yourself?" she whispered. She looked into eyes with pupils blown so wide she couldn't even see the ice blue of his irises any more. His mouth twisted strangely when she ran her thumb over that blue line again, and he shuddered. That scared her even more, because she couldn't even guess what was going through his head.

He edged one foot forward, then gave his head a sharp shake. He lowered her gently to her feet, carefully let go of her shirt, and stepped away. "I did what I had to do."

"That why you were out so long?" She pressed her hands against the wall for support, almost pulled over by the ache in her head.

"I had to... absorb it. Understand it."

"Did it work?" As if that was the most important question; it was the only one she could really bring herself to ask.

He nodded, mouth twisting as he swallowed. "If only you could... It has a song to it. I wish that you could hear. It pulls at me night and day, and I'm so... close."

Something about him seemed so lost. She'd never been the sort to offer comfort, to make gestures, but it tugged at her heart in a way she couldn't define. She left the safety of the wall, took up one of his hands with hers for a moment, trapping his smooth, pale fingers under her own, scars, grimy fingernails, and all. "You gonna be OK?"

He let out a short, sharp laugh, smoothing his hair back with his other hand. "I can stand against the Weatherman now. I will kill him."

"Didn't answer my question."

He squeezed her fingers, lifted one of her hands to his lips, brushed a light kiss across her knuckles like she was some sort of lady. "No, I didn't." He let go of her hand then, before she could pull away.

Hob took a few unsteady steps to the chair next to the window and sat as carefully as she could, trying not to jar her head. "So that's it? You gonna kill him, and that's the end of it?"

"Until they send another one." He sat down on the edge of the bed she'd been occupying. "Though I think I may need your help. I should be able to kill him. But he's got quite a few guards with him, from what I observed."

"Fifty by my count."

"So I *will* need help with that."

She gave him a little smile. "You askin' me, or you askin' *us*?"

"The plural you, as in the Ghost Wolves. I can pay."

He couldn't know they already had a contract for it. While some part of her insisted that it was dishonest, that she should own up, the razor edge of savvy that she'd honed from the time she could walk told her that getting paid twice for the same job was a damn good deal when she had people to feed. "What's the offer?"

"Oh, Hob. You become so businesslike."

"This here is a business deal, so I'd hope that was the case."

"I've got the cash boxes from the pay office in Pictou. I'll give you one of them."

"How many are there?"

He smiled at her. "It's not my job to help you with negotiations."

Life felt a little more normal, seeing just that hint of smug out of him. She smoothed down the front of her shirt. "Two cash boxes. The two lightest." Coin was popular now, but there were still bills around, and they were worth more – and weighed less.

"Lightest and heaviest."

"Done." She leaned back in her chair. Outside the room, a floorboard creaked. "Whoever it is, come in. I don't abide by eavesdroppers." And for a moment, she felt a flutter of hope in her heart, because who was the biggest eavesdropper of all but Coyote?

The door opened to reveal Freki and Geri. Geri stared openly at the Bone Collector. Freki had a flimsy folded into an envelope in his hands. "Nice to see you up," he said, handing the envelope to her.

"Good news or bad?"

Freki shrugged. "Complicated."

She opened the envelope, but the letters seemed to blur, run away from her eye. "How about one of you boys just give me the gist of it? I been havin' a rough day. Or…" she looked at Geri, who shook his head. "How long was I out?"

"More'n a full day," Geri said. "And what my brother here doesn't seem to want to tell ya is that it's a note from Raff. Supply train with explosives ain't comin' in to Ludlow for a week, and it don't matter anyway 'cause the Weatherman will be there three days from now."

She stared at him. "You said I was only out for a day."

"I did. Guess they decided to move the timetable up." He shrugged. "Good news is, they delayed a day already 'cause of what happened in Shimera."

Gently, she rubbed her forehead with one hand. "Dambala back with Coyote yet?"

"Not yet."

"Fuck me. What about things in Rouse?"

"Sent Lykaios up there. She said they just opened up a new vein last week and they're gonna be workin' it for a while. So they're full out, and won't be gettin' a resupply for at least two weeks, if not three." As Geri spoke about the mining operations, the Bone Collector's lips twisted with a hint of disgust.

"Shit. You got some good news for me?"

"'Fraid not," Geri said. "Other than, well, ain't you happy you're alive?"

She would have laughed a lot harder at that if her head hadn't hurt so bad. "Guess any day you're alive is better'n the alternative."

"What do you need the explosives for?" the Bone Collector asked.

"Stop the train afore it gets in to town so there're less people to deal with. But if we can't break the track enough, that's a fuckin' worthless plan..." She trailed off as the Bone Collector cleared his throat, tried to figure out what that long, hard look he was giving her meant until something clicked over in her brain. He could already tunnel through rock, tear synthcrete apart with his hands from beneath, and if he was stronger now… "Oh. Really?"

"Really."

"You sure?"

The Bone Collector laughed. "You'd better hope that I am."

"Mind lettin' us in on the joke?" Geri asked.

Hob glanced at the Bone Collector, who only shrugged. "I'll just say, I'm thinkin' it'll be justice to knock over that goddamn train with some proper witchiness."

"Mayhap I don't want to know after all," Geri said.

"You'll see for yourself soon, anyway." Hob started to pry herself out of the chair.

"I'll get things prepped," Freki said. "Already got 'em started anyway. Maps're in your office."

She sat back down as a wave of dizziness hit her. "I do appreciate it. Give me an extra day of rest, and I'd better be less of a fuckin' wreck tomorrow. 'Cause that's when we're gonna have to leave."

"And if Dambala's crew ain't back by then?" Geri asked.

"Then it's fifteen against fifty instead of nineteen. So you best keep your fingers crossed."

"Bigger payday with less people anyway." Geri and his brother turned to go.

"Geri, do me a favor?"

"Yessir?"

"Top drawer of my desk. Somethin' in there wrapped in a handkerchief. Send someone over with it."

He nodded, then shut the door behind him.

"I should probably go as well," the Bone Collector

said. "Let you rest, since we don't have much time."

"Bide a bit. Got somethin' to give you first." She let her head droop a little as a minute ticked by in silence. She didn't have a problem with quiet most of the time, but now it felt like there was something on the edge of her hearing, trying to get her attention. "Would I have been out longer if you hadn't showed up?"

He hesitated, then nodded.

"How much longer?"

"It's impossible to say."

"Impossible to say 'cause you don't know, or 'cause I wouldn't've woke up?" She looked him in the face when she asked. The man would probably be a champion if he ever learned to play poker. "What'd he do to me? It was like… he was just choppin' pieces out of my brainpan, just by lookin' at me."

"He's strong," the Bone Collector said softly.

"That gonna happen to me again, when we go up against him? 'Cause if so, I'm better off just sendin' Freki and Geri and plantin' my ass here."

The Bone Collector smiled. "He'll have other things to worry about when the time comes. Your concern is only the guards."

"I hope you're as confident as you sound."

"So do I."

A quick knock at the door and Raff let himself in, a rolled-up handkerchief in his hand. Hob shooed him away after he'd had a chance to see that yes, she was upright and mostly in one piece. She offered the handkerchief to the Bone Collector, making him stand to take it from her. She was tired of feeling wobbly on her feet for the moment.

"What is…" He unwrapped the handkerchief, revealing the charred finger bone of Old Nick. "Ah."

"Thought you'd want that, you two bein' such good friends an' all."

He bowed his head. "Thank you."

"Can you tell me what killed him? He wasn't doin' that bad, just up an' died."

Head still bowed, he rolled the bone into his hand, wrapping his fingers around it. He let out a long, heavy sigh. "Oh, my friend," he whispered.

Hob sat up a bit straighter. "What is it?"

When he looked up, his expression was smooth again, revealing nothing. "He was old, Hob, and sick. Sicker than you knew, perhaps."

She looked him in the eye and saw nothing but herself reflected back until she looked away first. "Guess that's a relief, then."

"Oh?"

"Ain't often that my paranoia don't turn somethin' up." She sighed. "Get on out of here now. I'm gonna spend the rest of the day sleepin' while everyone else preps. Tomorrow we'll head out past Ludlow and get ready for the show. So be here at dawn. You can ride with us."

"Riding. How… quaint."

She laughed. "I like my method of travelin' better than yours any day of the week."

The Bone Collector rose. "Some day, I think you'll come to appreciate it." He turned to leave.

"Hey," she said quietly.

"Hm?"

"Was that you? Were you… *Are* you my phoenix?" She couldn't shake the image of it from her mind, and she wasn't sure if it was comfort or curse. Because that phoenix had saved her, but she still carried the pain of it tearing out her eye.

He didn't answer with words, simply bent over her and pressed a featherlight kiss on top of her head. Then he was gone, door drifting shut behind him.

Hob wobbled her way back to bed, laying down with care. She had to roll onto her side to get the worst of the throbbing in her head to stop. "Somethin' ain't right with that man," she muttered. She closed her eyes and drifted off on a dizzy wave of sleep, to a place untouched by the Weatherman, but the phoenix circled and circled.

CHAPTER THIRTY-NINE

Hob slept for another sixteen hours, stirring occasionally to drink a little water, use the toilet, roll over onto her other side. Sometime in there, Dambala and his men returned with no Coyote. Sometime in there, Freki had all of the motorcycles checked, fitted, stocked, put at the ready with full combat equipment. The three big guns were cleaned and prepped, every spare round collected and properly boxed. Their collection of body armor was brought out, redistributed, repaired where needed. It wasn't enough for even half of them, a hodgepodge of pieces stolen from trash heaps or taken from dead guards found in the desert, but it was better than nothing.

All those things were done by the time she woke and wandered out of the sick room, chewing at her own tongue in a vain effort to rid her mouth of the rank taste that had built up over the last two days. The only light in the night came from the kitchen window and the moons overhead.

Lobo stood inside, getting breakfast in order. He dropped a frying pan on the stove, clutching at his chest when he turned and caught sight of her. "God, the dead have risen, it's the sign of end times."

"You're mighty funny." Hob pulled a rickety stool up to the counter and sat. "If'n you don't feed me, I might just try to eat your liver."

"Leftovers or breakfast?"

"Whichever's faster." He put a cup of inky black coffee in front of her. She took a drink and felt like it was going to eat the enamel off her teeth. But at least her mouth tasted slightly better. "Christ, how long's that been on the burner?"

"All night, just the way you like it."

She laughed. "I ain't turned into Old Nick yet."

"Could've fooled me. Most nights before we had a big job, he'd be right here, lookin' for a midnight snack because he couldn't sleep." Lobo slapped a sandwich onto a plate and put that in front of her, along with a glass of milk. "Milk's startin' to go a little off, but if you trade it with the coffee, you won't notice a thing. Just say when you want another sandwich."

While she ate, he caught her up on the news. Not even hearing about Coyote – or rather the lack thereof – put a dent in her appetite. She had to focus now on the job at hand, on what they'd be doing when they left in the morning. Coyote, she'd mourn later. Probably with a few other soldiers, before this business was through. "Dambala OK?"

"Good as you'd expect. He took it hard. But Bala don't get sad so much as he gets even."

"Harmony town still in one piece?"

"Town's fine. Some of the people ain't doin' so well, I hear."

She laughed without humor. "You gonna be ready

to ride in the morning, bein' up so early?"

"Don't worry about me, I been doin' this longer than you been alive." He gave her a gap-toothed smile. "Sharpened my favorite carvin' knives special, just for this occasion."

"I'm sure those Mariposa boys will be glad they're in the hands of a real craftsman." She took a drink of the milk and shuddered, immediately taking a long sip of the acidic coffee. "I only been the Ravani for what... less'n a month? The fuck am I doin'?"

"What every Ravani does." Lobo set a second sandwich in front of her, even though she was only halfway through the first. "You find us a payday and take us to it."

"Gonna lose some people today."

"Some of us are here 'cause we pissed off the wrong person. Some of us are here 'cause we just didn't want to be miners or farmers or company shills. But I don't think anyone's here 'cause he wants to play it safe."

Hob raised the coffee cup in the parody of a salute. "Absolvin' me of my guilt afore I even have it. Masterful plan, Lobo."

"Worked on Old Nick. It'll work on you too, if you'd stop overthinkin' things for five seconds. Eat your goddamn sandwich."

She laughed, and ate down the sandwiches. "You're a hard man to argue with."

"So I've heard. You fill that black hole in your belly yet, or do you need somethin' else?"

"Nah, I'm good."

"Then go get into some proper clothes. And I didn't want to say nothin' until you had a hearty meal, you bein' just back from the brink of death and all, but there's a powerful stench to you right now."

Hob looked down at herself; blood and dirt ground into her shirt, who knew what else. It hadn't bothered her before, but now everything felt stiff and crusty. She took an experimental sniff and grimaced. There was only so much a body could do, sweating day in and day out in a place where water was precious, but there was a certain threshold of stink they all tried to never violate. "Goin' for sainthood, you are."

Considering that there was a large measure more of blood and sweat and who knew what else in her future – if things went well – she wasn't concerned enough to take a proper bath. But she did rinse out her hair and replait it, and scraped the worst of the dirt and stink out of her skin with dry soap. After, she pulled on a fresh white shirt and black leather pants – good protection for her legs, and the extra heat it drank in would be that much more fuel for her fire now that she'd really practiced how to use it.

Her waistcoat was torn past all repair, so she dipped into the trunk of Old Nick's things still waiting to be given away or trashed. His waistcoat didn't fit quite right, since even the bare bit of chest and hips she'd grown was more than that man ever had on him, but it would pass muster and was far finer fabric than any of her own clothes. Her own coat was still in good enough shape, even if she'd bled all over it; there was a reason she favored black just as Nick had. It was forgiving about certain things.

She looked in the trunk again before shutting it, at the set of black ties, and the silver glint of Old Nick's pocket watch. Ties were out of the question, since there was no need to give someone an extra handle to grab in the middle of a brawl. But she picked up the pocket watch, running her thumb over its back. The silver had tarnished into faint stickiness, begging for a polish. Nick had carried that watch on every mission, the silver chain hanging at his waistcoat pocket. She popped the cover open. There was a faded picture inside: Nick and his brother as young men. She peeled it out with one fingernail, to give to Mag later. The initials *A. R.* were etched into the metal beneath.

"Wonder who you were, A. R.," she murmured, snapping the watch closed. "Hope you were a lucky bastard."

False dawn just touching the sky, she checked her reflection in the cracked mirror hanging behind the door. She looked a proper undertaker now, dapper even with that pocket watch. Except women never seemed to be undertakers, something about being more concerned with bringing people into the world and less with ushering them out.

Hob grinned at herself, showing more teeth than anyone decently should. There were a lot of things that just weren't done on her to-do list for the day.

The Bone Collector walked up to the gates as the sun showed a sliver above the horizon. The little base was a hive of activity, all of the motorcycles out of the garage and the men checking weapons and stowing gear. The larger equipment went on Lobo's trailer, the three big guns and their ammo boxes.

Hob waved the Bone Collector over and held up

one of their spare helmets. "You comfortable wearin'
one of these?"

"I'd rather not."

"Then you're gonna have to find another way to
tell me where we ought to stop. And I might say no,
since I gotta find good ground for us to fight on as
well."

He nodded. "If I think we ought to stop, I'll put
some pressure on your arm. If you don't wish to stop
there, then don't stop."

"Fair enough." She threw one leg over the
motorcycle, then paused to look him up and down.
"Think you'd better leave the staff behind."

He bowed his head slightly. "Fair enough." There
was just an edge of mockery in his voice as he copied
her inflections. "Where shall I leave it?"

"Corner of the garage. You can collect it when
you get back." Hob shouted to the men, "You boys
ready for a payday? And you ready to piss in the
company's ear while you're at it?" The men roared
and laughed; some of them threw back their heads
and howled. "Mount up!" she yelled, then put on her
helmet. Perhaps she should say more, about why they
were doing what they were doing, about stopping the
Weatherman meaning they were stopping TransRift
dead, for a while at least. But it would be redundant,
she realized. They all knew why they were here. All
of them, except for her and the twins, were already
once dead by the company, men who had been
blacklisted, had been thrown out of their own towns.
Give them money and a chance to spit in TransRift's
eye, and they'd go to their graves singing. She'd leave

the fancy speeches to Mag.

Hob signaled the Bone Collector to get on the back of her motorcycle. It certainly wasn't the first time she'd had a passenger, but this felt a special kind of awkward. "Raff, hang back and close the gate once we're all out," she said over the radio channel.

"Aye, sir."

Dambala laughed, "Wouldn't want eagles nestin' in here when we get back."

"Bird shit on your bed, I don't think anyone'd notice," Geri said, "'cept maybe the smell would improve."

She listened to the chatter with half an ear as they started engines and rolled out through the gate. If they were teasing each other, it meant that they couldn't be too scared. And why should they be, not knowing firsthand what the Weatherman could do to them? And hell, they were only outnumbered by a little more than two and a half times. What could be scary about that?

All of them were crazy. And she was the craziest, leading them out there.

CHAPTER FORTY

They rode for hours just to get to Ludlow, then cut a wide circle, picking their way through canyons to keep the dust cloud down. Out past Ludlow they hit another dune sea, making a long arc until they found the train tracks, a black thread in the red-gold sand. They sped along that line, following to a stretch of hardpan. The Bone Collector grabbed her upper arm and squeezed, there. She shook her head and didn't even slow. There was nowhere to hide on the hardpan, no cover.

More sand, and into another set of flat-bottomed canyons made of deep red rocks that the train tracks wove through. These canyons hadn't been made by any ancient and long-dead river; they were oddly straight and far too wide. Drifts of dust, too low to be proper dunes, made waves along the ground. Some had been cut in half by the passing of the last train. The last of the canyons held the least sand, talus spilling from the walls out onto another stretch of hardpan dotted with scrub.

Hob was already slowing before the Bone Collector had a chance to grab her arm. "Let's get some scouts

426

on a route up to the canyon walls," she said over the radio. "I want a place for the big guns. If you have to go more'n fifteen kilometers, just come back." Six riders peeled off, two circling to each side and two heading back into the canyon's mouth. "Let's get another party findin' me some good hidey places for riders on the ground." More moved out, coordinated by Geri. "Lobo, go ahead and set up, start cookin' us some dinner in the shade. Won't be anyone on these tracks for another ten hours at least. Grab whatever assistants you need."

She checked her odometer before pulling off her helmet. They were a good hundred and twenty kilometers down the train line from Ludlow, and probably another three fifty by track from the next nearest town. They'd have enough time to get the job finished and get the hell out before reinforcements could arrive. "This gonna work for you?" she asked the Bone Collector.

He slipped off the motorcycle and stepped out onto the hardpan, dropping to one knee and pressing his palms into the ground. "It'll do."

"Don't know how precise you can be, but if you can get the train stopped at the canyon mouth, that'd be best. Gives us plenty of room to work on the ground out here, but not too far away from the walls so I can have the big guns rainin' down."

"It's my first time derailing a train, but I'll do my best." He straightened, brushing the dust from his hands. "The bedrock is very close to the surface here. And there is an old fault here," he drew a line across the canyon mouth with one hand, "that I should be able to use."

"Where will you need to be to do this?"

"Here, on the hardpan. I will need to be close."

Hob paced around the tracks. Outside of the canyon, there wasn't much cover. "You flip the train, it's gonna get messy."

"That's the least of my worries, I assure you."

She glanced at him, then laughed. "Guess it ain't so scary, if you can turn to stone." A faint noise from her helmet caught her attention. She slipped it back on. "Repeat the last."

"Got a nice little place where we can shelter about ten men with motorcycles," Lykaios said. She had a low voice for a woman, easy to mistake for a man's. "If we get friendly."

"We're all a friendly sort. Head on back." She pulled the helmet off and tucked it under her arm, then started pacing the area, trying to get a good idea about line of sight and the best places to station the men up top.

"I will need quiet," the Bone Collector said.

Hob glanced over her shoulder. "Dunno if I can give you quiet. But I can keep all my yahoos from botherin' you."

He laughed, then lowered himself gracefully to his knees. "That will suffice." Head bowed, he rested his hands flat on the hard ground, fingers sinking into the hard salt crust like it was dough.

The scouts found a route up to the north wall of the canyon, but none to the south. Hob let the men get their late dinner, then counted off who would be riding, who would be firing the two .60 caliber machine guns and the .50 caliber sniper rifle, who would be running ammo or using regular rifles for cover fire. Most of the men sent to the canyon walls weren't necessarily the best shots, though she trusted them to not take out any of their friends; they were the weakest riders, the ones who shouldn't be trying to navigate around in a hot mess on a motorcycle. Though she did also send Maheegan up to take the .50 cal, since he'd been a sniper in his previous life. Seven men total went up the canyon walls to wait, and to watch for the lights of an approaching train or helicopter.

The Bone Collector sounded tired when Hob brought him his share of dinner: beans and rice that most ate with their fingers. He picked at his food when prompted.

"Lookin' mite peaky," Hob commented, sitting down on the hardpan across from him. She waved an evening fly away from her food.

"This isn't as easy as it looks."

"You gonna be able to do this and take on the Weatherman too?"

"Yes. This is the hard part, right now. I'm putting energy into the rocks, getting them ready to slip while holding them so they cannot. When the train comes, I'll merely be releasing all of that tension." He smiled slyly, picking beans off his plate with dust-coated fingers and eating them one by one. "If we succeed tomorrow, this will be... one for the history books, as I've heard your people say."

Hob snorted. She knew enough to not bother

asking if he had that kind of asshole smile on his face. "Depends on who's writin' that book." She pointed back behind him. "I'm gonna be there, on that little ledge among the rocks. So I can see things right away. Geri's hidin' place is good, but it don't have a view. That an OK place to be?"

He glanced over his shoulder. "As far as I'm concerned, it is. If the train decides otherwise... that, I cannot guarantee."

"Guess I'll take my chances. Because it's that or the canyon wall, and I'd be damn near useless up there."

"I doubt that."

"You never seen me try to hit somethin' with a rifle." She grinned at him and got a tired smile in response.

Not one to fill silence or be worried about it, she let it sit there, finishing her dinner and then laying the light plastic plate aside, looking out over the horizon. The sky went from deep blue to pure black quickly, bands and clouds of stars revealing themselves. When she looked back at the Bone Collector, his half-finished dinner was set aside as well, and he had his hands pressed against the ground once more. She ate the rest of his dinner for him and took the plates to be washed. She returned, though, to sit beside him and just listen to the quiet sound of him breathing, regular as a clock.

And maybe it was her imagination, but she felt a low rumble build. When she pressed her ear against the hardpan, it was the steady rush of her own heartbeat, echoing in the deeps.

CHAPTER FORTY-ONE

Technically it was a day off in Ludlow for the miners. Everything was shut down for the arrival of the Weatherman, and the night shift was even allowed extra time off so they could sleep. Mag suspected that piece of generosity was a way to head off excuses, not that anyone was given a choice about attending this to-do. She'd heard about the other towns, greenbellies checking houses and even sheds to make sure everyone was gathered and waiting.

Clarence left before sunrise, since it was up to him to get the workers on his shift organized, count noses and the like. He had to rub elbows with the company men. Mag was grateful for that; it made things easier for what she planned.

She woke Anabi as the sky went red with dawn. They made pancakes together, coffee, and fried a couple of eggs. Midway through breakfast, someone started hammering on the door, shouting to be let in. Anabi's face went pale and still, and she shot Mag a wide-eyed look.

"Don't you worry about it," Mag said. "Eat your pancakes."

The front door opened, the greenbelly coming in to search the house. He came around the corner rifle-barrel first, but looked relieved that it was just two women. He lowered his rifle. "You ladies need to get to the square."

"We're eatin'."

"You can eat it later."

"And when we're done with breakfast, we got sewin' to do. Don't have time for your nonsense today."

"You don't have a choice. You're both coming with me. I don't want it to get unpleasant."

Anabi stood up. Her face was sheet white, breath coming fast like a rabbit's.

"Sit down, Anabi. We're not goin' anywhere." Mag finished her coffee, waiting for Anabi to sink slowly back down. Something in the back of her head itched, a feeling that had grown stronger and stronger since Hob had rescued her from Newcastle. Instinct had been screaming at her that she could do this, that she had a stubborn will that was better than any weapon. She'd resisted it before now out of respect for Clarence and Odalia, and maybe out of fear. Well, no time left for fear, and she sure as hell didn't respect the greenbellies.

The greenbelly cussed, and took a step toward her. Mag set her cup down and tilted her head to look into his eyes. The motion felt strange, like she'd grabbed his hand instead of just looking at him, like there was a connection being made. Looking into his watery hazel eyes, she measured him up in a heartbeat, felt him telling himself he was just following orders, didn't matter anyway. He was a mouse of a man, just waiting to be told what to do.

Mag *leaned* into him, pushing at his brain with all her will like he was a wall instead of a man.

He stopped in his tracks, pupils blowing out wide.

Mag took in a shaky breath. Her heartbeat sounded loud in her ears. She planted one hand firmly against the table to steady herself, then pushed her empty cup toward Anabi with the other. "Mind gettin' me more coffee? I may be here a while."

Anabi knocked over her chair as she stood, snatching the cup up with a trembling hand.

"You're gonna forget all about this," Mag told the greenbelly, leaning harder and harder. Her right eye started to hurt, the vision clouding, but she didn't let her concentration waver. "Ain't nothin' in this house." For a moment he seemed to struggle, lips parting slightly, and she pushed, clenching her teeth. "Nothin' at all."

Something behind his eyes gave. Blood began to seep from the man's right nostril.

There was a rumble in the distance, like a collapse in the mine, only that was impossible; no one was working today. Dishes rattled on the shelves, and a cup tumbled off the table to smash on the floor. The guard reeled back, clutching at the doorframe vainly with one hand.

Mag smiled, sitting back in the chair. She knew what she'd paid the Ghost Wolves to do, and she knew Hob, like Uncle Nick, had a penchant to be showy. "Mayhap you got bigger things to worry about than a couple o' innocent ladies anyway."

CHAPTER FORTY-TWO

"Ravani, north wall has visual on lights." The voice was tinny and thin, a whine in the air by her ear. She'd dozed with her head pillowed on the helmet, listening for just that message.

Grunting as her hip complained about the bruising, uncomfortable hardpan, Hob rolled upright. The sky had gone from black to purple and red, the sun's rise hidden by the canyon walls. She stuck the helmet on and reached over to shake the Bone Collector's arm. "Can I get some confirmation on that?"

"Give me a second."

The Bone Collector lifted his head slowly, eyes dark with fatigue. She pointed out at the tracks and stood.

"South landing confirms it. Visual on lights, low to the horizon."

"Can you tell if it's a train yet?"

"Lights are bright, but can't tell for certain, not yet."

"Keep watchin' it. Geri?"

"Heard it. Had to kick a couple awake, but we're gettin' ready now. There an ETA?"

"Not yet." Again, she turned to the Bone Collector. "Gotta go get in my place. You gonna be OK?"

"I will be ready."

The two weren't the same thing, but this wasn't the time to argue. She tugged the spare revolver from her belt after a second of thought and offered it to him; he just shook his head. "Suit yourself." Her motorcycle awaited her; she coasted the short distance to her own position, then stowed it in a crevice where it would hopefully be safe from debris. The rocks were rough against her fingers, like warm sandpaper as she scrambled up to the ledge. She pulled back the faceplate of her helmet, brought up her own binoculars to watch. She caught a quick peep of lights in the distance, like they'd just bobbed over a hill. "Whatever it is, it's following the landscape," she said over the channel. "Ain't a chopper." She checked her pocket watch. "Time's about right."

The light bobbed into view again. "Maheegan confirms. Three lights in a triangle, it's a train." Someone on the channel whooped. Hob couldn't help but grin. "Comin' fast, but it'll be a while yet."

"Just let it come to us, boys," Hob said.

"Keep the updates coming," Geri said. His voice was dimmed with static even over the short distance. "We can't see a damn thing in the hidey hole."

The light crested another hill, and then it was steady, coming right at them. "They just hit the flats. They're speedin' up," Hob said.

"Confirmed. Look at 'em go," Maheegan drawled.

Overhead, the sky lightened pink and orange, the color climbing steadily to blue. Even better, Hob thought grimly, that they'd have the sun behind them. Put the company men at another disadvantage.

Every little bit helped.

"They just hit the edge of the hardpan. Five minutes at most."

"Get ready, Geri. But wait for my mark," Hob said. "No matter what you hear."

The train was a silver streak behind the lights, a bullet made giant. The tracks hummed and sang; thunder rolled up through her boots. She dropped low onto the ledge, not needing her height any more to watch. She turned to look at the Bone Collector, still sitting, seemingly oblivious.

Closer.

She gritted her teeth, willing the man to just move, because now she was starting to wonder if she needed to run down there, shake him, wake him up, anything. But the train was too close, only a few kilometers.

She tasted blood in her mouth.

The Bone Collector stood in one fluid motion, his hands coming up to clutch at the sky. His mouth opened to shout, but it was lost in the sound of the train echoing from the canyon walls. And then he dropped again, to drive his fist into the ground.

The hardpan rippled around him, rocks snarling like living things, and then the world *cracked*, lightning and gunshot and bone, a sound that touched her at the animal base of her brain and told her to *fucking run*.

Hob dropped the binoculars. They shattered on the ground below.

The train tracks bent, twisted, snapped like guitar strings as the earth beneath them contorted. The ground at the canyon mouth dropped four meters in an instant. The ledge bucked under her and she grabbed it with both hands, nails splitting as she clawed to hang on. A tinny scream came out of the helmet speakers, followed by cursing, hoarse shouting.

The train hopped off the impossibly warped tracks. The engine rolled, couplings to the cars behind it snapping, and then slammed into the new canyon wall sideways, bursting into a cloud of torn metal and a wash of fire as the fuel lines ruptured. The fire went up, rolled outward in a wave of blistering heat, flames licking up around the Bone Collector and turning him into a black cutout. More shouts echoed through the radio as the wall of heat washed up.

She had to do something or half of them would fry. It was fire, Hob felt the echo of it in her blood, and she tried something she'd never had the gumption to do before. She stood, held out her hands to the fire, and shouted with all her will, "Come to me!"

The inferno obeyed, swirling into a roaring wave that spun around her, boiled her blood and turned the air in her lungs into nothing but more fire. She screamed, the ends of her hair singed, but then she bit down and pulled all that flame through blood and flesh into her bones. The pain was worse than anything but the day the phoenix had spat fire into her skull, and her own wings of flame exploded from her back as she drank the fire in and tamed it. She left a smoldering shadow on the rock.

She was a goddamn idiot, she thought with the one neuron she had above all the nerves aflame. Every day of her life since Nick had taken her from the desert, she'd treated her fire like a parlor trick, for lighting cigarettes and dazzling dumbass kids. It wasn't a trick. It was in her. It *was* her. She was *fire*.

And still the three train cars kept tumbling, end over end, to slam into the canyon walls. Charred and twisted, they were barely recognizable when they came to rest, one of them propped on end against the north wall.

She could barely hear over the surge of her own heartbeat, but Hob could just make out the chatter, the men yelling at each other. "Shut up, all of you," she said, voice hoarse. "Geri, get movin'. Don't know how many survivors there'll be, but we can't be too safe. There's a... there's a nasty drop at the mouth of the canyon now, be ready to jump it. North wall, sound off." She heaved a smoky sigh of relief when seven came back. They sounded shaken. "Smile, boys. Near same thing woulda happened with explosives, and this we didn't have to steal."

There was reassuring if nervous laughter as she bolted down off the ledge and extricated her motorcycle from its crevice. There was a dent in the battery stack and the paint job would never be the same, but it was otherwise OK.

"Movement sighted, Ravani," Maheegan said.

She got the engine started, bursting around the ledge in time to see a man in green kick out a shattered door, crawl into freedom. His head burst in a flash of red, accompanied by the crack of a rifle shot.

"Neutralized," Maheegan continued laconically into her ear.

She pulled up next to the Bone Collector, who stood where she'd left him, hands hanging loose at his sides as he breathed heavily. The hair on one side of his head was singed, his cheek blackened with ash. "It still lives," he said.

Geri's group streamed out of the canyon, jumping down off the newly created ledge like a waterfall of metal, the morning sun glinting orange off the barrels of shotguns and pistols. "Then get to it." Hob revved her engine to a whine and started moving again, pulling the shotgun from the holster on the side of her bike. The fire beat at her blood, screamed to be released, but she didn't want to release it yet, because it was one more weapon in her arsenal, a hell of a lot more powerful than any gun.

Three more doors burst out in one of the passenger cars. She made out the black line of a rifle barrel in one. The shooting started in earnest.

"Keep 'em pinned!" Hob shouted. "Cover, let's get a couple people with grenades, go, get 'em in those doors as you go by. If you ain't sure of your throw, don't waste it!"

The motorcycles swirled around the wreckage; moving targets were harder to hit. Doors opened in the second car.

Someone went tumbling off a bike next to her. She dodged neatly around the fallen motorcycle and fired at the train car as she went close by. She didn't know if she got a kill or not, but the rifle disappeared from the door, dropping out of sight.

"Got a runner," Maheegan's calm voice came over the channel. "Neutralized. They're trying to get to the car to the east."

"Then that's where the Weatherman is." She looped

around, taking another shot at the train car. Her hand wobbled; she couldn't stay steady with everything still burning.

Pain hit her head in a wave, her ears ringing. She almost lost control of the motorcycle, had to lean hard into a turn before she ran into one of the cars.

A man in blue stood on the side of the east car at a crazy angle, black hair whipping in the wind: the Weatherman. His gaze swept over her, and she fought to keep herself in a straight line as he kept looking, going past, searching…

"Target acquired," Maheegan said. A flash of white heat popped in the air half a meter from the Weatherman's head. And in the same deadpan tone, Maheegan continued: "Oh fuck me." The Weatherman started to turn, looking up toward the canyon wall.

The Bone Collector's voice rang out, loud and pure and raised in song over the chatter of gunfire. Dust whipped around him in a halo. The Weatherman jerked back toward him, took one staggering step forward, and dropped onto the broken salt hardpan.

Pressure built up in Hob's skull, made her eyes blur. Her mouth tasted like electricity as she dropped the shotgun back into its holster and drew her revolver. "You can try one more shot now that our friend's got the Weatherman's attention, Maheegan." Her voice sounded strange to her own ears. "If it don't work, just let it alone. We got plenty of greenbellies to kill."

"Cover fire coming, east side of car one," Raff's light voice said. The chatter of the machine gun rolled in loud as thunder, short bursts. A security man screamed as another ducked back inside that car.

Hob caught sight of Lobo ahead of her; there was no mistaking his huge shoulders, or the mass of the trike under him. As he spun by one of the cars, a man in green jumped out of the doorway and slammed into him, taking him to the ground. The trike rolled to an idling stop seven meters distant. The two tumbled along the hardpan, and then metal flashed in Lobo's hand.

Dambala pulled up along one of the cars, firing his shotgun in rapid bursts, stuffing new cartridges into the barrel as fast as he could. Davey ducked around him, slowing enough to fling a grenade into one of the doors. Then he gunned it and slid away. Dambala gave the train car one more shot before he went skidding out. There was a burst of fire and then smoke billowed from the doorway.

"Gimme more of that!" Hob shouted.

A scream: another Wolf down.

And then a shout over the radio, "Bone Collector's been hit!"

CHAPTER FORTY-THREE

Shige had been put in the car with the Weatherman for travel, since Mr Green liked him. Very much, it seemed. Thankfully, it was more than just the two of them; there were several guards, and the same supervisor that had accompanied them to Primero and Shimera.

They were all drinking coffee and eating a light breakfast, just fruit and pastries – or rather, all of them but Mr Green – when there was a rumble, and–

–he lay against the wall, and everything hurt. Blood ran into his eye from a cut across his forehead. He tugged a handkerchief from his pocket and tried to press it against the cut, but his arm didn't seem to want to work right, his hand wavering before him.

Mr Green pulled himself from the shattered remains of their breakfast table. He looked completely unharmed and cheerful as ever, swiping splinters away from his lapels. "They're here! They're here. No more hide and seek," he husked.

Shige tried to ask him what he meant, but all that came from his mouth was a distressed little moan. Mr Green reached down and touched him on the head, then smiled. Something twisted in Shige's guts, and it hurt, but then the pain receded in a wash of relief.

"There. Now your intestines are back inside and you won't die." Mr Green walked away, pulling the door at the far end of the car open.

The sound of gunfire came into the wrecked car, strangely tinny. And then the sound of singing, which made absolutely no sense at all.

Someone else groaned, and wreckage crunched as it shifted. The supervisor, nearly as unharmed as Mr Green somehow, pulled himself out from under a pile of twisted chairs. He took a few steps, then went back, searching until he came up with his automatic rifle. He gave Shige a disgusted look, the expression skewed by a swollen cheek and broken nose. "All hands on deck, if you can stand to get them dirty." Then he, too, went to the doorway, where he stood and began to shoot. A moment later, he shouted, "Ha, got you, goddamn freak!"

Shige glanced around the car; there had been a few cameras, installed to track the Weatherman, now all smashed beyond recognition. No one else in the car was alive. Shige staggered to his feet. His insides twisted strangely again, not quite to the point of pain. He'd worry about that later. He paused next to the corpse of one of the guards, liberating a pistol from the man's holster, and walked quietly up behind the supervisor. Around the man, he caught a glance of the scene outside – chaos on one side, and before them on the hardpan the odd, pale man he'd seen at Primero. Only now, blood stuck his coat to his side, stained the hands he held outstretched toward the Weatherman.

Motorcycles buzzing about, and was that – yes, the so-called Ravani.

Shige calmly assessed the situation, weighing what would be best for him, for the mission in general. He was under deep cover, but that didn't mean he couldn't intervene, as long as he did it safely. He had assets worth protecting at this point.

He raised the pistol level with the supervisor's head and pulled the trigger.

"Stay on the greenbellies, goddammit! We ain't supposed to let that happen." Hob gritted her teeth as she braked hard, planted one foot on the hardpan to spin, and shot back toward the Bone Collector. He still stood, but blood spotted his duster, running freely down his back from just under his shoulder.

Even as she watched, he jerked again, more blood bursting from his side. He took a half step back, then pushed forward, like he was wrestling against something invisible and towering. His mouth opened like a scream, his eyes fixed on the Weatherman.

Two meters away, she hit a wall that wasn't there. She dropped the bike, sent it sliding across the hardpan ahead of her as she tumbled, hands clutching her head through the helmet. She couldn't breathe, and tore her helmet off. She staggered up toward the Bone Collector and saw a third gunshot hit him, this one in the leg. He fell to one knee, blood spraying over the hardpan.

But the sound of it. Without her helmet, she could hear the Bone Collector. Not a scream, but song, pure song, with words she'd never heard before, like the one he'd sung when they were going to get Mag. The Weatherman tore through that music, weaving discord with the notes, twisting them, trying to take control. The air writhed, dust clouds tearing into fantastic shapes, light warping and bending. The hardpan beneath the Bone Collector's knee cracked.

Hob caught sight of dark green in the tilted doorway of the car, and brought up her revolver, striding forward. If she concentrated, if she aimed, she could shut out everything else, the sound and feeling pounding at her head, the fire threatening to burst out of her blood and eat her whole.

The man in the doorway dropped forward, limp and dead before she could shoot. She thought she caught a flash of blue suit, quickly gone. She took a quick glance at the Bone Collector, at all the blood pooling around him, then aimed at the Weatherman and fired. A burst of white light bloomed by his shoulder, the bullet vaporizing.

The Weatherman's head started to turn toward her, that pressure digging into her brain again, but the Bone Collector shouted, twisting his hands, pulling the man back around like a puppet.

She fired again, the bullet bursting past his hip.

Even as he raised hands to claw at his own face, the Weatherman laughed.

laughs as the blood sprays and sprays and sprays, laughs you did this, you did this

He had no right to that pain, that personal horror. No one did. She'd paid for it a thousand times already. A scream of pure rage tore from her throat, the fire surging in her blood. That fire, the fire she'd eaten, the fire she'd never taught herself to use right. Well, it wasn't too late now. She fumbled to focus all that heat in like a magnifying glass, down to a single point. She looked down the barrel of that revolver, Nick's revolver, at the laughing face of the Weatherman, and all that fire flowed up through her arm. The metal of the pistol went red with heat, the bone butt singeing. Fighting with every ounce of strength she had to keep the pistol from melting – heat into the bullet, out of the barrel fuck she should have practiced more, why didn't she just practice more, she could do this, she *would* do this, *she was Hob Fucking Ravani* – she pulled the trigger one more time.

Instead of a bullet, the gun spat every bit of the fire from the explosion and her own blood compressed into one white-hot mote.

That mote screamed as it tore the air between them, and punched into the Weatherman's chest, where she'd tried to ruin him with a normal bullet before. For a moment his lips moved, and she almost heard him – *so pretty* – before she let that captive explosion go. Flames roared up, shot from his eyes and fingertips, turning him black and crisp and then to fine ash in an instant. Then there was only song for one perfect moment, the air going still and the gunfire retreating and she heard it, she almost heard it, the voice of the phoenix.

Come home, it sang. *Come home, come home, come ho–*

The song stopped abruptly as, behind her, the Bone Collector fell in a heap. Hob ran the short distance between them, hissing as she drew the heat back out of her revolver and into her skin before the damn thing melted. She dropped to her knees next to him.

"I think... I might have made a mistake," he whispered, voice barely audible. His lips were bright with blood. "He was stronger than I expected."

"Yeah, well, he's still dead now."

He looked at the dark smear of oily ash that now decorated the hardpan and the side of the train car. "Oh. So he is."

There was an explosion, a wash of heat. She glanced behind her quickly; smoke poured from the other train car. A man crawled from the door, started to run, and then dropped, flesh shredding under a burst from one of the machine guns.

The Bone Collector choked. She looked back down at his face, gave his shoulder a little shake. "You better not be plannin' to die on me."

"I'd rather not. I've... grown rather fond of this." He closed his eyes, swallowed hard. "Can you get me to the sands? I need to... I need to heal. Here would not be a good place."

Hob nodded. "If you can hang on, I can get you there." She stumbled to her feet and ran to where her helmet lay, then shoved it back on. "Tell me we're winnin'." Next she sprinted to her motorcycle, levering the heavy machine back up with hands that felt like they'd had the strength charred out of them.

"Just pickin' off stragglers comin' out of the two guard cars now," Geri said. "What about the Weatherman?"

"Dead." She scrabbled at the side panel over the engine, opening it up to make sure she hadn't cracked the batteries when she dumped the bike. She didn't much feel like exploding, having made it this far. "Careful about the third car. Dunno if anyone's still alive in it. But... if you see a man in company blue. Get a name before you shoot – if it's a guy named Rollins, he's... he might be on our side." Batteries whole, she started the engine back up; the hum felt unsteady, but it would get the job done.

"Ain't you gonna check it out?"

"Bone Collector's been hit. Needs me to take him out to the sands."

Geri hesitated, then said, "Gotcha."

"I'll be back fast as I can." She got herself over to the still form of the Bone Collector with a little squirt from the engine, then picked him up. He wasn't nearly heavy enough for someone who could be stone. "Can't put you on the back, can I?"

He cracked one eye open. "I... don't think so."

Awkwardly, she bundled him onto the bike's seat, laying him over the battery stack, and then slid on behind him. "Good thing for you I got such long damn arms and legs," she muttered. She lifted him back to lean against her and tied him in place with a scrap of rope. Then she burned out of there as fast as she could, cutting straight east, where the closest dunes would be.

Shige had retreated to the car rather than risk being hit by a stray bullet, though he tracked the battle as best he could with sound. The sudden silence from Mr Green, coupled with an explosion that blasted ash over the far end of the train car, told him that he'd been right to stay well back. A couple of explosions later, the gunfire went to almost nothing. Which likely meant that "his" side had lost.

He allowed himself a slight smile, because he could, without lying, say that he hadn't seen what had happened. Though he did hope he'd be able to convince the Ravani to tell him later how she'd done it.

The thin amount of light coming into the car wavered, and he looked toward the door, seeing the shape of a bulky man cut out in it. A bulky man with a gun. Shige carefully raised his hands over his head to show he wasn't armed.

"You Rollins?" the man called.

"Yes, that would be me." He gave the man a polite smile as he stepped closer, noting that he did not lower his gun. "And you are?"

"Geri." The man squinted. "Somethin' about how you sound…"

"My older brother is one of your fellows." He was more than willing to play that card in the hopes it would keep him in one piece. "I believe you call him Coyote?"

The man seemed less than impressed. "Coyote's dead. In Harmony."

Shige sighed. "He said he had it handled. Apparently he didn't."

"Hell of a thing, to leave your brother to die." Geri crouched down in front of him.

"I don't think it would do either of us a service to try to explain either my philosophy or my relationship with my brother. Are you planning to shoot me?"

"I'm considerin' my options."

"Please take into that consideration that I'm the one who gave your boss the information about which towns would be visited."

"Got anythin' else you'd like to share?"

He smiled brittlely. "Not at the moment. But if you kill me, I certainly won't in the future."

Geri rubbed his chin, hand rasping against stubble. "You make a fine point, friend." He straightened up. "So what do we do, take you into town and dump you?"

"I'm afraid that would be far too suspicious. What time is it?"

Geri cast around the train car, came upon a severed arm, and picked it up so he could take a look at the wrist watch. "Just gone nine."

"They'll be sending out reinforcements soon." Shige closed his eyes tightly for a moment, calculating the best way to play this. "I think I do need you to shoot me."

Geri let out a short bark of a laugh. "You serious?"

"Deadly. I need to be injured enough that they will believe I was unconscious and presumed dead for most of the fight. So that it isn't suspicious that I'm the lone survivor."

"Might be a couple of you left."

"But you understand my predicament."

"Not really, but I never let that stop me from helpin' a… friend out." Geri crouched again in front of him. "Where'd ya like it?"

"Somewhere that won't make me bleed out, please. Left shoulder, perhaps?"

"A man with a flare for the dramatic, I see." He

stood and backed up as far as he could, raising his pistol again. "Just say when you're ready. So long as you make it quick. I got people to tend to."

It felt strange, to be so close to the Bone Collector. Hob felt him breathe, felt his heart beating, so she knew he was alive. His blood seeped through her jacket; she'd half-expected it to be cold, since he'd always seemed so cool and collected. But it was hot, maybe hotter than her own blood. She kept their speed as high as she dared, because she could feel him slowing, getting ready to stop, breath and heartbeat weaker.

Dunes rose up over the horizon like a frozen ocean. She poured on more speed. At the bare edge of the sand, she slammed on the brakes, sliding sideways into a halt. With shaking hands, she undid the knots that held the Bone Collector, and then slid him over the side of the bike, dropping him onto the sand as gently as she could.

His lips curved slightly in a smile and his eyes cracked open. She knelt next to him, reaching out to touch his face, just to make sure he really was still alive. It wasn't satisfying, through a leather glove; she ripped it off, touched his cheek again.

"Your payment's in Pictou," he whispered. "Church basement."

She laughed, but it hurt, something twisting up around her heart. "Now who's all businesslike."

He covered her hand with his. His fingers were shaking, his hand sticky with blood. "Be well. I will… miss you."

She laughed, her eyes stinging. "Keep it up, I'll

start thinkin' you like me."

His only answer was a smile, and then the sand flowed around him, lapping like water. He sank until he disappeared from sight. It shouldn't have hurt so much, watching him sink away like drowning. But it had felt too much like *goodbye* for anything but a heartsick pain. She'd had too many damn goodbyes already in such a short time, and would have more soon, more men to burn while they mourned and shouted their victory at the same time.

She wrapped her suddenly empty hand into a fist, pressing it against her mouth. With her other hand, she felt from pocket to pocket, trying to locate her cigarettes. Her eye blurred again as she found Old Nick's silver case, pulled a cigarette out with shaking fingers. Just the act of doing it calmed her, let her unclench her fist. She lit the cigarette with a snap of her fingers and took in a deep, smoky breath, looking up at the endless blue sky as she pressed her knees into the sand that had just swallowed the Bone Collector whole.

A body could drown in that sky, could fly away and be free, could reach her arms out forever and never touch the corners of the world. That sky had terrified her into love, the day she set foot on this rock. And there, in the distance, she saw a mote of light as the phoenix circled and circled.

"Been a month and I already done the impossible you couldn't, you old bastard. Hope you're havin' yourself a good, smug laugh now."

She grinned, and even though it hurt, it felt like victory.

CHAPTER FORTY-FOUR

"Mr Rolland, in the past weeks, I have developed a... keen appreciation for your value to our organization," Ms Meetchim said.

Shige bowed, mindful of the sling holding his arm against his chest. He'd taken to doing that in lieu of shaking hands after Geri had so helpfully shot him in the right shoulder, instead of the left as he'd requested. *My left, your right*, he should have said. Hell. "I appreciate it, Ms Meetchim."

"You will be missed."

"Again, sir, my deepest appreciation. Though it is, of course, only temporary."

Meetchim smiled thinly. "Several months of having a series of temps sort my mail and make my coffee. I'm not certain I will survive."

Shige bowed again, ducking his head as if hiding a blush. "I'm merely honored that you selected me for this task."

"The late Mr Green liked you so much, I would feel remiss in not providing you as a companion for our next Weatherman. I'm surprised you wished to undertake the journey in your current state, but it certainly illustrates your dedication."

"I'll admit to a bit of selfishness," he said, offering her a nervous smile. "Nearly anywhere will have better medical care available. With the company's permission, of course, I'd like to stop into a decent orthopedic center, and that ought to fix my injury in a matter of days. Perhaps on Jeuno Prime or even Earth."

"I'm certain Corporate will recommend you to the best." Meetchim offered him her hand to shake, then laughed, shaking her head. "I am sorry. I forget. Have a safe flight."

"Thank you, sir. I will see you soon." Shige bowed one more time, and went up the embarkation ramp to the rift ship.

He had many reasons for volunteering for this task. Getting off Tanegawa's World would provide him with opportunities aplenty to report his initial findings to his family coalition – and a more careful version to his superiors in the Federal Union. And, he hoped, he would have a chance to investigate further once he reached the TransRift laboratories where he would be given their new Weatherman. He had a great many questions still to be answered. While he was beginning to grasp the uncomfortable reality that something on Tanegawa's World could act upon the people there and change them, that didn't answer how the Weathermen came to be in a lab so far afield.

He allowed a steward to show him to his private cabin on the *Kirin* and seated himself comfortably for takeoff, using belts and webbing. He would also have to pass on the unpleasant news if the opportunity presented itself that he'd not only found his family's prodigal son, but apparently lost him the same day. It was a shame.

"Would you like tea or coffee, sir?" the steward asked.

"Tea would be lovely. With lemon."

"Glad to be heading back to civilization, sir?"

He opened his eyes and smiled at the man, so neat in his blue company uniform, with his little cart of treats. "Something like that. It depends on how one defines civilization."

The steward set a white china teacup in front of him. "Somewhere they don't shoot people might be a start." He laughed nervously, glancing at the sling Shige wore.

Word got around. "Indeed. Thank you." He smiled, and the young man went on his way. The tea – just enough sharpness from the lemon – was everything he'd been missing on that dusty little planet. Tanegawa's World truly was the back of beyond.

But less civilized? There was a certain charm to a world that had shootouts instead of politics. Where warnings were heeded instead of reports ignored because they contained inconvenient truths.

Beneath him, the rift ship vibrated, the normal propulsion engines beginning to warm for lift-off. Shige sighed, resting the teacup against his leg for a moment, and contemplated the multitude of truths, each less convenient than the last, that were in his current report.

Yes, he was going to miss the little dustball, if only for that reason.

"What d'ya think?" Hob asked, sliding the poster across the table to Mag. Anabi stepped away from the stove, arms dusted with flour to the elbow, and leaned over Mag's shoulder to look as well. Mag's blue gingham dress was decorated with soft white smudges, where Anabi had touched her shoulder as if afraid she might disappear in an instant.

Mag grimaced. "I think for this much of a reward, they could hire a better artist." Her right eye was red and a bit swollen; she'd burst a blood vessel in it.

Hob laughed. The only real pictures of her were the ones Rollins had mentioned, of her breaking in to the lab. Apparently they didn't want to use those, where she was dressed like a company woman. "By the time they upgrade me to dead or alive, I bet I'll look downright artistic."

"Don't even say that," Mag said, covering the printing on the poster with one hand. "You need to lay low. Bribing people won't keep you hidden forever, if they keep cranking the reward up."

"I'll burn that bridge when I come to it," Hob said. She grinned at Mag. "I got my taste of pissin' the company off royal. Gotta say, I liked it."

Anabi took a stub of chalk and wrote on the little blackboard that always sat at the table: *I almost feel sorry for them*. She laughed silently and then underlined the word *almost* twice.

"Just be careful. Promise me."

"Careful as you'll be," Hob said. She grinned. "Don't think I haven't noticed you're up to your eyeballs in your own little plots. If anythin' you do ever comes to fruition, you'll be in more trouble than me."

Mag smiled at her. "If I lay my plots out right, maybe there won't be a company left to be all pissed off at me."

Hob raised her glass in a toast. "That's what I like about you, Mag. You may be quiet, but you never thought small in your life."

Mag tilted her own coffee mug up. "I am serious, though. Be careful."

"Got too much fire in my belly. Ain't room for careful." Hob said. She took a sip of her whiskey, rolling the smoky taste over her tongue. "Bein' bad pays too damn good anyway."

"You ain't bad, Hob Ravani."

"Oh, but I am. I'm just the right kind of bad." She raised her glass again, and drained it.

EPILOGUE

Thirsty.

There wasn't room for mission, purpose, name, nothing but the thirst that glued his tongue to the roof of his mouth. Sand shifted under his feet, trying to throw him to his knees again, but he knew its wiles now. He flowed like he was made of sand himself instead of blood and meat and kept going, one leaden foot in front of the other, right hand used for balance as necessary.

His left hand still clutched his side, covering the gaping hole there. The wound had stopped bleeding some time ago, but his hand seemed glued in place with tacky blood.

So thirsty. He squinted into the burning wind, almost blinded by the dust that coated lids and lashes, but he could still make out the lithe shape moving ahead of him: four shadowy legs, a waving tail, alert ears, long jaws. His side throbbed when he thought about those jaws.

Just a little further. Just a few more steps. And you'll never be thirsty again.

His feet met rock gritty with sand. The yawning

mouth of a cave opened to swallow him, breathing out *cool* and *damp*. He moved his tongue to speak, but had no voice between the screaming and sun and dust. So he simply followed, skittering and stumbling down the natural rock ramp, his shoulders scraping against the narrow passage.

It spat him out into a yawning cavern, so big that there were no echoes of his breathing, but he heard a thousand other sounds, sighs and laughter and chittering and the yelping of coyotes. It should have been dark, so far underground, but there was light everywhere, shining from the walls, the ceiling, reflecting the water. Reflecting the *water* instead of the other way around.

The water. It was bottomless, and full of stars.

He didn't care about the rest, couldn't think about it past the thirst. He threw himself to his knees at the water's edge and drank long from that deep, secret well. The black silvergoldredbluegreen water flowed into him, filled him, tasted like salt and iron and *light* and drank him in turn.

ACKNOWLEDGMENTS

I started writing this book back in 2005, when I was in Utah for one of the few writing retreats I've ever been on. I wrote what is now the short story "Fire in the Belly" (finally published in *Mothership Zeta* #2, March 2016) about Hob Ravani arriving on Tanegawa's World. In the year that followed, I wrote several halting attempts at more short stories about Hob's life. It wasn't until 2006, at another writing retreat, that I read another piece of Hob Ravani's life out loud and my friends pointed out to me that these really sounded like chapters, and maybe I should just write a novel and give them the whole story.

Eight drafts and eleven years later, here we are. And this book wouldn't be in your hands without:

Michelle Thatcher and Shannon Deonier, the friends who took me to that first retreat.

Molly Tanzer, who edited an earlier version of this book and made it good enough to submit to Angry Robot.

Alastair Mayer, who helped me figure out just how many of my darlings I had to kill.

Mike Wells, who read several versions of this book,

told me unflinchingly what didn't work, and spent many nights listening to my paroxysms of writerly self-doubt – and is still friends with me, even.

Phil Jourdan at AR, who destroyed and rebuilt my soul with one editing phone call.

The rest of the Angry Robot crew who have made this thing happen: Mike Underwood, Penny Reeve, Nick Tyler, and Marc Gascoigne.

DongWon Song, my amazing agent, who took me dumping this in his lap literally thirty seconds after I decided to be his client without even batting an eyelash.

My mother, who taught me to love books and take no shit.

My father, who was a chief steward in the Communications Workers of America (local 7750) when I was a child – and taught me to take no shit.

And the brave men and women of the United Mine Workers of America, who fought and died in the 1913-1914 Colorado Coal War. They lost that battle, but won their war. May we never forget, and may we retake the ground they paid for so dearly.

The union makes us strong.

Meet Riko...

"NECROTECH bleeds with raw & unapologetic badassery."

KEVIN HEARNE, NYT Bestselling author of the Iron Druid Chronicles

"It's like razors for your brain."

RICHARD KADREY, author of the Sandman Slim series

"Scalding and brutal as a radiation shower, punishing as a street fight, and as sharp as a blade to the jugular."

LILA BOWEN, RT Review Award-winning author of Wake of Vultures

"K C Alexander doesn't 'write' so much as she fires words into your cerebral cortex with an electromagnetic railgun."

CHUCK WENDIG, NYT Bestselling author of Star Wars: Aftermath and Invasive